Blind Men Don't Dial Zero

C.A. Larmer is a journalist, editor, indie publisher and the author of multiple crime series, two stand-alone novels and a non-fiction book about pioneering surveyors in Papua New Guinea. Christina grew up in that country, was educated in Australia, and spent many years working in London, Los Angeles and New York. She now lives with her musician husband, two sons and cheeky Blue Heeler on the east coast of Australia.

Sign up to her newsletter: www.calarmer.com

ALSO BY C.A. LARMER

The Sleuths of Last Resort
Smart Girls Don't Trust Strangers (Book 2)

The Murder Mystery Book Club
The Murder Mystery Book Club (Book 1)
Danger on the S.S Orient (Book 2)
Death Under the Stars (Book 3)
When There Were 9 (Book 4)

The Ghostwriter Mystery Series
Killer Twist (Book 1)
A Plot to Die For (Book 2)
Last Writes (Book 3)
Dying Words (Book 4)
Words Can Kill (Book 5)
A Note Before Dying (Book 6)
Without a Word (Book 7)

The Posthumous Mystery Series
Do Not Go Gentle
Do Not Go Alone

Plus:
After the Ferry: A Gripping Psychological Thriller

An Island Lost

A Measure of Papua New Guinea:
The Arman Larmer Surveys Story (Focus; 2008)

C.A. LARMER

Blind Men Don't Dial Zero

Sleuths of Last Resort
(Book 1)

LARMER MEDIA

Published by Larmer Media
Northern Rivers, NSW 2482
Australia

www.calarmer.com

Paperback ISBN: 978-0-6488009-4-1

Cover design by Nimo Pyle
Cover photography by Nimo Pyle, Krapels

Edited by The Editing Pen
& Elaine Rivers, with thanks

This one's for my son Nimo,
whose enthusiasm for the concept of 'Supersleuths'
inspired me from start to finish.

Sorry they don't don capes, honey, or have
actual superpowers, but I think you'll find
they come pretty damn close.

PROLOGUE

Fingers bloody, he grappled for the phone and stabbed in three zeroes, his breath like hiccups as he waited for a response.

"Emergency services, what's your emergency?"

"I, um… I'd like to report a… a murder please. Two murders."

There was a stunned silence, then a squeaky, "Can I have your full name and address please?"

The man cleared his throat. "Heath. It's Heathcliff Burlington-Brown. I'm… I'm at Harrow's Drive. Two thirty-five… Is that right?" A brief grumble, then, "Shit, I can't remember! We just call it Seagrave."

Like that would sort it out.

"Are you in any danger, sir? Are you injured?"

"What? Um, no… not yet. But I will be."

An inhalation. "I'm sorry, can you repeat that?"

"Look…" Annoyance now. "All you need to know is I killed both of them and now…"

"And now? Sir?"

"And now I'm going to kill myself, so… sor… sis—"

But his last words were lost behind the sound of a gunshot.

CHAPTER 1 ~
AN INVITATION

Meredith Kean tried very hard not to picture her sixteen-year-old snogging the school principal's son behind the recycling bins, where she was currently dumping a load of empty cans and boxes inside. That was a rumour. *Surely* it was just a rumour? She also tried not to notice that her nineteen-year-old's rusty old Mazda had gone AWOL, along with her nineteen-year-old, even though he *knew* her thirteen-year-old had scoffed down every last morsel of food like it was some sort of Olympic event, and she needed a lift to the supermarket pronto! And she focused instead on a slip of white poking through the letterbox out the front.

Oooh, snail mail. What a treat.

Creaking the lid open, Merry reached tentatively inside, half expecting it to morph into a bill but finding something else entirely— a crisp white envelope with her name handwritten on the front in a lovely black scrawl.

Her next thought was that it was *another* invitation to Las Vegas and she felt her stomach tighten, regret descend upon her again. Flipping it over she noted there was no address on the back, and her gloom evaporated as fresh theories began circling her brain.

A letter from her mother? Her ex? The aforementioned school principal! Drawing it to her nose, she hoped the scent might provide a valuable clue. It did not.

Eventually, reluctantly, Merry held up the white flag, pushed her pink spectacles back into place, and whipped it open.

~

Kila Morea heard the Uber pull up long before his guest did, and he gave her a gentle nudge. "That's you, my love."

The older woman groaned and reached for her dress. "Why can

3

I never stay, Kil'?"

"Aww, babe, you know what I'm like. Come on, little icon thingie says he's right outside."

She got up and glanced about for her bag, spotting it on the coffee table where she'd tossed it the night before amongst the empty wine bottles and crowded ashtray and coagulating camembert. As she stepped across the bedsit to retrieve it, she swished her hips and hair, and he couldn't help smiling. He knew what she was doing, but he wasn't going to fall for it this time. His head was hammering, and he had some serious sleeping to attend to.

"Aren't you at least going to see me out?" she said, her thick lips pouty, and he smiled, detangling himself from the covers.

"Here you go, my lady." He strode naked to the front door and swept it open. "Your chariot awaits!" Then he waved a hand towards the car idling at the kerb.

The Uber driver gave a little wave like he'd seen it all before, and the woman giggled at Kila's audacity and pecked him on the cheek, then lingered for a moment, smoothing back his unruly curls, soaking up his sweaty scent, before sighing deeply as she stepped outside.

"Sorry again about your license, Kil'," she said. "I mean, I never thought you'd actually be crazy enough to do it."

He shrugged like it didn't mean the end of his career and waved as she walked away, swishing her hips again. But Kila wasn't watching now. He was staring down at the envelope she had just stepped over. Eying it suspiciously for a moment, he glanced up and down the street, then snatched it, shut the door and dropped it atop the soggy cheese before returning to bed, where he promptly fell into slumber.

~

The moment Martin Chase noticed the envelope resting on the kitchen bench, he gave his nose an angry rub and dumped it in the garbage bin.

Piss off, lady, he thought as he strode into the bedroom to replace his sweaty cycling gear with skinny jeans and a T-shirt that read I'M SILENTLY CORRECTING YOUR GRAMMAR, then returned to the living area. His laptop was on the dining table and he slapped it to life as he dropped into a chair. He didn't have time for histrionics today. He had a very important manuscript to finish.

But it only took a few minutes, staring at the blinking cursor, to pique his curiosity, and he was soon back in the kitchen, scooping the letter from the bin and brushing some organic Tanzanian coffee mulch from the top.

"Is that another of those loony letters you've been getting?" his girlfriend asked, glancing up from the lounge where she'd been flicking through a gossip magazine.

"Mm-hmm," he mumbled, his nose wrinkling.

Was Tamara burning that hideous incense again? Or had her smell now permeated the place?

"Why do you even keep them?" she said. "Just put Return to Sender and be done with it; she's obviously got the wrong address, the nutter. Oh, and don't forget to call your agent. I think she wants to nag you again."

Well, you'd know all about that, he thought. He wasn't in the mood for another round with Tamara. She sensed it though and lifted one sculptured blond eyebrow skyward, but he didn't take the bait, just returned his eyes to the envelope and the florid cursive script.

Hang on a minute... This wasn't the mad woman's usual frantic scribble, and she'd got his name right this time. Perhaps it was fan mail, Martin decided, and opened it with a flourish.

~

Earle Fitzgerald was just shoving his thumb through the top of the white envelope when his wife appeared with some steaming tea in a chipped cup that read WORLD'S GRUMPIEST DAD.

"What've you got there, dear?" Beryl asked, plonking the cup down on the rotting wooden table in front of him.

"Not sure. Probably another wedding invite."

In their old age, it seemed like the Fitzgeralds' social life had been reduced to other people's weddings and funerals, although he'd see the inside of a coffin long before their Teresa ever walked down an aisle. She was a confirmed spinster, his daughter. Not that he'd use that word in front of Tess or her scary flatmate Fiona! They were both proud of their single status. Like it was a badge of honour. Buggered if he could work out why.

"Two eggs this morning? Or just the one?"

"Hmm?" Earle was so engrossed in the address peeking out from the top of the letter that he barely heard his wife speak. He looked up. Scratched his bushy white beard.

"Just the one, thanks, Beryl. Tummy's not getting any slimmer."

Then Earle patted his wide girth proudly as he wrenched the invitation out.

~

The croaky voice was just explaining how he'd "slipped the shank deep into the fucker's belly" when Francesca Josephina's almond eyes glanced across the invitation she had just plucked from the neatly split envelope.

She nearly dropped the telephone.

"You right, Frankie Jo?" the man on the other end said. "Told ya this'd freak you out."

"What? Oh, give it a rest, Shane. I'm fine. Keep going."

He sniggered, not believing her for one moment, and continued on. The bikie's story was riveting stuff, but that's not what had her quaking.

George Burlington was inviting her over. Sir George! The mining magnate himself!

Now here was one for the books. After months of pleading and camping on his doorstep, Mr Burlington was suddenly having her around for... She glanced at the invite again. "A brief consultation," whatever the hell that meant. No other explanation was provided.

She thought about that. Had he read her articles? Was he fuming? Perhaps he wanted to set the record straight.

In any case, Frankie could not have been more delighted. The Burlington story was still relatively fresh—gory true crime had no use-by date—but it was a pity he hadn't reached out earlier. Still, this could provide fodder for yet more "Frankie Jo exclusives", perhaps even a book. A probing tome. A brilliant bestseller. The diminutive blonde salivated just thinking of the publisher's advance.

"You even listenin' to me, sweetheart? Only got five minutes before they cut me off."

"Of course I'm listening, Shane. Don't be such a princess. I'm busy taking notes. Keep going."

Then Frankie's eyes wafted back to the invitation in her hand, and she was glad she was recording the conversation, because she barely registered a word.

CHAPTER 2 ~
A PROCLAMATION

Sir George Burlington's residence was not at all what Meredith had been expecting. Located in an ornate Victorian-era building that left the neighbouring Town Hall looking frumpy, the interior was surprisingly minimalist and über modern.

Stepping out of the elevator to the penthouse floor, she was welcomed at the door by a redheaded woman with a smart suit and a very subtle Irish accent. She introduced herself melodiously as Verity Vine, Mr Burlington's assistant, then led Merry into a polished concrete living area where three men and a woman stood, staring suspiciously at each other. The penthouse took up the entire floor and was full of glass and steel and lots of cold leather and sharp edges.

"Mr Burlington will be with you shortly," Verity announced before closing the door behind her.

"Thanks!" Meredith sang out, then repositioned her cat eyeglasses and smiled at the others, trying not to appear quite so exhilarated. They certainly didn't, and at least one of them looked almost maudlin. He was a forty-something in a statement T-shirt and black skinny jeans, with a perfectly sculptured nose and surprisingly dark hair, which he was now slicking back as he turned to inspect a bookcase.

The man looked vaguely familiar, Merry thought. She just couldn't decide from where...

The other two men were also dressed casually, and she was self-conscious now in her crisply ironed, pale blue skirt and not-quite-matching jacket. Her sixteen-year-old was right. She looked "so try-hard it's embarrassing." At least the other lady had made an effort in what was clearly vintage Chanel. Merry might not have money, but she did watch *Project Runway*, thanks very much.

"Hello there," said the oldest man, a portly Santa Claus lookalike, holding up one palm. "The name's Earle. Earle Fitzgerald."

"Hello, Earle," she called back. "I'm Merry."

"As in Merry Christmas?" asked the man with the slicked back hair by the bookshelf. Incredulous.

"Oh, goodness me, no!" She giggled, glancing at Santa and snorting. "As in Meredith Kean. It's short for Meredith."

"Well, I'm Kila Morea," said the third man as he dropped into one of the white lounges, his messy black curls bouncing along with him. "And no, it's not Killer as in murderer. It's Kila with an *a*." He directed that comment towards the bookshelf.

Bookshelf man just said, "Martin" like that was all that was required.

Merry glanced then at the smartly dressed woman who was tiny and blond and perfect. She was standing by the floor-to-ceiling window, looking downwards as she tapped furiously into her smartphone, not participating in the introductions.

"Any clue what the frig we're doing here?" said Kila.

Earle shrugged, and Merry giggled again. "I've been wondering the same thing!"

"It's obvious, isn't it?" the younger woman said now as she pocketed her device and sat in a lone armchair. She gave them a moment to catch up and then said, "The Burlington-Brown murders?"

"The whaties?" said Merry.

"Oh, right," said Kila, pushing a stray curl from his eyes.

"Surely not," said Martin while Earle just squinted as if trying to see down a shadowy corridor.

The chic woman turned her eyes to Merry. "Not a newspaper reader then, Merry?"

She smiled apologetically. "I've been a tad busy with my three kids. I'm a single mum. You know how it is?"

"Not at all." The blonde recoiled at the suggestion. Then, glancing back at the closed door, she said, "Last August. Socialite Tawny Burlington-Brown hosts her fortieth birthday party, then after the guests have all departed, she's shot in the head—by her twenty-one-year-old son no less! He also killed his father, then called triple zero, confessed to the ghastly deed before turning the gun on himself. Ring a bell?"

"Oh yes! I do recall that! Soz. You see, I was in Las Vegas last August."

"Vegas?" said Kila, nodding approvingly. "You don't look like a Vegas regular to me."

"Well, it was just the one trip, for the Clue—" She stopped, blushed. "Just a quick visit. I was away at the time."

"It's been in the paper for months!" said the other woman.

"Don't be offended because she doesn't read your columns, Francesca," said Martin.

The woman turned feline almond eyes upon him, pointedly staring at his obviously dyed hair and then down to his ironic T-shirt—this one read THIS IS NOT IRONIC—and said, "She'd be the only one then. And while we're swapping monikers, can I insist you call me Frankie Jo?"

"Frankie Jo the crime writer?" said Merry.

"*True*-crime reporter." Frankie Jo's eyes shifted once more to the man at the bookshelf. "Unlike the acclaimed Martin Chase here, I don't make it all up."

Merry's eyes were now saucer wide. *Martin Chase?* The famous mystery author? Her lips parted, but she was speechless. She had every book the man had ever written! No wonder he looked familiar, although she was sure his dust jacket photos showed a much younger man, more dapper. Less haughty.

She glanced around the group again, her excitement at fever pitch. What on earth was she doing with this illustrious mob? Now she was the one left feeling like the nearby Town Hall.

Only frumpier and far less useful.

Earle watched the exchange between the younger group curiously, wondering what he was doing there. He wasn't much of a crime reader—true or otherwise. Ironic, considering his life's vocation, but there you had it. He always found true crime too sensational and crime fiction a joke—autopsies done at lightning speed, DNA sorted in a matter of minutes, and amateur sleuths outwitting even the smartest of detectives.

In their bloody dreams.

Nah, since he'd left the force, he'd left crime behind, too, and focused on golf and gardening and getting out from under Beryl's feet.

She'd be impressed to hear he was in the same room as the best-selling author. And Frankie Jo for that matter. The missus was just quoting some story by the reporter that morning. Some interview with an outlaw motorcycle gang member. Like the cretin needed any more oxygen.

He was curious about Kila Morea though, the curly headed chap on the sofa. The others didn't seem to know him, but Earle did, by reputation only. Mad Dog Morea was a two-bit gumshoe, a private detective with a pretty appalling public record. Almost as bad as Frankie's bikie friend. He worked out of a crummy office in the heart of the city. Or he used to. *Hadn't he lost his license recently? Something about dodgy practices, interfering with crime scenes? Or was it sleeping with his clients?*

Earle heard a noise outside the doorway and checked his watch. He didn't know what was going on or how long they'd be there, but he did know Beryl would never forgive him if he didn't ask Chase for his autograph. He glanced at the man, then leaned back in his seat and shook his head.

Sorry, Beryl, but I can't give the smarmy bastard the satisfaction.

Where the hell is my name? Martin wondered, stroking the bridge of his nose as he scanned the books between Jane Austen and Agatha Christie. There wasn't so much as a Martin Chase in sight.

Now that was surprising. He'd assumed Mr Burlington was a fan. Why else would he be summoned? He frowned, rubbed a hand down his T-shirt—he liked this one, thought it was rather clever—then wondered if the snooty reporter was right. Were they here about the murders? He couldn't imagine what it had to do with him. Still, he wasn't about to miss an opportunity. The crimes alone would make a stellar plot for his next mystery. Maybe this would spark his creative juices! Get the words flowing.

Peeling his eyes from the shelf, he glanced around the room, soaking up the scenery, taking in every shiny surface. At the very least, he'd get a colourful setting for Flynn Bold's next adventure.

If only he could finish the latest one...

Frankie was also checking out the room, but more openly than Martin, and tapping everything into the Notes app on her smartphone—lest she forget. Here she was in Burlington's inner sanctum, and she needed to jot down every delicious detail.

Oh, how her peers would be green with envy! And the Boss too. The Boss would reward her richly tonight. Maybe even bring over a bottle of Veuve.

She smiled as she read over her notes: *Surprisingly modern. Palatial whites. Hermes chairs? Small Picasso, back wall (check that with art dept).*

Four others (check age/spelling): Martin Chase, author, trying to look twenty, dodgy dye job and Ts (WTF?). Kila More-ay-a, rumpled, handsome, Fijian perhaps? Earle Fitzgerald, old, quiet, distant rellie? Meredith/Merry Keen, dumpy middle-aged mum, utterly clueless.

"Scrambling to make the afternoon edition?" said Kila, batting his thick black eyelashes at her.

"Haven't had an afternoon edition for decades," she replied, not looking up as she resumed her tapping. "So glad you noticed."

Truth is, they barely had a paper. Half the staff had been laid off last Christmas, and the other half were all waiting for that ominous shoulder tap. But she didn't want to think about that now. Wanted to focus on a future book. That could earn her a true-crime gong, assure her future at the paper for life. Might even get out from under the Boss's thumb.

If she were lucky.

As the sexy reporter sat shimmering by the window, Kila wondered if he should try his luck. She was more stunning than her mugshot in the papers and slightly older too. Late twenties perhaps? That usually worked to his advantage. It was the just-ageing ones who let their guard down. Although he doubted Frankie Jo ever let anything slip. She seemed too slick for that. Pity really, because she had an extraordinary set of pins.

His eyes slid across to Merry's legs then. They weren't too shabby either—plump but shapely. He liked a shapely woman. Hell, he liked them all shapes and sizes. Merry was older than Frankie, certainly a lot sweeter. Too sweet for the likes of him.

Didn't need the guilt trip, not after this morning.

Merry noticed him staring and produced the most adorable blush before saying something inane about the weather. Then, more worriedly: "Do you think that's why we're here? Do they think maybe we have something to do with it?"

"*Do* you?" Kila asked, and she blushed even deeper.

"Me? Oh! No, I mean, of course not!" She giggled. "Like I said, I barely know the story."

"You should ask Frankie Jo. She reported on it."

"And what a load of codswallop those reports were," came a deep voice from the doorway, and they all glanced around to find an elderly man with a trimmed grey beard, thick tortoiseshell glasses, and a growly look upon his face.

It was the family patriarch, the formidable Sir George Burlington. And while he was seated in a wheelchair, there was nothing feeble about that look or his next words which echoed across all the hard glass and concrete.

"My grandson is innocent, and I have brought you all here to prove it."

CHAPTER 3 ~
MISSION IMPOSSIBLE

There was a moment of stunned silence, then Frankie almost dropped her mobile phone as she scrambled to her feet and said, "Mr Burlington! It's an absolute honour—"

"Sit down, Frankie, I haven't got time for sycophancy." His voice was like distant thunder. Not quite threatening, but you better have your wits about you. As Verity hovered nearby, he said, "Back away, Vine. I told you before, I'll call you if I need you."

The tiny assistant held her ground, giving him a pointed look, then nudged her eyes towards a sheaf of papers.

He groaned and added, "Okay then, get on with it."

Verity bowed her head and turned to the group. "Before Mr Burlington goes into any more details"—a quick glance at her boss that spoke volumes—"we have a little housekeeping to tick off." She handed each of them a set of stapled documents. "What I'm giving you now is a simple non-disclosure agreement, standard procedure, nothing to worry about. This ensures we keep the information provided here and henceforth between ourselves."

"A confidentiality agreement?" said Kila. "You serious?"

"Very," she replied breezily. "As I'm sure you can appreciate, there will be some sensitive and private matters discussed here today, and it is imperative that it goes no further than this room."

"I won't be signing anything," said Frankie, puffing herself up.

Sir George seemed amused by that. "I may not be a politician, Frankie. But I'm still capable of being misquoted, so I suggest you get on board."

Frankie looked suddenly stunned. She blinked at him mutely before visibly deflating back into her seat.

"And if we don't sign?" asked Kila, glancing between the two of them curiously.

Sir George nodded his head towards the elevator. "Then you may return to your desperate housewives, Mr Morea. Maybe check the fridge for leftover prawns on your way out."

"Prawns?" said Merry, confused, but Kila's expression now mirrored Frankie's, and he too shrank backwards.

Martin just looked incensed. "I don't sign any old thing! Not without my agent."

"It is just two pages, Mr Chase," said Sir George. "Even you can't be tripped up by the fine print, but if you wish to see your agent, you may also see yourself out."

"I... I'm happy to sign," said Merry, earning herself a glower from the author.

Martin snatched the pen Verity was now offering. "This is coercion," he grumbled even as he signed.

Eventually, with that task complete, the PA strode out of the room, leaving the door open behind her while Sir George wheeled himself into the centre and turned his chair around to face them.

He took a moment to survey the group, then placed his hands in his lap and said, "You'll forgive me if I don't offer you anything, but this meeting will be short and snappy. We'll have time for tea and niceties later."

"What exactly is this meeting?" Martin asked, his tone still petulant.

Sir George clapped his eyes on the author, who leaned back slightly.

"I'm offering you all the opportunity of a lifetime." He waited a beat. "There has been a grave injustice. My grandson Heathcliff is accused of a crime he did not commit. And I want you five to prove it."

While the others stared at him sceptically, Merry couldn't get past the name Heathcliff. Was that *really* his grandson's name? Such a bold choice. No wonder the kid went psycho!

A brief silence ensued, and then Sir George cocked a grey eyebrow and said, "Do none of you want to dispute this?"

"I suspect we'd be wasting our breath," Frankie muttered.

His expression lightened. "You would like me to get on with it?"

She smiled back. "If you don't mind. I am on deadline."

"Forget your deadline!" he roared now. "Forget everything on your plate! I want to hire you lot to investigate the murders and find my grandson innocent. Restore his good name. You can take as long as you need, and you will be paid handsomely for your services."

That, too, left them speechless except for Merry, who was holding a hand up apologetically.

"I'm sorry, sir. I just have one teeny weenie question, if you don't mind. I'm not really across the details, but didn't your grandson, er, take his own life?"

"He was murdered," he replied steadily. "I want the record corrected."

"Your grandson dialled emergency services," Frankie said, her voice also steady. "He confessed to the crimes."

"He was lying."

"And why would he do that?"

"That's what I've brought you here for. I want you to find out."

Martin stood up. "I don't have time for this nonsense. I'm on deadline too—"

"Sit down, Martin," Sir George boomed again. "Or should I call you Braxton?"

Now it was the author's turn to look like he'd been smacked over the head by an invisible hammer, and he, too, slunk into his seat while Merry just stared between them. *What was going on?* The iron-ore mogul wielded words like weapons, managing to disable the others with a seemingly innocuous sentence.

As if reading her mind, Sir George groaned and wheeled himself a little closer.

"I'm not explaining myself well. Vine tells me I'm like a bull in a china shop, so let me start over." He took a deep breath and rubbed gnarled fingers across his face. Exhaled loudly. "I know how this looks. I know what you all think. What the entire world thinks, goddammit. But I know my grandson, and I know he did not do this thing. Heathcliff was coerced. Somehow."

He waved a hand as if it were a mere detail. "The police are fools. They believe it is… What's the term?" His eyes were now on Earle, who hadn't yet said a word. "Open and shut?"

"There was that confession," Earle replied, clearing his throat before adding, "Sir."

Another dismissive wave. "Coerced," Sir George repeated. "Not worth the cost of the triple zero call."

"Actually emergency calls are all free," said Merry, "as they should…" She gobbled back her own words and stared into her lap.

"Mr Burlington," said Kila, "as you clearly know, I'm a private detective, but I'm not in the game anymore, at least not at the moment, so unless you're offering—"

"One million dollars."

Kila blinked back at him, gaping. They all did.

Then Merry said, "I'm sorry, could you repeat that?"

"I am offering each of you one million dollars to prove my grandson's innocence."

"Each of us?" asked Kila. "Or one of us?"

"Each of you. But only if you work as a team. Together. Or the deal's off."

"Hang on, *what?*" said Merry.

Sir George ignored her and added, "The person who makes the greatest breakthrough in the case will earn an extra million." He glanced at his watch. Frowned. "Time has snuck up on me. Story of my life." He sighed. "Vine will be back shortly to see to the details. I must be off."

Then he wheeled himself slowly towards the door like he hadn't just detonated a grenade in the room. The others stared at his back, all five of them now gobsmacked.

As he reached the door, Frankie called out, "And the person who does the least? What happens to them?"

Sir George stopped and smiled to himself. "Oh, that person will earn nothing. Not one red cent. You have forty-eight hours to decide."

Then he slid from the room.

"What just happened?" asked Merry.

"He's playing with us," said Martin.

"Could have dementia," whispered Frankie, glancing back at the open door.

"More like a demented sense of delusion," said Kila, not bothering to keep his tone down. "His grandson's a violent monster, and he's not willing to accept it. Don't you love the way the rich think they're above the law? That their progeny couldn't possibly have done it."

"I… I don't understand what's just happened," said Merry again.

"This is a joke," said Martin. "Nobody seriously pays that kind of money to prove a fiction."

"But what if he's right?" said Merry. "What if his grandson didn't do it?"

"Spoiler alert!" said Frankie. "Heathcliff *done it*. I know. I researched the story inside and out. There's nothing to see here. His grandson is a killer."

"Shouldn't we at least try?" said Merry. "He said he'd pay us a million dollars if we look into it."

Earle cleared his throat, and they all turned to stare at him. "No, actually, I think you'll find Mr Burlington said he'd pay us a million dollars *if we prove his grandson's innocence*. Quite a different thing entirely."

"So if we don't prove it…," began Merry.

"We get nothing," said Earle, his voice bone dry.

"And," added Martin, "even if we did manage to prove the impossible, one of us gets sweet F-all, remember? The one who does the least gets zilch. How is that even fair?"

"It's not; it's bullshit," said Kila, getting to his feet.

"You're just *leaving*?" said Frankie. "You don't even want to discuss it?"

The curly-headed PI shrugged. "You lot can do what you want. I'm not wasting any more time on a violent rich kid."

Merry looked deflated. "I haven't got that much on at the moment. I'm prepared to give it a whirl."

"Oh? No games of Cluedo on the horizon?" said Frankie, holding up her smartphone. "Yes, honey. I just googled you. Cluedo champion? Really? Is that what you bring to the table?"

And finally it was Merry's turn to deflate.

"Cluedo champion?" echoed Martin. "Is that even a thing?"

"Well, it's just a hobby really…," she replied. "I just happen to be pretty good at it. Bit of a fluke. But… Well, I can't imagine that's the reason I'm here."

"Then why are you here?" Frankie asked, hands on her hips, and Merry shrunk further. Frankie then turned her eyes to Kila. "While we're sorting out who's who and what's what, you're an ex-PI, Kila. I got that. And you, Earle? I can only assume you're a badge?"

"Was," he said. "For forty years. Twenty-five of them as a detective. Ten leading the Serious Crime Division."

"When did you last work a case?"

Earle hesitated and then said, "A while ago."

Kila groaned and began walking towards the door just as Verity reappeared. She had a set of business cards and was holding them out like a party favour.

"Thanks for your time, people," she sang out. "Should you decide to take up Mr Burlington's offer, he has asked that each of you be present at the address on this card at precisely nine on Monday morning. He will explain everything in more detail then."

"Nine?" said Frankie. "At least one of us has a day job, you know."

"I'd like to clarify an important matter please, Miss," said Earle. "If only three or four of us should happen to show up on Monday…"

"Then the deal is off," said Verity, her tone as matter-of-fact as her boss.

"That's a bit churlish," said Frankie. "I don't need a retiree and a pack of amateur sleuths to help me investigate anything. No offence, people."

"Oh, none taken!" gushed Merry, causing Martin to give her a withering look.

"I work alone too," said Kila.

"The instructions are quite clear," Verity replied. "All five of you have been carefully selected. You each bring certain… shall we say… *qualities* to the table. Mr Burlington would like you to work as one." She held her palm out. "Now, if you'd like to grab a card and follow me, I'll show you back out."

There was a bit of eye-rolling and some uncomfortable stares, then Kila said, "This is a joke" but took a card from the assistant's hands anyway, and the others followed.

"Tell your boss not to hold his breath," Frankie muttered, but as she snatched the card from the PA, she knew full well she'd be there.

She'd just clocked the word *Seagrave* and felt a jolt of excitement. That was the name of Roman and Tawny Burlington-Brown's home—the infamous murder mansion. And she'd happily show up for less than a buck.

CHAPTER 4 ~
THE AFTERMATH

By the time Frankie returned to the *Herald* office, her editor was on the warpath.

"This isn't the Holiday Inn, Frankie," he snapped at her. "You can't just clear off anytime you bloody like. We're on deadline, heard of that?"

"I know, I'm sorry! I was chasing up a lead."

His tone softened. "What lead?"

Frankie hesitated, not sure how much to say. She had already scripted the front-page headline on her drive back:

EXCLUSIVE! MINING MAGNATE'S MISSION IMPOSSIBLE
TO CLEAR HIS GUILTY GRANDSON

Now… Now Frankie was oddly reluctant to give anything away, and it had nothing to do with that irksome confidentiality agreement. She had a dreadful feeling it would all come to nothing. She'd put money on the PI not showing. Or perhaps it was a sense that this was bigger than one newspaper, even this one.

In any case, she simply shrugged and said, "Oh, turned out to be nothing. I'll get back to the dead mountain climber piece. I have a hunch her hubby pushed her."

The editor watched her for a moment as though not quite buying it, then said, "Well, make it snappy. Subs need something in ten."

Then he left her with her thoughts, which as usual were tangling in all directions, none of them towards the hapless hiker. Five minutes later a jaunty tune dragged Frankie back, and she glanced at her smartphone to see the Boss was calling.

"Piss off!" she hissed, then shoved it under some papers while she brought her computer to life. She hunted for her latest article but simply couldn't focus. Eventually Frankie reached for the hidden smartphone and pressed Return Call, then smacked a palm at her forehead as she waited for it to answer.

"Hey, gorgeous!" Frankie said a second later. "Sorry I missed your call. I was just in a meeting. Everything good?"

~

"So, will you take up the calling, d'ya think?" Beryl asked her husband as they sat, legs out before them, on the crackling wicker chairs in their backyard, enjoying their daily sundowner—a frosty lager for Earle, a clinking glass of scotch and dry for Beryl, a bowl of fresh water for their greying "bitzer" Gruff. (He was a bit of this, bit of that.)

"Hmm," he mumbled ambivalently as he reached down to scratch Gruff's upturned stomach. "There's something whiffy about it."

"Up to no good, you reckon?"

He placed his cold beer to his lips. "Maybe." He took a long, scorching gulp.

Something had been niggling at the ex-detective since the mogul made his grand announcement. It didn't feel quite right. Earle knew the case well. His old colleague Detective Inspector Andrew Morgan was on it, and they'd shared a beer soon after it happened. Morgs hadn't nursed a single doubt, and it had little to do with the lad's confession.

They'd both seen a few false confessions in their time. Plenty of nutters owned up to stuff they didn't do, and he knew at least two old colleagues who specialised in nagging, starving, or monstering a confession out of others—usually with the misguided belief that if the turd hadn't done this one, he sure as hell was guilty of something.

Nah, it was the evidence that made it stick. Or at least that's what Morgan had said. There was blood and plenty of it. The young bloke's bloody footprints were like a trail of breadcrumbs from room to room and body to body.

Yep, he was certain the kid was guilty and his rich gramps was just trying to protect the family honour, probably the mighty share price while he was at it. So why was he still mulling it over? Still considering showing up on Monday, despite all that?

"I'll grab us some chips, love," Beryl said, slipping her feet back into her shaggy slippers and then pulling herself up and back inside,

Gruff staggering to his feet to follow.

As Earle watched the screen door rattle on its rusty hinges and spotted the ripped screen flap through which Gruff was now sliding, Earle knew why. It had everything to do with that broken door and Beryl's crummy slippers and the fact that she was opening a packet of no-name potato chips when the gourmet version were her favourites.

Yep, no two ways about it. He was doing it for Beryl.

~

As she steered her trolley through the supermarket aisle, plucking the usual brands off the shelves at an alarming pace (Otis would be there soon to collect her), Merry couldn't stop replaying Frankie Jo's words in her head.

I don't need a pack of amateur sleuths to help me investigate anything.

Well, she didn't need Frankie Jo's disdain, thanks very much. She had plenty of her own to go around. Had absolutely no idea why she was included in that group; could not for the life of her work out why the lovely rich man had invited her.

Had to be a mistake, she thought as she reached for some gourmet muesli.

Perhaps he'd call soon and rescind the offer.

She plonked the muesli back and opted for a jumbo-size packet of Rice Bubbles instead.

The others had certainly looked at her like she didn't belong. And she *didn't* belong! They were all professionals in this field! She only knew her way around a Cluedo board—Clue to her American friends. It wasn't real life.

"You're a Cluedo world champion! You can solve anything!" Otis reminded her later that afternoon as he helped her unpack the green bags—and there were plenty of them.

Despite her reservations, Merry was already acting like she had an easy million and had bought all the treats she normally bought sparingly—chocolate iceblocks, quality steaks (not the cheap, fatty stuff) and even a decent bottle of wine instead of the usual half-price jobby. And yes, she had gone back and scooped up that lovely box of muesli.

"You need to think of it like a game of Cluedo," he added.

"How do you mean, beautiful boy?" she asked as she tried to find room for it all in their small, cluttered fridge.

21

"I mean, didn't it happen in some mega mansion? So why not set it up like a board game? Put the dead bodies in each room and work your way through it."

She was now sniffing what looked like a bowl of leftover curry. "I think it's a bit more complicated than that, hon."

"Popcorn! You never get popcorn!" squealed her thirteen-year-old, Archie, as he burst into the kitchen and atop the shopping bags.

Returning home with the groceries always felt a little like Christmas to Merry's three kids—unwrapping each bag, hopeful of something exciting and usually finding little more than the food equivalent of socks and undies. Today was different, and his smile widened.

"Go on then," she said. "But just one packet or you'll ruin your appetite. Tonight we eat like royalty!"

CHAPTER 5 ~
THE MURDER MANSION

Seagrave looked more like an aging royal residence than a family home, perched high above the plebs on the edge of a grand, chiselled cliff face in one of Sydney's wealthiest suburbs. How it came to be built there would make a story in itself, Frankie thought as she pulled her red Audi into the spacious, pebbled driveway out the front. Or back, really, because the premiere side had to be the one that faced that stunning ocean.

Frankie knew from her own research that Sir George had built this monstrosity just twenty years earlier. Designed to replicate the grand homes of his English ancestry, complete with ivy-clad pillars and crumbling sandstone walls, it could just as easily fit into an Agatha Christie novel, she thought. Certainly had the look of a creaking mansion. And now it had the ghosts to match.

Except there was already a ghostly presence.

Rumour has it the house was christened Seagrave by Sir George's much younger and ridiculously named second wife, Pookie, and no one quite agrees whether it was prophetic or just a very tragic coincidence that she died there less than two years after moving in. Some say she threw herself from a balcony into the roiling sea; some say it was just a terrible accident. In any case, the patriarch had promptly moved out and handed it to his eldest child.

Why Roman and his new wife Tawny would want to inhabit the home where the matriarch had met her demise was beyond Frankie, and she wondered who would want to inhabit it now. Would Sir George's remaining child, Susan, put her hand up? Or would they sell it quietly down the track to some foreign investor who cared more for stunning views than lingering ghosts?

Either way, the ambitious reporter wasn't about to miss an opportunity.

Thanks to a long, high-walled driveway on one side and impenetrable cliffs on the other, she had never got a chance to peek inside (and neither had a stream of paparazzi who'd given it their best shot). The closest Frankie ever got was back on the main road, behind the enormous gate, one hand on the buzzer, the other on her recorder, hoping a passing gardener would show her in and help embellish her articles. Yet there had never been so much as a crackled hello.

"Hello!" came a call from the other side of the driveway now, and Frankie looked up as she stepped from her car.

Martin Chase was leaning against a shiny silver Aston Martin.

Could he be any more cliché? Frankie thought.

"How the other half live, hey?" he said, nodding towards the mansion.

Like he could talk.

"Other one percent, I'd suggest," Frankie said, glancing around. Theirs were the only two vehicles in the guest parking area.

He read her mind and said, "Let's hope the others show."

A fresh bubble of annoyance rose in Frankie's chest. She didn't need four perfect strangers to take a fresh look at the case, two of them total amateurs, all of them riding on her coattails! Because, let's face it, *she* was the only expert amongst them. The aficionado of the murders. And she could do the job perfectly fine solo.

"Shall we?" the novelist said, sweeping a hand towards the Irish personal assistant, Verity, who was holding the front door open.

"After you," Frankie replied, resetting the scales.

~

Merry glanced at her watch, pulled her bag tighter and continued tottering her way up the steep street, past a posh private girls school with its impenetrable iron gate, and on towards the clifftop address on the card. She should have let Otis drive her all the way in, but she was damned if she was going to be caught hopping out of a rusty old bomb with a Provisional Licence plate. She was behind the eight ball as it was.

A car horn blasted, and Merry nearly toppled over.

"Sorry!" called a voice from within. It was the old guy, Earle, one arm slung across the steering wheel of his Holden sedan, the other reaching for the passenger-side door handle.

"Jump in. I'll give you a lift."

"Oh no, it's fine… I like to walk."

His car continued dawdling. "No, really, my dear. Time's almost up." He tapped his watch. "Jump in."

"Right, yes, that's probably best." She cranked the door open and clambered in.

"Car troubles?" he asked, steering them carefully back onto the road.

"Oh, I don't drive! That's what you have kids for."

"Really? My daughter, Teresa, doesn't drive me anywhere except up the wall." He chuckled at his joke and then said, "Strap yourself in, please. We're close, but that's no reason to be complacent."

Merry smiled, recognising the exact words she had used with her son earlier, and clicked her belt into place.

~

Sir George glanced up from the papers he was scanning as Verity entered the living room. She shook her head once, and his eyebrows tipped slightly.

"The PI," he said. It was not a question.

"We could give Mr Morea five more minutes."

"They all knew the rules." He shoved the papers into a manila folder. "Send them away."

Verity was just exiting the room when a bell chimed through the hallway, and she turned back and smiled.

Just in the nick of time.

~

Kila smiled benignly as he joined the others who were milling in the sunlit atrium at the entrance to the mansion. He offered no apology, just rubbed a hand through his tangled locks and said, "You're lucky my curiosity got the better of me."

They all replied with a frown, but it echoed with relief too, because Sir George was right. They did know the rules. And this clown's tardiness nearly cost them a fortune.

By the time they were marshalled through the glass entryway, past a grand circular staircase that led downwards, and into a gaudy yellow living room, they had forgotten about that and were busy marvelling at the decor.

The interior was more Jane Austen than Agatha Christie, with Provincial-style lounge suites and Louis XV armchairs atop exotic Persian carpets. On the ceiling hung a dripping crystal chandelier, at the windows were long velvet drapes tied back with elegant tassels, and all around them an extraordinary collection of books that reached from the polished wooden floorboards to the decorative plaster cornices.

Sir George gave them a moment to soak it up, his own eyes following theirs, appreciating their obvious awe and remembering the decades it had taken to build up his collection. Pookie's collection, really. She had been the book reader of the two, punctuating every work trip with jaunts to antique bookstores. Her favourite had been a tiny, dusty corner of Paris's Saint-Germain-des-Prés, and his eyes now flitted directly to the last book she purchased, the one before she died. Why he hadn't burned that one, he really didn't know.

He cleared his throat and shuffled the memory away.

"Shall we get started?" said Verity, eyes trained to her boss, and he must have nodded, however imperceptibly, because she waved towards a shiny sideboard loaded with a variety of food and beverages.

"Please, grab something to drink, then take a seat. We'll be here for a while."

"Oh goodie!" said Merry, clapping her hands together, and they all followed her across, helping themselves to tea and coffee, sponge cake and date slices, before spreading out across the lounges while Verity took the folder from her boss and stepped in front of a wide glass coffee table.

She hugged the folder to her chest and smiled. "Thank you for coming." She locked eyes with Kila. "I know our request is an unusual one, but Mr Burlington—Sir George as he prefers to be called—believes that a grave injustice has been done, and we're hoping you can correct it. Today I will be giving you a tour of the house so you can get the lay of the land, so to speak. But first I'd like to talk you through exactly what we know of that dreadful night last August."

And with that, anticipation rippled through the room.

The night of the murders was overcast and gusty, Verity told them, her pace slow, her voice crisp and clear. A storm was brewing and not just on the horizon. It was Tawny Burlington-Brown's fortieth birthday party, but it wasn't cause for celebration, she said, at least not for Tawny.

"Tawny hated the idea of turning forty," Verity explained. "She didn't want a fuss. Had invited only immediate family and twenty of her closest friends, choosing to hold it here in this very room, which we call the Yellow Room."

"Why would you call it that?" This was Kila and he was trying to lighten the mood, but nobody was laughing.

Sir George frowned at him and then addressed the others. "I was surprised my daughter-in-law did not choose to go large, fill the place up. I suggested the ballroom."

"You have a *ballroom?*" gasped Merry.

She earned a warm smile for that comment. "It was Tawny's favourite room in the house. Hell, she loved everything about this place." His rheumy eyes swept the walls like he was still trying to work it out. "She might have grown up on a surf beach, but she adored the glamour, our Tawny. Loved the grandiosity of it all."

"The party started at six p.m. sharp," said Verity, taking up the story. "Every guest had arrived by six-forty. All except a couple who had sent their apologies, and Charlie, of course."

"Who's Charlie?" asked Merry, now earning herself a withering glare from Frankie.

"Charlotte is my granddaughter," Sir George replied. "Heath's younger sister. She was at boarding school at the time."

"Boarding school?" Merry almost laughed. Was that still even a thing?

"Charlotte resides at Saint Augustine's Ladies College," added Verity. "Across the harbour in Potts Point."

"And she couldn't get a day pass for her mother's fortieth?" Merry was horrified at the thought of the poor child locked away while her family swanned about in here, sipping champagne without her. And why she wasn't at the girls school she'd just tottered past was another obvious question. It was just a hop, skip and a jump for goodness' sake!

"Permission was not granted," Verity replied, swapping a glance with Sir George. "It was not a lavish affair, so we did not push for it. And of course, in light of what happened that evening, we're all rather relieved."

"Oh, of course!" said Merry. "She really dodged a bullet that night, didn't she?"

Then she blushed at her clumsy wording, and Verity gave her a patient smile before continuing.

"By all accounts, the party was pleasant but relatively uneventful. The final guests had departed by midnight, the caterers and housekeeper left an hour later, and all that remained was the immediate family."

"Except Charlotte," said Merry, still trying to come to terms with the fact that the poor child had been banished from the fold.

"As I have already explained," said Vine, her smile now straining.

Frankie clocked the smile and glanced at Sir George, wondering what he thought of mumbling Meredith. She seemed to want to share every thought that popped into her silly little head, and Frankie couldn't imagine the old patriarch having patience for her kind, yet he didn't seem perturbed, so she decided to voice a question of her own.

"So what happened during the party?" she asked.

Verity blinked. "It was just a happy fortieth."

"No, no," Frankie persisted. "You said it was *relatively* uneventful. Something must have happened."

She knew she was on the money when she caught the quick look Verity gave her boss, who returned it with the slightest of nods.

"There was one thing," Verity conceded. "All we know, from guest statements, is that there was some kind of fracas in the kitchen about halfway through the party. Nobody knows the details, but Heath came out fuming, and then Tawny and Roman followed, looking somewhat distraught. When several guests enquired, they were told there was a problem with the hors d'oeuvres."

Martin snorted at that.

The assistant flashed him a look. "Indeed."

"So we have no idea what the problem was?" asked Frankie, who was surprised she hadn't already heard about this little fracas before.

"Your guess is as good as mine."

Better, probably. But she let it drop. For now.

"That was the last of it, and things seemed to calm down. Guests tell us everyone appeared happy enough, and the party went off without a hitch."

"Well, until the birthday girl got slaughtered."

That was Kila, and Sir George glowered at him.

Frankie smiled to herself. So the old guy had a soft spot for the ladies, hey? Forgave them almost anything, even the blathering ones. *Good.* She would use that to her advantage.

"The guests all left by midnight," Verity repeated. "The staff by one a.m. What we know after that is very limited because, of course, there were no witnesses left behind. We can only assume that at some stage Roman, Sir George's *son*"—a quick glance at Merry in case she wasn't keeping up—"made his way to the study, because that's where his body was located, while Roman's wife, Tawny, was found in her bed, in her nightdress. Their son Heath was located in the hall, slumped over the telephone, just wearing boxer shorts, and his bed looked like it had been slept in."

"Heath still lived at home?" asked Martin. "Wasn't he, like, twenty-one? Bit old for that, wasn't he?"

"Not at all!" said Merry. "My Otis is nineteen, and I don't want him going anywhere, thanks very much. Life's too harsh now to push them out of the nest, don't you think?"

She directed that question at Sir George, who gave her a warm, grandfatherly smile.

The assistant continued. "What we do know is that the emergency call was placed from the landline in the hallway between the bedrooms at exactly 2:35 a.m."

"By Heath," said Frankie. It was not a question, but Verity nodded.

"His voice was officially verified."

She reached for a tiny remote control and waved it towards one wall. A sudden crackling sound came through a hidden speaker, and then, to Frankie's delight, Heath's shocking emergency call began to play out.

"Emergency services, what's your emergency?"

"I, um... I'd like to report a... a murder, please. Two murders."

"Can I have your full name and address please?"

"Heath. It's Heathcliff Burlington-Brown. I'm... I'm at Harrow's Drive. Two thirty-five... Is that right? Shit, I can't remember! We just call it Seagrave."

"Are you in any danger, sir? Are you injured?"

"What? Um, no... not yet. But I will be."

"I'm sorry, can you repeat that?"

"Look... All you need to know is I killed both of them and now..."

"And now? Sir?"

"And now I'm going to kill myself, so... sor... sis—"

The group jumped in unison as the sound of a sharp gunshot filled the room followed by a heavy thud and then complete silence. It took just a second for the operator to find her voice, and as she began to ask over and over—somewhat naively as it turned out—whether Heath was still there, Verity clicked the recording off.

"There was no further response from Seagrave, and the call was disconnected exactly two minutes later."

"Pity," said Martin. "If they'd kept the line open, they might have heard if anybody else was at the house."

She shrugged. The point was now immaterial.

Kila asked, "What does Heath say at the end there? I didn't catch that."

Verity flashed another look at Sir George. "We're not quite sure. It is unclear, and we did ask the police to have it verified by an audiologist. They insist Heath's final words are 'so sorry sis.' We believe he was apologising to Charlotte."

"Well, that's something, isn't it?" said Merry, offering Sir George an encouraging smile.

"*So sorry?*" echoed Kila. "That's something you say when you accidentally bump into somebody, not when you slaughter half your family."

"What we know for sure," continued Verity, "is that the police arrived eight minutes after the call was placed, followed soon after by two paramedics, and then another two. No one could gain access as the house was firmly secured."

"What kind of security?" asked Earle.

"The front gate was locked as always and is accessible only by keypad. So, too, the front door. Both codes were changed regularly. The police had to break their way in." Verity took a deep breath and snuck another look at the old man before adding softly, "Everybody was declared deceased soon after."

Earle leaned back in his seat, and Kila emitted a long whistle.

Frankie agreed—it was quite a story.

"How was Roman's body discovered?" asked Earle.

"Slumped over his desk in the study," said Sir George, his expression hollow. "Still clutching his bloody biro."

"And the weapon?" Earle asked. "How did Heath even get hold of a weapon?"

"He didn't!" Sir George barked now. "Hence the reason I've brought you all here."

"It was a Smith & Wesson," said Verity, ignoring this outburst. "It belonged to Roman; he had a valid license. Shooting was a sport at his old alma mater. They have an undercover shooting range there."

Now it was Merry's turn to whistle.

Verity continued. "We believe the weapon was kept in the study safe, which was found wide open." Then as several eyebrows rose, she added, "As far as we could tell, nothing else was taken."

"Family jewels all present and accounted for then?" asked Kila, earning himself another glare from the patriarch.

"Who stands to gain the most from the murders?" asked Earle, still intent on fact-checking.

"Nobody gains!" boomed Sir George, and now Verity gave him a pointed look, and he sighed heavily. "Nobody gets anything until I'm in a casket, and last time I checked, my pulse was still pumping. So it can't be for the money. Has to be unrelated!"

Or perhaps he just didn't want to blame himself, thought Frankie.

Verity held up the folder she'd been hugging. "All the details are in here, and everything else you may need—the police and pathology reports as well as some photos we retrieved, taken by various guests at the party." She reached in and pulled out a large colour print. "I'd like to draw your attention to one image in particular."

Holding it up so they could all see, Frankie felt another ripple of excitement. It was a family portrait, clearly taken in haste, several people blinking at the flashing camera. She knew from her own research and the outfits they were wearing that this was taken on that fateful night, and Verity confirmed it.

"This is the last known image of the family together. Apart from the man just on the far right, who snuck into the shot inadvertently, this is the immediate family, sans Charlie of course, and Sir George who had left the party by then."

"I was tired," he growled, as though it was an issue he was yet to reconcile.

Verity handed the picture to Martin, explaining as he inspected it: "From left to right, we have Roman, then his wife Tawny, and beside her, Heath. Beside Heath is his aunty—Roman's sister—Susan, and then her husband Clement LeDoux on the end. Susan and Clem had also left the house by the time the events happened. And no"—she glanced at Martin—"they did not reside at this premises. They live on the other side of the harbour, not too far from Charlotte's boarding school, which is handy."

Frankie snatched the picture from Martin and studied it closely. As far as family photos go, it was a pretty bad one, she thought, and it had little to do with the distracting blur of the blue-haired photobomber. The smiles were forced, the cheeks ruddy, the clothes and hair ever so slightly dishevelled, like it had been a big night and not necessarily a good one.

Sir George's children, Roman and Susan, were both tall and angular like him, although Roman was carrying too much weight around the middle and had a balding pate. He was wearing a loose dinner shirt and dark trousers. Susan was in a classic black dress and pearls, her hair swept up in a tight chignon. She was attractive in a plain, horsey kind of way and quite the contrast to Tawny, who was short and curvaceous and glittered like the chandelier above them. Champagne glass in hand, Tawny was the only one smiling with any conviction, straight at the camera, while her brother-in-law Clem looked bored, arms crossed in front of him. He was also on the shorter side but trim and deeply tanned, with a full head of sandy hair and a suit that probably cost more than Frankie's Audi.

And then there was Heath, slam bang in the middle of the group, also dressed top to toe in something designer. He had a white T-shirt beneath his jacket and thick gold chains at his wrists and fingers, which he was holding in a juvenile rapper-style gesture. His hair looked short below a herringbone flat cap, and he was wearing thick, white-rimmed glasses. Half blinking, his smile was benign, not at all like a man who was about to slaughter half his family.

But then what would that smile look like, Frankie wondered? Could words ever sum that up? She would have given it a red-hot go if she'd had access to this photo before she'd written her articles. Still, she had it now, and more.

Reluctantly she handed the photo on to Kila and said, "We're going to need to talk to the LeDouxes and to Charlotte."

Verity nodded. "It has already been arranged."

"And I want to know who this bozo is that's photobombed the family portrait," said Kila.

Verity frowned. "We don't believe he's relevant."

"Sorry, lady, but I don't really care what you *believe*. He was there that night; he could be important." Then he pushed black curls from his face and said, "Unless of course there are some parameters we don't know about."

"I thought you ignored parameters, Mr Morea," Sir George growled.

Kila just grinned back at him. "Only the ones I don't like."

The old man stared hard at him for a moment and then said, "Nothing is off-limits as far as I'm concerned. This is why I've brought you here to the house where it happened. You can crawl through every inch of the place, check out the photo albums, fossick through the underwear drawer for all I care. And if you need to speak to someone—anyone—then Verity will arrange it. I need you to find the culprit."

"You mean *another* culprit," Frankie said softly, because as far as she was concerned the culprit had already been found and he was staring at them now in a David Beckham cap and oversized white glasses.

Earle had a hand up. He looked worried. "I hate to play devil's advocate here, but most homicide victims are killed by people they know. We could find evidence against another member of your family. What happens then?"

It was a good question, and the others all stared at Sir George expectantly.

His eyes narrowed. "Let me rephrase myself then. Nothing— *and no one*—is off-limits. I need to know who did this thing. I need to find the truth."

Verity looked worried for a fraction of a second before clapping her hands gaily and saying, "Time for the grand tour!"

Despite the patriarch's promises, the group did not get to "crawl" through the house today. Instead, Verity all but galloped them through, sticking to the main level where the murders had occurred.

On the northern side, to the left of the front atrium, was the business end of the house—the kitchen with a fridge you could live in, a dining room that could seat thirty, and an office that was textbook McMansion.

"This is the study," Verity told them, sweeping the door open to reveal a mahogany desk, Chesterfield sofa, and lots of polished cabinetry. "The room where Roman was located."

With barely a moment to blink, Verity was marching them back down the hallway, past the downward staircase, atrium, and what looked like a cosy library, to the wing that housed the bedrooms. There were six in all, although only two had been in use, and when Verity swept those doors open, it occurred to Frankie how markedly different the two rooms were.

The master bedroom where Tawny had been found was at the farthest end and void of all colour—no curtains, no personal possessions, the king-size bed stripped of everything, including the mattress. There wasn't so much as a toothbrush in the enormous en suite bathroom.

Yet Heath's room, just two doors down, was bursting with life. There were bright posters on the walls and clothing peeking out from the cupboards and a blue, billowy duvet on his bed. And on the cabinet beside it sat mementos of his life—a watch, his white glasses, a silver lighter, some magazines and a book.

As Verity swept the door shut again, it occurred to Frankie why Heath's room was still cluttered while his parents' possessions had been cleared away. This wasn't so much a shrine to Heath as evidence that it hadn't been awash with blood like the master bedroom.

This room was exactly as Heath had left it before he tiptoed out to perform his killing spree.

She shivered a little, then tapped the thought gleefully into her Notes.

CHAPTER 6 ~
MULLING IT OVER

"Well, that was an almighty waste of time," said Kila as they settled back in the Yellow Room and Verity left them to it.

"What were you expecting?" said Frankie. "A second gunman lurking in a cupboard?"

The PI smirked back. "I'd settle for a second *gun*. They gave us nothing. I thought they'd drop a bombshell. Some great revelation to explain why the old guy wants to put the remaining family through it all again. If anything, I reckon they proved their own case."

"How do you figure that?" asked Earle.

"The fight that night between Heath and his folks. The guy was a hothead. Seems to strengthen his motive, not weaken it. Plus there is the apology to his sister in his farewell call and the fact the place was locked up tighter than a nun's…" Kila glanced at Merry and let it drop. "I haven't changed my mind. I still think he's wasting everyone's time." He leaned forward. "But I'll tell you what he's not wasting. He's not wasting one cent of his own because we get nothing if we don't prove Heath's innocence. Zip, zero, zilch."

"Yes, yes, we have established that," said Martin, feeling irritable now because the slovenly private eye was right. Verity had just rehashed what most of them had already googled of the case last night, and there didn't seem to be any evidence pointing in anyone else's direction.

"Why don't we see it as a golden opportunity," said Frankie, her tone upbeat. "We're here, we're available, why not have a crack?"

"Planning more articles, are we?" said Martin. "A book perhaps?"

Frankie was too professional to blush at that, but she directed her next comments to Merry and to Earle. They both seemed undecided.

"Nobody gets this kind of access to a crime scene, right, Earle? Apart from you in your heyday, of course." She winked. *Flattery was always useful.* "Don't you think it'd be fun, Merry? I mean, what else have we all got on our schedule?"

"I thought you were on deadline," said Kila.

"Oh, I'm always on deadline; that can wait. Look…" She leaned forward, voice earnest. "Let's just commit to a quick look-see. Each of us takes one surviving family member and sees what they have to say. Maybe they agree with Sir George, might even drop us a clanging clue. We could meet back here in, say, another forty-eight hours. Wednesday arvo. How does that sound?"

"That sounds awfully quick," said Merry, eyebrows scrunched.

"That's a long time in the policing world," said Earle.

"And an eternity in mine," added Frankie. "So, what do you think? Kila?" Because he was proving mulishly stubborn.

Kila leaned back and shrugged, so Frankie clapped her hands and said, "Who wants to interrogate whom?"

"Hang on just a second there, lassie," said Earle, causing Frankie's eyebrows now to curdle. "I think it might be best if we take a breath and review the case properly before we all choof off in different directions."

"Didn't we just do that?"

"I've still got questions."

"Then google my articles. They explain everything—the whole kit and caboodle."

"Codswallop, you mean," said Martin, smirking.

Frankie ignored that and said, "What do you want to know, Earle?"

"Other potential suspects would be a start."

"It was a moot point. No one ever stopped to ask about suspects because Heath confessed and that was that. But my articles do explore the other four *W*s, particularly the why."

"The other four whaties?" asked Merry.

Frankie gave Merry a stiff smile. "If you'd studied journalism, as I have, you'd know that no story is complete unless you answer what they call the five *W*s—who, what, where, when and why. We already knew the first four, so there was really only one question left. Why? Why would Heath do it? What was his motive?"

"Or the *perpetrator's*," said Earle. "We need to keep an open mind."

"And what did you find?" said Martin impatiently.

"Exactly what the police found—young Heathcliff had motive

aplenty. According to my sources, Heath and his father did not get along. 'Locked horns' was how one witness described it. 'At each other's throats' came from another. Daddy dearest wanted Heath to join the family biz. Heath had other ideas. It all came to a head."

"Yet he was also fighting with his mother during the party," said Martin.

"Yes, I hadn't heard that before," said Frankie. "I wonder why. And it would not have had anything to do with smoked salmon blinis."

"Salmon what?" said Kila.

Merry giggled. "You've never had a salmon blinis? Blimey! You don't know what you're missing!" Then, noticing Frankie's frown, the Cluedo champ quickly said, "But I just wanted to say, you know all kids fight with their folks. At least all the kids I know."

"That is true," said Earle, recalling past run-ins with his daughter. "Especially at that age. They know everything at twenty-one."

Merry mock frowned. "When does that end?"

"Twenty-five if you're lucky. Never if you're my Tess."

He smiled sympathetically, and Frankie swapped a strained look with Martin and Kila. They weren't taking part in this parenting prattle, so she assumed they also had no kids.

"*Anyway*," she said, dragging them back on track, "Heath was a complete mummy's boy, or so the housekeeper said. A woman by the name of Lia Segeyaro."

"Segeyaro?" said Kila, lips wedged downwards. "Sounds like a wantok of mine. From my clan. Is she also from Papua New Guinea?"

"You're from PNG?" asked Merry.

He nodded. "Mum was born in Port Moresby. Dad's a Sydney boy."

"Goodness! How on earth did they meet?"

"Um, hello!" Frankie said, interrupting yet again. "Can we stay focused please? I'm not sure where the housekeeper's from, but I hardly think that's important. Lia's been in Sydney at least a decade. That's how long she worked for Tawny. Of all the witnesses I spoke to, she seemed the most upset. Worked her way through an entire box of tissues; could not come to terms with why Heath had murdered his mum, although she knew there was friction with the father. Lia used to live here full time in the staff quarters just below the pool. Claims she often heard Roman and Heath bellowing—her word—at each other long into the night."

"She's not here now?" asked Earle.

"Moved out just before the murders. Had already given notice, and the party was to be her swansong."

"That's convenient," said Martin.

"That's what I thought, but according to my sources, Tawny and Lia were close and there was no visible animosity on the night. Lia was strictly behind the scenes, helped the caterers clean up, then left with them. Had moved in with her boyfriend at the time, a bit of a geezer by the name of Wolly or Wacky or something like that. But you'd know all this if you'd read my articles." She directed that comment at Earle.

"Wolly or Wacky? Sounds like you need to read your own articles again, missy," he replied deftly. "So how long had they been at loggerheads? The boy and his dad?"

"Since adolescence I believe."

"If that's the case, I wonder why Heath didn't move out," said Martin, roughly rubbing the top of his nose like a genie might appear with the answer.

"Did Heath have independent means?" Earle asked. "His own job?"

"From what I could glean, just the odd shift at Grandpa's sailing club, but there was a grown-up job waiting for him at the family headquarters, which is right in the heart of the city. He was more interested in partying and playing music."

"Well, he was young," said Merry. "Plenty of time to find your calling."

"Or not, as it turns out," said Kila, making Merry blanch.

"Okay, so he hated his father," said Earle, getting them back on track. "Why kill his mother and himself for that matter?"

"Oh, it happens all the time," said Frankie. "Remember the Menendez brothers in the US?"

"Yes, but they didn't kill themselves. They did it for the inheritance. I wonder if he was a victim of child abuse…"

Merry's eyes widened, but Kila was shaking his head. "Not an excuse, mate. Not an excuse."

"Nothing of that kind came to light at the inquest," said Frankie. "I didn't hear so much as a rumour."

Martin listened to this exchange but wasn't interested in the backstory. "You left one out, before," he said to Frankie. "There's also the question of *how*. How did Heath achieve it? How could he move from room to room and carry out the murders without anyone stopping him or phoning the police during that gunfire? Guns are noisy weapons."

It was a problem he had encountered himself in several of his books, and you couldn't always add a silencer to the mix. That felt like a cop-out.

"Apart from the two victims, he had the place to himself by then and took out the strongest link first," said Earle, now flicking through the police file.

Frankie nodded. "That's what the detectives said. And Roman wasn't shot, you know? Verity glossed over the details, but the fact is he was struck from behind by an antique candelabra."

Merry sat forward with a gasp. "No way! A candlestick? Like in Cluedo?" Then she swallowed her delight and tried to look thoughtful while Frankie frowned at her like she was a fool.

"Whatever it was, it did the job. His head was smashed in, just one blow from behind so there'd be no time to cry out. And you have to remember, the study is on the other side of the house. These walls are pretty thick, and it was your proverbial dark and stormy night. Ideal conditions for murder."

Martin chewed his lower lip and said, "If Roman was killed at his desk, then that doesn't bode well for Heath either because it implies he was killed by someone he knew, someone who could get that close without him dropping his pen."

Frankie agreed. "Exactly what the detectives said. They believe Heath had some altercation with his father, probably over money as the safe was open and Roman's Will was out."

"His Last Will and Testament?" gasped Merry again.

She nodded. "Another thing Verity glossed over. Anyway, the police think they had a squabble over the Will, Heath fatally hit his dad in a fit of rage. Maybe it was unintentional, maybe it wasn't. In any case he then spotted the gun in the open safe and went on to shoot his mum while she was still sleeping. Maybe he wanted to cover his tracks or spare her the agony or something. Then he killed himself. Probably couldn't live with what he'd done."

Merry placed a shaky hand to her eyes like she was trying to block out the vision.

"It's not a pretty case, that's for sure," added Frankie.

"And not getting any prettier with us sitting here," said Kila, one foot tapping. "Let's get on with it. I bags the housekeeper, Lia. She sounds like kin to me. Besides, it's always the butler in these mansion murders, so she's the closest thing." He chuckled.

Martin frowned. *Was the deadbeat ever going to take it seriously?* "You just want to score the extra million."

"And you don't?" Kila shot back.

Merry had a hand in the air. "If it's okay with everyone, I think I'd like to have a little chat with young Charlotte. My daughter, Lola, is around the same age so…"

"So, because you're a mum, you're the only one capable of talking to a child?" said Frankie. "I was hoping to interview the granddaughter. I never had the chance before."

"Oh, sorry, I'm not saying—"

"I think Merry should do it," cut in Earle. "The poor child has recently experienced a tremendous trauma. She might relate to Merry better." He didn't seem to notice Frankie's reply scowl as he tapped the police file. "I'm going to have a quiet word with the detective who ran the case. He's an old mate."

"What about the LeDouxes?" said Martin, pointing at the family photo. "Heath's aunty and her husband live just a few suburbs from me. I'd be happy enough to pop in and see what they have to say."

Frankie dropped her phone on the couch beside her. "Oh, that's just fabulous. What will I do then? Paint my nails?"

"You could come with me," said Kila, eyebrows nudging up and down. "We could fetch a bite to eat afterwards."

She gave him a bored look. "That won't be happening."

"Why don't you have another chat with the Big Man," suggested Earle. "Sir George might know more than he's telling, and he did seem rather partial to you ladies."

Kila chuckled again. He'd clocked that too, but Frankie looked doubly offended.

"So I'm supposed to flirt some more information out of him, am I? That's all I'm good for?" She sighed and stood up. "Fine." She reached for her oversized Givenchy tote. "See you back here in two days."

"Hang on just a sec," said Merry, the only one still seated. "Shouldn't we, you know, discuss what to ask them?"

"I don't need lessons on interview technique, thanks, Merry," Frankie replied. "And I'd suggest if you do, you shouldn't be in this group in the first place."

Then she smiled blithely as she left the room.

~

By the time Martin had returned home, he was already rejecting the idea of turning Heath's crimes into another Flynn Bold story. It was just a distraction. Truth was, he wanted to write the Great Australian Novel, not another murder mystery.

He glanced at his books that now filled the shelves of his home office but felt no emotion. None at all. Once, they'd triggered a sense of pride. Now… not so much.

Martin remembered the exhilaration of his very first book deal, could recite every word his agent had uttered, telling him how, after three ego-crushing years of endless solicitations and stonewalling, they had finally found a home for his manuscript. Then he remembered his mood dampening when she said they wanted it to be part of a crime series.

"Say that again?" he'd asked, smile slipping.

"Well, your amateur sleuth…"

"My what?"

"Flynn Bold, who solves the murder."

"Oh, yeah, but Flynn's not a sleuth, per se. This is his life story, and he can't move on until he learns who killed his father. But that's a secondary plot."

"Well, don't tell that to the publisher!" His agent Lizzie had laughed. "They think Flynn Bold is going to be the next Jack Reacher."

"Jack who?"

She laughed louder. "Lee Child's creation! Goodness, you have been living under a rock!"

He'd balked at that. Of course he knew Lee Child, but he couldn't recall ever reading any. Literature was more Martin's thing, and he was disappointed to find that his book was being considered anything else.

"Don't get me wrong, they *adore* your prose, darling; even used the word *brilliant!*" Lizzie had quickly added, "But they love the mystery even more. They want Flynn back to solve another."

"But that doesn't make any sense. The whole point is by uncovering what happened to the patriarch, he frees himself from the shackles of his past and moves forward with his life."

"Yes! Exactly! They want him to move forward to find another corpse."

Martin wasn't feeling quite so jubilant anymore. Until she had talked him round.

"There're big bucks in genre fiction, Martin. Let's not get too snobby! You could pay your mortgage off with the advance. It's a three-book deal. Just write two more, then do whatever you want after that."

Two more? Seriously?

And yet he had done as he was asked, and much to his surprise, the series had become a global sensation, sitting alongside Child on best-seller lists. Not only had he paid off his mortgage, he'd bought a spanking-new pad, a luxury vehicle, and even traded up girlfriends—the last one as plain as his old hatchback.

And now here he was, clicking his computer on, trying to write Flynn Bold's twentieth adventure, and all he wanted to do was throw the guy under a bus and move on with something more literary. It's not that he didn't enjoy writing crime—turns out he was very good at it—but he couldn't believe he was now considered Australia's top crime writer. It's like his protagonist had taken over his life. Except where it mattered. He glanced at his mantelpiece and felt his stomach drop. There were plenty of awards up there but nothing of any value. At least not to Martin.

Six months ago, he told his agent he was writing Flynn's final chapter. The twentieth adventure would be his last. Lizzie had laughed and told him she had six months to talk him around. But she would not. Not this time. Next book he would do as he thought he had done the first time around—he would write a brilliant literary novel, but he'd be careful not to kill so much as an ant.

"Aperol spritz, hon?" came Tamara's voice from the lounge room, and he sighed.

Forget Flynn Bold, he should be focusing on a mystery of a different kind, calling the LeDouxes, setting up that first interview. He just couldn't find the energy.

It felt like another distraction.

"A bloody big one," he called back, deserting the blank page yet again.

~

Kila was also procrastinating but in a bar with strangers. Except for Trevor, of course.

The barman was sloppily wiping the counter when Kila took his stool, and he nodded hello and said, "The usual schooner of lager, mate?"

"I'm a creature of habit, you know that, Trev," Kila replied, reaching for his wallet, hoping it wasn't empty. "And don't forget the lemon squash."

Trevor frowned. "Do I ever forget the lemon squash?"

The lager and squash had been Kila's standing order when he first started coming to the Taboo Wine Bar three years ago. He never actually touched the soft drink, but that didn't stop him from ordering it each and every time. And Trevor was happy enough to oblige him even if it did feel like a waste of a good drink. Trevor also knew that the moment he placed Kila's order down, he'd be waxing lyrical about the state of the nation or the look of some winsome young chick in the corner. This time, however, he surprised him.

"What do you know about the Burlington murders?" Kila asked, and the barman's eyes widened.

CHAPTER 7 ~
FAMILY MATTERS

Merry squinted up at the gigantic marble statue of Mary that graced the cobbled courtyard of Saint Augustine's Ladies College in Potts Point.

Goodness me, she thought, before following the signs to the administration block. Girls were depressed enough these days without having a woman weeping down upon them!

It was now Tuesday morning, and Verity had kindly—and quickly—arranged Charlotte's interview for her. And so here she was in a school that felt a world away from her own children's public high school. Unlike that simple Besser Block structure, Saint Augustine's was a Gothic masterpiece, all pointed arches and flying buttresses, the kind of place she longed to go to when she was a wide-eyed lass.

Now Merry knew better.

As she waited in the creaky reception area with its spooky stained-glass windows, she wondered how they could possibly produce happy, modern women in such dark, miserable environs. Certainly couldn't imagine her Lola lasting more than a week here, although she might have threatened boarding school from time to time. *Must remember not to do that again!*

"Please, take a seat. The principal will be with you shortly," the receptionist told her, and she had barely sat down when a smartly dressed woman in her fifties approached.

"Hello there. I'm Sister Mary."

Sister Mary proved to be a lot less intimidating than her namesake, and Merry was surprised to see her hair was styled in a neat brown bob, not a habit in sight.

"I always feel like I'm disappointing people when I first show up," the head nun said, reaching a hand to her hair. "We haven't worn habits in many years, but perhaps I should bring it back?"

She was being facetious, and Merry chuckled. "Sorry. I don't know much about all this."

She was referring to the Catholic private school system, and Sister Mary smiled warmly.

"We're just like any other school except we have God on our side." She winked at another of her jokes and led the way down the dark panelled corridor towards her office where she sat behind an antique wooden desk and waved Merry into a stiff chair in front of it.

"So," Sister Mary said. "George has called and asked me to be helpful."

She smiled warmly while Merry thought, *George, hey? Isn't that a little familiar?*

"It's really not up to me," Sister Mary continued. "It's up to Charlotte. She's currently in a Modern History class, and I won't have that interrupted, but if she is interested, I have arranged for her to meet you in the boarders' common room after that. You may speak to her during recess break."

She glanced at the clock on the back wall, and Merry smiled politely, then there was a long, awkward silence before the nun said, "Until then, was there anything you wanted to ask me? Perhaps?"

"Oh! Right, of course, yes!" Merry cleared her throat and tried to think of something. "Um, well, I'm just wondering… um, how long has she been here? Young Charlie?"

"Charlotte has been a day student since Year Seven but only started boarding in third semester last year, just after the winter break. About a month before it happened."

"Well, thank goodness for that, hey?"

Sister Mary nodded. "Our Lord certainly wanted to spare young Charlotte. We give thanks for that daily."

"I bet you do! And she's Year Ten now, is that right?"

"Year Eleven, actually. Charlotte is young for her year, but quite mature, and applies herself diligently to all her studies. We may even have a future Dux in the making. She's quite exemplary. We have no issues."

"Even after what happened?" Merry's Lola had gone off the rails over a faulty hair straightener just yesterday, but the nun was nodding vigorously.

"More so now, I would suggest." Then, reading Merry's surprise, she added, "Sometimes the best elixir is busyness, Miss Kean.

Throwing yourself into your work, and I can see her study has helped. Of course, that's not to say it wasn't a terrible shock." She smiled grimly. "As I say, Charlotte is an extraordinary young lady. Very strong, clearly resilient, a true Saint Auggies trooper. As you will see."

Merry nodded, wondering if Sister Mary was giving her school the credit for all that. "Can I ask you about that night? Do you mind? I'm just wondering how Charlie found out about it. Like, did you deliver the news or…?"

"Yes, of course, with Charlotte's dorm mistress at my side. I received George's call very early that morning, just before the girls were due to wake up. It was highly distressing, but we put all the correct procedures in place."

"You have procedures for when a student's family is murdered?"

Merry regretted the words the second they sprang from her mouth, and the nun looked taken aback.

"We have procedures for when we have to deliver bad news to our charges. The murders were a first, I can assure you of that. We've only ever lost parents to things like farming accidents or cancer, may they rest in peace. In each case, we take the student to their common room and have a cup of tea on hand. Or would you prefer we shout it to the rafters in their dormitory, in front of the others?"

"No, of course not! Sorry, that, ah… well, it sounds like a really great way to… you know?" She smiled awkwardly and added, "And how was she? When you told her?"

Now Sister Mary looked inflamed. "Utterly distraught."

"Of course. Yes, of course!"

Merry felt like a right idiot. Her silly questions had taken her from joking with the convivial nun to combating with the enemy, and she was trying to think of something important to ask, something positive, anything that didn't sound like silly small talk when she heard the door of the office open.

Sister Mary looked as relieved as Merry felt.

"It appears that Charlotte is available," she said, getting to her feet. "Leanne will escort you to the senior common room now."

Merry stood up. "Fantastic, thank you so much, Sister Mary. And thank you for your time."

The nun smiled again as Merry left the office, but there was no warmth in it this time.

Charlotte Burlington-Brown looked straight out of Hollywood casting—tall, willowy, with a look of utter boredom on her perfect button-nosed face. Merry knew that look well. Lola might be from a very different school—suburb, dress size, bank balance—but there was something universal about the expression. It was Teen Girl 101: Feign boredom until your confidence catches up.

Merry watched as the student loped into the room and flopped down on one of the common-room beanbags with a dramatic sigh, not looking at Merry once. Merry would have laughed if she wasn't feeling so terribly for the poor child, and not just about the lack of confidence. To lose a family member at this age was unbearable, but to lose three of them, including both parents. In one bloody night! She couldn't even wrap her head around that. It wasn't just nerves Charlie was masking, it was unutterable trauma.

"I'm so very sorry for your loss," Merry began, but the girl continued staring at the wall. "I know that doesn't help in any way, shape or form."

Charlotte's eyes snapped across. "Why say it then?"

Merry giggled—her own attempt to mask her emotions—and nodded. "Good point! I guess it's just something adults say to make themselves feel better. We can be right idiots sometimes."

"*Sometimes?*"

There was a sliver of humour in Charlotte's tone, and Merry took that as her cue and nodded towards the neighbouring beanbag. "Do you mind if I plonk on down?"

Charlotte shrugged a bony shoulder beneath her crisply ironed tunic and watched as Merry dropped awkwardly into the velvety bag while Merry wondered how embarrassing it was going to look when she attempted to get up. Lola would be eye-rolling her about now.

"He talked you into it, did he?" Charlotte said.

"Sorry?"

Another sigh—a *keep up, woman!* huff. "Gramps. Pay you enough, did he?"

Merry almost blushed at that. Was that really why she was doing it? "So you know all about this mission of ours then?"

"He's a fool."

"Your grandfather?"

Another scornful look.

"Oh sweetie, you can't blame him for wanting to prove that your brother wasn't a monster."

"Heath *wasn't* a monster!"

"So you agree he didn't do it?"

"Oh, he did it all right," Charlotte shot back. "But he had his reasons." Then, reading the surprise on Merry's face, she quickly added, "I'm not saying they deserved to die! Oh my God! As if I would say that! My brother is, like, a total bastard. He took my parents from me, and I will never forgive him for that. Never."

Merry nodded again, offering a sympathetic look, but she waited, knowing there was more to come. When Charlotte remained stony-faced, she said, "But?"

Charlotte swiped at a tear that was plopping out of one eye. Merry wanted to reach out and hug her. Tell her it was okay to cry. She *should* be crying. Hell, she should be sobbing and weeping and gnashing her teeth! Yet Charlotte seemed too self-contained for that, and already the haughty, bored look was back.

"Gramps likes to pretend we were a happy family, but it wasn't like that. Not. One. Bit."

"What was it like?" Merry asked gently.

Charlotte ignored the question and said, "Is it true you're a Cluedo champion?"

Merry blinked. The girl was all over the shop!

"Guilty as charged," she said, waiting for the mockery that usually followed, yet Charlotte's eyes were wide and curious.

"I love that game! Everyone here prefers the Ouija board, but that's far too creepy."

"I agree."

"This place is so old-school. They switch the Wi-Fi off after nine, right—or think they do..." She sniggered but let that drop. "So we've taken up board games, and it turns out I'm very good at Cluedo. Perhaps I should challenge you to a game one day."

"I'd like that."

"Aren't you afraid I'll whop your arse?"

Merry smiled at her arrogance but had a feeling this was a test. "I don't think you'll beat me, Charlie, but I'd enjoy watching you try."

Charlie snorted. "Cocky, aren't you?"

"No, just good at Cluedo. It's the reason your Grandad hired me. I think. Do you mind if I ask you a few more questions about what happened at that time?"

Charlotte looked disappointed but nodded anyway.

"Can you tell me a little bit about your family? What was going on that might have led to… well, you know?"

Another shrug. "Just, like, lots of fighting and stuff."

"What was the fighting about?"

"Who *cares*? Dad and Heath were at it all the time, like they hated each other. It was sooo…" She mock snored. "Why do you think I'm even here? It's certainly not for the ambience." There was a splash of humour again as her eyes wafted across the bland-coloured furnishings and small kitchenette in one corner. Then, catching Merry's surprise, she said, "You honestly thought I was exiled here like all the other losers? Nah-uh! I chose to come here. I had to get out of that house and all the festering fights."

"Do you think that's how it happened? After a festering fight?"

The girl's eyes welled up again, and Merry felt dreadful for pushing. "I'm so sorry, honey."

"Stop saying that! I thought we'd agreed that's a stupid thing to say."

"You're right. It is. I'm sorry. Oops, damn, I did it again."

The girl's sliver of a smile was back but only briefly as a bell could be now heard through the open window. She leapt to her feet.

"Biology," she said as she headed for the door. "Snore." Then she stopped, twirled, and said, "Next time we play Cluedo."

Then she released a smile so dazzling it just had to be genuine.

~

Sir George didn't look exactly delighted when Frankie was shown back into his penthouse office, but he didn't seem perturbed either, just held up a palm and continued scribbling at some papers on his desk.

"Can I get you anything?" Verity whispered, and Frankie shook her head, thinking how wonderful it would be to have her own personal assistant.

Then she thought of the Boss and frowned. There were already six missed messages on her phone that morning, and not all of them were friendly. She'd better reply soon, or shit would hit the—

"Fancy seeing you again so soon," George said, breaking through her thoughts.

Frankie dropped the frown and smiled. "I know you're busy, Mr Burlington. Sir George. I do appreciate your time. I'm here to fill in some blanks."

"Off the record?" he asked, his tone teasing again, and Frankie tensed as her mind spiralled back to a drunken night in another lifetime.

She blinked. Breathed deeply. Told herself to focus. *Sir George couldn't know about that night, could he?* Unless he'd been talking to the Boss…

She gave herself a shake and sat in the chair in front of him. Another deep breath. Another exhalation. Then, "I'm curious about the tiff that was witnessed that night, the one between Tawny and Heath in the kitchen. Are you able to shed any more light on that?"

"I did ask Tawny soon after it happened. She insisted it was nothing."

"You believed her?"

"Of course I didn't. I'm not a fool. She rarely fought with Heath, adored the lad."

"And Roman?"

A smile played at his lips again. "Are you asking me if she adored Roman or if Roman adored his boy? Or if the two men fought? Which is it?"

Frankie smiled back now. "All the above."

"We were a normal family, Frankie. We had the odd—what did you call it? Tiff? But otherwise nothing worth killing for. Completely normal, I can assure you."

Normal was hardly a word Frankie would have used for the Burlingtons, certainly not twice in one breath, but she waited for him to answer the question.

Eventually he said, "My son and his wife had a very committed, honest relationship. They were dedicated to each other and to the rearing of their two children. It was their highest priority. They were a happy family. Content. I can assure you."

"And yet Charlie was sent to boarding school and Heath fought non-stop with his father, or so my sources tell me."

"Your sources are a disgrace!" he roared back before grimacing and glancing at the door as if Verity would return with one of her pointed looks. "Charlie was not *sent* anywhere; she asked to board at Saint Auggies. And if you're suggesting that Heath and Roman's squabbles led to murder, then by that measure my own father wouldn't have lasted past my fifteenth birthday." He leaned back in his wheelchair. "I know you're doing what I asked you to do, but there's nothing there, Frankie. Move it along."

She leaned forward. "Where should I move it to?"

"The boyfriend would be a good place to start."

"Tawny had a boyfriend?"

He stared at her. "No, I can assure you of that. I am referring to my granddaughter Charlotte's boyfriend. A lowlife by all accounts. Lad by the name of Igor. I can't recall the surname. Something Eastern European."

Frankie's eyes widened, and she reached for her phone to tap the name into her Notes. "You never mentioned him before."

"I can't make it too easy for you; where's the satisfaction in that?"

She smiled. "Why do you think this Igor fellow might be the culprit?"

"I don't, not necessarily, but you asked for a lead. He's one. He was spotted at the party, albeit briefly—"

"Hang on. Charlotte's boyfriend was at the party even though she was at boarding school?"

"My thoughts exactly. I never ran into the lad; wouldn't have recognised him if I had. The police never looked at him twice, but I have it on good authority that he's a bit of a ratbag. I was also informed that he left the party long before the murders. Was seen exiting around eleven that night. I wondered if my son grew some balls and kicked him out, but it was probably Tawny. She was the ballsy one in that family." He smiled sadly. "But still."

"Still you want me to check him out?"

He shrugged, said nothing.

"Got a contact number? Address?" Then she glanced up from her notes and said, "Never mind. I'll find it."

He smiled. "And now, my dear, you're learning."

~

By anyone's standards, Susan and Clem LeDoux's house was a mansion, but compared to Seagrave, it was little more than a granny flat—a fraction of the size and a lot less flashy.

Martin wondered about that as he stood in the driveway and rang the front doorbell, wondered too why they didn't have a massive fence and gate and intercom system. Susan clearly wasn't as fixated with security as her brother, and it felt horribly—tragically—ironic.

"Hello and welcome," Susan said as she swept the door open. Then she glanced behind him and said, "On your own?"

"Were you expecting others?"

"I did hear there were five of you, so perhaps I was." She smiled and twirled, and he followed her in.

Susan was more handsome than the party snap had indicated, with glossy auburn hair and long, shapely legs that flashed from time to time beneath a flowing silk dress as she swept Martin down the hallway to the other side of the house.

Turns out the house was also more handsome than first impressions, and Martin decided he preferred it to Seagrave. It was lighter, breezier and much more stylish, with none of the gaudy, antique furniture. It was as elegant and understated as Susan.

"Clem can't join us, sadly," she was saying as she flopped onto a wide, comfy-looking sofa. "He's busy teaching the riffraff how to sail."

"He's a sailor?"

She chortled. "Better not let *him* hear you say that! My husband is so much more than a sailor, dear. He runs my father's club, or he did before we got married."

"Club?"

"The Burly Sailing Club, just down the road from here."

Martin's lips formed a perfect circle. "I didn't realise that was you guys."

"In his heyday, Father was an avid sailor. Nearly won the America's Cup, don't you know? Missed it by *that* much!" She indicated an inch with her fingers, then winked. "He set up the club to give something back. Clem used to run it; now he runs an entire department down at HQ. He's so much more than a pretty face! But yes, occasionally Clemmie takes people sailing. Likes to keep his hand in. And yes, okay, he gave me some lessons; that is how we met. It was sunset, all very romantic. His French accent did the rest."

She said all of that matter-of-factly, like she was repeating a mantra or perhaps family lore.

"How long have you been married?" he asked.

"Twelve years, next March." She smirked slightly. "Is that

important? To all of this?"

He smiled back.

"Shall I fetch us some coffee?" Then without budging she said, "You know, I'm a little miffed with you lot."

"Sorry?"

"You're only here because Father insisted, and Father gets what Father wants." She leaned forward and grabbed a packet of cigarettes from a low glass coffee table, the offer of coffee completely forgotten. "The truth is I'm no fan of this ridiculous little project, and I really cannot imagine why you agreed to do it. It feels like you're taking advantage of an old man's grief."

Martin cocked his eyebrows at that. "You really think your father is capable of being taken advantage of?"

Susan stared at him hard for a moment and then laughed. "Oh, I like you," she said, pulling a cigarette out. Then her smile dropped. "My father might think he's a dynamo, but I do worry about his sanity sometimes. And all of you for accepting." Her head dropped to one side. "Why did you accept? You can't possibly need the money. If that's not Tag Heuer, I'll eat this cigarette."

He glanced at his luxury watch. "Maybe it was a challenge."

That rankled. "This is my family we're talking about, not some reality TV show. Although God knows we would have made a decent one."

"Lots of drama?"

"You don't get three corpses when life is dull, darling."

He watched her, wondering how she could be so flippant. "So can you tell me what you think brought it to a head? What drama?"

Susan retrieved a lighter from her skirt. "Where to begin…"

"You were there that night. At the party." He was offering a place to start, and she nodded, lighting the cigarette and then dragging on it long and hard before releasing a plume of smoke. He noticed she didn't ask if he minded her smoking and had a feeling it didn't matter. It seemed Susan got exactly what Susan wanted too.

"We arrived right on time as usual," she said. "My Clem loathes being late, although God knows Tawny was one for grand late entrances." She dragged on the cigarette again. "Anyway, all seemed fine. Tawny was a bit stressed, which wasn't like her." Took another long drag.

"Stressed? Do you know why?"

She released the smoke. "She was turning another year older. That'd do it. She always was very vain." It was a nasty comment, and perhaps because of that her eyes suddenly filled with tears, and she produced a hanky from somewhere and dabbed them away, giving Martin a grim smile. "I don't mean to sound like a bitch. We're all vain really." Her eyes skirted across his outfit, then up to his dyed hair. "No one likes to age. But... well, I think it was more than that. I assumed it was the party, hosting and all that—even though she liked to throw soirees and did them often. But now..."

"Now?"

"Now I have to wonder. Was there something on her mind? Did she have an inkling of what was to come? She did seem *haunted* that night..."

Martin didn't know what to make of that. "We heard there was a fight in the kitchen. Do you know anything about that?"

Her eyes narrowed. "No, I do not. Who was it between?"

"Heath and his parents, I believe."

"Really?" Her eyes were now staring out the window. "Interesting."

"Your father never mentioned it?"

Her eyes shot back. "Darling, if we gossiped every time that family fought, we'd have lost our voices entirely. I wouldn't read too much into it. I know Father likes to say we all got along and maybe as far as most families go, we did. We made an effort, mostly for his sake. Took annual holidays together, celebrated every milestone like we cared, but the truth is, my brother and I were chalk and cheese, and as for Tawny and my darling Clem?" She grinned. "Not even in the same shopping basket."

"Did anyone else have a beef against your brother?"

"Roman? I hardly think so! Poor Romy..." Her tears were back, and now she just looked annoyed at herself, her hanky swiping at them as they rolled down her cheeks. "Sorry," she said eventually. "I'm just so tired of crying. I'm exhausted by it! The fact is, I loved my brother dearly, but he was a pretty lame duck. Only interested in making money, keeping the family fortune intact. The only bold thing he ever did was marry Tawny. She was quite out of left field!"

"And Tawny? Any enemies that you know of?"

"Oh I'm sure she had her share. Like I said, she was a character, that one. Giant personality. Quite wicked when she wanted to be but not murderously so."

She reached for a glass ashtray and smashed her butt into it. "I'm sorry this is such a waste of your time, but it is nice to meet one of my favourite authors."

Martin's cheeks filled with colour, and she laughed—a deep, throaty chuckle.

"Oh dear, I've made the mighty Martin Chase blush."

"I wasn't sure you'd recognised me."

"I have several of your books, and if I were anyone but a Burlington, I'd demand a selfie, but that just won't do. So, can I help you with anything else?"

"Actually yes. If your dad's right and it wasn't Heath, who could it be, do you think?"

Susan looked confounded by the question. "There is no other possibility, and I am frankly offended by my father's attempts to point the finger at the rest of us." She frowned. "Look, I adored my nephew, really I did, but the truth is Heath could be a bit of an entitled brat. There, I've said it."

Susan looked almost relieved, like she'd unburdened herself, and then just as quickly offered Martin a defensive stare. "The boy slaughters my only sibling and I'm supposed to give him the benefit of the doubt? I just can't do it. I'm sorry. He could be sweet, he could be charming, but Heath was also lazy, entitled and, frankly, selfish. Refused to work for the family business even though we were crying out for a millennial perspective. It was all too hard, you see. Had dreams of stardom that did not involve the nine-to-five grind of Grandad's boring mining company."

She shot Martin a look then. "It wasn't really his fault, you know. His mother put him on a pedestal. Tawny could never say no to either of them, although why she let Charlie board at Saint Auggies when there are six perfectly acceptable bedrooms at Seagrave I cannot imagine. We even offered to take her in here. But no, the children got what the children wanted even if it meant dismantling decades of tradition, ignoring family commitments, ruining entire holidays!"

He cocked his head and said, "You're not talking about Saint Augustine's now, are you?"

She waved a fresh cigarette about. "Oh it's nothing. Really I ought to get over it." She sniffed. "Last winter. We all went away to the

Snowy Mountains, skiing, and stayed as we always do at the family lodge just on the perimeter of the Perisher Ski Resort. It's nothing glamorous, let me assure you. Grandfather Horatio bought it long before they made the really big bucks, but it had sentimental value to Father, and really it was perfectly suitable."

She stared at her cigarette. "But not quite suitable enough for young Heath. Too boring, or perhaps he couldn't lower himself to sleep on bunk beds anymore. Who knows? He lasted two days and said he was heading home, dragged cheeky Charlie with him. Ruined the entire holiday, which turned out to be our last! He was a sweet kid, but he was becoming a rather obnoxious man, I'm sorry to say."

"So you weren't surprised when it happened? The murders?"

"Of course I was surprised! Nobody suspects their nephew of that! But I'd be more surprised if you found anyone else who could possibly have done it. No, sorry, I think my father is wasting your time. The truth is, my nephew was utterly spoiled, and I suspect somebody finally said no to him and he spat the dummy."

"You're saying it was just a tantrum?"

She stared at him with a mixture of amusement and surprise. "I think we can both agree it was a little bit more than just a tantrum, Mr Chase."

~

Across town, Kila sat in front of his empty desk and stared glumly at his phone.

Come on, Sheila, call!

His lawyer, Sheila Bonneray, was taking his case to mediation today, fighting to get his PI license back. A chance to start over. He'd wanted to attend, but she'd quickly put him off. He was too off-putting apparently, or at least that's how most magistrates received him. Of course, if it was a woman, he might be in with half a chance...

The phone rang, and he leapt upon it. "Sheila?"

"What? This is Lia. Lia Segeyaro. Returning your call."

He blinked, trying to catch up, then remembered—Tawny's Papuan housekeeper. She was home from work and could talk to him now, but he vetoed that. It was always better to do these things face-to-face. So he scribbled down her home address and made his way over.

As he pulled his old utility truck in front of an equally old apartment block on the aptly named Dreary Road in Sydney's inner-west, Kila guessed Lia had come down a peg or two since she'd left Seagrave. This place looked like council housing. There was a patchy park on one side and no guest parking to be found, so he circled the block once, then pulled into a loading zone and cut the engine.

At the entrance to Lia's complex, he glanced around and then buzzed the apartment marked L. SEGEYARO, introducing himself before being informed it was on the fifth floor and hearing the door click open.

Expecting an islander version of Alice from the *Brady Bunch*— much like his dear old mum—Kila was pleasantly surprised when the door swung open to find a mini-me of Fran from the *Nanny*. In her mid-thirties, Lia was all big hair and luscious lips and clothing tight enough to make sure you didn't miss anything.

"*Apinun wantok*," he said, using a typical Pidgin English greeting, and she raised a pencilled eyebrow. He smiled. "Yep, Mum's from Moresby. You?"

"Goroka," she replied, her tone dismissive. "But I am from Sydney. Come…"

She ushered him in and into a mismatched lounge suite. "You want coffee, tea? Cold water?"

"Coffee'd be good." He watched as she sashayed into the adjoining kitchen and reached for the kettle. "I expect Verity Vine has explained what's going on. Why I'm here."

Lia was nodding even as she said, "No, Mr George, he tell me."

So she had a direct line to the old guy, did she? That was interesting.

"He's a good man," she added, stepping over to the sink. "He found me the new job with the Smythe-Turners. They're nice people. Decent hours, and I don't have to live in."

"You didn't like living at Seagrave?"

Lia looked around, kettle in hand. "I liked it! Why you say that?"

"You gave notice, didn't you? Just before Tawny's birthday?"

She looked at him as if to say *So?*

"I just wondered if—"

"I loved that family!" she shot back. "Especially Tawny and the kids! I barely saw Roman. But… well… everything was changing. Charlie was at school; Heath was out so much. It was time for me to have a fresh change, that is all. My job was done." She stopped, her lower lip trembling.

He wondered if she were about to fall apart and wished he'd brought a box of tissues. "What time did you leave the party?"

"I already told the police all this! Just before one that morning. I let the caterers out and followed them. I go to my boyfriend Woko's place. Sorry, ex-boyfriend." Her eyes slid to an android smartphone that was sitting on the nearby coffee table. "Now... Now I wish I had stayed. Maybe I could have stopped Heath. Maybe..."

"Or maybe he would have killed you too."

It sounded harsher than he intended, but she shrugged like the suggestion was not new.

"Heath would never hurt me. He liked me too much."

"He liked his mother too, didn't he?"

That did it. The tears were now tumbling down Lia's cheeks as she stood holding the empty kettle. Kila jumped up and took it from her, placing it back on its perch, then shepherded her to the sofa.

"I don't need a coffee, Lia. I'll ask what I need to ask and leave you alone."

She pulled out a crumpled tissue from her cleavage, giving her nose a wipe. As she did so, her phone buzzed, and they both stared at the screen where Kila noticed the face of another fellow islander, a man with dark skin and a shaggy yellow-coloured afro.

Reaching across, she switched it off. "Sorry." Blew her nose. "What do you want to know?"

He waited a beat, then said, "Sir George doesn't believe Heath did it. What do you reckon?"

"Oh poor Mr George, he loves his family, but..."

"You disagree?"

She shrugged, looked away.

"Did the family have any enemies that you know of? Could anyone else—"

"No! No one else. It was just Heath."

"Okay..." He frowned. "Your ex-boyfriend, Woko. He's Papuan, too, yeah?" Had a hunch it was Woko who'd just called her. Lia nodded. "When did you break up?"

She looked up sharply. "Why you care?"

He held up a palm. "Just filling in some blanks."

Her eyes narrowed.

"Not long after Tawny's birthday. Is no big deal."

"Fresh change?" he suggested, and she shrugged again. "Did he live with you at Seagrave before you broke up?"

Lia looked shocked at the suggestion. "No! I never took him there. Why I do that? Tawny did not like guests."

"So Woko wasn't at the party?"

Now she just looked confused. "It was Tawny's party, not Heath's. Why he be at the party? Why he do that?"

"So if it had been *Heath's* party, Woko would have been invited?"

She gave her dismissive shrug again, puckering her thick lips upwards. "They do some music together, Heath and Woko. An album. You know, rap?"

"So your ex is a musician, hey? Do you have a number for him?" He glanced at her phone. "Just so I can have a quick word?"

Lia shook her head firmly. "I not see him for ages." Her lips puckered again. "Why you care so much about him? He is nobody. He has nothing to do with this!" Her eyes had narrowed into slits. "Why you try to pin this on Woko?"

Kila frowned. Was that what he was doing? Planting it on the black fella? A wantok of his own country? No wonder she was getting testy.

"Hey, I'm not trying to pin it on anybody. I'm just fishing around."

"Well, you go fish elsewhere! This has nothing to do with me or my friends. Why you try to make trouble for me?"

He held a palm up to calm her down. "Sorry, Lia. Really, I don't mean anything by it." He stood up and pulled a business card from his wallet. "Look, call me if anything comes to mind, anything that might help the case."

She glared at the card he was holding out and did not take it.

"I'm sorry," he said more gently, holding the card to his heart now. "Really I am. I'm just trying to help your old boss out. That's all I'm doing." He held the card towards her again. "Forgive me?"

Lia's scowl slipped away, and she managed a small smile. "Only because you're a wantok," she said, then snatched the card from his fingers.

Back at his vehicle, Kila stared at the apartment block for several minutes, then reached for his phone and began googling the name Woko. If there was one thing he knew, it was women, and this woman was lying about her ex. And he couldn't help wondering why.

~

Earle didn't need to search for long to find his old colleague DI Morgan.

It was now six p.m., after-work drinks, so-called happy hour, yet the Wobbler's Arms hotel looked grumpy when Earle stepped into the front bar. There was none of the usual vigour he remembered from the old days, although the stench of stale beer and fresh sweat was familiar. So, too, the bulky figure hunched over a table, studying what looked like a form guide, a schooner of beer beside it.

"Place has lost its vibe," Earle said after grabbing his own lager and joining him.

"Never had one, mate. Retirement always comes with rose-coloured glasses," said Detective Inspector Andrew Morgan, laughing and reaching across to shake Earle's hand before pocketing the guide. "Good to see you again. I was surprised to get your call."

"Yeah, sorry for being so clandestine. I... Well, it's delicate."

"Oh yeah?"

Earle took a seat and a long slug of his beer. "Karen good? The kids?"

The detective smiled. "Karen's putting dinner on the table right now. Shall we get on with it?"

Earle smiled back. Morgan had always been impatient—it was a fault—and he wondered now if his impatience was also a factor in this case.

"The Burlington murders," he said, catching the younger man by surprise.

"What about them?"

"I've been hired to look into them again."

"You? By who?"

"The patriarch himself."

"Sir George?" His eyes were wide. He wiped a hand across his mouth. "Wow, okay, I guess that shouldn't be surprising. He never could admit his grandson was the devil."

"Be a hard thing to admit, don't you think?"

Morgan shrugged. "Truth hurts, right? Why you?"

"Ah, not just me, a crew of us."

"Like who?"

Now Earle was shrugging. "Wouldn't want to keep you from your lamb chops, mate. I just want to ask your views of the case. If you don't mind. Sir George seems to think his grandson is innocent. Tell me if you think he's dreaming."

"He's dreaming," Morgan said immediately, then pushed his empty glass away and added, "Is that all you need?"

Earle smiled. "Come on, Morgs, I think I left the force with the scales tipped slightly in my favour. Won't hurt you to give me a little more than that."

The copper frowned but he knew what he meant, and he exhaled loudly. "I hope he's paying you well for this waste of time. What do you want to know?"

"Any chance anybody else could've done it? Any chance at all?"

"The kid confessed, Earle. Had both victims' blood all over himself, gunshot residue on his hands, the same hands that produced the only prints found on the gun and the phone he used to make that confession." He smiled. "Did I mention the confession?"

"We've both heard false confessions before."

"Sure, but he wasn't in a police cell in the 1950s. He made the call all by his lonesome. Nobody beat it out of him."

"That we know of."

Morgan frowned again, then his features softened. "Bored with retirement are we, Fitzy?"

Earle knew it was a dig, but he smiled anyway. "Let's just say I'm spending a little too much time on the green..." He indicated swinging a golf club, then tapped his head and said, "And not enough time on the grey."

Morgan chuckled and stood up. "Good on you for giving it a second look, but there's nothing to see here other than a rich geezer trying to pretend his shit don't stink."

Earle tried not to grimace. He'd forgotten how crude his old colleague could be. "You might be right."

"I am right. You're barking up the wrong tree, Fitzy. Go home to Beryl. While you're there, give her my best."

Earle nodded and watched the DI stride away, but there was something Morgan just said that gave him pause for thought. He shrugged it away and stared down at his weathered hands, wrinkled and smattered with ageing spots. It's like a new one popped up daily. Looking around the pub now, he saw only young people, laughing and backslapping and drinking the day's hard work away, and he felt a sense of melancholy.

He checked his watch, polished off his beer, then headed to the bar for another.

CHAPTER 8 ~
THE GREAT UNRAVELLING

Merry was running late to the second meeting at Seagrave and envied the others their childless status—because grown-up kids who'd flown the nest didn't really count, right?

The envy didn't last long.

Glancing across at Otis, who was steering his car through the palatial mansion gates, she wondered what she'd do without him. He'd finished school two years ago. Had mentioned the idea of moving out of the family home with mates once or twice, but it never seemed to eventuate, and Merry was quietly relieved. She'd miss him terribly if he ever gave his wings a test flight.

"Thanks honey," she said as they pulled to a creaky stop beside Frankie's gleaming red Audi, and she reached over and hugged him. "Now drive home safely, and I'll give you a bell when I need picking up."

Then she grabbed her bag, jumped out, and headed for the front door, which was being held open, again, by Verity. Like she stood sentinel there all day.

"Hello, Merry," said Verity. "I do hope your time has been productive. The others are all here. Except for Mr Morea."

Merry giggled. "Why do I get the impression that's going to be a habit?"

Verity made no comment as she closed the door behind her and then led the way back to the Yellow Room.

Frankie was propped at a table, tapping away furiously at a laptop before her. She did not look up as she called out, "Hey, Merry."

Martin and Earle were seated at separate ends of one lounge, Martin looking bored, Earle flicking through a notebook with scribbles on every page.

"You've been busy," Merry said.

He glanced up. "What's that? Oh no, this is old. Lots of ancient cases in here. The stories I could tell."

"I bet! What's the most interesting—"

"Hey, guys!" Kila called out as he strolled through the door, offered them all a wave, then headed straight for the refreshments table.

"Please do all help yourself," said Verity. "I'll be back a bit later."

They joined Kila at the buffet and were soon nursing a range of beverages and sweet treats.

"Isn't it just delightful! I could get used to this," said Merry, waving a coconut slice about.

"God, I'd be the size of a house if I did this every day," said Frankie, looking Merry up and down. "So, what happens now?"

They all stared at each other.

Merry could tell the reporter was champing at the bit to run the show, but so it seemed was Kila.

He said, "We should shift to somewhere a little less comfortable. Perhaps the infamous study?"

"Where the first murder happened?" said Frankie. "I think not."

"In my experience, the best place to work is around the kitchen," said Merry, thinking of the kids and their homework.

"Oh, your *experience*?" said Frankie.

"Why don't we just stay where we are for now," said Earle, cutting in. "I suggest we each report back on our findings and see where we're at. Merry, would you like to go first?"

Merry blushed. He was trying to counterbalance Frankie's sarcasm with kindness, but she really wished he hadn't. She swallowed her nerves, along with a mouthful of slice, and cleared her throat. She hadn't thought to take notes! That would have been smart. She just hoped she remembered everything correctly.

"Okay then," she began. "I met up with Charlie at her boarding school. I can tell you, that place is a little scary. And the nun who runs it—Sister Mary—well, she's a force to be reckoned with!"

"Yeah, yeah, so how was Charlie?" Frankie asked, hands back on her keypad.

"Not great, I don't think, but pretending everything's hunky dory. She's sad, obviously, and angry with her brother."

"She thinks he did it?" asked Martin.

Merry nodded. "Doesn't blame him though—said there was lots

of fighting—but she didn't seem surprised, let's put it that way."

"That's the vibe I got from Susan," said Martin, glancing across at Frankie, who was tapping away. "Clem wasn't available, but Susan said Heath was lazy and entitled. Tawny could never say no to him; maybe she finally did. Or maybe his dad did; that's why he was in the study that night, asking for more money and it was refused. The cops' theory seems to fit." He stared at Frankie again. "I thought this was confidential?"

Frankie looked up from typing. "Doesn't mean I can't keep my own notes."

"Hoping to sneak out a bestseller when the old guy's not watching?"

"Oh, you're the only one allowed to sell books, is that it?"

"I'm just saying…"

"He's right," said Earle. "We need to be able to speak fearlessly and frankly. As far as I'm concerned, you're welcome to make notes, Frankie, but that's as far as it can go. I don't want to see my words come back to bite me in some book down the track."

"Some book?" She blew out a puff of air and shut her laptop lid again. "Fine. I'll refrain."

"Good." Earle turned back to Merry and Martin. "Get anything that will help this case?"

"I did learn one interesting thing." Merry paused for effect, proud of this little nugget. "Charlotte told me she chose to go to boarding school because the tension in the house was so toxic."

"That's what Gramps said," said Frankie. "But I didn't believe it. Why would she choose to be locked away with a bunch of nuns? And, more importantly, away from her boyfriend?"

"Boyfriend?" Merry repeated.

"Yes, Igor something or other." Her eyes narrowed. "You did ask about him, right?"

Merry looked flustered. "Ah, no, I didn't know there was a boyfriend. I mean, she never mentioned any boyfriend. I just assumed…"

"Oh. My. God!" Frankie slapped a palm against her brow. "This is exactly why I should have done the interview!" She took a deep breath. Exhaled loudly. "Sir George said that Charlie had taken up with some lowlife—his words precisely. Says this lowlife was spotted at the party that night."

"Why would he be there if she wasn't?" asked Martin, and Frankie flung a hand in the air.

"Exactly! Which is something I would have asked if I had been given the chance to interview Charlotte!"

"But she never said anything—"

"*Of course* she's not going to say it, Merry! You have to know what to ask. How? Dig deeper for goodness' sake."

"Go easy, Frankie," said Kila. "It's her first investigation."

"I know! That's what worries me! I'm sorry if I'm sounding harsh, but Charlie's a key player in this. The closest living relative, right? I did offer to do the interview, remember? But apparently I'm not *mumsy* enough!"

Merry recoiled at that and stared into her lap.

"Let's move on, shall we?" said Earle, giving Merry a reassuring smile. "Kila, what did you learn?"

As Kila began to outline what Lia had told him—that she was at the party but left ninety minutes before the killing—Merry slipped further into the sofa and tried to take steadying breaths. She could feel the tears spotting behind her eyes and tried to push them back. She was so excited by what she'd discovered; she thought she'd done well! But Frankie was right. She hadn't uncovered anything of any substance, and what were the chances Sister Mary would grant her access again? If only she hadn't barged her way into it! Hadn't let the child distract her with talk of board games and tears. If Frankie had interviewed Charlie, they might have the case wrapped up by now. She nibbled on her cuticles and felt about as useless as Sister Mary's discarded habit.

As Kila spoke, Frankie couldn't help seething. She knew she'd been harsh; she'd apologised, hadn't she? It's just that this wasn't a bloody board game! There was big money at stake here, not to mention careers and reputations.

As soon as word leaked about this investigation—because it would surely leak; it always did—she would look like a fool if her colleagues knew she'd been offered access to a key player in the Burlington murders and they'd handed it straight to a novice! A middle-aged mother who probably did little more than ask how she was feeling and make her a cup of hot cocoa!

Frankie jiggled her shoulders and tried to remember what she'd learned in her mindfulness classes. *Be in the moment. Let it all go…*

She breathed in and out, in and out, as she focused on Kila, but she had already explored that angle—the housekeeper and her boyfriend. She hadn't found anything of interest, and from what Kila was saying, neither had he.

"I wondered about Lia's so-called ex-boyfriend, some guy called Woko. She got defensive when his name came up but insists he was never at the party, never even been to the house. Which got me thinking…" Kila stopped. "Nah, don't worry. Feels like a bit of a stretch." Then he spread his arms wide to prove his point.

Earle was not perturbed. "No, no, tell us what you were thinking."

"Just that Lia says he wasn't welcome here at the Big House. Tawny didn't allow it. Maybe he took offence to that. I know I would."

"Would you slaughter them all to teach them a lesson in inclusivity?" This was Martin and he looked unimpressed.

"Like I said, it's a stretch."

"You also used the words *so-called* ex-boyfriend," said Frankie, who never missed a beat. "You don't think they've broken up? According to my research, they broke up just after the party."

"Lia said that too, but I'm not sure I believe her. It's just a vibe I got." He grinned. "I'm a bit of a pro at reading the signs."

"What?" said Frankie. "You can tell if somebody's got a boyfriend? Just like that?"

He grinned. "Yes, I can, and no you don't. Have a boyfriend that is. Which is why you really should let me take you out for dinner later. My shout."

She gasped. "This is sexual harassment, you know."

"Well, I was just thinking a burger, but if you insist…"

"Humph!" She turned her body away from him and tried to settle her breathing again while Kila's smile turned wolfish.

Earle now offered Frankie a reassuring smile and decided he'd step in if the frisky PI got too persistent. But the truth was, Frankie reminded him a little of his Tess. She was single too, despite being in her forties. He knew she wanted to settle down but wondered how she was going to achieve that if she stayed home every night with her flatmate and took every man's smile as a slight, every flirt like a fist to the face. He just couldn't get his head around it. *Wasn't that how courting worked?* Besides, he wanted to get back to this Woko fellow. He said, "Woko would have known about the party, through Lia. He might have expected them all to be half-tanked in their beds— easy pickings if you want to burgle the place."

"But one of them woke up," suggested Kila, and Earle nodded.

"So instead of scooting, he decides to slaughter the lot?" said Martin. "That's also what I'd call a stretch."

Kila said, "You're a bit of a prickly creature, aren't you, Martin?"

Martin scowled. "Oh sorry, mate, was I supposed to just sit here and agree with you? I might not be a private eye, but I've written a lot of crime—very creative, award-winning crime, in case you're not much of a book reader and you certainly don't look like one—and I can tell you that plot would not get past my editor."

Kila stared at him for a long, hard minute, then rubbed a hand across his stubble and stood up. "Pity they haven't got anything stronger than coffee," he mumbled as he strode back to the large buffet table.

Earle clapped his hands and tried to keep things moving along. "Okay, folks, well, I spoke with my old buddy, the man who was in charge of the investigation."

"And?" said Frankie eagerly. "Anything new to report?"

He dropped his hands to his lap and frowned. "No. Nothing new. He's adamant the grandson is guilty."

Then they all looked as deflated as he did.

Kila slugged his second espresso back and then turned to face the group.

"Allow me to do a recap," he said, standing as Verity had, between them all, in the centre of the room. "After two more days working for nothing—for one of the nation's richest men, I might add—we have exactly zero to show for our efforts. And I'm not just talking about a pay cheque. Not one of us has got a viable new lead. Everything still points to Heath."

"We have to keep digging," said Frankie.

But Kila shook his head. "Why do we have to? Richie Rich is not paying us. At the very least he should compensate us for the time we've already spent on this mission impossible."

"Those weren't the rules," said Earle.

"Then they were crap rules," Kila shot back. "I'm not hauling my arse halfway across town every day to prove what we all know can't be proven. The old geezer is wasting our time. He's probably hiding behind some one-way mirror, sniggering at us right now."

They began shooting furtive glances around the room, although Kila's eyes were on his mobile phone. He was waiting for a callback.

Why hadn't Sheila phoned?

Only that morning Kila had received two queries for work—one about another arsehole husband, the other a runaway daughter. He really wanted to get on to that one. The poor mother sounded distraught. Yet here he was chipping away at a case that had already been firmly cracked. And for what?

"Look," he said, "I'm not trying to play devil's advocate here, but all we've learned after two more days of slave labour is that the Burlington-Brown house was so toxic the housekeeper gave up a good job with free digs to escape it and the daughter willingly locked herself away in what amounts to a convent, while nobody else was very surprised when it ended in bloodshed. All the people who profess to love Heath the most are still pointing the finger straight back at him."

"Maybe they're doing that to deflect blame from themselves," said Martin.

Kila scoffed. "Maybe in one of your fairy tales, mate, but not in the real world. I've been in the biz too long. I know how to smell a non-event case, and this one's been whiffy from the start. Just because a man wants his grandson to be innocent, doesn't make him innocent. Seems to me, Sir George has got five pretty smart cookies working on this case, indefinitely, for nothing." He shook his head. "Maybe we're not so smart after all."

"We're not on it indefinitely," said Frankie.

"Really? You telling me you haven't thought about this case non-stop since we got it? Course you have. You're already preparing your book tour. What about the rest of you?" He scanned the group. "George has got us exactly where he wants us. Always thinking about his grandson, sniffing around on his behalf, the pot of gold just out of reach. Jesus, people, we could spend a year investigating and be no further along than we are right now. Well, I'm not buyin'. I'm not on some cushy salary or royalty package or pension plan. I get paid per job, and I don't work for nothing, certainly not for a mining magnate. My clients can barely afford their rent, but they have the decency to pay me for my time. This joker has given us nothing but a bit of attitude and some posh tea."

He made his way to the door, talking as he walked. "Sorry, guys, I know I'm disappointing you, but you'll thank me in the end." He reached for the handle and said, "I'm out."

"Hang on!" said Frankie, scrambling to her feet. "If you take off, Kila, then it's over for all of us. Isn't that incredibly selfish of you?"

"Hey!" Kila turned back to face her. "I didn't ask to be drawn into this little game of Sir George's. I was very happy thanks very much."

"Happy harassing unfaithful husbands for jealous wives?" said Frankie. "Really?"

He scowled. So she'd googled him too, had she? "At least those jealous wives pay me upfront whether I get results or not."

"Come on, people, let's not turn on each other," said Earle.

"It's all right for you," snapped Martin, who'd been quietly watching the tension rise. "You're retired. The rest of us have jobs, responsibilities."

Earle frowned at that but said nothing.

"I'm a single mum, three kids, and I'm happy to keep doing it," said Merry sheepishly.

"Oh, so your kids trump our careers again, do they?" he snapped back, and she held out a palm.

"No... I'm not saying—"

"You're seriously willing to lose a million dollars?" Frankie interrupted, eyes firmly on Kila.

He threw his hands in the air. "It's not about the money, Frankie! It never was. Sir George picked the wrong gumshoe, that's all. If I cared about money, I wouldn't be a bloody gumshoe in the first place. I work to live, not live to work, and I sure as hell don't work to save some poncy kid's reputation!"

And finally, with those parting words, Kila pulled the door open and walked out.

Martin sighed and stood up. "I don't need the distraction either. I'm so far from finishing my latest book I can barely see straight."

And he too left the room.

"And then there were three," said Merry, offering up a tiny smile.

"But that won't cut it," said Frankie, packing her laptop away. "I'm nothing if not a pragmatist. Looks like the deal is off." At the door she turned and said, "You want to tell Verity, or shall I?"

Earle shook his head. "The others ruined this; they can do the honours."

She agreed and left the final two, still seated and looking more despondent than ever.

"What are we going to do if they don't come back?" Merry asked.

"They won't be back, Merry. It's game over."

"Really? That's it? Couldn't we call them? Appeal?"

"There's no point them being here if they're not really *here*. Kila showed no interest from the start; should've expected this outcome. I don't want to get two months down the track and find him drop out again. Better to cut our losses now, hey?"

Merry tried to find that smile again, but her heart was feeling heavy. Deeply disappointed. Earle was right, of course he was right, yet she wouldn't have minded looking into the case for a few months, results or not. She enjoyed being here, doing something that didn't involve the children and the Parents and Citizens Committee and battling with her ex to pay some bloody maintenance. Merry hadn't felt so invigorated since the last Cluedo championship three years ago, and now... She sighed and turned back to Earle. He looked disappointed too.

"Now you can get back to that lovely retirement," she said.

He smiled, but it was forced. "And you can get back to those lovely kids."

Her smile was equally disingenuous.

"Come on. Let's get home. Need a lift?"

Merry checked her phone and shook her head. "I'll just text Otis, thanks anyway. Might grab another Darjeeling while I wait. Kila's right; the tea is posh. I just have cheap tea bags at my place."

He looked saddened by that, then stood up and produced a hand to shake. "It's been an honour meeting you, Merry Kean. Best of luck with those kiddies."

She smiled and surprised them both by jumping up and hugging him.

Later, after she'd summoned her driver and prepared another cup of tea, Merry stared at all the uneaten food on the table and wondered if she could sneak some cake home for her youngest. Archie was the gobbleguts in the family. But of course she didn't; she wouldn't dare. She just swallowed her tea, grabbed her bag and made her way back to the atrium at the entrance.

Verity was nowhere to be seen and Merry glanced around, wanting to thank her for the lovely tea at least. She noticed a light on in one of the bedrooms down the hall, so she headed that way, passing a Queen Anne-style telephone table that was positioned halfway along.

Merry pulled up with a start, staring at the corded landline resting on top.

Oh my Lord! This had to be where Heath made his final, fateful phone call. She hadn't noticed it before and shuddered wondering why it was all still here. Perhaps it was a priceless antique or a family heirloom. Still, she didn't care. If it had been her family, she would have incinerated the lot.

Wrapping her arms tightly around herself, Merry continued towards the light. It was coming from Heath's bedroom, and the door was wide open, yet Verity was not inside. Merry noticed several empty boxes on the bed and wondered if the shrine was finally being dismantled and what would happen to Heath's belongings, to the whole house for that matter. Would Susan and Clem move in? Or Charlotte when she came of age? Could any of them ever live here again? Or would they sell it at a discount rate—because who would pay top dollar for a house of horrors?

Merry glanced around but did not feel horrified. Not in the least. This room still had a heartbeat. She smiled sadly at the Eminem posters on the wall (her Archie had the same ones) and the discarded glasses on the bedside table, an opened book beside them. She stepped across to see what Heath had been reading—*The Shadow of the Wind* by Carlos Ruiz Zafon. It looked like Gothic crime. Not her cup of tea. Still, it might've been a clue the family had ignored.

Sighing wistfully, Merry turned away, then turned back just as quickly.

She reached for the white-rimmed glasses by the bed. They were Gucci. An expensive brand. She glanced back, then whipped her own glasses off and placed Heath's carefully on her face. The prescription was almost a perfect match.

"He loved those specs," came Verity's voice from the doorway, and Merry wrenched the glasses off and placed hers back on. "I'm surprised he wasn't buried in them."

"Sorry," Merry spluttered. "I was just…"

"I think it had more to do with the brand than the style to be honest," Verity added. "If you check his wardrobe, half is Gucci, the other half Tommy Hilfiger."

Merry smiled, collecting herself. "My youngest boy's the same, although in our case it's all knock-offs. It's only because the famous rappers wear them."

Verity raised her eyebrows as if she hadn't realised, then reached for an empty box. "I've got to get this room cleared out. Been putting it off."

"I'll leave you to it then," said Merry, but she didn't move, was still staring at the Gucci glasses. "Had he always worn specs? Heath?"

Verity looked up. "Since first year of high school, I believe. Why?"

Merry felt the shiver return. "Did he have several pairs?"

She shrugged. "No idea. Again, why?"

"Oh, nothing." Merry's heartbeat was beginning to rise. "Do you still have that police folder?"

"Of course. It's in the Yellow Room."

Merry was already dashing back down the hallway, past that creepy phone, heart now hammering in her chest. If her instincts were correct, she had just discovered their first real clue that could prove Sir George was right and young Heath was no killer.

She just had to work out how to convince the others.

~

Frankie was getting home from a late shift when she received Merry's frantic message—something about new evidence and can they meet up? Followed soon after by a missed call from Earle. She ignored them both as she closed her front door and leaned wearily against it, her eyes dancing around the whitewashed interior, soaking it up like the balm that it was.

Frankie Jo adored her inner-city apartment, really loved it. Which was just as well, considering how much debt she'd taken on to purchase and then redecorate it. Still, every cent was worth it—from the obscenely priced Florence Broadhurst back wallcovering to the genuine Fabienne armchairs. Most of all, however, she adored sharing it on Instagram so her colleagues and friends—critics and enemies—could see just how fabulous her life was.

Pity she barely had a spare moment to enjoy it. And pity she never found time to fill her enormous french door fridge, which she was now pulling open, her mind wafting back to Merry. Frankie wasn't sure she *would* return her call. Didn't hold much stock in what the bumbling novice had to say. Had already decided she would approach Sir George herself and beg to investigate alone. Why did he assume she needed the others? It was, frankly, insulting.

Sniffing at a chunk of cheese, she winced and then popped it back, glancing about. All that was left was a deflated tomato, last week's Indian leftovers, and a reusable container with something resembling dog vomit. Groaning, Frankie slammed the fridge shut, then reached for her phone, tapping a number into it.

It picked up on the first ring, and Frankie put a smile in her voice as she said, "Hey, Boss! Are you free? Do you think you could come over?"

"About time!" came the reply. "I'll be there in a tick."

~

Kila heard his phone ring and leapt upon it, hoping it was Sheila and finding, instead, the number he'd recently programmed in for Earle.

Give it a rest, mate, he thought, switching it off entirely.

Kila knew his desertion had just blown it for the rest of them, but he was doing them all a favour. They would thank him eventually. Heath Burlington was the killer, there was no other suspect, and he explained all this in laborious detail to the tipsy girl sitting to his right.

Back at his regular haunt, at a booth this time, he was trying to keep the young woman—Melody was it?—occupied as other blokes circled, smelling fresh blood. She did seem engrossed in his story, nodding and patting his arm from time to time, but when he returned after a brief stint in the loo, he found her slumped over the table, snoring.

He smiled. Wasn't the first time he'd sent a woman into a coma.

"Another one?" Trevor asked, clearing the shot glasses.

Kila smiled again, wondering if the barman was referring to a woman or a drink and said, "Yeah, why not?" to both. Then added, "And don't forget the lemon squash, thanks. Oh, and can you call this one a cab? We need to get her home."

He forgot all about his phone until he was returning home himself in a separate taxi later that night, his blood pumping with tequila, an older, more sober woman by his side this time.

"Shit!" he said, pulling it out and switching it back to life. A few seconds later the phone tinkled with missed messages.

"You're popular," said the redhead beside him.

"You don't know the half of it," he replied, knowing better than to bore this one with the details. When he scrolled through the calls, he noticed most were from Merry, including a text that said simply "Pls call! I NEED you!"

He smiled and tapped her number. Always was a sucker for a damsel…

~

Martin had just got off the phone with Merry and was wondering what to make of it.

"Who was that?" Tamara asked, head on her pillow, eyebrow cocked high.

"Oh, no one," he replied, dumping the phone on the bedside table.

"If I didn't know better, Marty, I'd think you were trying to make me jealous," she purred, sweeping her flaxen hair back and draping her long legs across his torso.

"Don't be paranoid," he said and turned his back on her as he switched off the light.

CHAPTER 9 ~
A GAME OF CLUEDO

Merry sat down at the table and waited for the others to join her, half-excited, half dreading how they might react. She tried not to think about that as she watched the waiter approach with a sweaty pot of Earl Grey.

"Good to see you again, Mez," he said, placing the pot and a cup down between the Ballroom and the Conservatory.

This was the Games Room Café, and every tabletop featured a different board—Chess, Scrabble, Monopoly, Badminton and, of course, Cluedo. Merry's favourite. They'd even tried to add a tiny plaque to that one, commemorating her achievements until she'd put them off.

That would be far too embarrassing!

Pouring the tea, Merry thought back to the first time she ever tried her hand at Cluedo. She was just seven years old, a mediocre kind of kid. Even at that age she knew she wasn't going to set the world on fire. Then, while camping with her cousins one Easter, someone brought out the board game and the flame was lit. Merry had fallen instantly in love with the elaborate floor plan—all those exotic rooms and eclectic-sounding characters! But it wasn't until a few years down the track that she realised she had a gift. Merry had not lost a single game since that first one on the sandy floor of the tent. It wasn't until she was married with her own kids that someone suggested she turn professional.

"How do you mean?" she had asked.

"Enter the Cluedo Championships. They run every year or so."

"They do?" She had giggled. The whole idea was absurd!

But of course she'd looked into it and then quietly sent off her application, and before she could say "Professor Plum in the billiard room with the dagger," she was being invited to a local meet.

The trick was to work your way up. And so she did.

Merry won her first state championship five years ago. Became Australian champ the following year. And then won the world event the year after that.

It was the happiest day of her life. Even happier than all three of her children's births if she were being honest, and she never was, not about birth. No one needed to know those gory details! For the first time in her life, Meredith didn't feel mediocre.

The joy lasted all of three days. Then she returned home, trophy in hand, to find her husband half-naked on the patio with his own trophy, a woman who drove taxis, apparently. And that was that.

Merry had not opened a Cluedo board since.

Now as she stared down at the room marked PATIO on the table, her smile began to waver and her confidence dried up, and she wondered that the waiter even remembered her order; it had been so long since she had been here.

"You look right at home," said Earle as he strode up. "Not your first time, I gather?"

She smiled lightly. "Thanks for coming. I'm wondering now if it was all a mistake."

He edged into the seat beside her. "Don't start doubting yourself, Merry. I've heard plenty of BS in my time, but you spoke sense last night, so just remember that."

She thanked him and smiled as she watched the others approach. Martin was frowning.

"Seriously? You dragged us here to play board games?"

"Sit down, folks," said Earle. "Give the girl a chance."

They all took their seats, Frankie also frowning.

"Did you do something different with your hair?" she said just as the waitress appeared to take drink orders.

When that was done, they all looked at Merry and then down at the game.

"You know, I've never played this one," said Kila. "Do we all get a room; how does it work?"

"There's a Miss Scarlet, isn't there?" Frankie said. "I bags being her."

"Who does she hook up with? I'll be him," said Kila, making Frankie frown again.

"We're not here to play games," Earle cut in. "Merry's put a lot of work into this, so let's hear her out, okay?" He gave her the nod.

Merry took a deep breath. "Thanks, guys, for coming. I know what we decided yesterday..."

"We?" said Frankie, her frown still on Kila.

"But I think once you hear what I have to say, you might think very differently. Or at least I hope you will." She looked at Earle, who gave her another reassuring nod while the waitress returned with their beverages.

After a fortifying sip of her own tea, Merry said, "Okay, so, here's the thing. Like the rest of you, I have been wondering what on earth I was doing in this illustrious group."

"Merry, I didn't mean to be rude—" began Frankie.

"Yes, you did," said Martin.

"But you were *right!*" said Merry. "The most exciting real-life thing I've ever investigated is who stole the last chocolate from the pantry." She smiled. "It was Archie. It's always Archie. The kid has a bottomless stomach." She giggled and waved a hand in the air. "Then I remembered what my older son said to me the other night— how I was once very good at Cluedo."

There was a subtle snort from Frankie as Merry reached for a small silver box in the centre of the table from which she plucked out a miniature blue figurine.

"You can't win Cluedo unless you're really good at strategising," she told them, "at looking at all the various pieces—the suspects, the weapons, the rooms—and determining who and what was where. Bit like your five *W*s, Frankie. I've been doing that for this case since we parted yesterday, and reading over the police report, and I'm here to tell you, the evidence does not fit. The pieces are in the wrong places."

They continued blinking at her, and Frankie said, "How do you mean? Exactly?"

Merry held up the little blue blob. "Let's pretend this is Heath, and let's pretend his bedroom is the Guest House, because for some strange reason Cluedo doesn't have normal bedrooms. I never did understand why. I mean, murders can happen just as easily in a bedroom as a kitchen or an observatory, right?"

She giggled as she placed the blue figurine into the square marked GUEST HOUSE. "Anyhoo, according to the police report, Heath was not found in his bedroom; he was found in the hall with the gun."

She picked up the figurine and slid it from GUEST HOUSE into the room marked HALL, then searched through the cache of weapons and plucked out a tiny silver gun, which she placed beside "Heath," then beamed back at them.

"So, in Cluedo speak, that means it was Heath in the Hall with the Revolver. Or at least that's where the final death happened, his own. Correct?"

They shrugged, they nodded, they looked at her like she had flipped.

"We do know this already, thanks, Merry," said Frankie, trying hard not to check her phone. "Can you get to the point please?"

"Sorry! Yes, okay… so… The point is, there was one piece of evidence that was missing from the report—or not missing so much as in the wrong room—and it makes a lie of everything else. There is a missing piece of the game. A pair of prescription glasses. Heath's prescription glasses."

"Glasses?" said Kila. "How do you kill someone with glasses?"

"Ah!" Merry smiled. "Perhaps a better question is: How do you kill someone *without* them?" She reached a hand to her face and pulled off the white Gucci spectacles she was wearing. "These are not mine," she said, squinting now as she leaned down towards the board and placed them in the GUEST HOUSE room. "These belonged to Heath, and yesterday I found them sitting on his bedside table. In his bedroom."

"I knew you looked different!" said Frankie. "They suit you. But we already know this too, or at least I did. If you'd read my articles"—a quick glance at Earle—"you'd know that Heath wasn't wearing his specs during the murders."

"Exactly!" Merry replied, like Frankie had just proven her point. "He was as blind as I am, which means blind as a bat. I'm not wearing any right now, and you're all just one big blur." She squinted as she looked around. "Seriously, it's all just really fuzzy."

"So?" asked Kila, still not comprehending.

"So, these glasses should have been located with Heath's body, down here, in the HALL." She leaned closer to the board and slowly slid her finger to the HALL. "Last night, Verity told me that Heath had myopia and got his first pair of glasses at the age of thirteen; has needed them ever since. He was short-sighted—that means he couldn't see distances."

"Yes," said Frankie, "but he killed them both up close, remember?"

"Without his glasses? I don't think so. Take it from me, peeps! I don't even get up to use the loo without popping my specs on."

She grappled for her handbag and pulled out her own pink glasses, which she thrust onto her face, smiling as the group came into focus before her.

Martin said, "This is all very interesting, Merry, but I'm a bit slow today. What exactly are you trying to say?"

"I'm saying the police report does not add up. I've read it from cover to cover. According to them, Heath got out of bed and met with his father in the study." She scooped up the tiny figurine and slid it to the room marked STUDY. "A fight ensued, and then he grabbed the candelabra"—she paused to pluck out the tiny silver candlestick—"and bopped him over the head with this. Then calmly reached into the safe where the gun was kept and loaded it with bullets." Now she picked up the tiny revolver. "He then walked from the study down the hallway to his mother's bedroom on the other side of the house, shot her in the head, then returned to the hall."

She shuffled the figurine all around the board, in various directions, before ending back in the HALL. "Deadly mission complete, Heath then picked up the hall phone, managed to type in three zeroes, and call emergency services before shooting himself."

"Heath in the Hall with the Revolver," Earle said, echoing her earlier comment.

She nodded, then tapped the glasses, which still sat looking giant-sized in the GUEST HOUSE room and said, "And all without his glasses? Are we really expected to believe that he would carry out a series of horrendous murders while flying blind? You just wouldn't do it."

"That's true," said Earle, tapping his own square silver spectacles. "I fall asleep with these on most nights. Drives my Beryl batty."

They all mulled that over for a few minutes. Then Kila said, "Maybe he was wearing them and he dropped them back by his bed before he made the call?"

"Why would he bother?" she said. "Besides, there are no traces of blood found on them. Not a single speck."

"Maybe he had another pair of glasses on or contact lenses," suggested Martin.

"Then where is this mysterious other pair? Where are these contact lenses? There is no mention of any visual aids, from the first responders to the pathologist's report. Nothing was located on or near the body."

"That is true," said Frankie, sounding more intrigued now as she picked up Heath's glasses and began inspecting them as though looking for blood traces.

Merry leaned forward. "Look, peeps, I don't know if it means anything. Maybe there is a perfectly good explanation and we'll stumble upon it. Maybe he was wearing contact lenses and they popped out along the way. I have no idea, but I do know that it's a sign that maybe—just maybe—there's more to this case than meets the eye. Excuse the pun!" She giggled again. "Heath just might be innocent."

"But… but what are you saying?" said Frankie. "That someone marched him around, blindly, and forced him to do it?"

"Or had already done it and just pulled him out of bed half-blind and forced him to make the phone call. Maybe he had been drugged so he didn't hear the commotion beforehand? I don't have all the answers, guys, but I have just discovered a fresh question."

She turned to Kila and said, "Yesterday you told us you weren't prepared to investigate without more evidence." She held the glasses up. "I think this is our second smoking gun."

Then she gave Earle a meek smile as she scooped up the various pieces and packed them away again.

Earle could not have been prouder of young Merry. Hadn't known her long but already saw her as the strongest link in the chain. Sure, she was a bit clunky, had none of the sophistication of the others, but she was made of stern stuff—had survived Frankie's smarminess and her own initial failures. Her little visual display was a work of brilliance. Not only did she prove her point, she proved her worth to the team, which was important in the light of what he was about to suggest.

But first he had to ease in gently.

Clearing his throat, the old detective sat forward. "You've done a stellar job, Merry, and you're right, those spectacles are a smoking gun, or at the very least, a loose thread—bloody great dangling one if you ask me. Something my old mate Morgan should've picked up.

It might come to nothing, sure, but it is worth investigating. And it's not the only thing."

He had their attention now.

"Morgan mentioned something the other day about Heath's fingerprints being the only set found on that hallway phone, so he must've done it. I didn't think too much of it at that time, and that's my mistake."

"Ah," said Martin, already leaping ahead. "There should have been more than one set, right? It was the main house phone, located in the thoroughfare."

"Oh, people use smartphones now," said Frankie, but Earle shook his head.

"At the very least the cleaner's prints should have been on there somewhere. In my experience, the absence of fingerprints is far more suspicious than a proliferation of them—it had been recently wiped clean."

"So why wipe the phone down only to put your prints back on there afterwards?" said Kila.

"My thoughts exactly," he replied. "Especially when I noticed from the report that the first murder weapon—the candelabra—was wiped clean. No prints on there at all. Why do that and then confess? The point here is that there are still questions to be answered. We got ahead of ourselves the first day, didn't stop to ask what exactly it was we were investigating. Part of the problem was that none of us quite believed Mr Burlington; none of us really accepted that Heath could be innocent, and that clouded our judgement."

Kila glanced between Merry and Earle. "Okay, so what is this really? An intervention? You want me to sign back up? Get back into line?"

"You wanted a smoking gun," Merry said again.

"*I'm* obviously interested," said Frankie. "I always was. But I want to re-interview Charlotte this time. No offence, Merry. You might be able to read a room, but I know how to lure stories out of people. It's what I do. If I could have another crack at Heath's sister, I could find out about the boyfriend, Igor. He was there that night, and she wasn't. That was never properly explained. Why was he there? What was that about?"

Earle smiled. "See? More unanswered questions. And you're right, Frankie. We have to work to our strengths this time instead of running off half-cocked. You're a crack interviewer. I've read your stuff. I'm not too shabby myself, and I suspect Kila here has plenty of experience sorting fact from fiction. So I think us three redo all the interviews and we do them properly. We ask the right questions this time."

"Oh great," said Martin, sulky again. "What do Merry and I do while you're running around earning all the brownie points? Keep playing Cluedo? I have a slightly more creative mind than that, you know."

"Actually, I'd like to, sort of," said Merry, choosing not to take offence at any of their comments. "Looking at the evidence is my strength—where everything is, who was where and when. And if you don't mind me saying, Martin, I have a feeling your strength is strategy too; your real genius is plot."

He snorted. "You want me to write a story about it?"

She giggled. "Kind of! But just in your head. Earle's right. At the start we all believed Heath did it, so our minds were closed. But what if he didn't? How could anyone else have pulled it off? You said it yourself; you write creative, award-winning crime. So, *who* would you plant it on if you could turn it into a Flynn Bold mystery?"

Martin still looked sullen. "I could do that easily enough, but it seems to me that I've got the least responsibility, which means I end up empty-handed. Or have you conveniently forgotten that even if we do solve this thing, only four of us get paid. One of us ends up with nothing."

"Which is why I have one more suggestion," said Earle before clearing his throat.

This was the part he was not sure they would agree to. The part he had been building up to. He leaned forward again and spread his palms on the table. "I suggest we pool the reward money and each get an equal share."

Martin's eyes squinted. "That's what, $800,000 each? Still an extraordinary amount of money in anybody's language."

"Actually," said Earle. "The real figure Sir George offered is five million—because one of us gets the extra mil, the person who makes the biggest contribution. Well, how do you work that out? I think we should agree that we work as a team and walk away with a clear million each. No matter who finds what. That's the only way this will work."

"Are we even *allowed* to do that?" asked Merry.

"He can't stop us from sharing the bounty."

They looked a little wary at the suggestion, especially Frankie. "I know what you're saying, Earle, but that doesn't seem entirely fair to me. Some of us will be doing the heaviest lifting. Sorry for being blunt again but sitting here staring at a few rooms is hardly taxing."

"Not necessarily," said Earle. "Look at what Merry's already discovered. It's given you your first question to Charlotte—did your brother ever stumble about without his glasses?"

"Yeah, Frankie," said Kila. "You wouldn't even be sitting here discussing payment if it wasn't for Merry. You'd be back at your desk earning bugger all."

"Hey! I make good money, thanks very much. At least I still have my job, unlike you."

"Easy, people," said Earle. "Can't you see? This is exactly what the old bastard wanted—us at each other's throats and competing with each other. He thought it'd make us work harder, but one thing I learned running Homicide: we have to work together. As a team. We have to come to it as equals, or we'll undermine each other at every turn."

Hadn't they already done that? Wasn't that part of the reason he hadn't mentioned the fingerprints before? Was he holding that back to earn extra points? He wondered now what else they each had been hiding.

Merry jumped to her feet and squealed, "I'm in!" She held one palm out in the centre of the table. "Come on, let's make a pact, guys. Who else is with me?"

Earle chuckled and stood up, then went to place his palm on hers before pulling back. "Just remember, Merry, we could work on this for months and still end up reestablishing Heath's guilt. Could still end up with nothing. That's okay for me. I'm retired, my girl's moved away, but that's a lot of wasted time away from your littlies."

"Oh they're not so little; they'll survive."

He smiled and placed his palm on hers as Frankie also got to her feet.

"Of course I'm in," she said. "Was never really out, if I'm being honest."

She winked as she covered Earle's palm with her own, and then the three of them stared down at Martin, who was slowly pulling himself up and out of his chair.

"Fine," he said. "I'll do anything to avoid writing my latest book." His palm went neatly over Frankie's.

Now it was just Kila sitting at the table, staring up at them, one eyebrow cocked. "You look like a pack of idiots, you know that, right?"

"Come on, Kila!" Merry sang out. "What have you got to lose?"

"Several months of my life that I'll never get back." He groaned. "Oh, fine…" He went to stand up, but Earle was holding his other palm up like a stop sign.

"Don't humour us, Kila. For the love of God—and my sanity—only do this if you're prepared to commit. No more late arrivals and holding it over our heads. You're in it one hundred percent, or you're not in it at all."

"Okay, old man, keep your hat on. I'm in on one condition." As they all began to groan, he said, "Forget this endless investigation. I can't work indefinitely for nothing. I say we give ourselves a stricter deadline."

Frankie glanced at the others. "Hmmm, not a bad idea. I work better to a tight deadline. What are you thinking? Two months? Three?"

"Two weeks," he said, and they all gasped.

"*Two weeks?* Are you insane?" said Martin.

"I'm impatient, and I'm lazy. You want me to commit, I can commit for a fortnight. After that all bets are off."

What Kila didn't tell them was that one of last night's missed calls was from his lawyer. The decision on his license had been deferred for a fortnight. "In the meantime," Sheila said, "keep your nose clean. Another misdemeanour, my love, and you'll be lucky to get work as a dish pig."

He'd made light of that and then gone into a panic, more worried about being idle than anything else. But they didn't need to know that. The others stared at each other dubiously.

"We'd have to get our skates on," said Frankie "but I'd probably prefer that to be honest. There's only so long I can string my editor out."

"Me too," said Merry, who was fibbing earlier and was not convinced her kids would cope without her for long.

Earle shrugged and gave a small nod, followed soon after by Martin.

"All right," said Kila, finally placing his palm on Martin's. "It looks like the Famous Five are back in business!"

CHAPTER 10 ~
BACK ON TRACK

When the "Famous Five" returned to Seagrave later that afternoon, Verity could see something had shifted. They had a steely determination in their eyes, and Merry was clutching a box of supplies. They looked ready for business, back on track, and she smiled to herself.

Good.

The PA was no fool. She had seen them all storm out separately the day before and knew there had been a mutiny of sorts; was not looking forward to calling Sir George about it. He had such high hopes for this motley crew. God knows it had taken her long enough to assemble the group.

George had hatched the idea of reinvestigating the case just after the coroner's verdict had come down and the blame had been placed squarely at Heath's feet. The patriarch simply wouldn't have it, would not accept the truth, was determined to find an alternative answer, and so Verity had been tasked with the job of putting together a fresh team to reinvestigate the case.

It had taken her two months and a lot of her own detective work.

The short list was originally twenty amateur sleuths, including a forensic scientist and a celebrity clairvoyant—her suggestion, quickly nixed by the boss. After much toing and froing, they had finally settled on these five. Verity had spent a lot of time combing through their respective lives and knew they would bring unique skills to the team but, more importantly, unique *needs*. A reason to say yes to such an impossible mission. Sure, the money was attractive, but they each had a secondary motivation that had lured them to the bait and would, hopefully, keep them nibbling as long as it took.

Not that she'd ever tell them that, of course. She was just here to keep a close eye on them for her boss. And she had to be subtle.

"So, how'd your leads go yesterday, folks?" she asked, feigning ignorance.

"Terrific," said Earle, flashing the others a look. "Just terrific. Listen, we'd like to set up properly in the library this time. Make it a bit more formal."

It was one of several new rules they'd agreed on before meeting again at Seagrave that afternoon, and Verity swallowed another smile.

"Good idea," she said, thinking, *hook, line and sinker.*

As the others settled into plush leather armchairs in front of walls of books, Merry placed her box on a low mahogany coffee table and began pulling out supplies, including a small whiteboard and some bright, non-permanent markers.

"Another thing I'm not too shabby at," she told Frankie, who was watching her curiously. "I'm secretary of the school P&C. Pretty good at keeping minutes. I know we can't go public with this, but I do think we should try to assemble the facts, make a list of suspects, that kind of thing."

"Smart thinking," said Earle just as Verity appeared, pushing in an enormous whiteboard on wheels.

"You wouldn't believe the paraphernalia stored in the old study," she told them. "Have you got sufficient markers?"

Merry nodded and then continued setting up, using the large board this time. As she added a dry-erase cloth to the lip at the bottom, she felt a rush of excitement, like she was on the set of her favourite TV show *Vera*—then tried to squelch it down again. This was a murder investigation. She really shouldn't be enjoying it so much!

Earle waited until she was ready, poised, then stepped forward. This was one more thing that they had all agreed on. Somebody needed to drive the investigation, and Earle was the obvious candidate, the only one in the group who had ever run a professional criminal investigation. Frankie's work might earn her awards, but Earle's was life and death.

"So," he said, staring up at the empty board. "If we're really to believe it wasn't Heath who killed his family, then we need to consider other suspects as well as possible motive, means and opportunity. I don't believe it could be the proverbial lunatic who stumbled into the house and wreaked havoc. There was no sign of forced entry. We've all seen the security here, been through it ourselves. An impenetrable gate, then a locked front door. All with keypads and codes, which we're told were changed regularly. We know there is no tradesman entrance or possible access at the cliff face, unless you're Tom Cruise in *Mission Impossible*, of course."

Merry giggled as he continued.

"We know from the police report that everything was secure when the first responders arrived. So it had to be someone already in the house or had, as Tom might say, the access codes. We should find out how often they were changed and who else had access. In any case, the perp then left the way they entered without so much as breaking a window."

"There had been a party earlier," said Martin, stretching his legs out in front of him. "Perhaps someone snuck in then, or it could be one of the caterers? They might have hidden away until the murders. I could look into them if you like."

"Good point," said Earle, turning to Merry. "Jot the word *caterers* down please, Merry. Might as well kick off our suspect list. Also better check the other guests while we're at it."

She nodded eagerly and began to scribble as Verity explained:

"There were eight caterers that night. Eighteen guests who showed up, excluding the family. Their statements are in the police file. That might satisfy most of your answers, but please understand, Tawny used the same caterers we've used for years. A group called Make It a Breeze. They're reliable, I can assure you. As for the friends? I really can't imagine any of them having a motive."

"Still, won't hurt to check them out," said Earle to Martin. "If you do find something, flag it and I'll see if any of them have a police record." He looked at Verity. "What about other staff? Gardeners? Pool boy?"

Verity shook her head. "None were there that night, nor would they have the code. The housekeeper, Lia, always buzzed them in."

"Wow, paranoid much?" said Frankie.

Verity shrugged. "Tawny came from a rough, working-class neighbourhood. I suppose she didn't trust people."

"Okay, but that still leaves Lia. I know she had an alibi, but that needs rechecking."

As Merry jotted down the housekeeper's name, Kila said, "I'm more interested in her supposed ex, Woko." He turned to

Verity. "Can't seem to get a Google hit on him. You don't happen to know his full name or where I can find him?"

"No, sorry. I don't believe he's in the police report either."

Earle was scratching his bushy white beard. "You're right to question their relationship, Kila. I mean, why lie about that? What's the big secret? Is she distancing herself from Woko for a reason? And if she is lying about that, what else is she hiding? Perhaps he was there that night in her room? All things to check out."

"What about the LeDouxes," added Martin. "I don't care what Sir George says. They stand to gain a bigger share of the inheritance down the track now that Roman and Tawny are dead. And they would absolutely have keys and codes to the house. Susan claims to love her big brother, but there had to be animosity between them. He got handed this place after Pookie died and Sir George cleared out. It's a $20 million property; that's got to hurt. Roman was also running the family business, the heir to the throne. Maybe Susan wanted to come first for a change. And with big brother out of the picture, she gets the lot."

"Not quite," said Frankie. "Charlotte gets a bigger share too. You'd better add her to the list."

Merry spun around. "No way! She was safely locked up in boarding school."

"Ah yes, but her boyfriend wasn't. He was there that night. Maybe they were in it together. Who knows? Put his name with hers."

"But he was spotted leaving early, remember?"

"Yes, but Charlie might have given him the code so he could return later. Go on, both their names please. It's Igor something."

"Ivanov," came Verity's voice from the back of the room again. "Unfortunately, that's as much as I know about him." Then she smiled brightly and said, "If you're questioning people with the access code, you'd better add Sir George and myself to your list."

Now Merry looked appalled. "Oh, I don't think that's necessary!"

But Earle was already nodding. "Without fear or favour, that's how you investigate a case." He nodded at the whiteboard, indicating that she should write the names up.

Still Merry hesitated, and that made Verity laugh. "I won't be offended, Merry. Especially if you find us innocent."

She was being coy, and Merry gave her an apologetic look before scribbling away.

"Also jot down DI Morgan," said Earle. "Not that I think he's a suspect, but I do want to have another word with him. I'll ask about criminal records and not just the caterers. I want to know more about this Igor Ivanov fellow."

"Can't you just phone Charlotte and quiz her yourself?" Merry asked Frankie.

Verity shook her head. "Charlie doesn't have a mobile phone. They're banned at Saint Auggies, it's very old-fashioned."

Merry wasn't sure she had that right but let it drop. After all, if Igor did have a police record, it probably wasn't something he put on his Tinder account. He certainly wouldn't have advertised it to his rich girlfriend.

"Well, I'm going to stay right here," she said, "at the scene of the crime. Go through it with a fine-tooth comb, see if I can't find more anomalies that need explaining."

Martin raised his hand. "I can do more than read through the caterers' statements. Any ideas?"

"Didn't you say Susan LeDoux was a fan?" said Earle. "Why don't you take another stab at her? See if you can get the hubby this time. I know what Merry's saying about your plotting prowess, but I think you could chew gum and walk at the same time. Head back to see Susan and take a few signed copies of your books, see if you can't get more out of her. Maybe take a bottle of bubbly while you're at it."

"Make it French," added Frankie. "She'd be used to top-shelf."

~

Half an hour later, Martin was grasping a bottle of Dom Pérignon and buzzing Susan's door again. Verity had organised the interview so quickly he barely had time to stop at a bottle shop, let alone go home and grab a signed copy of his latest novel. If she was such a big fan, she should have it anyway, he decided, as he buzzed the doorbell a second time.

"Sorry for the delay," Susan gushed when she finally answered. "We're out the back by the pool, having a sundowner." Then she grabbed the bottle from his hands and added, "Ooh, aren't you a darling! I guess you'll have to come join us."

She was in another floaty dress and whished him through the house and to the back deck towards a small plunge pool where a tanned, handsome man was seated in a sun lounge, a glass of something tall and icy in one hand, a cigarette in the other. He dropped them both as he stood up to shake Martin's hand.

"It is an honour," said Clem LeDoux, his voice laced with a heavy French accent. "Although I think I should be most jealous! My wife has spoken of nothing else since your last visit."

Martin smiled awkwardly. "Oh, right."

Susan laughed. "You are incorrigible, Clemmie!" She laughed again but did not deny it. "Cocktail, Martin? Or shall we crack open the sparkles?" Before he could answer, she thrust it at her husband and said, "Be a darl', will you, Clem? Flutes for all of us. There's some in the cabana."

He took another long drag on his cigarette, then strode to the other side of the pool deck to a small, Balinese-style cottage with thatch roofing and bamboo walls.

"Come and sit with me, Martin," Susan said, tapping the space beside her on her own sun lounge. "Let's try to make Clemmie even more jealous, shall we?"

Martin smiled stiffly, hoping she was joking and not liking the innuendo one bit. He was wondering whether Kila would have been a better interviewer. Flirting with the ladies wasn't exactly Martin's style.

As he perched on the edge of the lounge, she said, "So, what has brought the illustrious author back to my door so quickly?"

"Just a few more questions, and of course I wanted to meet your husband."

Clem was returning with three glasses of champagne then and sniggered. "You are a good liar, yes?"

Susan laughed again at that, and Martin felt increasingly uncomfortable. He wasn't a big fan of playing piggy in the middle even if it did spark up the couple's marriage, so he took a good swig of his champagne and said, "I might just launch straight in if that's okay."

"Please do," Susan purred, slugging her own drink back.

"Last time I was here, Susan, you said it did not surprise you that Heath did what he did."

"Oh dear, did I?" She made a mock grimace. "Don't tell my father that! He'd never forgive me."

"But he did do it, yes?" said Clem, looking confused.

"Not according to your father-in-law, no."

Clem looked incredulous now. "But he confessed!" He glanced to his wife as if wondering if he had that wrong, and she nodded.

"Yes, sweetie, but it seems Daddy Dearest doesn't buy it. Or *won't* buy it at the very least. So he's bought a crew of supersleuths to prove otherwise." She glanced at Martin. "What do you call a group of sleuths anyway? A murder? No, that's for crows…"

Clem was still gaping. "George does not think Heath was the killer? This is a revelation to me, quite a revelation!"

"I told you this already darling! Do keep up!"

"No, no, no. You did not."

As the couple bickered over this for a few minutes, Martin watched them curiously. They clearly didn't communicate well. What other reason would Martin have for visiting Susan twice in three days? No wonder the husband was jealous.

"We're just taking another look at it," Martin told Clem, breaking through the squabble. "In case the police got it wrong."

Clem's eyes were narrowing now. "But… you are an author, yes?"

He smiled, understanding the inference. "I've been employed for my 'leetle grey cells', apparently. I'm wondering who else might have done something so horrific to your family. And please—" He held up a palm. "Don't say Heath. Pretend I'm writing my next murder mystery, and I need to find Heath innocent. Who should I plant it on?"

Maybe Merry was smarter than he realised because they were already squinting their eyes and giving it genuine consideration.

Susan was sitting forward now, long nails tapping her glass, saying, "Oooh, this would be fun if it wasn't quite so gruesome." She offered up a grim smile. "Let me think… who else could possibly have done it?"

"Verity Vine!" said Clem, catching the others by surprise.

"Miss Efficiency?" said Susan. "Hardly!"

"Why would you suggest her?" asked Martin.

"Because she is the least likely! Is that not what you do in your books?"

He tried not to frown. They were a little more complex than that. "What would be Verity's motive?"

"I have no idea. You asked for a name, I give you one."

"Still," Martin persisted. "There must be a reason she popped into your head."

"Perhaps because she is always there, you know? Popping about in everyone's business. Who is she really? Just an assistant, and yet she has the access."

"To the house you mean?"

"To everything! To George, to the family. I just wonder..."

"Oh, he's being facetious, Martin! Ignore him," said Susan. "Verity's a treat! An absolute godsend. I'm not sure what Father would do without her. Or the rest of us. She's the only one who can keep him in line. No, I would pin it on the haughty housekeeper."

Clem looked surprised by this, but it made more sense to Martin who asked, "Why Lia?"

"Same reason I suppose. She was always *there*. Always had her sticky little nose in everything."

"Lia?" said Clem. "*Pft!* She is but a simple woman. She could not pull it off! No, Martin, you need to look deeper, I'm telling you. That Verity, she is a deep current."

There was admiration in his tone, and Martin said, "Duly noted," but felt like there was more to what Susan was saying.

"Why Lia?" he prodded. "And *how*? She was spotted leaving with the caterers."

She smiled. "Ah, but she could easily have snuck back in later. No one would've batted an eyelid."

"But they could say the same about us," said Clem.

"Not at all," she retorted. "We didn't have the codes that day, remember?"

"Codes?" he said, and Martin began to wonder if Susan's husband *was* just a pretty face.

"Access codes, darling! To get in. Which is probably a good thing, now I think about it. It does get us right off the hook, but still, it was insulting. My own family home and I had to be buzzed in at the gate like a common visitor, and by the bloody housekeeper!"

"Hang on," said Martin. "The codes were changed *every day*?"

She shrugged. "Apparently so."

He was about to enquire further when Clem tapped his Rolex.

"I hate to break up the party, but we will be late for our dinner with the Charlestons, *mon* sweet."

She groaned. "Oh, shoot me now. More boring prattle about the price of private education. Honestly, why have the little blighters if you don't want to cough up? Sorry, Martin, we must be off."

He nodded, feeling disappointed as Clem dumped his glass on the table and held a hand out to shake again.

"It was a pleasure to meet you, Martin, even if you have caught my wife's eye."

Martin went to object, but he turned to his wife and said, "Shall we take your car tonight, darling? I will pull it out. Please, do not be long."

Then he strode back inside while Susan watched Martin, smiling.

"Take no notice of Clemmie. He's just teasing. He loves it when other men flirt with me. It's a compliment to him, you see."

Martin wasn't sure he had been flirting but let it drop. His time was up, and he had more questions. "So these access codes, are you saying Lia had them?"

"Of course she had them." Susan paused as if holding something back, then leaned forward conspiratorially. "Look, Clem thinks Lia was just a cleaner, but he's as intuitive as a brick. There was more to it than that. They were like besties, Tawny and Lia. Thick as thieves. Which I think was unhealthy, frankly. Tawny trusted her too much. Told her absolutely everything, which she really shouldn't have done! I hate to sound like a snob, but I wonder whether Lia forgot her place sometimes."

Martin ignored the snobbery and said, "So why did Lia hand in her notice and move out? The party was her last job, right?"

Susan shrugged, then her eyes narrowed. "You know, that's a very good question. Something definitely shifted in that final month or so between Lia and Tawny. In fact, now I think about it, Tawny turned frosty with everybody. Like she had a bug up her arse." She leaned in again, her voice hushed. "I think something happened in that household, long before Heath went berserk with a gun. It's why Tawny started freaking out about security and changing the silly codes daily. Find out what that was, Martin, and you might have yourself another suspect."

"Any inkling at all?" Martin pressed, but annoyingly, she just shrugged.

"Lia does hang with a rather dubious group." Her lips smooched downwards. "Boyfriend's like a gangsta rapper or some such. I'd be checking them out if I were you." Then she drained the last of her drink. "Best get on. Clem will be hyperventilating, and not just about the hour. He'll be imagining us in all kinds of indecent reposes."

She laughed heartily at Martin's continued discomfort, then ushered him back through the house, scooping up a cream pashmina and a small black purse as they went.

Outside, Martin noticed a gleaming gold Mercedes sedan, Clem in the driver's seat, talking on his phone. He waved a hand at Martin, who waved back, then Martin turned and thanked Susan for her time. She leaned in and kissed him on one cheek, lingering there just a little longer than necessary.

Then she whispered, "I'm sorry we can't continue this over dinner, but if you have any more questions, feel free to drop in. Absolutely any time."

He stepped back quickly, shooting a glance at Clem, who was watching them, the sliver of a smile on his lips. Martin blushed, feeling like he'd just been served up on a platter and not liking it one bit.

~

Frankie was racing against the clock to make her interview with Charlotte. Verity had arranged this one quickly too, but she had stopped at work briefly to grab bait of a different kind—the teenage girl's equivalent of champagne.

As she followed the lay teacher through the labyrinth of dormitories to Charlotte's room, Frankie kept her loot close, lest the truth get back to Sister Mary. The head nun was grumpy enough as it was.

"I'm only doing this as a favour to George," she had told her, lips pursed. "You have exactly twenty minutes before the dinner bell rings. Get everything you need, please. There will be no third interview, not while the poor child is under my roof."

By the time they reached Charlie's door, there were less than fifteen minutes remaining, so she thanked the teacher and knocked on it loudly.

A minute later, the teenager peered out, her smile deflating. "Where's the Cluedo champ?"

"Sorry, but this time you're stuck with me. My name's Frankie—"

"I know who you are. I'm not illiterate you know."

Charlotte turned and threw herself onto her bed, where several textbooks lay open. They looked like strategically placed props to Frankie, but then what would she know? Perhaps Charlotte really was hiding her grief in hard work and study.

Closing the door behind her, Frankie glanced around. The room was bigger than she expected—a desk in one corner, cupboard in the other, a king single bed under a lacy curtained window, the walls plastered with images of models in couture fashion.

She approached the girl and said, "Studying hard I see."

That earned her a sarcastic sigh, so she decided not to dillydally, dropping her loot beside the textbooks.

As Charlie suspiciously eyed the bag, Frankie said, "I come bearing gifts. We get lots of crap sent to us at the paper. The blokes don't need it, or at least they don't *want* it, and I can't use it all."

Intrigued now, Charlie peered inside. Her eyes lit up, and she began pulling out glossy tubes of lipstick and eyeshadow and blush and the like.

"The real deal?" she said of a miniature bottle of Chanel perfume.

Frankie swept a hand to her heart. "Of course!"

"And you don't want it?"

"I already have several bottles, darling. All yours. There're stacks of lippies in there, half a dozen eyeshadow packs, plenty of skin stuff, moisturisers, even a straightening iron if you want one." She smiled as the girl rifled through. "Perhaps you could share it with your fellow inmates."

That word made Charlie smile, but she was also shaking her head. "They already have most of this. I'm the only one lacking. Mum still thought I was six. Never let me wear make-up even though she caked it on."

Charlotte's nastiness took them both by surprise, her eyes welled with tears and she pushed the bag aside and crumpled onto her pillow, suddenly sobbing. Frankie felt a flash of irritation.

This is all very sad, she thought, *but I haven't got time for this!*

She inhaled slowly and glanced around, noticing a box of tissues on the desk, which she grabbed and placed beside the weeping child. After another minute, she said, "Look, Charlie, I just have a few questions and then I'll leave you alone, I promise."

Like she was doing the girl a favour.

"You just want to sell more papers," Charlie shot back, looking up at her now through soggy eyelashes. "I read all your stuff, and it was rubbish." She sniffed, grabbed some tissues and wiped her nose. "Oh, just get on with it."

Frankie nodded. Fine. "Tell me about Igor."

Charlie wasn't expecting that. "How do you…?"

"Your grandfather mentioned him."

"Oh my God! He *knows* about Iggy?" Now the child was blushing.

"Yes, and he knows Igor was there that night."

"What night?"

"The night of your mum's party."

Charlie stared at her for a few moments as the colour in her cheeks faded away. Eventually she said, "So?"

"So, why would your boyfriend be there when you weren't? That seems odd, doesn't it?"

Charlie offered a careless shrug, but Frankie wasn't letting her off the hook. She leaned back and waited.

Eventually the teenager sighed. "Iggy would have gone there to make a point—show them that they should have invited me, their own flesh and blood."

"You weren't invited?"

"Course not! I'm stuck in here, aren't I?"

"We heard you didn't get permission to go."

"Well… um, you know, they could've fought for me harder. Grandpa has Sister Mary wrapped around his pinkie. She would've let me out if he'd insisted. But they couldn't be bothered."

Frankie understood her anger but also suspected that's what had saved the girl's life. Wondered why she wasn't more grateful.

Charlotte misread her thoughts entirely. "I know what you're all thinking, and Iggy absolutely did not do it! He might look hard, but he's, like, super soft underneath and stuff. And there is no way he hurt my family."

"Then who did, Charlotte? And don't say Heath. Imagine, just theoretically, that your grandfather is right and your brother is innocent. Who else would do such a thing?"

Charlie went to say something, then shrugged and looked away.

"Come on, Charlie. I know your brother had issues with your dad, but imagine if we could prove he was innocent."

"How? By stitching up my boyfriend instead?"

"Hey, I'm not gunning for Igor, but if he did it, sure! Wouldn't you want the truth to come out?"

"But he *didn't* do it! I know him; there is no way!"

Frankie held her palms up. "Okay, settle down, so who else then?

Just chuck a name at me."

"Lia," she said, then her blush returned.

"Lia? Your old housekeeper? You don't like her?"

"I do like her, it's just, like…" She sniffed. "I don't know… She just went weird, you know? Used to be so cool and fun and give me lifts to the city to meet Iggy after work and help me sneak him in when my folks were out."

Frankie must have frowned then because she quickly added, "I'm not a slag, you know! It was just so we could hang out at the pool and stuff. It's just that Dad didn't like me having a boyfriend. He thought I was too young, but I'm not! Iggy's almost twenty, and I'm really mature for my age!"

Frankie tried not to react to that one. "So why did Lia go weird, do you think?"

"How would I know? She just turned into a total *biatch*, looked at me like she hated me, and then she moved out."

"When was this, Charlotte?"

She shrugged. "A month before the murders, maybe?"

A bell began ringing in the corridor outside, but Charlie didn't look like she was in a hurry to leave, so Frankie persisted.

"Try to think back for me, please, Charlie. Do you have any idea why Lia changed?"

Another shrug. "That's adults for you. They can't be trusted. That's why I moved here. Everything was messed up. Heath was angrier than usual, Mum was all frosty, Lia… At least with the nuns you know where you stand."

"So, Lia—"

"Look, I can't think about all that now, okay?" Her eyes flitted to her books. "I have to focus on my future, not on the past. It's the only way forward." She chanted it like a mantra, and Frankie wondered about that. "I'm going to pore myself into my study," she continued, "and forget everything else. A fresh slate."

"What about Iggy?"

She gave her careless shrug again. "I'll see him in the break. I'm moving in with Sue and Clem then, and they won't try to stop us, not like my dad."

"You get on well with your aunt and uncle, hey?"

"Of course! They don't treat me like a baby. Give me my space. They're the parents I wished I had…"

Charlotte's voice choked up again, and the tears returned to her eyes. She might talk a big talk, but the girl was clearly wounded and using scorn and anger and schoolwork as a distraction, and who could blame her, thought Frankie.

The reporter stood up. "Dinner time, hey?"

"Mush time, you mean," said Charlotte, swiping another tissue as she got to her feet. Then, glancing back at the bag of goodies she said, "Thanks for the bribes."

Frankie smiled. The kid was savvier than she looked. They both stepped into the corridor where Charlotte began racing ahead when Frankie remembered what she'd promised Merry.

"Hey, Charlie! Just one more question!" Charlotte turned back at the corner, eyebrows high. "I know your brother wore glasses. Did you ever see him without them?"

Charlotte blinked for a moment, then shook her head and said, "They might as well have been tattooed to his face."

~

Across town, Kila wasn't feeling quite so smug.

He hadn't asked Verity to set up another interview with Lia because this one needed to be more clandestine than that, and so he had looked up her new employer—the only Smythe-Turners in the phone book—and then waited outside their McMansion for the housekeeper to appear, which she did promptly just after six.

"Thatta girl," he murmured as he slunk back in the seat of his beat-up Toyota four-wheel drive and watched her stride past him on the other side of the road, towards a rusty yellow hatchback. Knowing she didn't live in, he suspected she'd finish about now, and he hoped she was headed out, preferably towards her so-called ex. It was Thursday night, still a school night, but he knew a party girl when he saw one. Yet it didn't take many streets to realise Lia was heading for her own apartment on Dreary Road, where she clumsily parked and then disappeared inside.

"Damn it," he grumbled, then switched his car stereo on, sat back and waited.

~

After being escorted back to the main building and out, Frankie thanked the haughty dorm mistress and crunched her way across the pebbled driveway towards her own vehicle, which she'd parked near a side entrance. It must also be close to the dining hall she decided as she found herself following a stream of boarders who all sounded charged up and hungry, laughing and chatting and shoving each other, several clutching reusable water bottles.

Charlotte was nowhere in sight, but she did notice a few girls turning and staring at her as they walked. One seemed particularly fixated, and Frankie wondered if she was about to be accosted for career advice from a future wannabe reporter. It wouldn't be the first time, although it might be the first time she told them not to bother. Journalism felt like a dying career. She'd be lucky to have a full-time job in twelve months.

It was only as she reached her Audi that Frankie began to suspect this girl had ulterior motives. Slightly plump with eggshell-white hair, she was acting oddly secretive—had now dropped to the back of the throng and was giving Frankie a pointed look.

Frankie stopped and held her eyebrows high. The girl glanced around furtively, then began striding away from the others. Giving the campus her own furtive glance, Frankie followed and soon found herself at what could only be the music rooms, the clanking of poorly learnt piano scales cutting through the silence from somewhere deep within.

By now the girl was standing just inside the doorway, and as Frankie approached, she skittered off again, vanishing inside.

What was she playing at? Frankie wondered, feeling like she was in a spy movie.

"*Pst!*" came a voice from inside, and she followed the sound, down a dark, carpeted hallway towards a musty-smelling room where an upright piano stood against a wall, a bench seat in front of it. And to the side of the piano, the girl with the glacial hair.

"Did you want to speak to me?" Frankie asked.

She nodded. "Shut the door. I'll be in the shit if Scary walks in."

"Who?"

The girl frowned now. "Sister *Mary. Scary.* Get it?"

Frankie closed the door before asking, "What's going on?"

The girl seemed more relaxed now and took a seat at the piano, tinkling softly on the keys.

As she played a surprisingly skilful tune, she said, "I know you're a reporter. I was just wondering, you know, like, how your interview with Charlie went. And stuff."

Frankie frowned. "Why do you care?"

The girl kept tinkling away, still not meeting her eyes.

Frankie stepped towards her and asked a more pertinent question. "Who are you?"

Another tinkle and then, "No one."

Frankie sighed with impatience and was about to let loose when the girl said, "She's lying, you know."

"Who? Charlie?"

"She's a common little slut and a liar."

Frankie was stunned by her malevolence but tried to keep her tone casual as she said, "Okay. So, what is she lying about? Exactly."

The girl tinkled a little longer and went to say something when a door slammed somewhere, making them both jump. The girl held a finger to her lips as they heard the sound of footsteps and then laughter echo down the hallway outside. A door slammed again, and then there was silence.

"I've been gone too long," she whispered, returning to her feet. "Scary will be on the prowl."

Then she opened the rehearsal room door and peered out before plunging back into the dark hallway and towards the exit.

"Hang on!" Frankie chased after her. "You're the one who dragged me here. What are you trying to say about Charlie? What is she lying about?"

The girl stopped at the doorway and turned back. "I can't say any more; she'll know it's me." She turned, then turned back again. "Just ask her what she was really doing that night her parents were being slaughtered. I can tell you this, she wasn't tucked up in bed with her teddy bear, not unless the teddy's an older guy with really skanky tatts."

Frankie blinked rapidly. "Are you talking about Igor?"

The girl looked horrified. "I don't know his name, but that sounds about right. Urgh."

She mock gagged and within seconds was gone, nothing but a bulky silhouette heading back towards the dining hall. Frankie watched for a moment longer, then reached for her own smartphone and began to tap the entire conversation into her Notes app even though this was one conversation she would not easily forget.

~

Shadowing Lia had been more complicated than Kila expected. The housekeeper did reappear about two hours later, freshly coiffed and donning a shockingly tiny skirt but then led him straight to an inner-city terrace house where she was greeted at the door by a woman who was wearing a matching miniskirt and clutching what looked like a vodka bottle.

She ushered Lia in and slammed the door, leaving Kila groaning again as he turned the sound up on his Lou Reed CD and settled back into his stake-out. He would give them an hour, then assume this was a girlie catch-up and leave it at that. They were probably scrolling Netflix for a chick flick that very moment.

Ninety minutes later and Kila was still glaring at the door and telling himself to give it up, when it burst open and three scantily clad women, including Lia, spilled out onto the street, tottering and giggling.

From what he could see, they were all of Pacific Island origin and had clearly polished off that bottle, and then some. They teetered down the sidewalk in their stilettos, laughing and singing and egging each other on. He smiled. They looked like the kind of women he could get friendly with, but he shook the thought away as he watched them turn the corner.

Not bothering to lock his vehicle, he followed on foot, lingering in a darkened shop doorway as they first stopped to retrieve cash from an automatic-teller machine, then reapplied their lipstick before they locked arms and strolled straight past a queue of people outside a heaving nightclub called Bar Hola.

Offering the doorman little more than a wave, they plunged inside while Kila joined the queue.

It didn't take long to get inside. The doorman was checking identification and very little else, and Kila was promptly waved through. Once inside, it took him a moment for his eyes to adjust. Unlike his favourite haunt, this one was very dark and very loud, music pumping courtesy of a deejay set up in a shadowy corner.

Inside, he found Lia, not in the arms of a strapping ex-boyfriend as he'd hoped but still nestled in the midst of her girlfriends at a booth just to one side of the dance floor. Not a man in hugging distance.

Damn it, he thought, hanging back, watching. He noticed that Lia got up several times to request songs from the disc jockey, and it was only as she got up for a fourth time that it clicked. She wasn't requesting songs; she was keeping the guy company. Kila's eyes squinted as he checked the deejay out. He was dark-skinned and buffed, his shaggy afro bleached a lairy shade of yellow.

Hang on a minute...

He stepped a bit closer. There was a banner across the front of the guy's booth with the words DJ RASKO!, the exclamation mark replacing an *L*.

He smirked, thinking, *Woko by another name, perhaps?*

CHAPTER 11 ~
THINGS THAT GO BUMP IN THE NIGHT

Seagrave was little more than an ominous silhouette as Merry stepped out of Otis's car and pressed the gate buzzer. It was just on 4:25 the following morning, and for a few worrying minutes she thought Verity might still be home asleep, but then the gate cranked to life, and she did a little jig before giving her son the thumbs up, blowing him a kiss, then striding through.

By the time Merry got to the mansion's front door, the PA was holding it open, trying hard to suppress a yawn.

"Sorry to disturb your beauty sleep!" Merry called out.

"Nah, I gave up on that long ago. Come on, I've got the coffee brewing."

The accommodating PA had agreed to meet at the property in the dark. Merry wanted to simulate what the scene would have looked like at 2:35 that fateful morning, and 4:35 had been the compromise. It would still be dark then, and indeed it was, almost pitch-black, a tiny sliver of moon showing high above the ocean, the only light coming from deep within the house.

"I've simulated everything according to the police report," Verity told her as they made their way through the dimly lit hallway towards the kitchen.

Merry noticed the ceiling down lights were off and there were just intermittent wall lights glowing above the skirting boards.

"Tawny installed these when she moved in," said Verity. "Sir George kept the place dark as a cave at night—he hates to waste electricity."

"That's very green of him."

"More to do with saving money than the planet, but you didn't hear that from me. Tawny wanted the low lighting so everyone could move about safely at night."

"Or not," said Merry softly, and they both shivered a little at that.

After gulping down half her coffee, Merry said, "Do you mind if I do a re-enactment?" Then she chuckled. "I don't mean, an actual re-enactment, I just mean—"

"Go for it," Verity replied, waving a hand back towards the study.

In fact, Merry started in Heath's bedroom, beside his bed, where she pulled off her rose-coloured glasses, placed them in her pocket and then turned and made her way back into the hallway, hands reaching out, clasping onto the doorway as she went.

"Can't see anything?" Verity asked.

"I can, but it's blurry, and I think that's how it would have been for Heath."

She continued, hands out front, down the hallway towards the business end of the house. Along the way she stubbed one toe on the dreaded telephone table (it's like the monstrosity had reached out to kick her!), then tripped on two terraced steps that led from the hallway down into the study. Giggling at herself—this was a bit of fun!—she reached the study door, glanced in, and then made her way to the desk, before turning and feeling her way back out and up to the hall again. Once there, Merry continued on, back past Heath's room and into Tawny's—another crack of the knee, this time on the protruding bed base—and then out and into the hallway.

By the time she returned to the nasty telephone table, Merry's mood had soured. It was a grim re-enactment, after all, and she was a tad battered, but even she had to concede that Heath would know the layout better than her and be less likely to bump into things.

"Still," she told Verity, glasses back on in the kitchen, "the whole time, all I wanted to do was reach in and grab my specs. From what I can see, even if Heath did act spontaneously and stumbled sans glasses to the study to kill his dad, he had plenty of opportunity to correct his mistake. He has to walk back past his bedroom to get to his mother's room. He could have nipped in and popped his specs on in about five seconds and then kept going on his murderous mission. But he didn't."

Both women considered that as they finished their coffees, and it was only as Merry was placing her cup in the sink that she spotted the tiny square cupboard in one wall.

"What is that?" she asked.

"The dumbwaiter," Verity replied. "You know, a miniature elevator?" She stepped across and pulled it open, the door sliding up and then back to reveal a cavernous square-metre compartment.

"What's it for?"

"Carrying food and supplies down to the ballroom on the lower level and to the pool area on the other side. You know, so you don't have to traipse up and down the staircase."

"Oh yeah, that would be a grind," said Merry, tongue firmly in her cheek. She stepped across and began inspecting it as Verity said:

"The party was all on this level. The dumbwaiter would not have been in use that night."

"Or maybe it was in use and the killer left a souvenir!" said Merry, gasping excitedly as she pointed to something stashed in the farthest corner of the tiny lift.

~

By the time the sun had graced them with its presence, the others had arrived and were nestled on stools in the kitchen. They had agreed to meet for a dawn breakfast to go over their findings and discuss future moves. It would turn out to be a regular morning ritual, as much a chance to share news as to score a free meal, which Verity had now spread out across the marble bench tops—freshly baked bread for toasting, ham-and-cheese croissants already warm and melting, a variety of freshly squeezed juices, and a seemingly endless pot of exceptionally good, plunger coffee.

As the crew tucked in, smiles all round, Verity masked her own smile. She wasn't stupid. She knew at least one of the group was still smarting over the lack of payment and that there was nothing like free food to motivate the troops.

For his part, Earle was also appreciative. It was nice to eat something other than bland eggs and bowls of high-bran cereal. It reminded him of the buffet on the last holiday he took with the missus, the P&O cruise round the Pacific. As he helped himself to grapefruit juice, he wished they had the money to take another one, maybe try a fancier ship next time.

Merry was telling them about her blind walk-through in laborious detail, and he wondered why she'd bothered—hadn't they already decided the glasses were problematic?

"You know, Charlotte agrees with you, Merry," said Frankie, also keen to move on. "Her brother always wore his specs. We already know this, right?"

"I know, but I wanted to test it, just in case. Oh, and here's something new I discovered."

She stepped across the room and whipped open a door in the wall that no one else had noticed, and now she had Frankie's attention.

"This is interesting," she said, peering into the dumbwaiter with the others.

The space was big enough for a modestly sized person to hide in—albeit uncomfortably—and Merry explained her theory that someone could have hidden away in there only to reappear later when the house was quiet.

"And there is this," she added, pointing to what looked like a rollie cigarette butt in the far right-hand corner.

They all leaned in to inspect the item, one whiff revealing its true contents.

"Looks like we've got a stoner on the suspect list," said Kila, smirking.

Earle was not convinced. "That joint could have been left any time." He turned to Verity. "Any idea when this contraption was last used?"

"I'd need to check. As far as I recall, there'd been no big events since before they went skiing last July. The murders happened a month later, and the house was sealed up by the police after that. I was allowed in about a fortnight later to organise cleaners, but I can't be sure they even looked in here."

"And before the murders, how often would this space be cleaned?"

"You'd have to ask Lia that."

"So this might have been in there for some time."

"Or," said Merry, holding a finger up, "it could have been placed in there on the party night if someone was hiding in there, biding their time, waiting to strike!"

Martin preferred this version and said, "A caterer maybe? Or a guest?"

"Please tell me you haven't touched it," Earle said, and Merry shook her head proudly. "Good, I'll bag it and get it across to Morgan. I'm not sure this is going to reveal much, folks, but it should form part of the police evidence; there's not much we can do with it."

As Verity set about finding him a ziplock bag, Earle added, "Even if it was left here on the night of the murders, it's most likely by a caterer having an illegal smoke. Might've flicked it in when someone entered the kitchen. Doesn't mean they sat in there, waiting to murder anyone."

They all scowled. They all agreed. Now Martin wanted to move things along.

"Shall I tell you how my chat with Susan and her husband went?"

"That would be good," said Earle, "but let's relocate to the library first. Merry can continue keeping notes."

An hour later the group were all staring at the whiteboard, and one name kept popping out at them. Lia Segeyaro. This had Martin, for one, excited. Of all the possible suspects, hers was the name that had been circled several times and with good reason. The housekeeper had access to the place and the security codes, history with the family, and had handed in her notice just before it happened.

"I think Lia holds the key," Martin announced, and he wasn't just referring to the mansion's front door. "Both Susan and Charlotte said something changed in the housekeeper in the lead up to the murders. They both said Lia turned—what was the word—weird? Both said the household was not the same happy place it used to be, and then of course she left a perfectly good job to move into some dingy apartment."

"She just wanted a fresh change," said Kila, "and it's not that dingy."

Martin ignored this. "Maybe the honeymoon was over and they gave her the boot. Maybe she took umbrage to that."

Kila scoffed and stretched his arms out wide, causing Merry to giggle.

"What?" said Martin.

"He thinks it's a stretch," said Frankie, and that made Martin bristle.

Rubbing the bridge of his nose, he locked eyes with Kila. "You don't give up free board with ocean views for nothing. We need to find out why she packed up and moved out. Was it her decision? Was it theirs?"

Now all eyes were on Kila.

"Hey, like I said, she made out it was no biggie. Never mentioned any fight to me, not one that'd lead to mass murder." Then he scratched his stubble. "I really can't picture it to be honest."

"You don't think she could pull it off?" asked Merry.

"Too pretty, was she?" said Martin, snidely.

Kila smirked back. "I'm sure Lia could do anything she set her mind to, but killing the family that employed her for over a decade, one she bonded with?" He shrugged, giving it more thought. "She could've got help from her ex I suppose. I tracked him down, by the way. He was deejaying in a nightclub."

Kila told them about his evening's adventures, trailing Lia to the club and how he'd later googled Woko's stage name, DJ Rasko!, to learn he also traded as a music producer at Sanguma Studio in the grimy part of the city.

"His full name is Woko Wangi, and I reckon he's our best bet. Lia's a red herring. A cool cucumber but not a murderer, or at least that's not the vibe I got."

"You and your *vibes*," said Martin. "You could tell all that from lurking in the back of the club, could you?"

Kila smiled now. "You won't understand this, Martin, but if there's one thing I know, it's women."

Martin eye rolled that comment. "Lia's our best suspect at this point. With or without Woko. Both Susan and Charlotte implicated her."

Earle agreed. "If I were you, Kila, I'd talk to Lia first. Ask her why she moved out—the actual story this time. And ask about how things were towards the end there. Tell her what Susan and Charlotte reported; see what her response is."

"Happy to," said Kila, his grin turning lascivious now. "It will be my pleasure."

Martin tried not to glower. There was something about Kila that was beginning to grate.

As the clock ticked above the decorative mantlepiece, Frankie tried to quell her disappointment. Another twenty-four hours had passed, and they hadn't made nearly enough progress. Lia was a promising angle, sure, but Frankie was with Kila on this one.

She wasn't convinced there was much in it. Lia and her boss had probably just quibbled over a shoddy cleaning job. Having interviewed her in some depth in the past, Frankie had never heard a peep about any falling out. All she had seen was how devoted the housekeeper was and how devastated she had been by the murders. Could she really fake that? Perhaps she had moved out because, like Charlotte, all the quarrelling had broken her heart.

"There is one other thing I wanted to mention before I head to my day job," Frankie said, glancing at the clock again. Usually a fan of double-checking her sources, she decided it was time to spread the gossip from the snowy-haired tattletale. She explained how the girl had lured her to the music rooms.

"I don't know if it's true," she countered, "but she insists young Charlotte was in bed with her boyfriend the night her family was murdered."

"No way!" gasped Merry, lips wide. "She's locked up at nights. How on earth could he get in?"

"It's probably rubbish," said Martin. "Teenage girls can be right bitches."

This earned him a furious scowl from both women and Kila, and Frankie was shaking her head vehemently.

"I know teenage moral outrage when I see it, and I think she was telling the truth. The problem is, Merry's right. How on earth do you sneak a boy into your dormitory?"

"You don't," came a voice from the back of the room, and they all looked up to find Verity offering an apologetic smile. She was back at her post, sitting by the refreshments table. "Sorry, I don't mean to interfere, but I went to boarding school too. Not quite as posh as Charlie's of course."

"So what are you saying?" said Frankie.

"I'm saying she probably snuck *out*. Wouldn't be the first time a boarder did that."

"But how?" demanded Merry. "Surely the nuns would be onto that."

"Where there's a will..." Verity sounded almost wistful and then frowned. "Sir George will not be happy to hear this."

"Did *you* ever sneak out?" asked Merry, intrigued.

Verity's eyes lit up. "But it wasn't easy. You had to wait until the dorm mistress was snoring, then pad your bed with pillows and sneak out a back window or a door you'd sabotaged earlier. Then be sure to sneak back in before the morning wake-up bell."

"That's bolshie," said Frankie, looking at the woman with fresh eyes. "And you didn't get caught?"

"I didn't, but some of the girls did. Occasionally the dorm mistress would do a spot check at night. If the pillows looked too lumpy, they'd discover a girl or two missing."

"What would happen to them?"

"Expulsion." Her smile dropped. "So it had to be worth it."

Frankie was now doubly impressed, while she could tell from Merry's horrified expression that she would be checking under her daughter's duvet tonight.

"Okay, so what do we think?" said Martin. "Charlie snuck out that night to go to her mum's party?"

Verity frowned. "I didn't see Charlotte there and neither did Sir George. Of course, she might have arrived after we left, which was around eleven thirty."

"But?" said Frankie, who could sense a *but* a mile off.

Verity folded her arms over. "Sorry. I'm interfering."

"No, go on," said Frankie. "You think that's not likely?"

"I think it's not *typical*. Like I said, it had to be worth it, and no offence to mums everywhere"—she flashed Merry a look—"but I don't know many teenagers who would risk expulsion to go to their mum's fortieth."

"We know Igor was at the party, so maybe Charlie said happy birthday to mumsy then hooked up with him," said Frankie. "In any case, it tells us Charlotte lied about her whereabouts the night her family was killed. And if Charlotte was lying, then what else is she lying about? Worse, where does that leave her rock-solid alibi?"

Merry's eyes were saucer-shaped again. "My goodness me! You can't honestly think Charlie snuck out of school to kill her family. Why would she do such a thing?"

"They did banish her to boarding school," said Frankie. "Don't know about you, but that would make me feel murderous! She might claim it was all her idea but she never would have left if it had been a harmonious household."

"Hang on just a minute there, Frankie." This was Earle and he, too, wasn't buying it. "Are you suggesting that the girl snuck in after the party was over, killed her parents, and somehow held a gun to her brother's head—her bigger, older brother—and got him to confess to the murders before killing himself?"

"Maybe Heath adored his sister and willingly took the blame. Maybe he thought it was justified... I don't know, do I?" said Frankie, irritable because he was right. It sounded ridiculous. "The siblings could have been in it together for the inheritance, but then she double-crossed him."

"Again, how does a scrap of a sixteen-year-old girl overpower a twenty-one-year-old man and force a confession out of him?"

"She does have an older boyfriend at her beck and call. Maybe Igor didn't leave the party—he hid in that dumbwaiter smoking his joint—then let Charlie in later and they did the deed together."

"All speculation," said Earle. "I really need to speak to Igor, but DI Morgan's not returning my phone calls. Verity, any luck finding the lad's address?"

"Not his home address, no, but I heard he works at a cinema complex somewhere. That's all I've got."

"The city," said Frankie, recalling something Charlie had said.

"Thanks, I'll check it out," said Earle, jotting something on his notepad.

Frankie said, "While you do that, I'll try to wangle the truth out of the girl—who is actually a six-foot-tall woman, I might add—and find out why she lied to everybody about her whereabouts that night. If indeed she did."

Verity looked worried. "I'm not sure Sister Mary will give you access again."

Frankie cocked her heard to one side and said, "I don't need Scary Mary for this one. I'm going to take a leaf from your book and break the boarder out."

CHAPTER 12 ~
FROM HOMICIDE TO HIP-HOP

The Serious Crime Division was bustling with life as Earle made his way through the open-plan office, and he tried to ignore the tug of regret he felt as surprised ex-colleagues welcomed him back and shook his hand.

"Miss you in here," several of them said, and he laughed them off, noticing that at least one of them felt differently and was staring at him now, a flash of irritation in his eyes.

"No games of golf today, hey, Fitzy?" Morgan said, managing a belated smile as Earle approached his desk.

The retired detective ignored the condescending comment. "Just need to check some things around the Burlington case."

"You still on that?"

"It has only been a few days. Mind if I?" He indicated the chair in front of Morgan's desk and didn't wait for a reply as he sat straight down. "Need to check if anyone present at the party had a criminal record. Maybe one of the party guests or caterers perhaps?"

"The criminal was Heath Burlington-Brown. He was all we were concerned about."

"What about the housekeeper's boyfriend, a Papuan by the name of Woko Wangi?"

"Never heard of him." At Earle's frown, he added, "Was he at the party?"

"Not that we know of."

"Then why would I check his record?"

Earle nodded. "Fair enough. What about the granddaughter's boyfriend, young lad by the name of Igor—"

"Ivanov, yeah, what of him?"

Earle tried to keep the impatience from his tone. "He *was* at the party. Got a record we should know about?"

Morgan shook his head. "I mean, he might have been done for a spot of theft. Nothing more than that."

Earle sat forward. *Finally some traction.* "*Might* have? You looked into him, right?"

"What for? He once stole a Bentley, didn't put a bullet in anyone's head. Just a dumb thug with champagne taste in cars. And chicks for that matter. Besides, nothing was reported stolen from the Burlington place, and—oh, there is this bit—he wasn't the one wielding the gun. That was your client's grandkid."

Earle smiled and let that one go to the keeper. "I'm also wondering about drugs in Heath's system. Did you ever check for that?"

Morgan looked at him like he was mad. "You're joking, right?"

Earle frowned. "I didn't see anything in the pathology report."

"Course you didn't. I told you before, Grandpa's living a lie. Heath was no saint, spaced out on all kinds of shit. A bit of MDMA, some hash, plenty of alcohol. That page of the report must've slipped under the billiard table."

Morgan sniggered at his own joke while Earle tried to mask his disappointment. *Why the blazes was that information not provided?* Verity and Sir George had never mentioned a word about drugs in Heath's system. Had they held that information back deliberately? Then his irritation subsided as he realised it *assisted* his case, and he told Morgan that.

"If Heath was spaced out, how could he pull it off?"

"That's why he pulled it off, or at least I hope it is. Wouldn't want your kid to slaughter you sober." He grinned. "It wasn't out of character, you know. Heath was a known party boy. Big Ecstasy user; loved his coke too. Oh, and here's something else the old bastard probably didn't tell you. Had to be done by one of the occupants of the house because they changed the codes to the doors—"

"Regularly, yeah, I know that."

"Not just regularly. They'd been changed that very day. Nobody else had them. Apart from Sir George, everyone who knew the code is now six feet under. Take my word for it, Fitzy, it's your classic murder-suicide. Better yet, take your easy million and run." Then he chuckled at Earle's sudden discomfort. "You're not the only one with sources, mate. I heard you've got a very handsome payola coming your way. No wonder you're rooting for Heath's innocence."

"You better double-check your sources then because I haven't received one red cent for my efforts." It wasn't strictly a lie, but it only seemed to delight Morgan further.

"Then why are you here, mate, when there are holes-in-one out there to be enjoyed?"

Earle had reached his limit. He hadn't intended to start a war with his old colleague, but his patronising attitude had worn thin.

"*Mate*, the only holes I can see are the ones all over this case."

That lowered the wattage in Morgan's smile. "What holes? What are you talking about?"

Earle leaned in closer and dropped his voice. He wasn't particularly fond of Morgan right now, but he didn't want to embarrass him publicly either. "We found Heath's eyeglasses, sitting by his bed. No obvious signs of blood on them."

"So?"

"So we know that despite his youth, Heathcliff was as blind as the proverbial bat. Useless without his specs, I'm told from several reliable sources. Doesn't it seem odd to you that he wasn't wearing them the night it all happened?"

"Could've been wearing contact lenses."

"At two in the morning? So was he?"

The copper said nothing, and Earle frowned. "No word of it in any of the reports. Or did I miss that report too?"

"Maybe they dropped out during his long night of slaughter."

"So why weren't they found at the scene, these mysterious contact lenses? Oh, I know, because you just waltzed in and took it all at face value, didn't do your due diligence—secure the scene, check for any other alternatives to the bleeding obvious."

"He fucking confessed!" Morgan shouted, catching the eye of nearby comrades. He grimaced and lowered his voice. "How many times I gotta say it, the kid said he did it and was going to kill himself, and then, lo and behold, he does."

"Kid could've been coerced, and you know it. It's been done before. Or someone could've impersonated his voice."

"Ah, another thing your boss neglected to tell you. *Sir George* is the one who identified the voice from the emergency recording. Confirmed it was his grandson's. I really don't know why he's wasting his time. Oh, hang on, he's not. He's wasting yours. And mine." He picked up a pen. "I do still have my job, Fitzy, so if you don't mind…"

"It's not the only hole we found."

Morgan flung his pen back on the table. "Now what? Somebody forget to pop in their hearing aid?"

Earle almost smiled at that one. "The daughter, Charlotte."

"What about her?"

"Her alibi doesn't stack up. We have reason to believe she was not at boarding school that night. A witness who says she'd snuck out."

Morgan looked genuinely worried this time, but he tried to mask it with bluster. "So what? Now you think the granddaughter did it?"

"I don't know, Morgs. All I know is you missed the glasses, and you missed the fact that the only surviving member of the immediate family, the suspect with the most motive—the heir to all that fortune—has no alibi. Oh, and that's right, her criminal boyfriend was spotted at the scene of the murders that very night. Witnesses say he left the house, but did you ever check that? Did this known criminal lie in wait for the opportune time? Did someone else? Someone you haven't thought of?"

Earle dug around in his jacket pocket and retrieved the bagged joint, then flung it across Morgan's desk. "Found that in the dumbwaiter in the main kitchen. It might have been left at the house that night. If I were you, I'd at least get it checked for prints. Check everyone who was present at the party, starting with Igor Ivanov."

Morgan stared at the bag and sighed. "Mate, give me a break. You know as well as I do this isn't *CSI Miami*. And we don't have a bottomless bank account like the Burlingtons either." He sighed again. "Look, I get it. None of us leave here with a golden parachute, let alone a gold watch. So I don't blame you for chasing the rainbow, but that's all it is—a mirage. There really is nothing to see here. We didn't check every little thing because we didn't have to. I've never had such a straightforward case my whole career. Why're you trying to make it all wonky?"

"I'm trying to get it to make sense."

"The kid hated his parents. One night he explodes. It's as simple as that. You don't need eyeglasses to put a gun to a sleeping woman's head and pull the damn trigger. But you do need to be a coward, I can tell you that for nothing. Worse than shooting someone in the back, you ask me. The kid does not deserve the benefit of the doubt. Just let it go. Just take the money and invest in a nice new set of putting irons, okay Fitz?"

And there it was, the condescending tone again. Earle stood up and shook his head.

"I might be out to pasture, mate, but it doesn't take prescription glasses to see there's a lot more to this case than meets the eye. You better hope it's not you who ends up being put to pasture because of it."

Then he turned and stormed out as quickly as his creaky limbs would allow.

~

Across town, Kila was feeling a little long in the tooth himself. He was standing in the grimy laneway outside Sanguma Studio, staring up at some band posters pasted on the brick wall that were splattered with what looked like red paint. Kila knew Sanguma meant sorcery in his language, but there was nothing frightening about these baggy-clad hip-hop artists. Several wore black balaclavas, gold chains around the necks, fingers thrust awkwardly towards the camera. To Kila, they looked like scrawny teenagers posing as burly LA rappers and about as ferocious as his cousin's labradoodle. Had probably been dropped off to the photo shoot by their grandmothers.

He sniggered and checked his watch. It was now close to midday and seemed a safe time to visit a recording studio. Martin and Earle had wanted him to go back to Lia, but he didn't take orders from anybody. He followed his gut, and his gut told him Woko Wangi had the answers. Might be able to help dissect Heath's final triple zero words, too, if he was such a hotshot sound guy. Besides, he thought, smiling to himself, he could always drop in on Lia later. He worked better at night, especially with the ladies...

After several stabs at the intercom, it finally crackled to life and a voice yelled out, "Yo?"

Kila explained he was an acquaintance of Lia's and was investigating her boss's murder. Could he come up?

There was silence on the other end, and then the door was beeped open with a crackly, "Third floor! On the right!"

Sanguma Studio was as dingy as the street below, with the same comical posters on the walls of the tiny reception area. There was nobody at the front desk, but Woko was just coming through a side door marked LIVE ROOM—STFU!

The man was smaller than he'd looked up in the deejay booth, older too. Probably in his forties.

"Who'd you say you are?" he said, stepping towards Kila.

"Kila Morea. Private investigator, working for the Burlington-Brown family."

"That's right, Lia said a wantok was onto it." Woko scratched his yellow afro and looked impressed. "Okay, come through."

He led him into the inner studio. The room contained a faux-leather lounge, a large mixing board and a dazzling array of computers, but not an instrument in sight. Kila spotted a microphone in a smaller, adjoining room, and a grubby duvet strewn across the floor. He wondered for a moment if that was soundproofing on a budget.

"Nice place you got here," Kila lied, but the man beamed at that.

"Top hip-hop studio in the South Pacific. Do mainly rap. Bit of funk and dembow. We did Newkie's last album."

Most of that meant nothing to Kila, and he wondered if half of it was bullshit, but he tried to look impressed anyway. He was old-school. Give him a vinyl rock track any day.

"So what do you need, brother?" Woko asked, slouching into a shabby office chair in front of the mixing board.

Kila sat on the sofa facing him, shifting a stack of bills and correspondence to one side. "I want to ask about the kid, Heathcliff. Lia said he'd done an album with you. Was a rapper or a hip-hop artist or something?"

"He wasn't a hip-hop artist's arsehole," he fired back. "But yeah, sure, I let him come in and cut a few tracks. See if he might surprise me."

"And?"

"There were no surprises. Kid went to some fancy school but could barely string a sentence together. Had to give him my own thesaurus, man." He chuckled. "Those *dim-dims*, hey? White people think hip-hop is all for dumb arses and gangstas, but it's poetry, brother. Piss all over Shakespeare and Keats. Harder, too, cause you gotta do it to a beat."

Kila clearly couldn't hide his scepticism because Woko jumped up and placed a tune on. As the words began streaming out—something about "smoking a blunt and freaking the funk"—Woko said,

"You tell me that's not poetry."

Okay, *that's not poetry*, Kila thought but kept it to himself. "So, back to Heathcliff. He came in, cut some tracks and was lame. Then what? You had to break the news to him? Tell him to find another vocation?"

Kila wondered now if this was what ticked the guy off. He still couldn't move past Heath as the culprit, but Woko was cackling.

"Nah, man, I booked him in for an EP. He was no poet, but he had the next best thing." He rubbed his fingers together like he was playing with cash and cackled again. "Also had a lot of blow. Rich kids always do. That'll get you in the door every time."

"Big drug user, was he?"

"Isn't everyone?"

In this industry, probably, Kila thought. "So when was this? That he did the EP?"

"'Bout six, seven months ago. Few weeks before he went postal."

"Can I hear some of his stuff?"

He reached over and produced what looked like a blank CD. "This is as far as we got. But it'll give you a good laugh."

He tossed the CD across to Kila, who quickly scanned the song titles that had been scribbled on the front with clever names like "Shutter Out" and "Rock Spider Scissors", when the studio door cranked open and three very large men bedecked in even larger, baggier clothes stepped in, filling what was left of the space. They looked Tongan to Kila, who watched as Woko jumped up and gave each of them a fist pump.

Then he turned to Kila and said, "It's PatPela and the crew. Gotta make tracks."

"I'll show myself out then," said Kila, disappointed.

At the studio door he stopped and turned back. "Hey, Woko. You never asked why I was investigating. Do you agree with the old man—that Heath didn't do it?"

"Nah, Heath did it."

"Why, do you think?"

He made the cash miming sign again and Kila said, "But he killed himself too."

Woko sniggered. "I told you he wasn't bright, right?"

He cackled as Kila suddenly remembered the thumb drive he'd asked Verity to copy for him just that morning. He pulled it from his pocket and held it out.

"Wonder if I can ask a favour? This is a recording of the emergency call Heath made from the house the night of the murders. Heath says a few words at the end that, well, let's just say they're drowned out. Any chance any of these newfangled machines in front of you could dissect it? Clarify?"

Woko was shrugging. "I can give it a crack, sure."

He flipped the thumb drive across to Woko, who caught it and then gave PatPela another fist pump as Kila showed himself out.

On the way to the elevator, he heard a sound pumping out from behind him. PatPela's latest track was all about crack mothers and gangster hoes. Shakespeare and Keats must be shaking in their graves, Kila thought.

CHAPTER 13 ~
HOME TRUTHS

Martin scanned the report in front of him and then scowled, shook himself out and turned his eyes back to the top of the page. He had just one job to do today and that was to go over the names and statements of the caterers and other guests at the party. But he couldn't concentrate. For some reason Kila was still under his skin, and he couldn't work out why. It didn't help that *she'd* written to him again, the pathetic, needy woman who'd been sending letters now every month. The latest more desperate than the last. Or that Tamara had jumped on him the moment he walked in the door, demanding to know where he'd been and if he was seeing someone else. The question had caught him by surprise, but his answer—or lack of one—was even more surprising. He had turned completely coy, even evasive, refusing to outright deny it, and Tamara had stared at him with horror, then stormed out in a whirl of tears and curses while he sat at his desk and wondered what the hell he was playing at.

Tamara was a bombshell. Blond hair down to her waist, legs that went on forever. A right catch. Everybody said it, stopping just short of adding, "How the hell did you score that one?"

Of course the answer was obvious. His fame was a magnet. The fortune was just as powerful. He'd been batting off babes since his third hit book, sometime between those first awkward morning television appearances and purchasing this luxury apartment. Tamara was one of many, but something about her had stuck. He liked to think they were compatible, that it had nothing to do with looks. But the truth was, it was *all* about looks—the ones he got from Kila-types whenever she draped those long legs around him in bars and restaurants.

He jumped as she slammed a door somewhere deep in the apartment and wondered again what he was playing at. Was he trying to make her jealous? His mind flitted to Susan LeDoux then and the way she had flirted in front of her husband.

Was she just playing games too?

He groaned, gave himself another shake, and pulled the police report closer.

~

Earle was too old and creaky to pound the pavement, so instead of wandering the city cinemas, searching for Igor, he headed home to have lunch with Beryl and then let his fingers do the walking. He knew there were four cinemas in the CBD, two of them major complexes, and he struck gold on his second phone call.

"Yes, we've got an Igor Ivanov working here," said the man at MovieStars on Pitt. "Why? What's happened?"

Earle assured him all was fine, then spoke for a few more minutes before hanging up.

"Got your tuna sandwich here, love," said Beryl from the doorway.

"Thanks, dear. I'll be out in a sec," he replied, before making another call. "Hello there," he said to Merry. "Fancy catching a film?"

~

It took just one glance for Merry to recognise Igor, and she had never met the guy. Earle was about to ask the manager to point him out, but she had a hunch the usher loitering by cinema six with his head shaved short and dyed a Matchbox-blue had to be their man.

"I'd recognise that shade of blue anywhere," she said. "It's the photobomber!"

It took Earle a moment to catch up, then he thanked the manager and they made their way across. "Good work, Merry. You're right. He was the one walking through the family portrait that night of the party."

She beamed as they approached. She was finally getting the hang of it! Still, she had so much to learn...

Igor Ivanov was stunning in a terrifying kind of way, and Merry already knew that Principal Roger's pimply son wouldn't stand a chance if her Lola ever clapped eyes on this guy, which Merry hoped she never did. The nineteen-year-old embodied every parent's worst nightmare, and it wasn't just the lurid shade of locks. He had luscious red lips and thick, dark eyebrows and a neck that was crammed with tattoos that reached beneath his shirt at the southern end and stopped just below his chiselled chin. She couldn't believe the Burlington-Browns had ever let this creature into their home, let alone into their daughter's bed—although they might not have known about the latter.

Merry was sure she could make out the letters CBB in decorative scrawl amongst the tattoos. Charlotte Burlington-Brown, perhaps?

She wondered if Charlie had a matching one somewhere—she certainly hadn't seen it—but it suggested they were thicker than she'd realised. Still, how long could this doomed *Romeo and Juliet* relationship last? She wasn't sure about Igor's motives, but Charlotte had to be dating this guy to piss off her dad. He was textbook Rebellious Boyfriend. And now that Dad was gone, she wondered if Igor's days were numbered and he'd soon be regretting that tatt.

For now, he seemed free of any kind of remorse, just staring at them blankly as Earle outlined the purpose of their visit.

"Still got two cinemas to clean out," Igor told Earle, who shook his head.

"Your manager's given us ten minutes, buddy. Got somewhere quiet?"

Without waiting for a response, Earle led them back into the empty cinema and pointed the kid to an aisle seat while he and Merry stood in the row in front of that, staring back at him.

Earle said nothing for a few minutes, and Igor did the same. It made Merry want to jump in and fill the void with chatter, but she kept her lips shut.

She'd been thrilled when Earle had called. Was halfway through another grocery shop (it was shocking how quickly the food evaporated) and had promptly abandoned the trolley to meet him here. Although she wasn't quite sure why he'd asked. Did Earle want a mumsy type to help disarm Igor? Or was this training? In any case, she bit her tongue and waited. And Igor did the same, his blank look still in place.

Eventually Earle said, "We know you were at the Burlington house the night of the murders. We'd like to know what you were doing there."

No small talk then, thought Merry, taking mental notes.

"Was invited, wasn't I?" Earle must have given Igor a look

because he added, "By Tawny."

"Well, isn't that convenient? She's not around to contradict you."

"Not my fault." Then, "Although it looks like you're trying to pin it on me."

"Why would you say that?"

He scoffed. "You're here, aren't ya?"

"Did you go to the party with Charlie?" Earle asked, changing tack.

Igor leaned back in his seat, crossing his long legs and smiling. "You know I didn't."

"How would I know that?"

His smiled dropped. "She was stuck at that nunnery they put her in. I went alone. And I left alone. End of story."

Merry opened her mouth to dispute this, but then Earle coughed so she took that as a warning, her lips snapping shut again. Igor noticed this, his eyes resting on Merry as if to say, "What's Mum doing here?"

Or maybe she was just being paranoid.

Earle said, "You really expect me to believe you turned up all alone at your girlfriend's mother's birthday party—a middle-aged woman no less—for the fun of it?"

"Who said it was fun? I was doing my girl a favour."

"How so?"

He nudged a shoulder upwards. "She couldn't get there. I went in her place. Simple as that. Besides, Tawny was cool." He flickered another glance at Merry as if to say "Unlike this one" and added, "It's not a crime to go to someone's party, is it?"

"Nah, mate, but it is to kill them. You kill them, Igor?"

"What the *fuck*!" Igor flinched, as did Merry.

That was rather abrupt!

But Earle looked as cool as Igor's hair colour as he said, "Mind your language, lad." And nodded towards Merry.

Igor scowled at her. "Course I didn't kill them!" He made a dramatic sighing sound. "Typical! Pin it on the proletariat. Couldn't possibly be the heir to the throne even though he rang the cops and told them he did it. Nah, let's not believe that! Has to be Daddy's little jodhpur girl's bit of rough."

He rolled his eyes and folded his arms and looked almost wearily at Earle, like he'd heard it all before, and Merry felt sorry for the kid.

He was probably used to being pulled over by the cops every time he hit the streets. Of course, he'd be left alone if he removed the hair dye and popped on a pair of glasses and looked more like Prince Heath, but she wasn't about to mention that.

"You have a criminal record, buddy. Want to tell me about that?"

"I stole an old bomb. Needed a quick ride. Jesus, I didn't kill my girl's family. Why would I want to do that?"

"Money."

"What money?"

"Seems to me the jodhpur girl is now a free agent. No Daddy around to set her straight. She comes with a nice pile of bricks, plenty of dough. She give you money, does she, Igor?"

He snorted and waved a hand around the cinema. "Yeah, I'm loaded. That's why I'm cleaning up this shithole. So, what, because she comes from money and I don't, we're not allowed to like each other? What are you? The Class Police?"

Merry began to giggle, then caught their frowns and gobbled it back down.

"Charlotte's a bit young for you, isn't she?" Earle said. Persistent.

Igor snorted again and swept his eyes to Merry. "I could say the same about your bit of rough."

Merry gasped at that, but Earle didn't take the bait—another good tip for Merry—and said, "Why were you really at the party?"

"I told ya! Tawny asked me, so I went. No biggie. I think she wanted to get to know me better but didn't get a chance. She was always kind to me, didn't judge me like the others. She didn't come from money, see? She was like me, she said; we weren't like the others. We were from, what did she call it? Good, honest stock."

"What about the others then?"

"What about them?"

"I can't imagine Charlotte's dad wanted you there. Or Sir George."

"Couldn't give a flying frig what those weirdos wanted, and now, as it turns out, I don't have to."

"That's convenient," Earle said, and the boy just smooched his luscious lips to one side and said nothing.

"You ever sneak into Charlie's boarding school?" Earle asked. "Sneak her out perhaps?"

Igor crossed his arms now and said nothing.

"Did she meet you there that night? At the party? Was that the arrangement?"

Igor stared at him calmly and said, "No comment."

The cinema door whooshed open then, and the manager appeared, looking harried. Igor couldn't get to his feet fast enough.

"Hang on, sorry, do you mind?" said Merry, a finger high. "I just want to ask one thing."

It was Earle she was speaking to, but Igor turned to her with another weary look, so she said, "I'm just wondering what you most like about Charlotte?"

The question caught both men by surprise, and Igor's face suddenly softened, his lips even flickering into a smile.

"What's not to like?" he said. "She's a fucking goddess, my ChaCha, heart of gold. Deserves a lot more than that family ever gave her."

Then he shot a withering look at the old copper before scuttling out of the cinema.

As Earle drove Merry back to her house later, he asked, "Why did you ask that? What he likes about Charlotte?"

Merry grinned across at him. She mightn't be an expert at interrogation, but she did know a thing or two about early crushes.

"I wanted to see if Igor could answer the question, whether he genuinely likes Charlie or was using her for the money. His answer seemed pretty spontaneous to me. I reckon he's smitten."

Earle nodded and turned his eyes back to the road. "Doesn't mean he wasn't using her," he murmured, wiping the grin back off her face.

~

"Sir George will have my skin for garters if he knew I was doing this," said Verity as she stood staring up at the seemingly impenetrable sandstone walls of Saint Augustine's Ladies College.

It was late Friday night, just at midnight. The devil's hour, and they hoped the nuns were doing as all good nuns should be doing and snoring blissfully in their beds.

"You're not as brave as you once were," said Frankie, trying to calculate which of the windows above belonged to Charlotte. She was wearing an overcoat, despite the warm evening.

"Are any of us?" Verity shot back. "Look, I'm pretty sure it's the first floor up, fifth one along. You said it's beside a bathroom, right? Well, that small window has to be the bathroom. There's a fan thingie just beside it."

Frankie laughed. "Don't ever consider a career change to plumbing. But yep, I was thinking the same thing." She grabbed a handful of wooden chips from the small garden bed on the sidewalk and raised one when Verity caught her arm.

"You'll break the window!"

"Got a better idea?"

Verity released the arm, and Frankie began lobbing the chips towards the relevant window. The first two missed, benignly bouncing off the brickwork, but the third hit with a rattle. They waited and heard nothing, so she flung another with the same precision. Still the window remained firmly shut.

After two more attempts, they were just considering giving up when they heard a creak coming from a lower window on the ground floor and then spotted a blond head just inside the metal bars. It was clearly Charlotte, her hair in messy tangles around her head, glimpses of strawberry-pink pyjamas underneath. She was scanning the sidewalk and looked past them for a moment, then swept her eyes back, and even from a distance the disappointment was obvious.

"Expecting someone else?" said Frankie, rushing up.

"Shh!" Charlie glanced briefly back into the shadowy room behind her.

Frankie could just make out what looked like the side of a fridge and wondered if this was the common-room kitchen.

"What do you want?" Charlotte hissed. "Why are you even here?" That last question was directed at Verity, who stepped back and let Frankie do the talking.

"We know you snuck out that night, Charlie," Frankie said. "To meet with Igor—"

"What? No, I didn't!" Charlie's hiss had turned high-pitched, and she was looking behind her again, as if Miss Hanson would suddenly appear. "You need to go away. I'll get in trouble."

"Nope, not going anywhere," said Frankie. "Not until we talk. Can you get out? How does that work?"

"In my PJs? Are you *deranged*?"

Frankie whipped her coat off. "You can wear this." Then noticing the look of horror, she added, "Don't be like that; it's genuine

Burberry. Come on, there's a café open down the road. My treat."

Charlie sighed, glanced around again, then gave the bars one quick yank, and the entire thing miraculously gave way.

Verity gasped. "Sir George pays top dollar for that security!"

"Don't worry," said Charlie as she clambered out. "I'll put it back."

The dimly lit café was bursting with a mixture of bored backpackers, sleepy shift workers and late-night revellers, all with a case of the munchies by the look of the half-empty pastry cabinet that Charlotte was now studying like a textbook. She eventually settled on a jam-filled donut and then ordered an iced chocolate with extra whipped cream, reminding Frankie that despite it all, Charlie was still just a kid.

As they retrieved their order and then squeezed into a small table at the back, Charlotte glanced around furtively as if looking for familiar faces.

"You girls often slip away to come here?" Frankie asked, but Charlie smirked.

"As if we'd sneak out for this dump."

Frankie ignored the knowing smile Verity was now offering and said, "But you did sneak out often, right?"

"Not often!" Charlie responded, glancing at Verity.

"That night then. Your mum's fortieth."

Charlie blinked rapidly, then stared at the table, not answering.

"We know you snuck out, Charlie. The question is why. Did you do it to see your mum, or was it to catch up with your boyfriend?"

The girl's mouth gaped and then she gaped again and said, "*Of course* it was to see Mum! *Cor*!"

She took a large bite of her donut and glared at the two women, chewing like she was taking her anger out on the treat. After swallowing, she said, "I wanted to say happy birthday. It was a big surprise for her. What's wrong with that?"

"Hey, I think it's kind of sweet," said Frankie. "I just don't know why you lied to everyone about it."

"Because I broke out—you got that bit, right?" She looked at her like she was dim again, then flashed a frown at Verity. "And because, well, after everything that happened... I thought..."

"You thought they'd pin it on you?" said Frankie.

"God no! Why would they do that? No, it just didn't seem to

matter. Like it would only make things worse for Gramps. I would disappoint him, and he was sad enough as it was, so, you know…" She took another bite of the donut.

"I didn't see you at the party," said Verity, and the younger girl flinched.

Frankie's eyes narrowed. "Neither did your grandfather."

"Doesn't mean I wasn't there. I, um, I snuck in around the side and surprised Mum in the butler's pantry. Gave her a hug and a pressie and shit, then headed back to school again."

"And how did you get the access codes?"

She blinked. "Lia gave them to me."

Verity was more interested in the setting. "The butler's pantry?" she said, and now she was getting the dim look.

"Yah! It's got an exterior door, remember? I snuck in that way. It was just a quick hello. If Gramps had seen me, he would have had a spaz." Her eyes squinted at Verity. "Are you going to dob me in?"

Verity sat back and said nothing.

"Did you come straight back here?" Frankie asked, trying to get the girl's attention off the PA and wondering if she should have come alone. "To school I mean?"

Frankie said nothing, and Verity rolled her eyes. "Of course she didn't. She hooked up with Igor."

Charlie folded her arms and flashed her a filthy look. "We love each other, you know."

Verity sighed softly. "No, you don't honey. You just think you do."

Charlotte's jaw dropped at that, and she unfolded her arms like she was ready for battle, so Frankie jumped in and said, "Sorry, I like to get things straight. Occupational hazard. Explain it to me properly please, Charlie. Did you catch up with Igor at the party? And if so, how did you get there? I mean, it's a bit of a hike from here, across the bridge to Seagrave."

The teenager pulled her eyes from Verity and then shrugged. "I don't know. Got an Uber. Who cares?"

"Er, I do, Charlie. The timeline's not adding up. You snuck out from here at what time?"

"About midnight, I guess. I couldn't sneak out until Hanson the Horrible was asleep, could I?"

"But Igor left Seagrave at eleven."

She shrugged.

"Ah," said Verity. "He didn't leave, did he? He went down to the butler's pantry and waited for you there."

Charlotte ignored this too. She dropped the dregs of her donut to the plate and dusted her hands off as if it was no big deal. Then she picked up her glass and began to spoon the cream off the top and into her mouth. How the girl managed to consume that much sugar and stay painfully thin was beyond Frankie.

"Then what?" she asked her.

"Then nothing. We hung out for a bit, and then I got an Uber back."

"And Iggy?"

She frowned. "He came with me, got dropped at his place in Kings Cross."

"So what time did you and Igor really leave Seagrave?"

Charlotte looked up from the glass she was now draining, bat her eyelids a few times, then said, "I don't know, around two I guess."

Frankie leaned in. "This is important, Charlie. What time exactly, do you remember?"

According to the police report, the murders happened around two thirty, and the emergency call was logged five minutes later. She wondered if Igor had time to wave goodbye to Charlie, then return to the mansion.

"Like I said, two-ish. Why does it matter? I had nothing to do with it, and neither did Iggy."

Frankie watched her for a moment and then said, "Why was Igor at the party hours before you?"

Charlie looked confused. "What? I don't know. He told me Mum asked him and he was being polite."

Verity scoffed. "Why would your mother want your boyfriend there?"

Charlotte's scowl dissolved, and she seemed genuinely bewildered. "It surprised me too, to be honest. I didn't even think Mum *liked* Iggy! I mean, I thought that was partly why she let me come to boarding school, to get me away from him, but… well, she obviously realised he's a good guy because about a month before the party, she changed her tune; really encouraged him in the end. And he is a good guy! Like, the best guy ever! Not like the toffee-nosed juveniles the prudes at my school go out with." She shrugged her head towards

Saint Augustine's. "They're pigs those boys. Barely open a door for you. So entitled, so *aristo!*"

"Aristo?" said Frankie.

"Aristocratic," murmured Verity.

"Iggy's different," said Charlie. "He's, like, a gentleman and a grown-up."

"Doesn't sound very gentlemanly to me," said Verity, reaching for the bill. "Rooting you downstairs in a pantry."

"We weren't rooting! Oh my God! You're so disgusting! We love each other!"

"My bad. Sorry, I keep forgetting."

"We're celebrating our nine-month anniversary next week, you know!"

"Oh, well then, you're practically married," said Verity, her voice laced with sarcasm.

"Better than being a dried-up old spinster," Charlie shot back, and Verity's expression turned icy.

"Okay, let's get you back to school," said Frankie, seriously regretting inviting the PA along now, "before Sister Scary catches us."

Charlie blinked. "How do you know we call her that?"

Frankie blinked back. "Oh, I just assumed... Seems the logical nickname." She hadn't particularly liked the white-haired tattletale, but she never revealed her sources.

That's something she had learned the hard way.

As they escorted Charlie back to the window, the girl said, "Maybe next time you want to talk, you could, like, text me or something. Might be easier."

"I didn't think you had a mobile," said Frankie, eyes turned to Verity.

"As if I wouldn't have a mobile? Oh em gee, it's not 1978!"

"That's my bad this time," said Verity. "I didn't think you were allowed devices. At least that's what your grandfather told me."

She coyly lifted a shoulder. "Uncle Clem gave it to me."

"So what's the number?" asked Frankie, pulling her mobile out.

Charlie's eyes narrowed. "Only if you promise not to say anything to Grandad. About my night out with Iggy, I mean."

She was appealing to Verity, who just looked at her blankly. "It will come out in the end, you know? It all comes out in the end."

Charlie shrugged, like she didn't care about the endgame. She was living for the moment, and as Frankie tapped the number Charlie was now reciting into her phone, she wondered if that's all this was—a young girl playing nookie with her boyfriend. Or if she was all about the endgame and playing them just as she was playing Sister Mary and Sir George and everybody else who thought she was currently tucked up asleep, sans an iPhone.

Or perhaps the real player here was the man who could get a young heiress to desert her warm bed in the dead of night—and risk expulsion, no less—all with the flick of a pebble.

CHAPTER 14 ~
FOOD FOR THOUGHT

It was a stiflingly hot Saturday morning, and the crew were gathered again in the cool interior of Seagrave's library, enjoying another buffet breakfast. As before, they'd each shared their previous findings and were comparing notes. Martin, however, was feeling grumpy. And not about Tamara, who was still stomping around the apartment like she was checking for termites.

He had read and reread the statements of everybody present at the party that bloody night and found nothing of any significance, not one interesting morsel. The police certainly hadn't noted anything, but Earle quickly explained that they wouldn't have because they were wholly focused on Heathcliff.

"DI Morgan refuses to see beyond the bleeding obvious, so we're on our own, folks."

They all nodded. They had always assumed as much.

"So, how d'you go with Lia then?" Martin asked Kila.

Surprised, he glanced up from his coffee. "Lia? Oh, she was babysitting her boss's kids last night, so I'm going to see her tonight."

"What are you, a vampire? Can't visit her during the day like a normal person?" said Martin. "Get her on her lunch break?"

"Hey man, nothing normal about the way I operate. When it comes to the ladies, night-time is my theatre." Kila grinned at that, but Martin wasn't amused.

"You're the one who put this tight deadline in place, do I need to remind you of that?"

"Chill, Marty babe. I'll get what I need out of Lia. It'll happen. I did track down the infamous Woko Wangi and confirmed what Lia said. He was recording a rap EP with Heath about a month before the murders."

He produced the CD that Woko had given him and tossed it on

the table beside the police file.

Merry grabbed it and glanced across the titles. "Any clues in the lyrics?"

"No idea. They couldn't pay me enough to listen to that shit. Oh hang on, they're not."

"I'll do it!" Merry popped the CD into her handbag. "I don't mind a bit of hip-hop. My Archie is into drill rap, whatever that means."

"I think that means he's headed for a life of crime," said Frankie, who also knew her music. "You reckon there'll be a song on there from Heath about slaughtering his whole family?"

She giggled. "Hope not or we'll be out a million bucks!"

"So, Kila, did you get one of your infamous *vibes* about whether this Woko clown was a killer?" asked Martin, still intent on moving things forward.

Kila shrugged. "He's short on cash; that could've been the motive. Had a few red-letter bills lying about, and I spotted a bit of bedding. Have a hunch he bunks down in his studio, can't afford a rental."

"Oh, that's well spotted! You are so good at this!" said Merry, and he pushed his top lip up, Elvis Presley-style.

"Thank you, thank you very much."

She giggled.

Martin stared hard at him, softly stroking his nose. "Considering nothing was pinched during the murders, Kila, how exactly is that a motive?"

Kila shrugged and held his gaze.

Earle watched the two bucks going at it, their strikes still subtle at this stage. It reminded him of his old colleagues, always tussling for the top spot. Two alpha males in one room were never easy. He cleared his throat, as he was prone to do, and cut in before things escalated.

"Frankie, how did you go with young Charlotte?"

The reporter had been madly tapping away at her smartphone but glanced up then and across to Verity, who was replacing the coffeepot, and said, "Hmmm, not sure to be honest."

She proceeded to describe their late-night escapade, explaining how Charlie was clearly an expert at sneaking out of school, and confirmed that she had indeed lied about her whereabouts on the night of the murders.

"She admits she snuck out around midnight and caught an Uber to the party, admits to a quick hello with her mother and a rendezvous with Igor in some pantry, and then insists she tucked herself back into school before the murders."

"Hang on just a moment," said Earle. "Are you saying Charlotte met Igor at her mother's party? He told us he never saw her that night."

"Oh, he just lied to protect his girlfriend," said Merry dismissively. "He didn't want to snitch."

Earle frowned. She really had to get over her natural motherly bias. He'd met enough charming young villains to know it was wasted energy.

Frankie said, "That's probably where Igor went when he left the party at eleven—to hide in the aforementioned pantry. Probably smoked that joint while he was waiting. In any case, Charlie insists they left together in an Uber, and she was back at school around two a.m. Which means Igor could've easily returned here by the time of the murders. Providing he had the security codes to get in. Charlie could've given him those because she said she got them from Lia."

"I'm more interested in the timeline," said Earle, "and why Ivanov was at the party earlier. He claims Tawny invited him, but I'm struggling to buy it."

"Actually, Charlie's confirmed that," said Frankie. "Says her mother did a U-turn on her boyfriend about a month before the murders."

Kila squinted. "A month, you reckon?"

She nodded, and he just said, "Huh," then dropped his head to one side.

"There is one other thing I wanted to mention," said Verity, still lingering. "It's kind of off the track a bit."

"Nothing is off the track in a murder investigation," said Earle, thinking of the pathology report and how Sir George had never mentioned the drugs in Heath's system. He hadn't brought that up yet and wasn't sure he would. Perhaps he could use it as leverage later; perhaps it was not important.

Glancing at Frankie, Verity said, "Charlotte claims she surprised her mother in the butler's pantry the night of her birthday, right? But there is no butler's pantry on this floor. The only butler's pantry is downstairs at the far end of the ballroom. It's just below the kitchen, where the dumbwaiter ends up. One door opens to the kitchen in the ballroom, the butler's pantry we call it, the other to the pool outside."

"So?" Frankie said, not following.

"Maybe it's nothing, but that's quite a hike, and there would be no reason for Tawny to be on the lower floor. The party was held on this level. So either Charlotte prearranged to meet her mother down there, in which case she lied to us about that, or…"

"*Or* maybe her mother was down on that level and that's where Charlie found her!" Frankie jumped in. "In which case, what was Tawny doing down there all alone? If indeed she was alone."

The two women blinked at each other while Earle's mind drifted back to Igor and a timeline that still looked as messy as the lad's tatts.

Kila tried to focus on the chatter about posh pantries, but a timeline of a different type was circling through his head. As they paused to replenish their coffees, he said to no one in particular, "Why does a month before the murders keep coming up?"

"What's that?" said Frankie, snapping a low-sugar sachet against her cup.

"Lia says she gave notice to Tawny *about a month* before the murders. That's also when Heath recorded his EP with Woko."

"Mmmm," she agreed. "That's when Charlotte booked herself into boarding school too."

"And when Susan said things turned weird between Tawny and Lia," added Martin. "Could all be a red herring, of course, a coincidence."

"I've never been a fan of coincidences," said Earle. "I think you're onto something there, Kila. Be good to find out what happened the month before the murders that brought on so many changes. When was that?"

"Murders were last August, August 30 to be precise, so it had to be late July," said Frankie.

Earle looked at Verity. "Any idea what happened back then?"

She pulled a phone out of her jacket. "Let's see…" She opened her Calendar app. "Last July… Hmmm… Okay, here we are. So, George had a shareholders' meeting, can't be that… Roman had a quick trip to the Pilbara mines for work… Oh, and that's when the family went on their annual skiing holiday to Perisher—the last week of July." She glanced up. "That's about the only thing I can see of any significance."

"Maybe something happened after the ski trip?" suggested Merry.

"Or *during* it," said Martin, "because Susan told me the two kids left the holiday early. She said they were bored, but maybe there was more to it."

"Good point," said Frankie, glancing at Verity. "Can we ask Sir George?"

"He may not know. He opted out this year. His first concession to old age, I'm afraid."

"Pity," said Frankie. "Okay, then we need to ask the people who were there. I now have Charlie's number so will call her, and you should ask Susan if she knows more, Martin."

The novelist's lips twisted downward. "That's assuming she'll tell me the truth."

"*Of course* she won't tell you the truth; she's family!" said Kila. "Look how much Charlie has lied already. You lot need to stop playing by their rules and speak to an outsider, a third party. A snitch." He gave Merry a wink. "Is there someone who works at the ski lodge who can dish the dirt?"

Verity looked appalled by the suggestion but eventually conceded that there was some overlap with the staff. "One or two of the lodge's winter staff go on to work as instructors at Sir George's sailing school during summer, so they could be there now if you want me to make enquiries. I will need to check with Sir George first, of course. It could take time."

"Tell him he owes us one," said Earle as the doorbell started chiming through the house.

As Verity strode off to answer it, Frankie's brain was in overdrive, her mind spiralling back towards the pantry, but it wasn't Charlie she was seeing locked in an embrace with Iggy. It was her mother Tawny.

Could the two have had an illicit affair? What other reason would Igor have to be at the party before Charlotte? It might also explain the fight in the kitchen. Perhaps Heath caught them at it. Perhaps the truth came out that night.

Earle seemed to be thinking along similar lines. "I want to look into this Ivanov fellow a little more. Find out what he did to suddenly ingratiate himself to Tawny."

"Good plan," agreed Frankie, excitement bubbling up as it always did when a good story came together, or better yet, a bad story started unravelling before her eyes.

It took just three words for the bubbles to evaporate.

"Well, hello there!"

Frankie froze as the others looked around to see a short, portly woman standing at the entrance to the library, a massive bag under one arm, a blanket of frizzy hair fluttering around her like a cape.

"So *this* is where you've been hiding!"

Frankie felt her throat go dry. She took a deep breath, forced her lips into a smile, and turned to face the music. "Jan! Hey! What are you doing here?"

The woman stepped forward and dragged Frankie into a tight embrace. "Oh, like I'm not welcome?"

"*Of course* you're welcome—"

"Actually," Verity said, standing behind them, index finger up. "Sir George has asked that only you five be allowed access. I have already explained this to your friend and—"

"Door bitch is chucking me out," said Jan, causing Frankie to wince. "I've got two minutes, then she's giving me the boot."

"Oh, right," said Frankie turning to the others. "Everybody, this is my friend Jan."

"*Best* friend," Jan said. "But you can all call me the Boss."

Frankie smiled stiffly as the others stared between them surprised, then introduced themselves while Jan turned her attention to the buffet.

"No wonder you're not returning my calls! Who needs me when you have all this?"

"Feel free to help yourself," said Verity, "then, if you don't mind…"

The PA tapped her watch as Jan gave a quick Hitler salute.

Kila chuckled at that, but Frankie was not impressed. After last night's adventure, she had come to like Verity and didn't need the Boss undermining her in front of the others.

"Come on," she said to Jan. "Grab a croissant and let's head off. I'm running late for work as it is."

"On a Saturday? Really?" said Merry.

Frankie nodded vigorously. "Making up for all the time I've spent here."

"And how will you make it up to me?" said Jan, chewing on a croissant as she talked, her eyes firmly on Frankie.

Frankie looked flustered suddenly and was relieved when Earle said, "Why don't we all have tomorrow off, folks? It's Sunday after all. I know we're on deadline, but one day won't hurt. Give us a chance to catch up with our other lives."

They all agreed, then watched as Jan grabbed a serviette and piled more pastries into it before waving at the others and shuffling out, Frankie behind her, Verity nipping at their heels.

"What's the deal with those two?" said Kila as the sound of Frankie's stilettoes echoed down the hall. "Don't look like besties to me. You think they might be a couple?"

"What?" said Merry. "No! I mean... I doubt it. Didn't she say she was Frankie's boss?"

"You're pathetic, Kila," said Martin. "Frankie gives you the brush-off, so she must be a lesbian, is that it?"

"Only explanation I can think of," Kila replied deftly.

"Well, whoever she is, she seems really nice," said Merry. "But I want to get back to the butler and his pantry. Anyone want to toddle on downstairs with me, see how it's all laid out, whether Charlie's story adds up?"

Truth was, Merry was really interested in the ballroom. She'd never been in an actual ballroom before, at least not outside the Cluedo board game, and was desperate to have a squiz.

"I'll show you," said Verity, who had now returned. "Anyone else for a tour of the lower level?"

"Nah," said Kila, reaching for another coffee. "Merry's our strategist; she can suss it out and report back."

Merry took that as a vote of confidence and followed Verity, beaming.

The ballroom, as it turns out, was rather disappointing. Sure, it had shiny parquetry flooring and looming leadlight windows, but there was nothing in it except an empty stage at one end and more gaudy chandeliers, hanging like forgotten promises from the high ceiling above. What a silly thing it is to have a ballroom, Merry thought now. Such a massive waste of space! If it were up to her, she'd fill it with beanbags and ping-pong tables, a trampoline or two.

At least the adjoining butler's pantry was useful, she thought, as she peered into the small kitchen with the dumbwaiter against one wall and a sliding door to hide the mess from waltzing guests. There was another door that led out to the terraced pool deck, which featured a kidney-shaped pool on one terrace with a purple mosaic waterfall just below it and the stunning blue sea beyond that.

Merry sighed wistfully and glanced around. One thing she knew for sure—this was quite a hike from all the action in the Yellow Room upstairs.

"I guess Tawny could've come down here to grab supplies for the party," Merry suggested, nodding at a box of serviettes just inside the door.

"That's why you hire caterers," said Verity. "They do the running around."

Merry chuckled. "That makes sense! I've never had the luxury, I'm afraid. Okay, so Charlie must have prearranged the reunion with her mum down here, which only seems to lead to more questions like: Why make it so secretive? Wouldn't she be welcome at the party? And if not, who exactly was she hiding from?"

Her eyes widened, and she stared at Verity. "Do you think Charlie was scared of somebody?"

Verity frowned. "How do you mean?"

"I mean, why did she not feel welcome at the party? I know she snuck out of school, but this *is* her family home. It was her mother's fortieth for goodness' sake! So why did she feel the need to hide down here, and who, pray tell, was she hiding from?"

CHAPTER 15 ~
THREATS AND ATTITUDE

Frankie tried to douse her frown as she watched Jan wedge her large station wagon into a tiny parking spot behind her Audi, just outside *Herald* headquarters, then fling the door wide. She hadn't asked how Jan had found her, wasn't sure she wanted to know—was her bestie following her now? But she did need to do some back peddling. And fast.

"I'm sorry, Boss," Frankie said, using Jan's self-appointed nickname as her friend strode towards her, bag hanging from one arm. "I would've told you about the investigation, but I wasn't allowed. I signed a confidentiality agreement."

"And you didn't pass it by me? Are you *insane*? What else did you sign?"

"Nothing! And I'm perfectly capable of signing my own agreement."

Jan stepped closer and placed a hand on her shoulder. "Honey. We all know you can write a killer article, but legal stuff is my forte, right?"

Frankie nodded, looking contrite. "I know. You're right."

Jan's eyes squinted, getting lost in folds of cheek. "So what's this story about then?"

"Like I said, it's confidential. I promised I'd keep it to myself."

"Oh, well, you wouldn't want to break a promise now, would you? Or repeat something off the record?" Jan's tone was light and breezy. "It's not like you've ever done *that* before."

Frankie frowned. "What do you mean by that?"

"Nothing, honeybun!" Jan plucked a stray strand of hair from Frankie's jacket. "Just don't forget we're in this together, hey? We have been from the start."

"I know." Frankie glanced around. "I've really got to run."

Jan released her hand and plunged it into her bag, pulling out the pilfered pastries. "Eat these," she said, thrusting them towards her. "You're too skinny. It doesn't suit you."

As Frankie rode the elevator upwards, her reporter self told her to stop being neurotic. Jan always turned snarky when she was feeling left out. Her long-time best friend was jealous, and she couldn't blame her for that. Frankie *had* been neglecting her of late, preoccupied with the Burlington case. But she'd make it up to her somehow. It would all be okay in the end, because it *had to be.* Jan was all Frankie had. She didn't call her "the Boss" for no reason. Jan was everything to Frankie, the only person in the world she trusted.

The keeper of her secrets.

Of course, it didn't take a jealous PI to notice they were a curious match. Frankie Jo was petite and blond and coiffed to within an inch of her life, while the Boss was all big hair and wobbly body and oversized linen garments, a large calico bag permanently hitched to one shoulder. What exactly was in that carryall was anyone's guess, but it seemed to Frankie that it contained the world.

"Hungry, honey?" the Boss would say, then out would come a container of nuts, a muesli bar or some chocolate. She had every mood food required. And that was just the beginning. The second a cloud appeared, an umbrella would pop out. Then another for herself. If Frankie was feeling down or bored or angry, Jan was the one who dropped everything at a moment's notice.

She'd been her rock since university where Frankie studied journalism and Jan did legal studies. Was ambitious too, Frankie remembered, but then all that faded, and by third year, Jan had dropped out and devoted herself to Frankie—prepping her for exams, writing half her essays, even helping her land her dazzling cadetship at the *Herald.* If it wasn't for the Boss's intervention, she never would have got a look-in.

She knew it; Jan knew it. And now she just needed to tick this story off and get everything back to normal, because her life depended on it. Or at the very least, her career did. And, after everything she'd been through, she wasn't going to risk that now.

"Hey, Frankie, what brings you in?" a colleague called out as she stepped from the elevator on level sixteen.

Several others were tapping away at their computers and also looked surprised to see her. The paper did not sleep, but Frankie usually got a chance to, rarely working weekends, her copy always delivered long before then. She mumbled something non-committal and headed straight for her desk. Might as well cross a few things from her to-do list while she was in here.

The first was the call to young Charlotte, who did not sound thrilled to hear from her.

"My God, you're worse than Scary! I'm on my way to netball. What do you want?"

"I won't keep you long. When you went skiing with your family last July, you and your brother returned home early. Why?"

There was a long pause. "I don't know. Just bored I guess."

"Of skiing?"

"And all the fighting. Although…" Another pause amidst the sound of a bus roaring. "This time Heath wasn't fighting with Dad. It was Mum he was cranky at."

"Any idea why?"

"I told you before, the bickering makes me snore. All I know is Heath was disappointed with Mum for some reason and said he wanted to bail and did I want to come? Like, does the Pope shit in the forest?"

"You don't like skiing."

"It's not that; it's just, Perisher is so… Well, it's not Aspen, is it? We only go to keep Grandpa happy, but he wasn't even there, so what was the point? Besides, that gave me a chance to see Iggy."

"If you were so keen to see Iggy, why did you then book yourself into boarding school at the end of that winter holiday? I know you sneak out to see him, but it's hardly ideal, is it?"

There was another long pause, and for a moment Frankie thought Charlotte had hung up, but then she said, "Look, here's the thing. I don't know what happened at the ski lodge, but Mum returned all gnarly and took it out on me. Don't ask me why. Like I said, it was Heath's idea to leave early, not mine! Still, I was the one who got punished and sent to boarding school."

"Hang on. I thought you said you *chose* to go." *For the love of God, keep your stories straight!*

"I did. Sort of." Charlie sighed, sounding frustrated with the dumb reporter. "Mum wanted me go to some stupid finishing school in Switzerland somewhere."

"Those places still exist?"

Charlotte snorted. "I know, right? So *of course* I said no way. But, like, if you're trying to get rid of me, why don't I go and live with Aunty Sue, and she wouldn't have that of course. Can't have me happily living with the sister-in-law she despises."

"She despised Susan?" *This too was new.*

"Maybe not *despised,* but there was tension between them, that's for sure. Anyway, that's how I ended up boarding at Saint Auggie's. The happy compromise. Not."

"So you had no idea why your mum wanted to send you away?"

"I just said that, didn't I?" She suddenly yelled out, "Claudia! Clauds! Wait up! *Jesus!*" Then she lowered her voice again and said, "Look, Mum was different after that holiday. Heath and I obviously hurt her feelings by leaving early." There was a sudden sniff on the other end of the line, followed by another. "It's like I disappointed her, or she didn't *like* me anymore... or something."

"Oh, Charlie, I'm sure that's not true."

"I think she thought I was turning into a brat. She said she wanted me elsewhere until I had matured."

"Matured?"

"Yah! Like I'm a piece of cheese or something. She said, 'I don't want you back here until you're old enough to see the wood for the trees,' whatever that means." There was another sniff and then she said, "What *does* that even mean?"

In this context, Frankie didn't have a clue, but her mind was back on Igor and that cosy butler's pantry.

~

Martin had left the sleuths' meeting back in grumpy mode. He didn't want to take the rest of the weekend off as Earle suggested. He wanted to avoid his petulant girlfriend and his frustratingly unfinished manuscript and instead get stuck into the Burlington case, but the thought of interrogating Susan again made him feel nauseated. There was something about the woman that put him off. It was just six months since half her family had been slaughtered, and she seemed so oddly flippant. Happier to flirt with him than uncover the facts. He shuddered again, thinking of her flirtatious banter. How disconcerting it was—and something else that he couldn't quite articulate. He regretted ever volunteering to interview her, really should have flicked her across to Kila. *He'd* know how to handle a woman like that, he thought, and it irked him. How could Kila possibly be a hit with the ladies when he looked and acted like a buffoon? The guy was a shabbily dressed loser with signs of grey stubble, yet he acted like he was an islander version of George Clooney. It infuriated Martin, and he wasn't sure why.

Oh, who was he kidding? He knew *exactly* why. Kila reminded Martin of all the footy heroes at his high school, the ones who were constantly lauded in the school newsletter and scored all the cute chicks even though they could barely string a sentence together. Meanwhile, Martin had to work hard to get noticed. If it wasn't for his bestsellers, he'd be lucky to have a girlfriend at all, even one as needy as Tamara.

Poor Tamara. She was probably still sulking at home, waiting for him to explain himself. But he just couldn't do it, and it had nothing to do with the confidentiality agreement.

He groaned, wondering if he should stop somewhere for a stiff drink, when he noticed a large sign for the Burly Sailing Club. Before he knew what he was doing, he had applied his left blinker and was turning in to their car park.

He'd show Kila who was the rule breaker.

The club was small but grand and perched on the edge of the marina, and Martin tried to think on his feet as they dragged him towards the entrance. Somewhere between taking the turn and parking his car, he'd decided that he wasn't waiting for Verity to organise anything. If there was staff overlap between the ski lodge and the sailing club, he would find it.

"Can I help you?" said a woman at the front desk, wearing a cap with the letters BSC stitched across it.

"Hello there. Martin Chase is my name, and I'd like to take a sailing lesson."

"Of course, sir. Are you a member here?" The receptionist turned and started clicking at her keyboard. "Chase was it?"

"Yes. Martin Chase. And no, I'm not." She stopped tapping, her expression blank, and it was clear she was no crime reader, so he added, "Sorry, I didn't realise you had to be a member."

"Yes, I'm afraid so. Members only."

He tried a different angle. "Oh well, that's a pity." Sighed dramatically. "I'll have to tell Sir George I gave it a red-hot go."

Now *that* name rang a bell, and her eyes lit up. "You're a friend of Mr Burlington's?"

"Well, I was at his place just the other day." It wasn't strictly a lie. "He said to drop in here, see about some classes, but since I'm not a member…"

The woman was now nodding fervently. "Oh, I'm sure we can make an exception for a friend of Mr Burlington's. We can absolutely help you with that. Have you ever sailed before, Mr Chase?"

He waggled a hand in the air. "I'm very rusty. George calls me an abomination, suggested I come in and get my skills up."

He hoped he wasn't overdoing it, but she didn't bat an eyelid as she began scrolling through the computer in front of her.

"Let me see who we have available for lessons…"

"Actually," he said, "last time I was at his Snowy Mountains lodge, George introduced me to one of his staffers—can't recall the name—said they worked here in summer and would be the perfect instructor for me. Just my speed."

She glanced up, flummoxed. "Oh, okay… I wonder who that could be. Did you catch a name?" He shook his head and she held up a finger. "If you'll give me just a moment, sir, I'll ask the manager."

Shrugging like he couldn't care less, Martin watched as she vanished into a side office, then felt his heart skip a beat. Was she checking his story with someone? Calling Sir George that very minute? He considered making a quick, graceful exit when the receptionist returned with her lovely warm smile back in place. He exhaled.

"I think perhaps you're referring to Timothy Langer," she said before her smile slipped slightly. "Unfortunately, Timmy's not scheduled on until tomorrow. I can find you another instructor, sir. I assure you they are all very competent."

"No, no, let's stick to the man George recommends, hey? Or I'll never hear the end of it. You know what the old guy's like?"

He laughed heartily and she smiled politely back. "Shall I book you in then, sir? Say, ten a.m. tomorrow?"

"Perfect," he said, "Tallyho!"

Then he knew he was overdoing it and scuttled for the exit.

~

Earle was also feeling antsy that day, not in the mood to hang around the house. He'd already missed tee off with his mates, and Beryl had three gossips coming over under the guise of playing bridge.

He needed to get out.

And so it was he found himself returning to the Wobbler's Arms, his eyes scanning the crowd for Morgan. He wasn't looking forward to butting horns with the fellow again, but what choice did he have? He needed to verify Igor's alibi, because right now he was the ideal suspect and there were too many inconsistencies in his statements.

Earle had already checked the official police report, and that had Ivanov home at 2:35 a.m. when the murders occurred. But there was no corroborating evidence. For all they knew Igor kissed his girl goodbye at two, then returned to Seagrave to bump off her family.

So here he was, staking out the pub again, hoping Morgan was as bored with his home life as Earle was. And sure enough, there was the detective, perched on a stool at the back of the venue, watching as someone lobbed a dart towards a heavily battered board.

Earle smiled and headed straight for the bar, ordering two beers, one of them a bribe.

As Earle walked towards him, Morgan was no longer feigning politeness. He sneered as the older cop approached, but he did take the beer and Earle took that as a concession of sorts. Figured he had until the glass was empty, then all bets were off.

"Igor Ivanov," Earle said, not bothering with niceties either. "Your report has him at a share house in Kings Cross at the time of the murders."

"Yeah, Fitzy. I wrote the report. You don't need to tell me what's in it."

"Fair enough, then I'll tell you what's not in it. No witness statement to verify the alibi."

"That's because it wasn't an alibi," he shot back. "You keep forgetting, nobody else was under suspicion."

"So why interview him at all?"

"He was at the party. Everyone at the party gave a statement. That's the job."

"Oh, *the job*? Good-oh. I was worried for a moment there that you'd forgotten all about what the job entailed."

This inflamed the detective, and he dumped the beer on a side table. "Oh bugger off, Earle. I don't need some washed-up has-been

BLIND MEN DON'T DIAL ZERO

to tell me how to do my job."

Earle had his palms out. "I'm just trying to make it look less wonky, remember? What you obviously don't know is that there are some hours that are unaccounted for. Charlotte Burlington has confirmed that she snuck out of school on the night of the party, around midnight, and went straight to Seagrave where she met up with both her mother and her boyfriend. That means Igor Ivanov had to be at the mansion around twelve-fifteen, twelve thirty at the latest. So why did he say he left at eleven? And if he really did leave, what did he do for that extra hour? Search the house and find the weapon, perhaps?"

Morgan took the darts now being offered to him and didn't say a word.

Earle continued. "Charlotte also states that they were both at Seagrave until he dropped her back to school around two a.m. What I want to know is, did her criminal boyfriend return to the mansion?"

Morgan held a dart up. "What's your bloody point?"

"You never verified that Ivanov was at his home in Kings Cross when the homicides happened, and you should have because the guy is a pathological liar. He lied about the time he left the party, he lied about seeing his girlfriend, who's to say he's not lying about his alibi?"

"Or maybe it's not Igor who's lying," said Morgan. "Maybe it's his girlfriend. Ever thought of that? Or does that not suit your boss's agenda?"

"Hey, I'm just doing the maths. It doesn't add up."

"The only thing that doesn't add up is why a tired ex-detective would leave his happy home and wife to waste time on a case that's going nowhere fast. Sounds like somebody needs to get a life."

Then Morgan turned towards the board and began lobbing his darts like the board was Earle's head.

Earle watched him for another moment, then drained his glass and began to move away when Morgan called out his name.

"He's lying to you, you know."

Earle looked back. "Sorry?"

"Your boss, Sir Bullshit Artist. He hasn't told you everything. He's left out the best parts of this story."

"What parts? What are you talking about?"

Morgan shook his head. "Just go home, Fitzy. You're pathetic."
And then he looked away.

~

Kila didn't need Martin's derision to know it was time to have
another word with housekeeper Lia. It was as overdue as his rent.
Still, he waited until the witching hour to finally make his move. He
tried Lia's apartment unsuccessfully at first and then took a punt and
headed for the terrace house he'd trailed her to a few nights earlier. It
was now Saturday evening, and if he knew Lia as he thought he did,
she'd be topping up with her wantoks again before they headed out.

After buzzing the doorbell and finding it didn't work, he rapped
loudly and was pleasantly surprised when Lia herself answered it, a
slinky dress on her voluptuous body, a glass of something bubbly in
her hands.

"How you find me?" she asked, eyes narrow, but she did not look
disappointed.

"I'm a private dick, Lia. It's what I do. Got a sec?"

He didn't wait for an answer, was already brushing past her and
into the house.

Two other women sat on the couch, both in various stages of
undress, and one jumped up, squealing when she saw Kila.

"Hey! *Yu no ken lukim mi*!"

"Sorry, I'm not here to perve." He held up a palm, as if blocking
the sight. "Just want a quiet word with Ms Segeyaro."

The women shared a look with Lia that spoke volumes, but Lia
was laughing. "I'm fine. This is just Kila. I told you about him. Go!
Finish getting dressed. I talk to Kila alone."

They still looked suspicious but did as instructed, giggling a little
as they headed for their bedrooms. Lia sat on the sofa and did not
offer Kila a chair, simply stared up at him with wide eyes, so he took
one anyway.

"I won't take long. I know you have some partying to do."

"You like to party?" she asked, her tone flirty, her eyes darting to a
bottle of cheap, sparkling wine on the coffee table. "Have a drink,
come party with us if you like."

His smile widened. He'd seen Lia's half-dressed friends, and
would like, very much indeed. But shook the thought away. "I need
to talk to you about last July." Lia's own smile dropped. "Something

happened when the Burlingtons went skiing in Perisher."

"I didn't do anything last July! Why you say this?"

"I'm not talking about you," he said. "I'm asking about the ski trip. Did something happen on the slopes or at their winter lodge? Something that set everything in motion?"

Lia blinked. "I don't know what you mean."

She sculled her drink and looked away, and he almost laughed at her obvious lie, which was now catching up with her in the form of a creeping blush under her glossy, dark cheeks.

"You really should tell me," he said. "It might be important to the case."

Lia shrugged and poured herself another glass. By the time she met his eyes again, she had regained her composure. "Nothing to tell."

He smiled. "You didn't go on the trip, right?"

"I never go skiing. Only family."

Her tone was just on the cusp of sulky. Did she believe she was *entitled* to a ski trip after all her years of service? Was that what the falling out was over?

"You not good enough to go with them?" he asked, poking the bear.

She shrugged again like it wasn't an issue, but he sensed she was bluffing, so he tried a different tack.

"The two kids came home early. Any idea why?"

Her eyes slid away again.

He said, "Tawny shoved poor Charlie off to boarding school then, like she didn't matter."

"No, not like this!" Lia's eyes had snapped back. "Tawny was a good mother! She loved Charlie!"

"So why'd she send her away?"

Lia went to say something and stopped.

He leaned forward. "What happened, Lia? I know you know. Something happened around that time, and you have to tell me what it was."

Lia was blushing again, her eyes ablaze. "It's nothing! You stop, okay? Just leave it alone."

"Leave what alone?"

She growled like an angry beast. "I'm telling you! Let it go!"

"You okay, Lia?"

This was one of her friends, only minimally more dressed, standing in the doorway, hands on her hips, ready for battle.

Lia nodded, smiled and waved her back in.

"Come, Violet," she said. "Come join us. It's time to party!"

Then she gave Kila a wary glance as she reached once again for the bottle.

~

Merry adored being at home, finally catching up with the kids, but she barely had a moment to spend with them as she hung out the washing and emptied the dishwasher and put together a veggie lasagne. Otis appeared at one point to help her in the kitchen, then Lola swept in to gripe about Jasper Rogers.

"He's so *straight*, Mum, I think I'll have to dump him!"

"Jasper sounds perfect to me, darling," she'd fired back, thinking of Igor and shuddering.

The principal's son now seemed like a right catch.

It was not until after dinner, as she grabbed her mobile to recharge for the morning, that Merry noticed the CD Kila had given her and pulled it from her handbag. Then made a beeline for Archie's bedroom.

Her youngest boy was watching YouTube clips on his computer but waved her in happily enough and turned it all to mute. She loved that about the kid. Unlike Lola, he was never disappointed to see her.

"How's the case going?" he asked. "Found any more corpses?"

All three children knew what Merry was doing; she'd ignored the confidentiality agreement entirely. After her husband's lies and deceit, Merry didn't want any secrets between them. Her sister Beth often accused her of telling the kids too much—treating them like her partner—but they *were* partners now, the four of them. A tight little unit. And she wouldn't apologise for that. She was sick to death of apologising.

Hadn't she spent her entire marriage starting every sentence with the word *sorry?*

"Sorry I put on so much weight since our wedding."

"Sorry I'm so needy and never learned to drive."

"Sorry I did so well at Cluedo and you turned to someone else."

Well, she wouldn't do it. Not anymore. She wasn't sorry about anything. She liked her extra weight; it made her feel womanly.

And she was *happy* she couldn't drive. It meant quality car time with Otis. In fact, her hubby's departure meant more time with *all* the kids, and that was something to celebrate! And she sure as hell wasn't sorry her kids took an interest in her exciting new mission, as macabre as it was.

She held the CD up and said, "Can I give you some homework?"

Archie mock gagged, and she laughed and assured him it wouldn't be too taxing. "This was recorded by the guy who supposedly killed his family."

"Mr Wuthering Heights?"

She laughed again. "Heathcliff, yes! Good to see your English classes aren't a complete waste of time!" Then she stopped and leaned on the doorframe. "Maybe I should've been more ambitious with your names. Gone more literary."

"Nah, look how that worked out for him." He beamed. "You want me to take a listen? Maybe play it backwards and see if it's satanic?"

Merry started to laugh again when she noticed something on the screen behind Archie. "What's that?"

He glanced towards his computer. "Nothin'. Just watching YouTube videos."

"Can you put it on full screen, add the sound?"

He shrugged and did as she asked, and that's when she saw it again, the familiar purple mosaic tiles and fountain before it was obscured by an obese black man with two busty white women gyrating on either side of him.

"Who is that?" she asked.

"Just some rapper. PatPela. Why?"

But it wasn't the rapper she was staring at, and now her brain was gushing faster than the water feature behind him.

CHAPTER 16 ~

SEX, LIES AND VIDEOTAPE

It was just past nine a.m., Sunday morning. Kila peeled his eyes open and waited for the world to come into focus. Slowly, gradually, he spotted the glossy shoulder half-hidden beneath the sheet and felt his stomach drop just as his phone vibrated. He pounced on it, then glanced back at the sleeping form before shifting out of bed and quickly making his way through the apartment to the tiny balcony at the front, where he stepped out to answer it.

"Hey, I hope I haven't woken you?" came Merry's dulcet tones at the other end. "Are you busy?"

He scraped fingers through his tussled hair and said, "Not anymore, I'm not."

Half an hour later, Kila was stepping out onto Seagrave's windswept terrace and towards the swimming pool where Merry was standing. He held a hand up to block the sunlight. It was way too shimmery for his hangover, and he grappled for his sunglasses.

"Verity said I'd find you here," he mumbled. "She's upstairs if we need her."

"Oh, we don't need her, no siree!" Merry sang out. "Come!" She beckoned him closer. "I want to show you something!" Then when they were both poolside, she pulled out her smartphone, and as she waited for a page to load, she said, "How d'you go with Lia last night? Did she say anything interesting?"

He shrugged. "Not really. What've you got there?" Then before she could answer, he noticed the music video that was now playing on her device and said, "I know that guy. Saw him the other day. What's this about?"

She blinked. "You saw PatPela? Where?"

"At Sanguma studios. He's a client of Woko's, I assume.

Why, what's going on?"

"Look at the background!" Merry's voice was at fever pitch. "Does *that* look familiar to you?"

Kila peered at the screen, using his fingers to zero in on one corner. Then he yanked off his sunglasses and stared across the pool, his hangover now forgotten.

~

Martin glanced down at his boat shoes and hoped he'd fit in. *Did people even wear boat shoes on yachts these days?* He wouldn't have a clue. The closest he ever got to a yacht was the one that nearly capsized his dad's rusty little dinghy twenty years ago. He'd taken his father out on a fishing expedition, but it wasn't Flathead or Whiting he was hoping to catch. Martin just wanted the truth, a chance to set the record straight. What he got was a broken nose, a wounded ego, and a lifetime of silence.

He would never make that mistake again.

Stroking his reconstructed nose, he shook the memory away and strode into Burlington's sailing club early that Sunday morning. Was relieved to see he looked just like every other man in the place. They were all of a certain age, certain income level, certain stature.

Here at least he could outshine the likes of Kila. And leave his dad in his wake.

"Ah, Mr Chase," came the receptionist from the day before. She had clearly been looking out for him and was now waving at a young man in a matching BSC cap who promptly stepped forward. "This is Timmy Langer. It's a lovely day for sailing, and you're in very good hands, so I'll leave you to it."

Timmy smiled broadly and offered his hand to shake, then led Martin through the club and out to the creaky marina, making small talk as they went.

They were halfway down the pontoon when Timmy said, "So Mr Burlington recommended me personally, yeah?"

"Oh, well, just in passing. You know, while I was at his place last week."

At least half that sentence was true, and he hoped the kid didn't enquire further, but Timmy seemed more intent on using it to his advantage.

"With a reference like that, I might have to ask my manager for a pay rise." He chuckled as they reached a lightweight, thirteen-foot, fiberglass sailboat. "So, this is our training boat."

Martin nodded and watched as the kid began to prepare the rig. Then he said, "I know another way you can make a bit of extra cash, Timmy."

Timmy looked back at him, "Huh?"

Martin smiled. "Let's take her out shall we, and I'll tell you all about it."

~

Frankie woke late Sunday morning to the sound of tapping at her front door. She sat up in bed and listened as the tap became a hammer.

"Okay, okay, I'm coming!"

Pulling on a kimono dressing gown, she staggered through to open it and found Jan standing there, her arms laden with groceries. Before she could say hello, Jan was sweeping in and dumping the bags on the kitchen bench, then reaching for a frying pan.

"I'm making us both a decent breakfast—no poncy pastries for you today! Then you're going to tell me all about it."

Frankie muffled a groan and shut the door behind her. She pulled out a kitchen stool and said, "I keep telling you, Boss. I'm not supposed to."

"Yes, darling, but you weren't *supposed* to repeat the words that drunken politician told you that night at the college bar either, but..." She shrugged and opened the cutlery drawer. "Well, that never stopped you. And look where you ended up!"

She pulled out a spatula and waved it around Frankie's apartment.

Frankie's jaw dropped. *So, she was bringing this up again, was she?* It had been a good year since she'd mentioned the politician, but now the gloves were off.

"That minister was corrupt, Jan, and you know it. He was stealing from the public purse and boasting about it. Not my fault he told me everything. I was doing the country a favour, getting the truth out, and you know very well that I didn't make up one single word in that article!"

"Yes, sweetie, but I also know that everything he told you was—and I quote—strictly off the record. He didn't even know you were a journalist, hmm? You don't have to be a journalism major to know that's not ethical. Isn't it, like, number three in the Code of Ethics, or something?" Then she glanced around from the pan and said, "Hey, don't look so distressed! It's okay. I was there. I backed you up, remember? Everybody believed your side of it, then you went on and won that fancy award and then you got the *Herald* job… It all worked out swimmingly in the end."

Not for him, it didn't, thought Frankie, but she pushed that horrendous memory aside and tried to remember her breathing. After a few deep inhalations, she said, "What are you saying, Jan?"

"I'm just saying I've got your back, sweetie. You know that. Always have, always will. We are a team, and I wish you'd remember that. It's really important you remember. Okay?"

Frankie stared at her, horrified. "Are you *threatening* me?"

Now Jan was the one looking horrified. "Of course not, sweets! I'm making you some eggs. How do you want them? Scrambled like always?"

~

It was still mid-morning when Kila and Merry reached Woko's studio, but they suspected that didn't matter. Kila had a hunch the producer would be tucked up snoring under that duvet he'd seen earlier. Not that he was judging. He'd be lucky to own a sleeping bag by the time the lawyers were done with him.

It was a surprise then to find Woko awake and leaning against the graffitied wall down in the studio laneway, chewing on something. He frowned as they walked up.

"Aw, come on, brother! I'm working! Give me a break."

"Doesn't look like work to me," Kila replied, staring at the bag of white powder in Woko's hand.

He offered it to Kila, along with a strange green nut, and Kila shook his head, then laughed at Merry who looked mortified.

"Relax, Mez, it's just *buai*—betel nut, mustard stick, lime powder. Big in Papua New Guinea. It's a stimulant when you chew it together; it goes that funny colour."

"Gross," she said as she watched Woko spit a stream of sticky red stuff towards a bin, missing it entirely.

"What do you want?" said Woko, ignoring her reaction.

Kila grabbed Merry's mobile phone and brought the YouTube clip to life.

It only took one bar for Woko to pocket the betel nut and say, "Okay, come up."

Back in the studio live room, Woko looked half-dead.

"Big night, bro?" Kila said.

Woko scowled. "It's a studio, man. Every night's a big night." Then, "Didn't think you were into rap."

"I'm not." He waved a hand at Merry. "Meet Meredith Kean, mother of a rap fan."

Merry smiled giddily at Woko, who scowled deeper and made his way to the studio couch.

Kila and Merry followed.

"So," Kila began, "care to tell us what PatPela was doing at the Burlington place?"

"Don't know what you're talking about."

Kila looked disappointed. "Come on, we're both too hungover for bullshitting." He held out the phone again. "That's Seagrave's swimming pool, and that's your mate PatPela. We've just come from there. We're not morons."

Woko shifted in his seat and stuck his lower jaw out. He didn't speak for many minutes, and when he did his tone was defensive. "We didn't sneak in. Got permission from the family."

Kila made a buzzing sound. "Try again. We already know from Lia that Tawny didn't allow guests. You're gonna have to do better than that."

"It was Heath who gave permission. He said we could use the space."

Kila scoffed. "When exactly did Heath give you permission?" He held a hand up. "No, don't tell me. Was it a month before the murders?"

Woko's eyes narrowed. "Maybe."

He glanced at Merry. *There was that timeline again.*

"Did you pay to use the space? Get a receipt?"

"Didn't have to. Heath said I could just come in and go for it. No biggie but you can always check with—"

The deejay stopped and Kila smirked. "Heath? Is that what you were gonna say?" He looked at Merry. "Pity dead men don't talk, hey, Mez?"

She nodded eagerly. "We could always check with Lia. She'd know."

Woko frowned, and Kila noticed, saying, "Maybe I'll do that, Mez. Might have another word with Lia tonight. Over a few drinks, like last time. She's a lot of fun, Lia. Really knows how to party."

He was riling the ex-boyfriend, and Woko was looking increasingly edgy. Although that might have had more to do with his crashing hangover.

"Here's our problem, Woko," said Kila. "We've already been informed that around the time of this shoot, a month before the murders, something happened in the household that turned everything to shit between Tawny and Lia. Was that you? Did Tawny find out you were illegally filming on her pool deck? Did you cause the rift between Lia and her boss? Is that why Lia broke up with you and moved out?"

He shrugged. "I don't have to speak to you." Then he turned over on the couch, facing the wall, and said, "See yourselves out."

Merry didn't need a confession to know Kila was on the right track. "He's lying through his bloodstained teeth; I just know it," she told him as he dropped her home.

"Yeah, but I'm not sure it has anything to do with the murders."

"It's a perfect fit! He was filming there illegally and got busted by Heath and Charlie when they returned from the ski trip early. They told their parents, and the parents threatened to take legal action. So he broke into the house and killed them."

Kila looked at her sideways, so she said, "I know it sounds extreme but think about it! Woko knew the house, could easily have got the access codes from his girlfriend. It certainly explains why Lia got turfed out and things turned frosty between her and her boss. Remember, Tawny's fortieth was Lia's final day, so if they wanted revenge, that was their last chance!"

Still Kila looked unconvinced, so she sighed and said, "I'm sorry, but I'm struggling to believe the Burlington-Browns would ever let a gang of burly rappers take over their pool deck."

"Except Heath might have," said Kila, his tone grouchy. "The kid wanted to break into the industry. It's not implausible that he'd suck up to the studio producer, offer his home as a set. That's probably *why* he left skiing early, to get back in time to sneak them all in while his folks were away. But whether it set off a series of murders? Hmm… Nah."

"We should go straight to Lia now, ask her," said Merry, but he was shaking his head.

"Nah. Let's leave Lia for now. Besides, aren't we supposed to be having the day off?"

"Fine, we'll do it tomorrow." Then she groaned. "Earle's not going to like any of this. It's one of those things he despises."

"Questions?" said Kila.

"Coincidences," she corrected.

~

It took a few tacks around the bay and a rather tacky bribe to make young Timmy talk. Martin had explained that he was working for the Burlingtons, investigating the horrific murders, but that it was all hush-hush, super confidential, and at first Timmy wasn't buying it.

"How do I know you're really working for the Burlingtons?" he called out as he pulled on the jib sail. "Maybe you're a journalist."

Martin smiled and produced two fifty-dollar notes, grasping them tight as they fluttered in the wind. "I'm not a journalist. Like I said, I'm here on behalf of Sir George."

"Why grease my palm then?"

"Just paying you for your trouble. But here…" He held out his mobile phone. "Why don't you call George, and I'll take back my hundred."

Martin didn't actually have the man's direct phone number, but he also had a hunch, like the club receptionist, Timmy was not about to call Mr Burlington directly, and he was right.

"Better not disturb him on his weekend, hey?" Timmy said, pocketing the bribe. "What do you want to know?"

Martin smiled again. "I need information on their last ski visit, last July. George was not there, so he can't fill in the gaps. But you were working at the lodge then, is that correct?"

Timmy nodded as he steered the boat towards open water. "But not full time. I was on call for Angus, the lodge manager. I also worked at Bunny's, the café down in the village nearby."

"Okay, close enough," Martin said, returning his phone to his pocket. "We know something happened that week. We just need to know what."

Timmy looked back at him. "Why do you think something happened?"

"Call it a hunch. We believe something big went down between

Heath and his mother."

"Can't help you there. Heath'd cleared out by the time I got to the lodge. Never saw him or his sister. Pity that. She's fit. I'll tell you that for nothing."

Martin grimaced. That was a waste of good money. He tried a different tack: "Any idea why the two kids took off? Was there any talk about what caused them to leave early?"

Timmy adjusted the rudder, then said, "Not that I heard, but then I'd be the last to find out. Angus isn't exactly the gossipy kind. I think that's why he's held that cushy job for so long." Then, sensing Martin's disappointment or perhaps fearing he'd have to hand the cash back, he quickly added, "Something happened *after* Heath left though. That was kind of interesting."

Martin pushed his glasses up. "Interesting how? Like sinister? Sneaky?"

"Sleazy maybe."

Martin's eyebrows shot up, and Timmy glanced furtively back towards land, to the yacht club that was now little more than a blob on the horizon. "Look, all I know is I went to the lodge during one of their ski days—"

"When was this? How far into the trip?"

"Third day in, I think. Watch the boom!" He paused to perform a tricky tack, then continued. "It was the day after the kids bailed, I remember that. Angus needed me to put some shutters up, do a bit of maintenance. It was the middle of the day, good layer of powder the night before. I should have had the place to myself, but I didn't." He gave Martin a knowing look. "Mrs Burlington-Brown was there. She seemed surprised to see me."

"Tawny?" He nodded. "And why was that such a surprise?"

"Told you, there'd been a heap of snow, and they skied every day, that lot, even when it was sketchy. Was like some kind of rule the old guy insisted on—no lazing around the lodge." Then he must have remembered Martin's so-called affiliation and quickly added, "It's a good rule though. I mean, why else are you there, right?"

Martin ignored the back-pedal and said, "But Tawny wasn't skiing that day. So what are you saying? You caught her wagging; she was worried you'd tell Sir George?"

"Oh, I reckon it was more to do with the fact that she was half-naked." He sniggered like a schoolboy, then yelled, "Ready about!"

Martin ducked under the boom again, then said, "How do you mean?"

"I mean, the lodge might have been heated, but she was in a… like a lacey thing, a… what do you call it?"

"Negligee?"

"Yeah, that's it. Slinky black number. Very yummy mummy. She was in the kitchen, grabbing a drink, and she demanded to know what I was doing there. I explained I had to install some shutters downstairs, and she said, 'Okay, well hurry up.'"

"Did she explain why she was skimpily dressed?"

He looked at Martin like he was thick. "The rich don't explain themselves to me." Then he gave Martin the once-over. "She just went into her bedroom and shut the door."

"You think someone was in there with her?"

He sniggered. "She took two glasses in. You tell me."

"Do you know for sure though? Did you hear something?"

"No, but I *saw* something. Something else that proves it." He leaned in, pulling at a rope. "While I was downstairs, right, putting the shutters up, I noticed two sets of ski boots, two sets of soggy socks." He gave another knowing look. Then, in case Martin really was thick, he added, "There was definitely somebody else at the lodge that day."

Martin thought about that. "She is married, Timmy. Could've been the husband and her sneaking back for some afternoon delight."

"That's what I thought, but it wasn't Roman." He smiled. "I was embarrassed for her to be honest, and I wanted to give her a chance to finish up, so I yelled out that I was heading off for a coffee and would be back in an hour." He leaned in closer, like they could possibly be overheard from land, and said, "You'll never guess who I spotted ahead of me, queuing at Bunny's."

"Don't tell me. It was Roman."

Timmy's smile turned lascivious. "And he was wearing his ski boots. Mind the boom!"

CHAPTER 17 ~
CHEWING IT OVER

"Tawny was having an *affair*?" gasped Merry, not sure if she was thrilled with this new information or not. It certainly blew her poolside discovery out of the water.

It was Monday morning, and the day was as stunning as the view from the lower terrace where she'd gathered the group to share her video. Yet no one noticed the vista; they were too dazzled by Martin's news.

"I can't say for sure," said Martin, reaching for some fruit Verity had placed on the outdoor table. "But that's what the guy was implying."

"*Implying*?" echoed Verity, who most certainly wasn't thrilled with this news. "Timmy practically accused her of infidelity. It was extremely unprofessional of him. For all he knows there could have been a spare set of boots in the mudroom for days, or maybe someone else from the group came back with Tawny and was resting in their room."

"Resting's one way of putting it," sniggered Kila, but Martin was staring warily at Verity.

"Timmy was doing me a favour," he told her. "You can't repeat a word of it to Sir George. He'll lose his job."

"And so he should! That information was private."

Earle's eyes narrowed. "I thought there were no parameters."

She blinked rapidly, then turned back towards the buffet.

"It could be anyone of course," said Martin. "Her lover might have snuck in from the village. Could be someone we haven't even come across yet."

"It could be Clem!" said Frankie, coffee cup at her lips. "You know what those Frenchmen are like? I wonder if Heath caught them together at the lodge earlier…" Her eyes lit up. "Maybe *that's* why he left and took his baby sister with him. That could be why things turned frosty." She dropped her cup and said, "Or, even more excitingly, it could be Igor."

She gave them a knowing grin, but Merry did not look happy. Not one bit.

"Charlie's boyfriend? Having an affair with Tawny? No way! Besides, was he even on that ski trip? Do we know?"

"They'd been dating a few months by then, so maybe," said Frankie. "Even if he wasn't, he could've secretly rendezvoused with Tawny there while the others were skiing. I've also been thinking it might explain why he was at Tawny's party without Charlotte and why there was that bust-up in the kitchen that night. Maybe Heath caught Tawny and Igor together and had it out with his mum?"

Earle cleared his throat. "I'm sorry to bring all this, er, speculation to a grinding halt, but you're forgetting what it is we're trying to do here. None of this explains the murders."

"I haven't forgotten," said Martin. "I don't know *who* Tawny was sleeping with, but what if she had called off the affair and the lover wouldn't take no for an answer and lashed out? Or, better yet, what if *Tawny* was the one who wouldn't give it up? Maybe she was threatening to go public, and her lover needed it to stay quiet. He could be a good family friend or a politician or—"

"Clem or Igor!" said Frankie.

"Right. In any case, Tawny was murdered to keep her quiet, and the others were just collateral damage."

Frowns were forming on the faces around Martin, so he sat forward and said, "How about this then? We already know from Timmy that Roman was at the café near the ski lodge that day. What if *Roman* discovered Tawny's affair and wanted revenge? Maybe he caught her again at her fortieth; maybe that's what brought it to a head. In any case, he'd had enough. He waited until his wife was asleep that night, then shot her, then went to his study to write out his confession or whatever, but, meantime, Heath woke up and discovered his mother's body. He confronted his father, smashed him over the head, then took the gun and shot himself out of remorse."

They were all staring at him like he was insane, and Martin sat back, hand at his nose again. "I *was* asked to think laterally."

"That's so lateral it's loony," said Frankie. "And all it does is take us back to square one. We're trying to get Heath off the hook, not plant him on it, remember? Besides, if Roman wanted revenge, he'd kill the man his wife was sleeping with, not her, surely?"

Martin groaned and helped himself to some fruit.

Merry took that as her cue. She sat forward and opened the laptop she had placed on the poolside table earlier, then clicked on YouTube. "Kila and I have another theory if you want to hear it."

"God yes," said Earle, like Merry was holding out a flotation device.

Just three minutes and a poorly performed video clip later, the group was looking inspired again. All except for Verity, whose outrage had returned.

"Tawny never would have allowed that video to be shot here," she said. "The family doesn't like strays on the property, hence the reason I had to throw your friend out, Frankie. I can't even have guests here, so I don't know why Lia would."

"That must hurt," said Merry, eyes narrowing.

Verity brushed her off. "It wasn't personal. The Burlingtons are extremely private people. They've knocked back plenty of commercial opportunities too. Film shoots, fashion magazines, *Vogue Living*…"

"There is a chance Heath gave the green light with or without Tawny's permission," said Kila. "They were recording an EP together."

"We believe the clip you just watched was filmed while the family were at Perisher," added Merry. "It might even have been the reason Heath nipped back early—to let them in. Of course we can't check any of that now because, lo and behold, Heath is dead."

"Okay," said Frankie. "What does Lia say? She was house-minding at the time. She must know what was going on."

Merry swapped a look with Kila, who said, "Haven't spoken to her about this yet."

"Why not?" Frankie demanded.

"Hey, I did try calling last night, and she didn't pick up." His tone was a little surly. "Anyway, I thought we were supposed to be taking yesterday off, or did I get that wrong, Earle?"

Earle nodded and held a palm up. He was not as excited by all this as the rest of them.

"Hate to sound like a broken record again but *motive*, folks? Do we have one? Even if Woko did sneak in, how does that end in the murder of three people a month later?"

Merry's hand was up now, waving about. "Ooh, ooh! I have my own theory if you want to hear it!" Earle smiled wearily back at her. "What if *Lia* snuck Woko in without permission while the family were at Perisher? Heath came back early and busted him out here, mid-shoot. Maybe *that's* why Woko was producing an EP for him— as payback. Maybe Heath was blackmailing Woko, and Woko had had enough. Knew it wouldn't end with the EP, so he took Heath out and the rest of them while he was at it. He hangs with some pretty heavy-looking rappers. Maybe they helped?"

Earle rubbed his jowls. "That's quite a story but not very likely, Merry. Trespassing is not an indictable offence, especially during daylight hours. I'm not sure you'd kill three people to avoid a non-custodial sentence."

"Oh, right, yes, of course." She sat back, looking as deflated as Martin.

Earle patted her hand and then addressed the group. "These are all good theories, team, but it's pure conjecture. We need solid evidence, and short of that, we needed a reliable witness. And I think that witness is Lia."

All eyes turned back to Kila, who squirmed again. "Okay, okay, I'll see her tonight."

"Not tonight, buddy, see her today. After this," urged Earle. "She's the link. She'll know whether Woko got the requisite permission to enter the property. Might also know about Tawny's supposed affair, if they were as close as Susan suggests. But this time, forget the charm and get straight to the point, hey?"

Kila reached for his phone and said, "Fine. I'll tee something up now."

Frankie was also preoccupied with her device, so Earle addressed Martin. "I know you're not keen, but I think you really need to speak to the LeDouxes again. See what more they can tell us, especially regarding Tawny and any indiscretions."

Martin groaned. "Couldn't you do that? I was hoping to follow up the ski lodge angle, maybe head up and speak with the manager, Angus."

"Yeah, I suppose I could," Earle agreed, "but you're the one who's fostered a relationship with the couple. I'd just be starting from scratch. I'd suggest you talk to Clem first, *mano* to *mano*. See if you can get a feel for whether Frankie's right and he really is Tawny's mystery lover."

"Like he's going to confess to that!" said Merry.

The only reason her husband confessed to anything was because she caught him in a tryst on the patio couch, and even then he tried to pretend it was a minor mishap. Like he'd just fallen into the woman's naked body by chance.

"Worth a try, I reckon," said Earle. "Then speak to Susan. Separately, if you can. Tell her what we've discovered, what Timmy told you about the affair, see how she reacts. Just feel them both out."

Martin sighed resignedly while Earle turned, finally, to Frankie, who was still staring at her phone. "You still with us, Miss Josephina?"

She looked up. "Sorry. Something's brewing at the news desk. What were you saying?"

"I think it'd be mighty helpful if you could talk to young Charlotte again. Ask about the ski trip and why her mother might have been lurking in the lodge half-naked."

Merry gasped at that, and he held his palm up again.

"I know, the poor child might not know anything about any affair, and we may have that wrong, so you'll have to be subtle, use a bit of tact. But it's worth exploring." He paused as Frankie glanced down at her phone again, then said, "Also, ask about this video clip. Charlotte came back early with Heath. She might know something." He cleared his throat. "Earth to Frankie."

The reporter was still mesmerised by her phone and held a finger up, then tapped something into it, before dropping it on the table. "I heard you, Earle. I'm to ask Charlie if her brother snuck gangsta rappers into the house and if her mother was a slut."

He looked as horrified as Merry had earlier, and she winked.

"Don't worry, I'll tread gently. But listen, I agree with Martin. Someone should get up to the ski lodge, chat to the manager there."

Now the PA was the one looking worried. "Is that really necessary?"

"I'll do it!" said Merry, hand in the air again.

"But you don't drive," said Earle.

"*You don't drive?*" said Frankie, looking aghast.

"Well… no, but maybe we could go together, Frankie. You know, like Thelma and Louise!"

"No way," said Frankie, leaving Merry feeling deflated until she realised the reporter was staring at her phone again. "No, no, no," Frankie repeated as she began madly scrolling.

"What's going on?" Earle asked, but Frankie shook her head and kept reading, then she stopped and stared sharply at Kila.

"Where does Lia live?" she asked, and he looked up from his own reverie, blinking slowly.

"What?"

"Lia!" she yelled now, clicking her fingers at him. "Isn't she on Dreary Road?"

He nodded warily. "Why?"

"I'm just getting reports of a woman found dead in her apartment on Dreary Road."

He stared at her, eyes wide, just as Earle's mobile phone began to sing out.

CHAPTER 18 ~
THE PARTY'S OVER, BABY

Lia's hand was stretched outwards as though grasping for something, and as Earle surveyed her living room, he spotted her mobile phone on the kitchen counter and wondered if she had been trying to reach it, and what she would have said if she had made it. Because Lia would no longer be talking.

Someone had made sure of that.

The woman's lifeless body had been discovered that morning by her sister. The pathologist was close to finishing up, and Earle knew he did not have much time. The fact that Morgan had even called and invited him to inspect the scene was a miracle in itself, and he wouldn't waste a moment of it.

"So what do you think?" Morgan asked, his expression inscrutable.

Earle stared at the corpse. Soaked it all up. Lia was lying facedown on a patch of carpet, her silky red dressing gown hitched up on one side, but there were no obvious signs of sexual assault, just a deep, bloody gash to the back of her head and several thick scarlet splatters strewn around her. He recoiled a little at that. Hadn't remembered blood being quite so vibrant. It was like someone had let the special-effects department loose with the red paint.

"There's evidence of blunt-force trauma," Earle told Morgan.

The detective scoffed. "Yeah, I did get that, thanks, Earle. I mean, could this be related to your investigation?"

Earle turned back. "I thought my investigation was a complete waste of time?"

"Just answer the question."

He shrugged. "You know how I feel about coincidences."

Morgan nodded, then immediately shook his head. "I'm not saying Heath isn't guilty, so don't start shopping for new golf sticks just yet, but I have to wonder whether your poking about has unleashed an entirely new beast."

Now Earle was scoffing. "Has to be the same beast, surely? Unless you believe in ghosts, this proves that Heath is not the killer you thought he was. At the very least, there was someone else involved. A third party."

"I don't see that," Morgan replied, frowning. "Like I said, this could be completely unrelated. We can't take anything for granted at this stage."

"Then what am I doing here?"

Morgan turned back to him. "Yeah, about that."

As he continued speaking, it was Earle who was left frowning.

~

Frankie was vox-popping an excitable neighbour at one end of Dreary Road when she spotted Earle exit Lia's apartment building, so she thanked the woman and then raced up to him, recorder in hand.

"Don't even try," he said as other journalists turned to watch.

"Can you tell me anything? Anything at all?"

He stared at her. Hard.

"Okay, off the record then, for our investigation."

"Where are the others?"

"They're all waiting at the pub on the corner. Champing at the bit to know what's happened. Did Morgan say when the police will make a statement? They've kept us out here for ages. All we've got at this point is that a woman of Pacific Islander appearance has been found dead in that complex. But I know it's Lia, so you might as well come clean. I'm going to find out anyway."

He looked around. "Put that bloody recorder away, Frankie, then wait five minutes and follow me to the Hog and Toad."

The clock had just struck two when Earle strode into the Hog and Toad Hotel, Frankie hot on his heels, and the group were slouched at a window table cluttered with drinks, some of them alcoholic, most of them Kila's. Several of the group jumped up when they spotted Earle, but he waved them back down.

"She's dead, isn't she?" Merry burst out. "Lia? The poor darling! She's dead!"

He placed a hand on her shoulder and said, "Take a few deep

breaths, Merry." Then he looked down at the others. "Everything I say here is off the record. I need you all to agree to that, or I will walk straight back out."

Everyone nodded except for Frankie.

"That includes you, young lady, and your grubby paper."

"Hey!" she cried before rolling her eyes. "I'll find out anyway, but fine, have it your way."

She pulled up a chair, and so did Earle, his expression heavy.

He took his own deep breath then said, "Yes, it is Lia, and yes, they believe she's been murdered."

"Oh my God," gasped Merry. "H-how?"

"It's early days, but all signs indicate she was struck across the head by a blunt instrument. Haven't located the weapon yet."

"When did it happen?" Martin asked. "Do they know?"

"They're still nailing it down, but she was in her dressing gown, so they're thinking mid-morning Sunday, at the latest."

"She's been lying there since *yesterday*?" said Merry, horrified, her eyes darting towards Kila, who was staring into his beer glass. "But... but that's when we were going to see her!"

"Pity you didn't," said Earle, "she might have been found faster. She didn't show for work this morning, so her boss called Lia's sister—"

"Lia has a sister?" This was Frankie. "Do we know her name?"

He ignored that and said, "The sister has a key, let herself in, found Lia facedown on the living room floor."

"Oh that's just awful!" said Merry, glancing at Kila again, but he seemed reluctant to look up from his drink, his face like a stone statue, his eyes boring a hole in the glass.

She squinted. She knew that look. Had seen it not so long ago, on her patio, soon after she'd returned from Vegas.

Earle noticed too and said, "Kila, you okay?"

He looked up then with a start. "What? Course I'm okay. Why wouldn't I be okay?"

"You met her, mate. You interviewed her on our behalf. Just the day before. It's normal to be a bit thrown."

He shrugged and stared back into his drink while Martin now looked worried. He was back to his trademark nose-stroking.

"Do they think we've stirred something up? Do they think there'll be more murders?"

"Oh God, I hope not!" said Merry.

"Well, of course we all hope not," said Frankie, eyes rolling again. "We can't be blamed for this, Martin."

"That might be true," said Earle, "but we *can* be blamed for what we do next." He rubbed a hand across his beard, preparing himself for some pushback as he added, "I'm sorry, folks, but we've been asked to stand back."

"What?" said Martin.

"What do you mean?" echoed Frankie.

"I mean, DI Morgan wants us off the case." He folded his arms across his chest. "I know that million bucks was close, but for now at least, it's over."

As Earle leaned on the bar, waiting for his order to be filled, Frankie turned to the others and hissed. "They can't stop me from investigating this. It's my job." She glanced out to the street. "I need to get back soon. I haven't got long."

"He's not talking about the paper, Frankie, and you know it," said Martin. "He's talking about this little investigation of ours."

"Little?" said Kila, his tone sullen. "If the cops had bothered to make it a bigger priority the first time around, Lia might not be lying in a pool of blood."

"Poor, poor Lia," said Merry, still trying to get her head around it. It was all very well for Frankie and Earle, but corpses weren't part of her daily regimen.

"I can understand it," said Martin, referring to Morgan's demand. "He doesn't want us muddying the waters."

"We weren't muddying anything! We were making it clearer last time I looked. You ask me, this proves we were on the right track."

"*Frankie,*" growled Earle, who was now standing by the table, drink tray in hand. "Morgan's request is standard procedure. You can't have civilians racing about interrogating the suspects, and everyone we've been talking to is a viable suspect. They all knew Lia; they might have motive."

"And they might also have been the person who killed Heath and his parents!" she shot back. "You're really going to let those incompetent cops take over again?"

He sat down and began handing out the beverages. "It's not up to me, Frankie. I'm just a civilian now. But, yes, we do have to stay out of it. I'm not saying it's over entirely. Let's just give them a week or two and see what they find. Then, if they stonewall, we can consider jumping back in."

"We've only got a week left," said Merry, turning to Kila. "Haven't we?"

Kila shrugged like he no longer cared.

"The question we should be asking is how is it all related, and why?" said Frankie.

"Ah, no, no we should not," said Earle. "I already told you, we can't do this."

"Oh, just chillax, Earle! It's not illegal to have a chat over a few drinks!" Frankie waved one palm around the room. "What do you think everybody else is talking about?" She turned to the others. "Lia obviously knew something about the Burlington murders, and she was silenced."

"Or someone just thought she did," he shot back.

"Let's look at the facts as we know them," said Frankie again. "We know that something happened seven months ago. Something life-changing. Something that ended in murder a month later."

"That's pure speculation," said Earle beneath his breath.

Frankie ignored him. "At this stage we know of two such events. Tawny's affair—"

"Alleged," added Earle.

"And Woko's *alleged* trespass of the family mansion." She shot Earle a smirk. "In both cases, Lia might have known something, or at least someone thought she did. So they had to shut her up."

"But why wait until now?" said Martin. "That all happened months ago."

"You said it yourself," said Kila, his tone heavy. "Our investigation stirred things up." It was a statement. As far as he was concerned, it was a fact. He looked at Merry. "Woko said he had permission to use the pool, and we threatened to check his story with Lia. Maybe he had to muzzle her before we got there."

Merry cringed. "Oh thanks, Kila, that makes me feel so much better!"

Earle shook his head. "Like I've said before, would you really kill three people—now four—for trespassing? At worst it's break and enter. But it's still a moot point because Woko can always say he had lawful authority to enter the premises and Lia knew nothing about it.

Heath's not around to dispute this. There was no reason to kill Lia."

Martin nodded. "I'm not buying the Woko angle either."

"Has to be related to Tawny then," said Frankie.

"Ooh!" said Merry now, her enthusiasm getting the better of her again. "What if Lia *did* know about Tawny's affair and suspected her lover was the murderer all along? Maybe Lia was blackmailing him or threatened to go to the police or tell us or something?" She flashed a look at Kila, who was back to glass-staring glum.

Frankie nodded firmly. "It's as good a theory as any, Merry. We have to find out who was in the lodge with Tawny that day. It could all come down to that." She stared at Martin. "Here's your chance. Want to take that road trip?"

But Martin was already shaking his head. "Sorry, guys, but I'm not convinced the lover angle is any stronger. Lia wasn't even at the lodge, and how many people go on to kill four people to protect their reputation? That's spy-thriller stuff. Too outlandish even for me."

Frankie scowled. He was right. Of course he was right. She groaned. "This is infuriating."

"And officially not our concern," said Earle, getting to his feet. "I'm heading home, and I suggest you all finish up and do the same."

"And Sir George?" said Merry. "What do we say to Verity?"

He hesitated, reading the anxiety on all their faces. "We don't have to say anything at this point. Let's lie low for a bit, and I'll stay in touch with Morgan and see how far they get. If they show any signs of stuffing this one up, we can consider our options then. Okay?"

He was waiting for universal agreement, but Frankie was also on her feet, tapping at her phone, bringing her digital recorder app to life.

"Press conference is about to start. Gotta run." Then she turned to Earle. "I will be investigating this case. It's called freedom of the press, and there's nothing you or your mate Morgan can do to stop me. And I don't just mean Lia's murder. I mean all of it." She glanced around the table. "And I hope the rest of you do too, at least for Lia's sake."

Then Frankie rushed outside and towards the entrance to the apartment block where the other reporters were beginning to circle like white pointer sharks around two detectives.

As they watched the journalists tear into DI Morgan, the remaining sleuths fell into a sullen silence. Each of them had been enjoying the momentum of the case, had felt that they were getting close to providing, if not an exact solution to the Burlington crimes, at least an alternative theory or two. But now...

Now they were supposed to pack up their trench coats and get back to their lives, and most of them weren't enthusiastic. Despite their early reservations, they were enjoying the process, enjoying working together, already daring to hope that they might just solve this thing. Might come away with a million bucks while they were at it. Now they had to get back to their desks and couches and meagre bank accounts.

"I should get home to my writing," Martin said eventually.

Merry was relieved to see him go. She needed to have a quiet word with Kila. Get something off her chest. After buying a fresh round of drinks, she said, "Hey, Kila, I'm just wondering—why didn't we go and speak to Lia yesterday?"

"What?"

"Sunday, when we interviewed Woko at his studio. I suggested we pay Lia a visit. You were adamant we leave her alone. What was that about?"

"Nothing. I just didn't think it was urgent, that's all." He slurped the froth from the top of his beer, then glanced across it towards her. "You don't think I feel bad enough about this, Merry? You don't think I realise that if we had gone to see her, she might still be alive?"

She nodded. She'd been thinking the same thing too. But that's not what she was talking about. "You were with her when I rang you yesterday morning, weren't you?"

He stared at her now like she was bonkers. *"What?"*

"Lia. You were with her early Sunday morning. Before she died."

Slowly Kila placed his glass down. Slowly he met her gaze. When he spoke, his tone was cool, dispassionate. "Don't know what you're talking about. I was home alone when you dragged me out of bed."

Merry's expression turned from steely determination to sad disappointment. "Please don't lie to me, Kila. I was married to a liar for twenty-one years. It taught me two things. One, I'm an idiot. And two, how to pick a lie a mile off. And I'm sorry, honey, but you're lying. I just need to know why." He continued staring, mutely, so she sighed. "Oh, Kila. You looked guilty that morning we met up at the Seagrave pool, and you look guilty now. I know the signs."

Kila's deep brown eyes turned even darker, and his hands were now fists beside his drink. "You think I killed Lia?" he said slowly. "You think I could *do* something like that?"

"What?" Now Merry was affronted. "No! Of course not! Jesus! I'm saying you looked guilty because you slept with her! As if I would think you'd *killed* her!"

Kila exhaled loudly like he'd been holding his breath, and he straightened his fingers out, almost smiling, although the point remained.

Merry said, "Why didn't you tell me? Why all the secrecy?"

"Because my private life is none of your business."

"It is when you're sleeping with one of our suspects!" She scanned the room and lowered her voice. "I don't need to be a cop to know that's a conflict of interest. Geez Louise, what were you thinking?"

"We just had some fun, a bit of a laugh." He shrugged, tried to produce one of his flirty smiles, but she wasn't buying it. "I promise you, Merry, she was alive when I left her. I had nothing to do with this."

"You need to come clean. Tell the police everything."

"Yeah right!" He shook his head, curls flopping into his eyes. "If I come clean, the investigation will come to a grinding halt and I'll be their number one suspect."

"Oh for goodness' sake, you're just being paranoid."

"Really? What would you know, little Miss *Dim-Dim*?" She gulped at him, and he added, "You're just a lovely white girl. You're clueless."

"Kila…"

"Ever been stopped on the streets by the cops for no apparent reason? Get checked every single time you go through an airport or a shopping centre? Have women like you hold on to their handbags tighter whenever you pass them on the street?"

Merry blinked back at him, tears forming at the back of her eyes. "Kila, come on now…"

"Ever been hauled into a copshop to answer questions about shit you know nothing about just because they need to plant it on somebody and your skin colour is the perfect match?"

She reached a hand over and clasped his in it. "That's all happened to you?"

He pulled his hand back. "And plenty more. So don't tell me I should just wander in and feed myself to the lions. That's what they want: a big black guy to pin it on. You might be able to get away with murder, but if DI Morgan finds out I was one of the last people to see Lia… I'm toast."

Merry felt a tear drop down her cheek and wiped it away. She knew what he was saying; she understood his bitterness and wariness, and she didn't blame him. But she also didn't want to see him locked up, and she had a feeling his righteous anger and bitterness were as dangerous to him as his skin colour.

She pushed her glass aside. "You're right about one thing, Kila." She stood up and reached for her handbag. "I wouldn't have a clue. I've never been pulled over for no reason by the police, never even come close. But *you* have, so you know exactly how this works. DI Morgan will find out what you did; he'll find out anyway. So let me give you the advice I give my kids. If you don't put your hand up first and 'fess up to something that is, I agree, no one's business and perfectly innocent, then everyone will think the opposite—that your silence equals your guilt and you're hiding something. And then you really will be toast."

"*Oooh*, this is all very tense," came a voice behind Merry, and she swivelled to find Frankie standing there, mobile phone in hand.

Kila drained his glass and got up. "I'm outta here," he said and marched away.

Frankie turned back to Merry, who had slumped back into her chair.

"What was that about?"

"Oh nothing," Merry mumbled, now feeling complicit in the lie and wondering who she was betraying more—the rest of the sleuths or poor Lia.

Frankie watched her for a moment and decided to let it drop. "Look, I'm heading into work now, got to file this story fast, but I'm glad you're still here. I've just spoken to Verity, and I've got a proposition for you. For both of you. If you're free."

Merry stared at her suspiciously, and Frankie added, "You can be Thelma and Verity can be Louise."

CHAPTER 19 ~
MEANWHILE BACK AT
THE STATION

Earle felt every one of his sixty-six years as he strode into homicide headquarters the following morning, and it wasn't the Burlingtons' fault entirely.

He'd had words with Beryl last night, and they were still ringing in his ears.

"It's on hold, love," he'd told his wife when he returned from the Hog and Toad. "There's been a development. Morgan wants us off the case, at least for now."

She'd shrugged like it didn't matter and said, "Oh well, never mind."

That got him miffed. Because he did mind, very bloody much! And she would too if she understood what was at stake. What they'd now lost. He'd worked hard his whole damn life, and what did he have to show for it? Very bloody little. And here she was casually dismissing his one chance to turn their fortunes around. Score them a cruise on a fancier boat. He almost wished the old bastard had never waved the money in his face in the first place.

He'd said all of that to his wife, and she shrugged nonchalantly again. Told him to keep investigating if he wanted to keep investigating—like it was all up to him—and then turned to load the dishwasher!

But it wasn't up to him. Nothing was up to him anymore. He had no control over his life, no sense of purpose, and it pissed him right off. Truth was, Earle had enjoyed the work. Loved every minute. Sometimes, as he watched Beryl fetch him yet another cup of tea and he farted about on the computer, pretending to be busy, he wished he hadn't retired from the force quite so quickly.

Morgan wasn't that much younger than him but was still hard at it, nose to the grindstone. At first Earle didn't understand it. How could the bloke drag himself in there every single day? Wasn't he done with shifty criminals and upstart recruits and the plods at the top who did very little but managed to look very busy?

Now? Now he knew. And Beryl knew too.

As he watched her shuffle around the house, repairing a curtain, compiling a shopping list, putting another load in the wash, he envied her the tasks. Their Tess called him a dinosaur and kept pressing Beryl to hand over half the housework now that he was retired.

"He gets to put his feet up," Tess said more than once. "You should be able to too, Mum!"

"Oh, it's fine," Beryl had replied. "I don't mind, you know that."

And he had tried not to smirk at his frowning daughter—always too much of a feminist for her own good. But now he wondered whether Beryl held on to her wifely duties not out of habit but out of necessity. At least she had *something* on her schedule. She wasn't going to give away her sense of purpose, no matter how mundane.

And now *his* fresh sense of purpose had been wrenched from him. The other sleuths might call him a stickler, but he wasn't ashamed of playing by the rules, and the current rules precluded him from doing any more investigating, so that was that. The ship had sailed…

Or so he'd thought.

It was an early-morning phone call from Morgan that got Earle's hopes up. The DI wanted him at headquarters ASAP, and so here he was, strolling through, but the mood today had darkened. Perhaps it was his imagination, or perhaps it was because of Lia, but there was definite tension in the air. Not one old colleague stopped to greet him this time as he made his way to Morgan's desk.

"Thanks for coming in so quickly," Morgan said, waving him into a chair.

He nodded but felt his defences rise again when Morgan's trademark smirk appeared and he tossed a piece of paper across to him. Earle read the report, his hope diminishing with every line. "What is this?"

"What does it look like?"

"It looks like you're trying to stitch up my mate Kila."

Morgan's eyebrows shot up. "*Mate*, hey? Wow, Fitzy. You used to have a better dickhead barometer." His eyebrows lowered, and he nodded at the report. "Fingerprints do not lie, you know that.

And Mr Morea's were smattered across the scene of the crime."

Earle tossed the paper back on Morgan's desk. "I'd be more suspicious if they weren't. Told you yesterday, Lia was a person of interest. Kila was the one who went and interviewed her on our behalf."

"In her bedroom?" Morgan asked. "Did he *interview* her in her bed, touch her bedhead while he continued *interviewing* her? Switch her bedroom lamp off after the post-*interview* cigarette?"

Earle's frown deepened. Morgan was all class. So was Kila, judging from this report.

"We've already spoken to her friends. We know the two hooked up Saturday night. They all went drinking. The last anyone saw Lia she was heading home with Mad Dog Morea."

"So, Kila slept with her. Big leap from lothario to murderer."

"Maybe he was trying to get the truth out of her, went too far."

Earle scoffed now. Didn't bother commenting on that. "How did you even get his prints?" He shook his head. "Don't answer that. I don't think I want to know."

Morgan was right. Earle had grown to like the larrikin PI, wasn't keen to hear his past transgressions.

"He's no innocent." Morgan said. "Almost lost his license multiple times—illegal entry, trespass, illegally accessing mobile phone records without a warrant or consent. Claims he was snooping on his sister's dodgy new boyfriend that time."

Earle almost chuckled. "So, he goes the extra mile."

"I don't think it's amusing, Earle. He ended up beating that guy into a coma. Can't believe he wasn't up on assault charges for that one. He's before the courts now, right? His current fixation appears to be shoving seafood products under the bonnets of unsuspecting victims' cars."

Earle blinked back at him. "What?"

"Yeah, I'm telling you, the guy's a bloody psycho. Teflon kid too. Nothing seems to stick."

"And this won't either. I can assure you of that. You'll be wasting your time. But look, let me talk to him first."

"Yeah, nah." Morgan sniggered again. "You know how this works. We're bringing him in now. We'll know soon enough. I'm just giving you the heads-up so you can tell your new boss. Smooth the waters, so to speak."

"How kind of you," Earle said, drily. "I thought for a moment there you were telling me so you could gloat."

~

The road to Perisher was long and winding, and Merry knew she should be enjoying the mountain vista, but all she could think about was Kila and the noose that would no doubt soon be tightening.

"Penny for your thoughts?" came a voice from the driver's seat.

Merry glanced across to Verity behind the wheel, her eyes firmly on the road, and smiled. "Just hoping my eldest gets my youngest to school on time and in one piece," she fibbed.

"I can't believe we let Frankie talk us into this," said Verity, but she looked pleased enough to be heading away. Had collected Merry at the crack of dawn, a takeaway coffee and baguette already waiting for her as she climbed in.

Merry said, "She says I'm to interrogate Angus like he holds the key to the missing chocolate in the pantry. And you're to help me."

Verity had heard about Lia's murder but knew nothing of DI Morgan's moratorium, and the less said about that the better.

"Really? I thought I was just the chauffeur."

"No!" said Merry. "You're so much more than that! But thanks for taking me."

"I noticed you don't drive. Any reason why?"

Merry shrugged. "Never had a need for it. There's plenty of public transport, and well, my eldest son drives, so he gets me where I need to go."

"Doesn't that annoy him?"

"Sorry?"

"He's a teenager. Doesn't that cramp his style?"

Merry blinked. "Oh, he's studying part-time at the moment, plenty of free time to drive his poor old mum about. No, really, he loves it." She was *sure* he loved it. He hadn't ever complained… She drifted into thought then, chewing on her lower lip.

Was her ex-husband, right? And her sister for that matter? *Was* she too needy? Did she ask too much of her kids? Was Otis simply too polite to tell her to find her own way? Worse still, was she giving her youngest son nightmares, involving him in this ghastly case?

"Don't mind me," said Verity. "What on earth would I know? Never had kids."

Merry blinked the worrying thoughts away and glanced across. "Never wanted any? Never had the opp?"

"Married to the job, I think they call it. But don't feel sorry for me. I've loved working for George. I really have."

Merry waved out at the stunning scenery that had changed from rolling green valleys and plump farmhouses to rocky slopes littered with towering pine trees as the car climbed upwards. "The perks of the job are certainly divine!"

"Oh the lodge is strictly a place for the family. No ring-ins allowed."

Merry got that. She rarely let her kids drag their friends along on camping holidays. She wanted the munchkins all to herself. Still it got her thinking…

"What about boyfriends? Would Igor be invited to the lodge?" *Was he there, having a tryst with Tawny as Frankie suggested?*

"Not without a ring on his finger he wouldn't," Verity replied. "At least, Sir George would not have invited him. It's been a family tradition for ions, you see. Long before my time. They always block off the last week of July to go skiing—no matter how heavy their commitments or how sparse the snow. They never miss a year."

"Except last year," said Merry. "Didn't you say Sir George was absent last winter?"

She nodded, frowned, then turned her eyes back to the road.

"It must have hit him very hard then, when just a month later he lost half his family! I mean, he must now wish he'd gone."

"Of course! He acts stoic. Half of it's a lie."

"And he had no inkling that there was all that tension between Heath and his parents?"

"Oh he knew. Of course he knew. But I don't think he knew the extent of it. They generally behaved themselves around him."

"Keeping it civil for their beloved Gramps."

"Keeping their names in the will more like it." She flung a hand to her lips. "You did not hear me say that!"

Merry giggled. "Don't worry, what happens on the road stays on the road." Giggled again.

Verity flashed her a quick relieved smile. "Thank you." She frowned. "I don't blame them, you know. It is a whopping inheritance, and I guess I'd want a cut of it too."

"You're not in the will?" Merry flung a hand to her own lips.

"Sorry, is that too personal? I'm always asking inappropriate questions!"

Verity laughed. "No, and no. I would not be in the will. Like I said, staff was staff and family was family, and never the twain shall meet."

"Except didn't Susan marry a staff member?"

"Yes, but you have to wonder if she was doing that more out of rebellion than romance." Verity threw a hand to her lips again. "Goodness, you bring out the bad girl in me! Scratch that comment too. The point is, family is everything to my boss. And not just family. Loyalty."

"Yikes, that sounds a little lofty! What does that mean exactly?"

"It means if one of them kills the others, he refuses to believe it." She gave her another sideways glance.

"You don't believe Heath is innocent?"

"It's not my place to believe. I'm just George's assistant."

Merry made a scoffing sound. "I think you're a little more than that! What about disloyalty then? What if Sir George discovered that one of them was unfaithful?"

"I know what you're getting at, but there was one thing he wanted more than loyalty, and that was for his kids to be happy, and if a French sailor could make you happy, then…" She smiled. "You have to remember, George's first wife left him, and then his second… well, she left too."

"Didn't she… you know?" Merry screwed up her face apologetically and said, "Commit suicide?"

"No! It was just a terrible accident. Her foot slipped…" She trailed off. Sighed. "At least that's what the coroner said. The point is, George just wanted his kids to find the right partner, have children and be happy. It's as simple as that."

"Nothing simple about that," said Merry softly as she watched Verity take the next exit.

And there was nothing simple about this family, she thought to herself. Merry was now more convinced than ever that Frankie was right, but not about Igor. *Clem* had to be Tawny's mystery lover; he ticked every box! He *was* at the lodge last winter. He was also family. Also held to the same lofty standards as the others. Had a very good motive to want to keep any affair a secret. If the truth got out, he'd be back to sailing school and miss out on all that lovely inheritance. Perhaps he had a billion reasons to kill Tawny and everyone in her inner circle who might know the truth, including Tawny's beloved housekeeper...

~

Kila glanced around the small, beige room impassively. It wasn't his first interrogation and would no doubt not be his last. It wasn't just his Papuan heritage. Cops seemed to take great pleasure in hauling private detectives in for questioning. Like they were jealous that PIs got to play by a cooler, looser standard. Although it was a fine line, and he might've just crossed it. He squirmed thinking about his lawyer. Sheila will have a fit when she finds out. It's why he hadn't called her. Better to handle this one alone...

Kila's mind wandered then to Lia, to the last time he'd seen her. To the things he'd done and should've done. To what she clearly knew. Lia was so close to spilling the beans on that dysfunctional family, and he had blown it. What a fool he'd been, putting his libido first. That had paid dividends in the past—get them in bed first, then get what you need afterwards. But it was working less and less these days. Women were getting bolshier, savvier. Smarter. And he didn't blame them, blamed himself entirely. And lovely, ditzy Merry if he was being honest. Because the truth is, he would have got the facts out of Lia if it wasn't for Merry's early-morning phone call, dragging him from Lia's bed to the Burlington pool deck. He had to stop being a sucker for the needy ones. Should have stayed with Lia, made her a decent breakfast, and got the truth out of her at last.

Now...

Now he'd left his run too late, and now it was too late for Lia and the three earlier victims. Because he finally believed, without a shadow of a doubt, that Heath was also innocent. Kila just didn't know how and why. And he could've known those things, if only he'd kept his pants on and his phone switched off.

"Well, well, well, Mad Dog Morea," said Morgan as he stepped into the room, a junior on his heel.

"DI Morgan," he replied, his tone light and polite.

Morgan slammed a plastic A4 folder on the table. "Care to explain this?"

Kila didn't bother looking at it. Said nothing.

Morgan sat down and pulled the folder towards him. "Fingerprint report, mate. Yours are all over the Dreary Road crime scene. All over Lia Segeyaro and her cheap Ikea bed. Now, I have to wonder why."

Kila shrugged. "You know me, Morgan. I can never resist a pretty chick."

"Ah, no, but did she resist you? Is that what happened?"

He smiled. "Nobody resists me. I'm too charming."

"You forget the charm this time, Kila? Things get a little too rough? You wouldn't take no for an answer?"

"Seriously? That's what you think happened?"

Morgan shrugged. "You tell me. Wouldn't be the first time your fists got away from you."

Kila's expression darkened, and he had a sudden vision of his sister—his beautiful baby sister with her springy black curls and bad taste in drinks, even worse taste in blokes—and tried to keep his breath steady.

Do not take the bait, he told himself. *Do not do it.*

He cleared his throat and leaned forward. "Look, we're both too long in the tooth to play this game. You know I have a right to a lawyer, but the minute I ask for one, you'll say 'But what are you hiding?' and I'll say 'No comment.' So let me fast-track this whole boring process. Here are the facts and nothing but the facts. I met with Lia last Saturday night. I went to her friend Violet's house to ask some questions on behalf of my client Mr Burlington. We ended up partying at a club called Bar Hola. Not my usual scene but we had fun, regardless. Then Lia invited me back to her place. I stayed over. We had sex." He paused, smiled and added, "Thrice. I left just after nine on Sunday morning, right after Merry called and requested my presence at the Burlington-Brown residence. When I left Lia, she was very much alive. Smiling even. As they always are."

Morgan stared at him deadpan. "And how can you prove that?"

Kila smiled. "I don't need to, see, that's your job, not mine. And I'm going to say my farewells and leave you to it."

He stood up and earned himself a look of contempt.

"What makes you think I won't arrest you here and now, you cocky bastard?" Morgan said.

"Because you would have arrested me by now if you had more than a few smudged paw prints. Oh, and because there's the very teeny matter of motive. I don't have one. I liked Lia, am bloody sad to see her go, but it wasn't me who done it. And you know that as well as I do. I'm a known flirt, some might say a bit of a sleaze, but I've never so much as looked angrily at a woman, let alone raised a hand to one, and I never will. Women have always been my favourite people. They shit all over us blokes. So you're barking up the wrong tree."

Then he turned and walked out, as tall as an oak despite the tiny, hollow feeling inside.

~

A wall of Beech trees camouflaged Sir George's beloved winter lodge, and it was not until they were halfway down the driveway that Merry finally got a good look at the place. By Burlington standards, it was ordinary, to say the least. Built of slate and faded timber with a traditional triangular roof, it didn't look big enough to house the entire extended family and could certainly do with a lick of paint.

The interior was not much better.

After being met at the gate by Angus Johnson, the manager, a short stocky fellow with a fuzzy red beard, the two women had dropped their overnight bags inside the front door and then taken a look around. Verity might not be a frequent visitor, but she led the tour, guiding Merry first down a thin hallway to the bedrooms at the back of the house. There were four of those, three with double beds, one with a variety of single beds and bunks. None of them had an en suite bathroom or a view of any kind, and all were as basic as Charlotte's school common room. Worse even, because the furnishings were like something from the *Brady Bunch*—lots of mismatched fabrics in fading oranges and greens and browns.

Back past the front door, Merry was led through a sizeable working kitchen to the living room at the front, with its equally lurid collection of lounge suites and chairs, some facing a wide, sooty fireplace, others looking out at the view.

And what a view it was.

"It must be *soooo* stunning when the mountains are blanketed in snow," said Merry, stepping across to soak it up. It also helped explain the drab interior. Who needs bling when you have this outlook?

"Come on," said Verity. "I'll show you downstairs."

The lower level was purely functional with a dazzling array of ski gear, including skis, poles and boots, as well as a large cement sink, a washing machine and dryer.

"How does Sir George get down here in a wheelchair?" Merry asked.

"The chair's fairly new," Verity told her as she stepped across to a door by the sink and swept it open. "But there's a ramp from the front door down to this one. It also means the family can ski right up to the house and dump all their wet gear here before going upstairs." She tapped the sink. "It's quite literally a mudroom."

Merry's eyes lit up. "This must be where Timmy spotted the extra set of ski boots!"

Verity made no comment as she moved on to another door, which was hanging open.

"And—shock, horror—this is the only loo in the lodge," she said, pointing into a bathroom with an antique venetian pink china bathtub and matching sink, a poky shower with a plastic curtain, and a toilet that had seen better days.

Merry wondered how the Burlington women coped!

"This must be Timmy's handiwork," said Verity, reaching up to some white wooden shutters that covered a large glass window. She pushed them aside to reveal a timber walkway that encircled the exterior of the building and met up with the ramp by the exit door. Beyond the walkway was a high, thatched fence that concealed most of the towering forest beyond, and Merry wondered why Timmy had bothered with the shutters.

"Help yourself to the amenities," Verity said. "There're fresh towels in the cabinet by the sink. I'll see if there's anything edible in the kitchen."

By the time Merry returned upstairs, Verity had managed to make two steaming cups of hot cocoa.

"This will have to do for now. Angus will be back later with supplies for dinner, so why don't you just relax and enjoy some hard-earned R & R?"

"Good thing I brought my book then," said Merry, reaching into her bag for Flynn Bold's twelfth adventure, the only one she hadn't read.

Still, she couldn't help feeling disappointed. Relaxing wasn't on the itinerary; she needed to interrogate the manager. Frankie would never forgive her if she came back empty-handed. She watched

Verity over her oversized mug and wondered, *Had she sent Angus away deliberately? Or was she just being paranoid?*

An hour later and things were back on track. Verity was preparing a stew in the kitchen while Angus took a seat beside Merry, facing the view.

"So," he said, his tone solemn. "I hear you have some questions for me?"

She nodded and glanced down at the notes she'd prepared with Frankie last night. On the notepad below the questions, she'd scribbled Frankie's final advice: "Don't take no for an answer!"

Smiling nervously she said, "I promise not to bite."

He didn't return the smile. "I'm happy to help."

As it turned out, Angus was not helpful in the slightest. Yes, it was unusual for a family member to be home during a skiing day, but no, he had not heard of any *indiscretions*, and his handyman should not have jumped to the conclusion that he did.

"You don't think Tawny was having an affair?" she asked outright—another Frankie tip—and he looked confounded by the question.

"It's not my place to think, ma'am. I just keep the home fires burning."

He sounded just like Verity. "But did you ever *see* anything?" she persisted. "Any indication that she might be unfaithful?"

He shook his head quickly and firmly, and she had a feeling he wouldn't tell her even if he did. She tried a different angle.

"I understand that Sir George did not encourage the family to bring in extra guests." He nodded. "Did you ever happen to see any strange men here, especially during the day when only Tawny was about?"

He knew what she was doing, and he shook his head firmly again. "As Verity has no doubt explained, it was rare for anyone to be at the lodge during the day. Apart from arrival and departure days, they spent every bit of daylight on the slopes."

"What about Clem?"

He frowned. "What about Mr LeDoux?"

"I hear he's a sailor. I just wonder how he handles all the skiing."

"He's also French. They do have a few alps over there, Merry. He was a very proficient skier."

Of course! Right! She felt like an idiot, but still she persisted.

188

"Did he ever take the day off? That you know? Ever hang here with Tawny?"

He smiled again. It said, *Nice try, bucko.* Aloud, he said, "If Mr LeDoux was going to *hang* anywhere, it would be with his wife. But as I said, they skied every day. That was the routine."

She shrugged and closed her notepad, trying hard not to feel like a failure. "They must love their skiing," she said, glancing out. "And be super athletic. One day on the slopes would cripple me, let alone seven!"

He laughed finally, a muffled little chuckle, and said, "Truth is, there was the rare mutiny. Tawny and Susan stayed back once or twice. But they didn't try that often. Didn't want to upset the apple cart."

Then he gave her an awkward smile, and she smiled back. "Yes, except we heard there were often fights—between Heath and his parents. That must have upset Sir George."

Angus just looked disappointed with her now. "These were happy family holidays, Merry, I can assure you." Then he waved a hand and said, "Look at that view. What's not to be happy about?"

She followed his eyes and nodded, but all she could see now were deep, dark shadows beyond.

~

Kila was deep into his sixth round of drinks, and the barman was getting worried.

"Ease up a bit, mate," Trevor said. "You'll be legless before you get a chance to rescue that cute brunette in the corner."

He waved a loose hand about. "Nah, I'm off chicks, mate. Done with them."

"Well, there's one for the books. What about the case? How's that going?"

He shrugged. "It's going... going..." He fluttered a hand in the air. "Gone!"

Trevor looked at him, had no idea what that meant. Went to leave when Kila grabbed him by the arm and said, "I'll have another round thanksh, Trev. And don't forget the lemon squash."

Trevor shook his head and went to fetch the drinks.

"Hey stranger," came a voice beside him, and Kila shifted his gaze to find Frankie standing there.

"Hey! Ish the sexy reporter girl!" he said, his words slurred and tumbling into each other. "How dishu know where to find me?"

She smiled. "I'm the sexy reporter girl, yeah?" She laughed. "Mind if I pull up a pew?"

He shrugged. "Shhhhure... pull away."

Frankie slipped onto the empty stool beside him as Trevor appeared with the drinks and gave Kila a look. Kila laughed.

"What can I shay? I just have to sit here and I attract 'em..."

Frankie scoffed. "In your dreams, Mr Morea." She glanced at Trevor. "A gin and tonic for me thanks. Put it on his tab."

Trevor laughed and headed off again as Frankie stared at the lemon squash.

"You have a sweet tooth or is that chick bait?"

Kila grabbed the drink and placed it out of her reach, sloshing it in the process. "It's for my sister."

Frankie glanced around. "Oh? I didn't realise you had company. I'll try to be quick. So, you want to tell me about it?"

"What? What are you talking about?"

"I'm talking about your little interlude at the cop shop today."

"How did you—"

"I'm sorry, have we not been introduced properly? I am a reporter, Kila. I find things out; it's what I do. It's why Sir George invited me to the group. I'm still trying to work out why he asked you."

Kila leaned back. "Thanksh a lot, babe."

She laughed. "Sorry, but sleeping with a suspect? Really?"

He shrugged. "Sheemed like a good idea at the time."

"She tell you anything? Before you got her kit off?" He shook his head glumly. "You got any ideas?" Shook his head again.

Frankie watched as Trevor placed a tall glass before her, then took a long sip as he walked away. "Merry called. She's had no luck at the lodge."

He made a *pft* sound, like he didn't care or simply expected that of Merry, so she added, "We're running out of leads, Kila. But I think I know where we might find some."

Then she produced her trusty smartphone, tapped open a Facebook events page and said, "Got a decent black suit?"

CHAPTER 20 ~
RISING SUSPICIONS

The sound of a door slamming woke Merry from a deep slumber, and she sat up and wondered if she needed to wake the kids yet. Then she remembered where she was and lay back and thought, *I could get used to this.*

The lodge might be old and dated, but it wasn't a bad place to spend a holiday.

After a few more minutes of luxuriating under the covers, Merry grappled for her glasses, pulled herself up and out and then opened her bedroom door. Verity was at the dining table with Angus, going through what looked like an accounts ledger, and there was a strong scent of cinnamon in the air.

Merry fetched her bath bag and a change of clothes and stepped out. "Might just duck down for a shower," she said.

Verity looked up. "Go right ahead, Merry. There's coffee and rolls in the kitchen when you're done."

Merry thanked her and headed downstairs.

The water spat and spurted as she took a shower, and Merry glared at it angrily, then curiously, wondering why one of the country's wealthiest families couldn't install a better system. Or get a swankier lodge, for that matter. She understood sentimentality— really she did—but if she ever made the million, the first thing she'd do is sell her old pile of bricks and upgrade the kids to somewhere nicer. Didn't they deserve it?

At least the water was steaming hot, and as she stepped out, she noticed the bathroom now felt and looked like a sauna. Wrapping herself in a towel, she pulled the shutters further back and opened the window a crack to let the steam out, noticing again the thick, thatched wall that circled this side of the house. Merry stared at it a moment longer, peering this way and that.

Why install shutters, she thought again, when there's already a thatched wall for privacy? There was no way anyone hiking or skiing across could see past the wall into the bathroom. The only thing the shutters did was block the view from the internal walkway, and the only people using the walkway were those already at the lodge. So why would you even bother?

And that's when Merry finally saw what was staring at her all along.

This was the only secluded room in the lodge, the only one with a lock! Tawny must have installed the shutters so she could carry on her affairs down here in private! The shutters were there to hide the view from her husband and no one else!

She gasped, dressed quickly, then grabbed her things and dashed out.

Merry was just reaching the top of the landing when she heard Verity murmuring to Angus, their footsteps heading to the front door. She thanked him for his time and then said something that stopped Merry in her tracks again.

"No, they suspect nothing, so let's try to keep it that way. For George's sake."

Merry flattened herself against the wall and peeled her ears for more. She heard the whoosh of a door opening and a bird call in the distance.

There was an inaudible murmur, then Verity said, "You too! And thanks for your discretion," before swinging the door shut while Merry slid down onto the step, her brain back in overdrive.

On the journey home, Merry was feeling jumpy and barely able to look Verity in the eye. She hadn't mentioned a word of what she'd overheard, and Verity seemed equally distracted, so they simply tuned into the various radio stations of the local villages they passed and settled into strained silence.

Merry could not get Verity's words out of her head.

"They suspect nothing... Thanks for your discretion."

It made Merry's stomach lurch and her skin crawl and her nerves turn to jelly. She snuck a look at Verity then and looked away again. What exactly didn't they suspect? What was he being discreet about? Tawny? Clem? Or something else entirely?

"Everything okay?" Verity asked, making Merry jump.

"Oh! Yes... of course," she stammered, then jumped again as her mobile phone sang out.

Verity watched her curiously as she snatched it up and read the incoming text from Martin. He was passing on a message to meet them all at an impromptu memorial for Lia that evening. He posted the address, then finished with the words *"Any clues at the lodge?"*

Merry shot Verity another glance, and Verity returned it, now frowning.

"Everything okay?" she said again.

"Oh, yeah, no problems! Just the kids. You know… family stuff."

Verity's eyes narrowed, then she returned them to the road while Merry quickly texted Martin back with the words:

"Can't talk now, but Angus and Verity are definitely hiding something, and I think all roads lead to Clem."

~

Martin reread Merry's text, his brain ticking over. Okay, that was interesting. And slightly alarming too. He was now seated outside Clem's office, waiting for a prearranged interview, and suddenly the pressure was on.

He stroked his nose forcefully. Was he about to face off with a murderer?

"Mr Chase?" A voice cut through his thoughts, causing him to jump. "Sorry, I didn't mean to startle you," said the cherub-faced receptionist. "Mr LeDoux is ready to see you now."

He smiled awkwardly, slicked his hair back, and made his way through.

Clem's office was like any plush, executive office except for one addition, or dozens, really. There were so many framed photos Martin didn't know where to look. Many featured a dapper-looking Clem—on a yacht, holding up a marlin, shaking hands with what looked like a younger version of Gerard Depardieu. But most were of Clem's wife and her family in various different poses.

Clem noticed Martin staring and said, "Family is very important to my father-in-law, and so it is for me. Please take a seat. Shall I organise some coffee? Some tea?"

"No, thank you, I think I'll get straight to it." He had to keep the momentum going or he just might lose his nerve.

"Of course." Clem took his own seat and leaned back, his hands prayerlike against his chest. "It has all been a very big shock, this latest news. And now my wife, she feels terrible."

"She was close to Lia?"

He scoffed. "She suspected Lia! The last time we talked. Do you not recall? She accused the poor woman of murder. Now she is riddled with the rue. Is that how you say it?"

"Riddled with regret. Yes. Well, I did push her for an answer, so…"

"And now you are back to push for some more answers, *oui*?"

"Yes. I'm afraid so." Martin took a deep breath. "I might as well cut to the chase, Clem. No pun intended." He tried to smile at his own lame joke, but Clem just looked at him bemused, so he forged on. "We wonder whether Lia was killed because she knew something. Something about Tawny, perhaps." Clem continued blinking at Martin as if not following so he said more slowly, "You see, we believe Tawny was having an affair with someone."

Clem's eyebrows lifted at that, but he did not look surprised. He gave a very slight shrug as if to say "So what? Who cares? Move it along."

Martin took another deep breath. "We think someone caught Tawny and her, er, lover together at the ski lodge last July."

Clem's lips swished to the side. "Okay, this is interesting, but what has it to do with me and Susan?"

Martin waited a beat. The guy couldn't be this stupid! Surely he had to be connecting the dots by now? But still Clem stared at him blankly, so he sat forward and said, "Here's the thing. We think the affair was with someone from the household. Which, um, I'm sorry to say, brings us back to you."

Clem leaned forward. *"Moi?"*

Martin smiled stiffly. The guy was not going to make it easy. "Clem, I know this is awkward and may seem like none of my business, but your father-in-law has made it my business, so I do have to ask. Did you and Tawny have an affair last winter?"

Now Martin was leaning back, hand at his nose, half expecting a counterattack, but Clem continued blinking like he really was confused, and then instead of exploding with rage or indignation, he dropped his head backwards and began to laugh.

"You… you think it was me?" he said when he finally collected himself. "At the lodge with Tawny? This is hilarious! I must call my wife. We must share this little joke!"

Martin frowned. It was not the reaction he was expecting. "Well, it's just... we know Tawny was having an affair with someone. It had to be someone from the household, so... I mean... it has to be you."

Clem made a *pft* sound. "I do not see this! You are not as bright as George thinks you are. You say it happened at the lodge? During the day?" Martin nodded. "She could have easily invited somebody back with her, someone from the village."

"Yes, I suppose so, it's just..."

"It's just ridiculous! You take that theory to George and see how he laughs at you!" Then he shook his head and his smile drained away. "I can assure you, Mr Chase, Tawny was not for me. She was too low for me." He grimaced for good measure.

"I'm sorry, I don't follow."

Clem sighed, almost irritably. "You have money, yes? So I think you can understand this. It is one thing to have money, but it does not always buy you class. She was... how you say? Mutton dressed up as the little lamb. No class at all." His face wrinkled again, and there was no faking his obvious disdain.

Martin recognised the expression. Tamara had used it recently, so too Frankie. He pushed the thought away and said, "How do I know you're not lying, Clem? I mean, you would lie about such a thing."

Clem shook his head again and reached for a photo that was sitting on his desk, facing towards him. It was another family portrait, a better one of a happier time by the look of the genuine smiles on all the faces. There was a banner behind the group that said HAPPY SIXTEENTH, suggesting it was probably for Charlotte's birthday as she was in the centre. Clem held it up and tapped a finger at the woman pictured to the right of Charlie.

"Look at my wife, Martin. Look at my elegant Susan in her classic Chanel suit and pearl earrings. Then look at Tawny." His finger moved to the woman left of centre, standing with one arm around her daughter, the other around her son. Tawny was wearing a suit too, but it was a little too low-cut at the front and a little too high above the knees. Her hair had large, chunky blond highlights and was straightened stiff around her thickly made-up face, and she had two enormous silver hoops in her ears.

"Tawny was no match for my Susan. Tawny was... How do you call it? *Cheap*." He spat the word out like there could be no greater insult, then he looked at the photo again and sighed. "I am sorry for Tawny. I did not wish her dead, you understand this, yes? I am sorry for all of them. It is terrible what has happened, but you have to believe me. It has nothing to do with me or with my elegant Susan."

Clem placed the picture back in its prime spot on his desk, and Martin realised that he did believe him. Annoyingly. Because Frankie was right and so was Merry. Clem made a terrific suspect. He had means and opportunity. But motive? Not so much.

Martin exhaled, feeling almost relieved, and thanked Clem for his time, apologising for the accusation.

"No, no, it is fine," said Clem, a small, amused smile now playing at his lips. "But you give me lots to laugh about with Susan tonight. Tawny and *moi*? *Pft!*"

Martin copped that on the chin and saw himself out, thinking the only thing Clem LeDoux was guilty of was being a frightful snob.

CHAPTER 21 ~
A MEMORIAL TO REMEMBER

It would be some time before Lia's body would be handed back to the family for burial, but that did not stop her older sister, Eva, from organising a memorial, which was now in full swing in the scrappy park beside her apartment block.

The place was packed, mostly with Pacific Islanders, and Kila felt relieved as he made his way in. He was keen to blend in, considering he'd been one of the last to see poor Lia alive. Oh, and the minor issue of being accused of her murder didn't help.

"You okay?"

Kila turned to see Merry standing behind him, backpack slung over her shoulder. "I came as soon as I could."

"Thanks." He nodded his head. "Martin's finding a car park, and Frankie's lurking behind a tree somewhere, trying to sneak a few photos for her paper. Not sure about Earle."

"He's lurking too," said Merry. "I spotted him near the side entrance. Looking a bit cranky."

He shook his head. "We're not breaking any rules being here, Merry. It's a public park. My concern is for the family. Do *they* want us here? I know I wouldn't."

As if on cue, two young Papuan women approached, and one of them grabbed Kila by the forearm and said, "Kila? Are you Kila Morea?"

He took a step backwards, unsure whether to 'fess up, but she was dragging him forwards again and into a bear hug.

"Oh, Kila! Lia really liked you!" the woman said before breaking into gulping sobs. "It is such a pity. Why she no meet you sooner?"

Kila patted her gently on the back and stared at the other woman whom he recognised as Violet, Lia's friend from the other night. She mouthed the word *Eva* and he nodded, hugging the crying woman tighter. It was Lia's older sister, and she clearly didn't believe—or know—what the cops were thinking.

Eventually Eva pulled herself together and stepped back, and that's when he quietly introduced her to the other sleuths, who had now gathered around as if drawn by a magnet.

"I hope you don't mind," he said. "But we wanted to pay our respects."

She glanced at them vaguely, smiled as if dazed, then was pulled away by the friend and into another hug, this time with an elderly member of the congregation.

Kila exhaled loudly and shoved his hands into his pockets.

"You okay?" Merry asked again, giving his arm a rub.

He nodded, cleared his throat. "How d'you go on your road trip? Tell me you got some answers."

Merry waggled a hand in the air, first explaining about the shutters and how that felt like more proof of Tawny's infidelity. "But if Angus knows who she's been sleeping with, he wasn't telling me. He's a loyal mutt, that one, clearly protecting the family." Then she pulled her shoulders back and added, "And so is Verity."

After filling them in on the conversation she'd overheard that morning, Merry said, "I think Verity was thanking Angus for not spilling the beans on Clem and Tawny."

"Clem wasn't sleeping with Tawny," said Martin, causing Merry's smile to deflate. Then he gave them the abridged version of his conversation with Susan's husband.

Frankie scoffed at that. "As if Clem's going to tell you the truth! He's clearly lying."

"I don't think so. He was so *superior*, like he wouldn't lower himself to sleep with Tawny, and I think that was genuine. He came off looking like an arrogant tosser, but he definitely seems devoted to his wife. I think the devotion was genuine."

"If that's true, it's a great shame," said Frankie, "because we're running low on suspects." She glanced about. "Okay, enough idle chatter. Let's get busy, team. We haven't got much time. We need to do what the cops do at these shindigs and look out for someone suspicious. Find ourselves more culprits."

"I've got one in my sights right now," said Kila, his tone turning snarly. He'd spotted Woko in the distance, surrounded by a bevy of PatPela-types. "Excuse me, guys. I can't put this off any longer."

As Kila headed towards Woko, Frankie also noticed a familiar figure on the other side of the park.

"Charlotte's here," she said. "Fancy that! And is that Susan LeDoux beside her?"

The others followed her gaze to find the two women standing awkwardly, talking to a middle-aged Papuan man. Charlie was in her school uniform, which made her look very young, Susan in a demure black dress beside her.

"Yep, that's *elegant Susan*, the apple of Clem's eye," said Martin, his own tone droll.

Charlie glanced around at that very moment and locked eyes with Frankie, giving her a quick wave. She then said something to her aunt, who stared across, a blank expression on her face.

"I'd better say hello," Frankie told the team and headed off in their direction.

Frankie wasn't sure why she was so surprised to see Charlotte and Susan at the memorial. They had more right to be there than she did; had known Lia a lot longer after all. At the very least they would be paying their respects on behalf of the family.

"How are you?" Frankie asked as Charlotte approached, meeting her halfway. Susan was still talking to the older man, although glancing back, curiously, from time to time.

"Devo'ed!" the girl said, her tone back in *duh!* mode.

"I know. It's terrible. I'm glad Sister Scary let you out for the day."

"Oh, I've been staying with Aunty Sue since it happened." Charlie's voice broke then. She sniffed and wiped her nose with a tissue. "The whole world's gone completely berko!"

Frankie didn't hesitate this time. She dragged the teenager into a hug, noticing the girl stiffen, then melt ever so slightly, and they stood like that for a few minutes until a discreet cough pulled them apart and they found Susan standing there, a sad smile on her face.

She held one hand out. "I'm Susan LeDoux."

"Yes, of course," said Frankie, shaking her hand warmly. "I'm—"

"Frankie Jo. Yes, I read you religiously."

"Really?" The day was full of surprises. "Condolences to you both," Frankie added. "I know Lia was a big part of your lives."

"Well, not mine so much," Susan qualified, "but Charlie, yes. She's been most upset, haven't you sweetie?"

Susan grabbed Charlie's hand and squeezed it, then she turned her eyes back to Frankie, and the look she gave her now made the reporter take a large step backwards. She smiled politely and thought *Okay, that's also rather surprising.*

Earle stood back at the memorial, watching as objectively as he could manage. He hadn't intended to come. Had berated Frankie for even suggesting it, but he couldn't stay at home. He was still feeling grumpy. Had a feeling Morgan would be grumpy, too, if he knew they were all here, sticking their noses in.

Still, these events were often a gold mine for a homicide enquiry, and it didn't surprise him to see an undercover cop loitering by the gate, also surreptitiously scanning the crowd.

The kid was young, green, his suit looked lumpy on him. Earle hoped he was up for the task. Morgan would skin him alive if he didn't come back with something. He almost made a beeline for him to give the lad some tips, but then he noticed a squad car slide into an illegal park just outside the park entrance. Its siren and lights weren't on, but they might as well have been blazing because half the crowd had now turned to watch as Morgan stepped out from the passenger side of the vehicle.

The detective had a suspiciously determined look in his eyes, and Earle felt his stomach drop. He glanced at Kila, who was almost the only one who hadn't noticed. He was deep in conversation with a short, muscular chap in baggy black clothing. As he watched the detective stride, first to the young undercover cop, then in the direction of the PI, Earle wanted to intervene somehow— stall Morgan, warn Kila to remain silent—but he stayed rooted to the spot.

It was not his job now. He had promised to stay out of it, and so he could do nothing but watch benignly from the sidelines. Morgan was right. So was Tess. He was as useful as Beryl's mangy slippers.

Kila spotted the squad car pull up in his peripheral vision and knew he didn't have much time. It had taken all his energy to approach Woko without punching him in the face. He didn't know if Woko knew anything of his dalliance with his ex, but he didn't care about that now. And he didn't care what the others said. Kila felt complicit in Lia's murder, like he'd stuck a red light outside her door for the killer to find. He wondered if that killer was Woko and if their last conversation had forced the guy's hand.

For his part, Woko was playing the bereaved ex-boyfriend to a *T*. He looked utterly broken, his eyes rimmed red, his features haggard, yet he seemed keen to talk to Kila, too, and brushed aside the small talk, dropping his voice and leaning in close.

"You gotta look into this, bro. Lia did not deserve that. After everything she did for that family. She did not deserve to go that way."

"You're not talking about housekeeping now are you, Woko?"

"Shit no," he snapped back. "She kept secrets for that family, secrets that kept them safe."

"What secrets?" Kila tried to keep his tone steady, but he needed answers fast. Morgan was out of his car now and heading over.

"I don't know, swear to God I don't. She wouldn't tell me. Said it was for my own safety. But look where that got her! She should have said something. And all to keep those rich bastards safe!"

"Sir George? What are you saying, Woko? What's this about?"

"I don't know the details, honest. But I know she gave her life for that family, and it pisses me off." Woko glanced around then and must have noticed the detective closing in because he quickly added, "About the call. I know what he said now."

Kila was confused. "Call? What call?"

Before he could explain, DI Morgan was barking Kila's name. Kila rolled his eyes upwards, then turned to face the music, his wrists coming together instinctively, preparing for the handcuffs.

"Step aside, Morea," Morgan bellowed as his eyes swept past Kila and locked onto Woko.

Kila frowned. "What?"

"Woko Wangi?" Morgan bellowed again, and Woko nodded reluctantly.

Morgan turned to his lacky and waved him forward with the handcuffs. "Woko Wangi, you are under arrest for the murder of Lia Segeyaro."

"What?"

This was both Woko and Kila in unison, but Morgan was not yet done. As the officer slapped Woko's wrists together, the detective continued bellowing, "You are also being brought in for questioning regarding the deaths of Roman Burlington, Tawny Burlington-Brown and Heath Burlington-Brown…"

Morgan's deliberately raised voice was a waste of energy. He had the crowd's attention the moment he pulled up, and they were now staring wide-eyed at Woko, whose own eyes were wild with shock and fear and something else entirely. Kila stared back at him, baffled, surprised.

He searched the crowd for the others, thinking, *What the hell just happened?*

CHAPTER 22 ~
THE PARTY'S (REALLY) OVER

"We just got gazumped!" said Frankie, arms wrapped tightly around her torso, her eyes aflame. "And by a bumbling fool of a detective. I cannot believe it!"

The sleuths were back at the pub down from Lia's apartment and huddled around a wobbly table, nursing strong drinks and stunned expressions. Frankie had just called in the report to the news editor on duty, sending in the images she had managed to snap, while Earle had spent the past half hour interrogating his sources, and it did not look good for Woko. Or their bank balances for that matter. Because they knew the score. Despite all their effort, according to the police gossip, there was evidence aplenty to pin all four murders on the deejay/producer.

That meant Sir George got the answer he wanted and the sleuths came away with nothing.

Frankie could barely sit still she was so enraged. Kila too. Merry just sighed wistfully—she never really believed she'd see that kind of money—and Martin, while cranky, was also thinking wistfully, already resurrecting Flynn from the dead in his next book.

Earle just looked deeply disappointed.

"They really think Woko did it?" said Merry, eyes darting from Earle to Kila and back. "All of it? All four murders?"

"God *damn it*," groaned Frankie. "How did they come to suspect Woko? His name wasn't even in their initial report!"

Earle swallowed hard. "Sorry, folks. I think you can blame me for that one." They stared at him, waiting. "I might have mentioned the name Woko to Morgan once or twice. Told him Lia's ex could very well be a suspect."

"Why would you do that?" demanded Kila.

"Because he was a viable lead. I didn't think he'd follow it up."

"Your police friend must've already known about Woko, surely?" said Merry, trying to help Earle out.

He shook his head. "If he did, he showed no interest to me, didn't seem to know who I was talking about when I first brought him up. Not until I…" Earle paused. Groaned. Knew how this next bit would be received. "Not until I handed him that joint butt and asked him to get it tested."

"You think that's how they caught Woko?" said Frankie. "That had his DNA?"

"A partial fingerprint, apparently. At least that's what my sources tell me. Matched it to other prints they'd taken from the Burlington-Brown house immediately after the murders."

"Well, they would do!" said Kila. "He shot a video clip there back in July; we already knew that. Doesn't mean he's a killer."

"I'm not just talking the pool deck. Woko's prints were located in Tawny and Roman's master suite. Morgan had a bunch of prints taken after the murders but never bothered to get them analysed before because, well, they were tunnel-visioned by Heath."

"Until we came along," grumbled Frankie.

Earle exhaled. "It will probably only be a matter of time before they find Woko's fingerprints in the study. Fool didn't think to wear gloves."

Kila looked up from his drink. "That's a dead giveaway he's innocent, surely? Why go to the trouble of wiping down the murder weapons and the hall phone but not the master suite?"

"Not all crims are smart, Kila," said Earle. "They miss stuff."

"Woko can just say he was there with Lia at an earlier time," Kila persisted.

Earle shook his head. "Lia's already on record saying she never brought friends or family to Seagrave. And now Lia's dead and can't change her statement or back him up. Even if Woko didn't do it, he's in a mighty tight corner."

"He didn't do it," said Kila, surprised by his own conviction. "I just know it. He's innocent." There was something in the guy's eyes, something in his voice, something in what he'd said just before he got arrested.

He sat forward. "I need to speak to Woko. He was trying to tell me something earlier. I think it was about Heath's triple zero call." He looked directly at Earle. "Can you get me access?"

Earle frowned. "He's just been arrested, Kila. I don't have a lot of pull these days, you know."

"Just try, please. I think he knows something important. He may not even realise it."

"My, my, haven't you changed your tune," said Frankie, just as her phone began to beep, followed soon after by everyone else's devices. She glanced at her screen and felt her heart drop.

They had all received a group message from Verity, inviting them back to Seagrave first thing in the morning, and they knew it was not a delicious breakfast she was about to deliver.

Earle stood up. He had a steely look in his eyes. "I'm heading back to police headquarters. Tonight. I need to find out just how serious this arrest really is."

"What about the meeting with Verity?" asked Merry.

"I'll see you there tomorrow. Just don't haul out the white flag until I arrive."

~

Earle was not expecting to see the whites of Morgan's eyes when he strode back into Homicide headquarters an hour later. He was just hoping to see a friendly face, coax a little more *intel* out of someone, maybe plant the seeds of a possible meeting with the suspect. Hell, he'd settle for a cuppa.

The ex-detective had stopped home first for dinner as he'd promised Beryl he would but came away empty-stomached. They'd had another run-in. Well, more like a mighty great blue if he was being honest.

"Sausages won't be long, dear," she'd told him as she stood in the living room, ironing in front of the TV. Then, noticing his look of despair, she'd said, "Now what's happened?"

And so he told her. Morgan had a fresh suspect. The case was officially kaput. "I'll check in at headquarters later, love, but it's over. No money for us I'm afraid."

Then she'd offered him one of her breezy smiles and said, "Oh well, who needs a million dollars anyway?"

And so he'd hit the roof.

"*That's it?*" he said. "That's all you can say? After everything I've done for you?"

Beryl looked up from the iron, stunned.

"Me? You're doing this for me?"

There was something dark in Beryl's tone, but he was too charged up to notice. "Of course I'm doing this for you! Who else? Why do you think I took this impossible case in the first place? Why I worked all those hours, all those years? I've spent my whole working life, trying to get you out of this dingy old house and into some decent clobber, give you something better to cook than sausages and mash. And what do I have to show for it? We're back where we started—with absolutely nothing!"

Beryl placed the iron down calmly and said, "Nothing? You think we have nothing?"

Before he could answer she had stepped out from behind the ironing board towards him, and he felt himself step back.

"Earle Thomas Fitzgerald, don't you pretend for one bleeding minute that you're doing any of this for me. I was never the reason you worked hard all those years, and I'm not the reason you've been working hard now. Don't you dare throw me under the bus! Don't you do it!"

"Hang on," he'd spluttered. "I'm just saying…"

"You're saying our life is worthless, and I'm sorry, but I beg to differ! I don't know if those rich folks have rubbed off on you, but I quite like my clothes, thanks very much, and I'm awfully fond of sausages and mash. And I would never call the home we raised our daughter in *dingy*! I'm proud of this place, and I'm even prouder of Tess, now we're on it—even if you can't bring yourself to love her for who she is. And don't look at me like you have no idea what I'm talking about. I'm no fool, and neither are you. Maybe if you accepted the poor child, she might just feel welcome in this *dingy old house*!"

Then she turned to walk out, but she wasn't quite finished yet. She grabbed hold of the ironing board and said, "Don't you see, Earle? You've just belittled everything *I've* worked for, for forty years. And I thought you loved it too. But I'll tell you one thing for certain. You didn't take that job for me. You took it for yourself. Or at least I hope you did, otherwise you've been wasting all our time!"

And then she did storm away, leaving the board rattling almost as much as Earle was now just thinking about it.

A loud voice tore him from his reverie, and Earle looked up to see Morgan waving at him from the other side of the office.

"Fitzy my man!" Morgan sang out. "Come to congratulate me, have ya?"

He was surprised to see the lead detective sitting at his desk, feet up, his posse in a huddle around him. He made his way over and wedged a smile on his face.

"So," Earle said. "Woko Wangi, you reckon?"

"Well, that's what the evidence says, but feel free to reinvestigate in your own time," Morgan replied, snorting as the guys around him chuckled.

Earle sucked it up. "Has he made it nice and easy and confessed?"

"Aw I'm letting him stew for a bit. I'll interrogate him in my own damn time. You know how this works."

"Yeah, I do know how this works, and you have to have a fair bit of evidence to pull a stunt like that, arresting him at his ex-girlfriend's memorial in front of everybody. You must be mighty confident. So, what have you got?"

Morgan leaned back further in his chair. "You know very well that's classified information, Earle. You're not a badge anymore, mate. Why should I tell you?"

"Because it will give you tremendous satisfaction, I suspect."

Morgan sniggered. "Damn straight it will!" He laughed properly now and indicated for Earle to take the seat in front of him as the other officers peeled away.

"Let me take you through it, nice and slow, old man, so you can keep up." Morgan raised his forefinger. "First, the guy has no alibi. Home all alone at the time of both sets of crimes. That's always helpful. Of course, home was his studio, so that's even more telling."

Earle mirrored the finger and said, "It's evidence of nothing but a lack of clients and a social life."

Morgan smiled and held up a second finger. "He left his DNA behind. Lots of it."

"He went out with Lia, remained her friend. His DNA *would* be all over her place."

"Nah, mate, *fresh* DNA, and it's not what you think." Morgan was beaming now as he leaned in and lowered his voice. "Ever heard of a little substance the Papuans like to chew called betel nut?"

Earle frowned, nodding, his mind flashing back to the crime scene, to Lia's body, to those thick scarlet splatters on the carpet beside her that seemed too bright to be true.

"Turns out the guy's not just stupid, he's a bastard. He struck her over the head, then leaned down and spat on his dying girlfriend's body. Found traces of betel nut on her night gown, the rug, even her bed." He sat back and said louder, "What kind of monster does a thing like that?"

There was a murmur of agreement from the officer at a desk nearby, but Earle was trying to get it straight in his head.

"But Lia's Papuan, so were most of her friends, judging by the memorial. It could've been anybody's."

"We're not morons, Fitzy. Getting it analysed right this minute, but it'll be his. I know it."

"Just like you knew Heath killed his family?"

Morgan was in too good a mood to reply to that. He held up a third finger. "Want the best bit? The motive bit?"

"That'd be helpful. Especially if you can explain the other three deaths while you're at it, because at this stage, I'm not seeing it."

Morgan smiled. It was almost a leer. "Jealousy and rage, my friend, the oldest motives in the book. Young Lia had been putting it about a little too much for Woko's liking—and I'm not talking about your Papuan PI. Who'd be jealous of that slimeball? No, he found his girl bats for both camps. Couldn't handle it."

This too was unexpected. "Lia? She was *bisexual*?"

"Oh, I'm sorry, Miss Marple, did you not uncover that?" The nearby officer started chuckling again. "Yeah, we suspect she'd been shagging her boss for years. Woko caught them at it. His fragile ego did the rest."

Earle blinked. "Lia and Roman were having an affair?"

Morgan shook his head knowingly.

Earle sat forward. "Hang on... are you saying Lia and *Tawny* were in a relationship? You're serious? Who told you that? Where's your evidence?"

"Don't need it, mate. It's not exactly a well-kept secret. You've lost your form if you didn't work that one out. We know for a fact that Tawny was a lesbian. Ask your boss. It's not a stretch to assume her loyal lackey was too. But we don't rely on guesswork like you. We received a tip-off about Lia, good policing did the rest."

Earle blinked rapidly now. He still couldn't get his head around the fact that Tawny was a lesbian. Tawny, of all people! He certainly hadn't picked that. But then he shouldn't have had to. If it was true,

Sir George should have told them. His blood began to boil. "Tip-off? From whom?"

"That's also classified, mate. I will tell you this though. We suspect Woko found out about his missus and was incensed. Here's the family that worked her to the bone, the family that kept her from him, that wouldn't allow him to stay at their mega mansion, and now he finds out why—because the boss wanted to sleep with his woman. That must have driven him psycho. We now think Lia broke up with Woko *before* the murders. We believe he took his revenge out on the Burlington-Browns. Waited until they were distracted with a drunken party, snuck in, hid in the downstairs kitchen where he smoked his joint—" He stopped, winked. "Thanks for that, by the way; that was a great help. Then, while they were sleeping, Woko slaughtered as many of the family members as he could get his hands on. Then when Lia threatened to bring it to us, he had to kill her too."

He smiled and added, "If Woko gets bail, you'd better tell your mate Kila to watch his back."

"Kila can take care of himself," Earle said, his mind tangling in all directions. It was the kind of theory the amateur sleuths would present to him, not a professional detective. It just seemed too outlandish. "And you know for a fact that Tawny was a lesbian?"

That's the bit he was still struggling with, and the question delighted Morgan further.

"Oh, diddums," he said, mock pouting. "I told you your boss was keeping shit from you. He's been playing you from the start. It's the family's dirty little secret, Earle. I unearthed it last year. Didn't see how it was relevant at the time, so I told George I'd keep it on the down-low, didn't think it was anyone's business frankly, but since he has the audacity to bring my investigation into question, that little nugget can go far and wide for all I care. Hey, where's that cute reporter you've been putting it about with?"

Earle ignored that. He was struggling hard to gain his equilibrium, feeling both furious and let down. No, Sir George had *not* mentioned his daughter-in-law's sexual proclivities, not a single word. And he bloody well should have! If Tawny really was a lesbian, they should have been informed. From the very beginning. It was vital information. It painted everything in a very different light. And it made him think of something else. Something closer to home...

"You okay, mate, need a cup of tea and a lie-down?" Morgan said, his tone condescending again.

Earle brushed a rough hand over his face. "Okay, well, you certainly got me there, Morgan. You're right. I never knew that about Tawny, or Lia for that matter. But I'm struggling to see how it brought about such a bloodbath, and it certainly doesn't explain how Woko got Heath to confess to the murders."

"You said it yourself, Fitzy. Coercion. He must've pulled a drug-fucked Heath from his bed and forced him to make the confession, then shot him in the head. Which makes him smarter than I give him credit for and even more of a monster."

"What about the murder weapon? How'd he get it from the safe?"

"Same way we thought Heath got it. Roman had already opened the safe that night. He got lucky."

Now that did sound ridiculous. It was a coincidence, and he didn't buy it. "And Lia?" he asked. "Why not kill Lia back then? In the moment of passion. Why wait six months?"

Morgan looked at him like he was stupid again and said, "Oh Fitzy, Fitzy, Fitzy. Revenge is a dish best served cold. Even you must know that."

CHAPTER 23 ~
A PALTRY PRIZE

There was no avoiding it. It was time to face the music. And so the five sleuths gathered, as requested, back at Seagrave where Verity's grim expression confirmed what they were expecting.

"It's over," she told them. "I'm sorry."

"That's it?" said Frankie.

Verity produced five envelopes from her jacket. As she handed them out, she said, "A small token of Sir George's appreciation."

Frankie ripped hers open to find a cheque made out in her name for $5,000. It wasn't close to a million bucks, and she wasn't close to finished yet.

"This is insulting," she told Verity as the others eyed off their money.

"I'm sorry you feel that way," Verity replied. "But it has been less than two weeks. That's a pretty decent hourly rate." Verity took a breath. "Look, I know it's disappointing, and I know you've all gone above and beyond, and we're really grateful for that. But Sir George wanted to find the culprit, and that has now happened, regardless of your efforts."

"But Woko didn't do it!" Kila spat back. "He might be found innocent for all you know."

"Sir George believes he did it, so does the DI. We're leaving it at that."

"Oh, for goodness' sake, the DI thought Heath did it initially!" Frankie said. "He got it wrong once, he can get it wrong again." Verity shrugged, and Frankie's eyes narrowed. "He doesn't care, does he? Sir George just wanted another name. Any name. Now he's got one."

"Not just a name, Frankie," Verity replied. "He wanted evidence, and DI Morgan has provided plenty. It's over, folks. I'm sorry."

Then she smiled and added, "But on the upside, you all get your lives back."

"Oh, don't be so patronising!" said Frankie, glaring at the woman.

"Okay, but what happens if the cops are wrong?" said Martin "What happens if a court finds Woko didn't do it. Does Sir George think he can just click his fingers and we'll come running back?"

"Of course not. He would never expect that of you."

Frankie's eyes narrowed further. "Don't you get it, guys? Sir George couldn't give a damn if Woko is found guilty or not. He just wanted some doubt thrown at Heath's case, another name bandied about that wasn't his own. Now that he's got that name, we're no use to him."

Verity's smile dropped. "I'm not sure that's a fair assessment—"

"I'll tell you what's not fair," Frankie spluttered. "The king himself not bothering to come down here and sack us in person!" She began glaring up towards the corners of the ceiling. "Are you up there somewhere, you old bastard? Watching us and laughing? If so, we are not impressed! You used us shabbily! If it wasn't for us, Morgan never would've looked at Woko. He wasn't even on his radar!"

"So what happens now?" asked Merry glumly, her eyes on the PA. "We just go quietly into the night, do we? Act like this never happened?"

"I'm not going quietly into anything," Frankie snapped back. "I'll be writing about this, every minute detail—from that first invitation to this pathetic attempt to buy our silence!" She flicked a finger at the cheque, and Verity looked disappointed.

"Need I remind you of the confidentiality agreement you all signed?"

"It's null and void," came a low voice, and they all turned to find Earle stepping forward.

Earle had been watching from the sidelines, but now it was time to show his hand. And he wasn't doing it for the money.

Verity's eyes had narrowed. "I'm sorry, Earle. What do you mean by that?"

"I mean, we were misled and more than once. Mr Burlington promised there would be no parameters. Nothing was off-limits. Yet vital information was withheld from us from the very start of this investigation. We were never told of Heath's drug habits—that part of the pathology report was removed. Deliberately, I suspect. More fool me for not noticing."

Verity had the decency to look chastened.

"But more importantly," he continued, "we were never informed that Tawny and Lia were having an affair."

"*What?*" said several of them while his gaze remained glued to the PA, whose eyes had now widened again.

"That information was relevant to the case. It might have helped us solve it. It certainly helped Morgan, who was in possession of those facts."

"Tawny was a lesbian?" said Merry, although she didn't sound surprised.

Earle stared at Verity. "Were you ever going to tell us?" he asked. "That was crucial information. Integral to solving the crimes." He looked at his shocked fellow sleuths now and explained. "DI Morgan's entire case rests on information he received that Tawny and her housekeeper were in an extra-marital relationship. He claims Woko discovered this relationship and that's what led to the homicides. He lashed out."

"Lia wasn't a lesbian!" said Kila, and Martin scoffed as though about to ridicule him, but then he simply clamped his lips shut and stared at Verity.

Her arms were crossed, her expression defensive.

"So tell us, please, why were we not informed?" Earle persisted. "As far as I'm concerned, we were hired under false pretences."

She dropped her arms to the side. "Look, it's not what you think. I mean, sure, we knew about Tawny's, er, predilections. But not about Lia. I assure you. That was news to us."

"So why didn't you tell us about Tawny? We've been wasting our time, searching for a male lover when all along—"

"I wanted to tell you, really I did! But George was keen to maintain his family's privacy. He believed it was not relevant."

"*That was not his decision to make!*" Earle roared back, catching them all by surprise now.

He had never spoken above a low growl, so his sudden fury was breathtaking, but it wasn't just George and Verity Earle was furious at. They had made him a laughingstock in front of his old colleagues, in front of that egomaniac Morgan. The fact that he had never realised Tawny's secret made him feel like... What were the words

Frankie used at the pub last night? A bumbling fool of a detective. That's all he amounted to.

No wonder his wife looked at him with pity and his daughter with disdain. And no wonder Sir George didn't front up and face them himself.

"Your boss deceived us from the beginning," said Earle, "on multiple fronts. He's wasted our time and all for what?"

Earle held out his cheque and tore it in two, then watched as the pieces fluttered to the thick Persian carpet. Kila soon followed, and so did Martin. Frankie shrugged and tore hers up as well, and then Merry sighed sadly and reached for hers.

"Come on, guys," said Verity, "you don't have to do that."

As Merry watched the money drop away, she felt a deep sense of melancholy. She loathed confrontation, did everything she could to avoid it, and wasn't in the mood to drag this depressing final chapter out any longer than she had to, yet she felt doubly betrayed by Verity after their road trip away.

Like she'd just been taken for another ride.

"You've deceived us too, Verity," she told her, wedging her glasses into place. "Pretending to be Little Miss Helpful, driving me to the Snowy Mountains, when all you were really doing—all you've been doing from the start—is keeping your boss's dirty laundry covered."

"No, Merry, that's not true!" Verity said, looked genuinely crestfallen now.

"I heard you, Verity, that morning we left the lodge. You thanked Angus for his *discretion*." She gave her a pointed look. "That's the only reason you agreed to the drive. You wanted to make sure the truth didn't come out, that it wasn't a man Tawny was having an affair with last winter. It was a woman."

"No, that's not—"

"Hang on," said Martin, interrupting Verity. "Are you saying it was *Lia* in the lodge with Tawny that day?" He gasped. "No *wonder* Clem laughed me out of his office yesterday! I accused him of sleeping with a lesbian!"

Merry shrugged, she really had no idea.

But Verity was shaking her head furiously. "You have to believe me, Merry, I never set out to deceive you. I had no idea about Lia.

Honestly, I didn't. And it was news to me when Martin learned about Tawny's winter affair. I didn't know anything about that either." She held up a palm then. "But, yes, okay, Tawny *has* had relations in the past. With other women. That's what I was talking to Angus about. The family... well, we tried to keep that out of the papers. Didn't want it splashed about. But I always thought Lia was straight. Look..." She sighed. "I didn't mean to deceive anyone, and I don't believe Sir George did either."

"Codswallop!" said Frankie now, using the very word he'd thrown at her. "I can't hear any more of this bullshit. I'm out of here." She held a finger up. "And don't think I won't make a song and dance about all this. This is all going to come out."

"But the confidentiality agreement...," Verity spluttered.

"So, sue me! I'll countersue for... What did you call it, Earle? Employment under false pretences?"

She swept past Verity and out the door, and the others quickly followed.

"Please," said Verity, "it doesn't need to end like this. I can have those cheques drawn up again!"

But no one was listening to Sir George's loyal lackey anymore.

~

The group stood around the cars in the guest car park, stewing. No one wanted to leave just yet. They all had questions for Earle, and he tried his best to answer them, but he was more interested in questioning Kila.

"Did Lia say anything to you about her sexuality? Did you get any inkling she'd had an affair with Tawny?" Kila shook his head firmly. "Then that's our next step," said Earle. "Half the DI's entire case rests on the assumption that Lia and Tawny were in a relationship. We need to disprove it."

"I could talk to her sister," Kila replied. "Eva seemed pretty friendly."

"*Kila*...," said Merry.

"Hey, I'll talk, that's all. I promise!"

She smiled while Earle pulled a cotton handkerchief from his pocket and wiped his face. He wasn't in the mood for jokes. "Good, do it. Second question: Did you ever see Woko chewing betel nut?"

"Betel nut?" said Martin, his tone quizzical.

Earle brushed him off, also not in the mood for a cultural lesson, and just waited for Kila's response. Kila was looking at Merry, and they were both nodding.

"Woko was chewing it last time we saw him," Kila said. "Why?"

Earle deflated like a burst tyre. "That's the other half of Morgan's case, damn it. Some fresh betel nut was found at the crime scene. I was hoping Woko didn't touch the stuff."

Kila's eyes narrowed. "Jesus, that's hardly incriminating. Loads of Papuans chew it."

"If it contains his DNA, it's game over. I need to get access to that report when it comes back."

"So, hang on a second," said Merry, "does this mean we're continuing with the case? Still investigating?"

"Why do you think I ripped up the cheque?" said Earle. "Yes, we're continuing, or at least I am. I can't force you folks to do anything. I don't know if Woko is the killer, but I'm willing to keep trying. You said it yourself, Frankie. They got it wrong once; they could have it wrong again."

"You really want that money, don't you?" she said.

"It's not about the money." Although a million dollars *would* buy a lot of apology flowers for Beryl.

"So what do you suggest we do?" Frankie asked.

"I suggest Kila talk to Lia's sister while I try to get access to Woko and also have a little chat to my mates in pathology." Earle glanced at Merry. "You could come along with me if you like? I could give you a lift home afterwards."

Merry shook her head. "Sorry, I thought this was all over, so I've already arranged for Otis to collect me. We have a… well, a *thing*. I really can't miss it."

"No worries. You do what you have to do, Mother Hen. What about you, Martin?"

"I'm going to talk to Susan again. I've put it off long enough. If Verity knew about Tawny's affairs, then she must too. I want to know why she kept that from me."

"I'll come with you," said Frankie. "I think you're right, and I have a feeling it's not the only secret Susan's keeping."

Merry waited until they had all driven off, then took a deep breath and returned to the main house where the front door was wide open. She wasn't fibbing about the *thing* with Otis, but there was another reason she wanted the place to herself. There was something about Verity, something that reminded her of a book she'd recently finished.

Retracing her steps, she found Verity still in the library, staring at the whiteboard with Merry's scribbles all over it.

"Admiring your handiwork?" she said.

Verity turned abruptly, one hand to her heart. "Oh, Merry! You gave me a fright! I thought you'd all left."

She smiled grimly. "I can't help wondering if we played right into your hands. Delivered poor Lia to you on a platter."

Verity blinked back at her, looking puzzled.

Merry thought, *Nice acting, lady, but it won't cut it, not this time.* She pointed at the board. "There's two names on that list we never looked into but really should have." She waited a dramatic beat and then pointed to the words *Verity* and *Sir George.*

Verity looked across at her sharply, hand back at her chest. "You *cannot* possibly think we had anything to do with this?"

"Seems crazy, right? Except, gee you'd make terrific suspects. It's just like in Martin's book *Better Be Bold*—the one where the person who hires Flynn ends up being the killer. It was so unexpected because they were the least likely. Well, guess what, Verity, that's you. And Sir George. I almost didn't write your names down, remember? It seemed so far-fetched. But the more I think about it... the more the clues all fit."

Verity's eyes narrowed. "I don't see how."

"Let's start with opportunity, shall we?" She grinned. She was getting good at the terminology! "You said yourself you had the access codes, but Roman would have happily buzzed you back in even if you didn't. He'd never turn away his dad's loyal PA. I'm not saying you worked alone. Maybe Angus came down and helped you, or maybe Sir George hired someone. He'd also know the code to the safe so you could access the gun. That's means *and* opportunity."

Verity stared at Merry for another moment, looking stunned. And something else. Amused maybe? "And what about motive, Merry? What possible motive would I have to do this?"

"Loyalty, of course. You told me how important that was to your boss. Did it extend to his dirty work?"

She rolled her eyes. Now she *did* look amused. "I can assure you I don't get paid nearly enough for one murder, let alone four. Okay, then what's Sir George's motive? Why slaughter his own family?"

"Again, loyalty. Perhaps some family honour thrown in the mix. You see, I'm struggling to believe that the mighty patriarch would really accept Tawny's—what did you call it?—*sexual predilections.* I wonder whether he found out about the affair at the lodge—his sacred family sanctuary, no less—and that was the final straw. He must have been outraged, especially when the only person who was punished at the end of it all was his beloved granddaughter, who was bustled off to boarding school."

Verity almost laughed at that. "Are you seriously trying to say that George would slaughter them all for that? Because his daughter-in-law was fooling around. Something he already knew about? And how, pray tell, is any of that Roman's fault? Or Heath's for that matter? Why kill them?"

"Maybe they were complicit to the affairs, turned a blind eye, and he found that unforgiveable. Or maybe his hitman went too far."

Now Verity did laugh, clearly comforted by how stupid that sounded, even to Merry's ears.

"Goodness me, I'm glad I never read that book of Martin's before we hired him. Sounds absurd." She laughed again, then shook her head. She seemed to be enjoying this now. "What about Lia? Why kill Lia months later? And why hire you lot? These are all loose threads, Merry. Earle will not be happy."

She frowned. "Well... I guess... Sir George didn't know about Lia at first. Just heard rumours of an affair from some lowly staffer and was incensed. That's why he hired us. To find the third party. To deliver Lia to his doorstep."

"Oh for goodness' sake!"

Verity fell into a chair in front of the board and didn't look amused anymore, and Merry frowned again. Wasn't this the part where the criminal started to break down and confess to everything?

"You honestly think after all the time we spent together, Merry, that I could do such a thing? That I'm a killer?" The look she gave Merry mirrored the one Kila had given her a few days earlier—both disappointed and offended.

"I'm sorry...," Merry spluttered. "But... you know... you had access to everything we learned, were with us every step of the way.

We thought you were being helpful. Perhaps it was to report back."

Verity sighed. "If my boss really wanted to punish Tawny for sleeping with Lia, there were much easier ways to do it. He could have stripped Seagrave from her. It would have killed her; she adored this place. As for the others? Writing them out of his will would have done the trick. A lot less bloody too." She stared up at Merry's scribbling. "I can assure you, Merry, you have it all wrong. But then what would I know? I'm just a *lowly staffer*. But you're right about one thing. Sometimes I'm a little too loyal for my own good, just like Angus."

Then she cocked her head to one side, still staring at the board.

"Well, I'm watching you," Merry told her, pointing two fingers at her own eyes before pointing them at Verity's. "You and Mr Money Bags are both on my radar."

But as she walked out, Merry had a feeling this case was nothing like Flynn Bold's twelfth adventure, and it was Verity who was no longer listening.

CHAPTER 24 ~
TRUTH AND LIES

The moment Susan opened her front door, she swept fingers through her hair and brushed a tongue across her lips, and Frankie knew she was on the right track.

"Thanks for agreeing to see us again," said Martin, oblivious to Frankie's thinking.

"Oh, the pleasure's all mine," purred Susan as she led them to the living room. "Please take a seat. I'll grab us some coffees, be back in a jiffy."

This time she came through with the offer and returned with three cups of frothy lattes on a silver serving tray, a delighted look on her face. She handed the drinks out, then sat down on the sofa closest to Frankie.

"I've just been on the phone to the detectives. It's all rather shocking, isn't it?" Susan said, referring to Woko's arrest.

"You think they have the real culprit this time?" asked Frankie and Susan shrugged like she really didn't care. Just like her dad, thought Frankie.

These people were unbelievable.

Susan took a dainty sip of her coffee, then said, "I'm surprised you lot are still working on the case though. I thought Father was wrapping it up."

"We just have a few loose ends to clear up," Martin lied.

She placed her cup demurely in her lap, turned her body towards Frankie, and said, "Shoot."

Frankie smiled, ignoring the bad-taste pun, and went in for the jugular. "When did you all learn that Tawny was a lesbian, and why did you not think to inform us of the fact?"

"Oooh, straight to it, I see." Susan looked even more delighted. "Frankie Jo in action! It's quite something!" She laughed and then lifted one shoulder. "I've known about Tawny for some time but not as long as Roman. He knew from the start. I really couldn't pinpoint the moment Father found out, but really, it was no biggie."

"*No biggie?*" gasped Martin. "Are you saying Roman tolerated his wife seeing other women?"

"Didn't just tolerate it, darling, he encouraged it." She chuckled. "Oh, don't look so shocked! I told you poor Romy was dull. He really had no interest in sex, none whatsoever. But he wanted a wife who could pad the nest and provide the proverbial heir and spare and glitter while she was doing it. And Tawny certainly glittered!" She smiled at some memory. "Besides, it's so much less ego-crushing when your wife is not attracted to other men, don't you think?"

"I'm also struggling with the fact that Sir George knew and was happy about it," he persisted.

"Oh, I'm not sure my father was happy about it. I never said that. But…" She sighed and sipped her coffee again. "Father married for love—twice—and we all know how that turned out." A crinkle crossed her face. "My mother left him for an even wealthier man, and Pookie… Well, let's just say she was never content, and poor Father was utterly clueless. Of course, the fact that Pookie was reading *The Tibetan Book of the Dead* the week before she died was a bit of a giveaway but, well…"

She shook the memory away. "I think father just wanted his son to be content. That's all he ever wanted for both of us. And if Tawny made him content, sex life notwithstanding, then so be it. Father accepted it just like he accepted my choice of husband—a handsome French sailor I could flirt with." She winked at Frankie.

Frankie smiled back, then waited a beat and said, "Okay, let's move on to Lia. I interviewed her for several hours for my articles, back when it all started—"

"I know you did, you wicked girl!" Susan's tone was sulky. "You did make us out to be a bunch of rather cold fish."

"I'm sorry about that," Frankie replied. "I misread you entirely, and I also misread Lia. Which is odd. I usually have a pretty good gaydar, and I never picked Lia for a lesbian."

"Oh, that's because she's not," Susan said, waving a hand dismissively. "The idiot cop has got it wrong again." That had both sleuths' eyes widening, and she quickly added, "I'm not saying Lia's fellow *didn't* do it! Sounds very much like he did, to me. I think he might be a *gangster*. But if he did it out of jealousy—caught Lia in bed with Tawny as the detective seems to be saying—then he was misled. There was absolutely no way Lia was into women."

"Really?" said Martin. "You sound very certain."

She looked at him like he was a young child—innocently stupid. "Like I told you before, Martin, Lia was more like Tawny's bestie than her housekeeper, but they certainly weren't lovers." She paused to consider it and shook her head. "At least that's not the vibe I got."

"But how do you know *for sure*?" Martin persisted.

She smiled again, her eyes flitting back to Frankie. "Because Lia always gave me the same vibe Frankie is giving me now. The 'I'm Not Interested So Back Off' vibe. It's utterly charming."

Then both women laughed at that comment while Martin darted glances between them, a blush creeping onto his cheeks.

Susan dropped her cup to the table and stood up. "Shall I fetch us something stronger, Frankie? Looks like our illustrious author might need it."

~

It took just two seconds with Eva for Kila to find out the truth. No drinking, no flirting, everyone's clothes still firmly in place.

"Lia was as straight as an arrow!" Eva proclaimed the moment she opened the door to him.

He'd tracked the sister down to Violet's house, the very place where he'd started to interrogate Lia before lust got in the way.

As Eva showed him through to the kitchen, she kept saying it, over and over. Then she added, "The stupid *polis*!" And reached for the kettle. "They get it all wrong! You know this! You can tell them! She loved her girls—Tawny, Charlotte, all these girls here too." She waved a hand to the living room where Violet had remained. "But she didn't love them *like that*." Her lips curled up. "Never! No way! Nuh-uh!"

Then she turned to him just as her sister had done not so long ago, tears in her eyes, empty kettle in her hand. And just as he'd done with Lia, he took the kettle away and dragged her to a chair.

"Tell me about her relationship with Tawny then. They were friends?"

"Yes, I'm telling you! But not lovers."

"And Woko?"

She hissed. "Why Woko want to kill Lia? She was like a sister to him. He would never hurt a hair on her head."

He nodded. Okay, he got that. "Woko said something to me about a secret that Lia was keeping for the family. Did she ever tell you what that was?"

Now the woman's face did crumple with a heady mix of sadness and regret. "No. She never tell me anything, but I knew it. I knew something had turned evil in that house. There was dark, dark energy there. Why do you think Lia moved out? She was not kicked out! Tawny begged her to stay, but she was scared of something. I know this. I could smell it."

"Was she scared of something or *someone*?"

"I don't know. I don't know! She would not say." She sniffed, and regret was now overwhelming the sadness. "I thought Lia was being a drama queen at first. She could be a drama queen, yes? But then I could tell. There was something very wrong that was troubling my Lia. Oh no. Why didn't I make her tell me?"

Then she dissolved into tears while Kila filled up the kettle.

~

Merry took her foot off the brake and squealed as the car lurched forward. She slammed her foot back and winced at Otis, who was laughing.

"Come on, Mum, you can do this! Be brave."

She winced again. "What if I crash?"

He stared outwards at the empty car park of the abandoned shopping centre. "Into what? The trolley bay? There's no one here. Come on, you got this."

She took a deep breath and released her foot again, more slowly this time and giggled as the car began to roll forward.

"I think we can go a little faster than that. Just tap the right pedal. Just give it a try. *I can't ask for more than that.*"

He was repeating the family mantra, and she giggled as she drove slowly to one end, then turned the vehicle around and began driving in the other direction.

"Nice ten-point turn," he said, laughing. Then, "Nah, you're doing good."

"And so are you, honey. Thanks for teaching me. It'll be one of the last things I ask of you, I promise."

"Hey, it's all g." Merry knew that was code for good. "I'm happy to help." He turned the music up on the dashboard and said, "Why *did* you suddenly ask? I thought you told Dad you never wanted to learn."

She shrugged as she turned the steering wheel again. "Ah well, it's long overdue, isn't it? I'm only just working that out. You won't be around forever, so…"

"Where am I going?" He sounded defensive. "You kicking me out?"

"No, of course not, silly! But you do need to spread your wings eventually, and I need to learn how to let you. I have to stand on my own two feet."

"Start by pushing your right foot down just a bit harder, Mum, or we'll never get to the other side. You're going so slowly!"

"Just being cautious," she said as her phone began to beep. She grappled for it and noticed it was a text from Frankie.

"That's an instant fail," said Otis. "Nothing cautious about touching your phone while you're driving."

"Sorry, honey, I just need to…" She pulled the car to a complete stop and cut the engine, then glanced at the text again.

It read: *"Susan is a lesbian. Just like Tawny."*

Merry's jaw dropped. Whoa! Okay, that was really interesting. Tawny *and* Susan? Whoever would have said?

And that's when it hit her, like they'd just smashed into the trolley bay. Someone *had* said it. Only recently. A memory flashed to the fore. It was her conversation with Angus up at the ski lodge. She'd asked if the family ever stayed back during the day, and the silly man had practically given the game away, his words still clear as day: "Tawny and Susan stayed back once or twice."

Tawny and Susan. Susan and Tawny.

Did they stay back *together*? On purpose? Did they have more in common than sexual persuasion? Was that why Tawny was busted in a black negligee? Was it her sister-in-law she was hiding in her bedroom, not some mysterious stranger? Not Lia!

And was *that* why Verity thanked Angus for his discretion the morning they departed? He wasn't just hiding Tawny's *predilections*. He was hiding Susan's too.

"Mum?" said Otis, not for the first time, and she looked up from her lap with a start.

"Sorry, honey, I'm going to have to cut the lesson short."

"But you were just starting to get the hang of it!"

"I know, and I was really enjoying it too. But I'm too distracted now. It's not safe."

She wasn't just distracted, she needed to get home and call Verity. It was time for some straight talking. Then she giggled at her pun and handed the keys back to her son.

~

Frankie pocketed her mobile phone as Susan returned to the living room, this time with three glasses of champagne in hand and said, "Getting me drunk's not going to change anything, Susan."

That made the woman chuckle while Martin took his glass and shifted in his seat. He never thought of himself as conservative, certainly not a prude, yet the chemistry Susan was directing at Frankie was throwing him. It was almost *lewd*. And there he'd been thinking she was flirting with him last time he visited.

As if reading his mind, Susan said, "I don't believe in boundaries or labels. Clemmie says I'd fall for anybody as long as they had a pulse."

"So it was you in the lodge that day with Tawny?" he asked. "The day the maintenance guy came to put in the shutters?"

She held a hand to her breast. "Poor lad! Tawny said he went positively crimson when he busted her half-naked in the kitchen. Didn't know where to look, the poor darling!"

"And your husbands? What did they think?" Martin was thinking mostly of Clem and his adoration for his wife.

"There wasn't much *to* think! We just played around because we were bored. I told you before, Roman couldn't care less and Clemmie doesn't mind either." She smiled. "You can see now why he laughed when you suggested it was him at the lodge with Tawny! He's a faithful hound, my hubby. Too faithful, really. Sometimes I wish he'd break out, make me feel a little less naughty. Although he does like to watch occasionally, especially when I'm in the cabana with someone else. That's a little naughty."

Then she threw her head back and barked with laughter, and Martin tried hard not to react. She was enjoying his discomfort enormously. Eventually she wiped tears from her eyes and reached for a fresh cigarette.

"Oh Martin, I'm sorry. I'm just teasing. The truth is I'm all talk. I rarely stray, and Clem knows that. I much prefer to flirt with both men and women, in case you hadn't noticed. Foreplay is so much more satisfying than the real thing. Of course, Tawny always said I hadn't yet met my match." Her eyes slid across to Frankie again, who shook her head firmly and chuckled.

Martin sighed. *Would the innuendo never end?* "So you and Tawny? How—"

"There was no me and Tawny, darling. How many times must I say it? It was just a one-off, a bit of a lark. To be honest, Tawny was too much even for me."

"And definitely not Lia?"

"*Definitely* not. Lia used to roll her eyes at her boss and tell her men were the only game in town. So, no, the dim detectives have got that part terribly wrong."

"Your father believes them," said Frankie.

"Oh, Father will believe anything that will get young Heathie off the hook. At least now he can get on with his own life or what's left of it. Let it all go."

"Does he know about you and Tawny?" Frankie asked, and the smile suddenly drained from Susan's lips. "He doesn't know does he, Sir George?"

Susan wasn't looking amused anymore. She placed her glass on the table, then her hands prayerlike in front of her. She glanced between them and said, "Look, like I said, there wasn't much to know. It was a mistake. A bit of flirting. Just the same, I'd really rather my father didn't find out."

She glanced at the doorway like he might miraculously appear. "We were all rather stunned when Father gave Tawny and Roman his blessing. Like I said, he just wanted Roman to be happy. But I'm not sure the same courtesy would be extended to me, you see. I am his *little girl* after all. I can't imagine he'd be too thrilled to hear about any of this. There's only so much poor Daddy can handle, and really, this might be a bridge too far. Even for him."

Then she took a long gulp of her drink while Martin and Frankie swapped a conspiratorial smile.

"She did it!" said Martin as they made their way back to their cars.

"Maybe *Clemmie* helped her, maybe he didn't. But she killed them all to hide her dirty secret from her dad. You saw it—the minute you mentioned him, she turned skittish."

"Yeah, I got that," said Frankie, "but Sir George already knew about Tawny. Surely this wouldn't be such a revelation."

"I disagree. Entirely. Like she said, it's one thing to have a frisky daughter-in-law, but your own flesh and blood? The heiress to half your fortune?" Martin scoffed. "Remember what Verity told Merry about the loyalty he expected from his children. His blood relatives no less. Sir George would not have liked any of this, not one bit. Perhaps that was what they were all fighting about that night in the kitchen at the party? Heath had obviously caught his mum *in flagrante* with his aunty, and maybe he was going to tell his grandfather, or maybe Tawny had decided to bring the affair out into the open. Susan says it was nothing, but how can we believe her? She's lied to us from the beginning. Maybe Susan needed to shut Tawny up and all who knew the truth."

Frankie thought about this as they both leaned against his Aston Martin. "She says she didn't have the codes, had to be buzzed in, remember."

"As if she wouldn't have access to the family home!"

"Or maybe Lia gave them to her that night, which is why Lia needed to be silenced. Because she knew that the only outsider with access to Seagrave was Susan."

"Now you're thinking," said Martin. "Lia could have been blackmailing Susan or maybe just threatening to go to the police. So she had to shut her up." His smile suddenly dropped. "Except, she just defended Lia in there and blew the cop's motive out of the water. Why do that if you want to deflect your own guilt? She should have agreed with the police theory about Tawny and Lia and kept the focus entirely on Woko."

Frankie groaned. "Yeah, that's odd. Doesn't add up." Then she glanced across at Martin. "And would you really kill half your family to keep a bit of flirting a secret?"

Martin groaned and opened his car door. "I don't know, Frankie, but look how hard we're working to get a million bucks. Makes me wonder how far you'd go to hold on to your share of a billion."

Then he said goodbye and headed off down the driveway. Frankie was checking her phone messages as she stepped across to her own vehicle when a car whooshed up beside her, making her jump. It was a silver Tesla, an electric vehicle so quiet she hadn't even heard it approach. Clem was behind the steering wheel, Charlie in the passenger seat beside him. He offered a wave but did not appear to recognise Frankie, while Charlie acted like they were old buddies, jumping out and giving her a hug. A heartfelt one this time.

"Clem was just dropping Iggy back. I went along for the ride," Charlie explained as Clem continued on into the lock-up garage, the door closing behind him.

"You're still staying here, with Sue and Clem?"

"Yeah, I might do for a bit longer... We'll see. It's like a win-win, really. They give me my own space, a whole cottage to myself to do my homework and stuff, and they don't carry on when Iggy stays over. They are so, so cool."

"Iggy stays here with you? Overnight?"

She smiled. "Yah! I told you they were cool." Then she produced some house keys, did a little pirouette and said, "Coming in?"

But Frankie didn't hear her. Her mind was galloping in a new direction, a startling direction, and Charlie had to repeat the question before she said, "Charlie, that night of your mum's party—"

Charlie groaned. "*Oh God.* Must we?"

"You said you met your mum at Seagrave in the butler's pantry. But you didn't go there at all, did you? That was a lie."

Now Charlie looked startled. She took a step closer to the front door.

"Verity picked it," said Frankie. "You must have thought the party was in the ballroom, so that seemed like a logical place to mention. But your mother was nowhere near the butler's pantry that evening, and neither were you. You didn't sneak out to see your mum; you snuck out to catch up with your boyfriend, and you didn't do it at Seagrave." She waved a hand towards Susan's house and said, "You met up here! In your own private Idaho."

There was the look of a deer caught in a headlight, and then Charlie dropped, just like she'd been punched, slumping onto the front stoop and dropping her head onto her knees. "Oh, no, no, no..."

"Charlie?" said Frankie, leaning down towards her.

"I'm sorry... so, so sorry! I never knew that would happen... If I had known, I would have gone. Really, I would have! I promise!"

"So you admit you weren't at Seagrave that night?"

"No… no… no. But oh how I wish I had! If only I'd gone to see Mum! If only I'd known that would be the last time…"

"You couldn't have known," said Frankie, patting her back again. "But you shouldn't have lied. Your first alibi was a lie, so was your second—"

Charlie looked up, aghast. "Alibi? I don't need an alibi! I didn't kill my parents!"

"So why all the lies?"

She stood up and grappled for her keys again. "I'm not lying now. I snuck out of school at midnight and came straight here. Igor was already waiting for me. We stayed a few hours, and then I returned to school. If you don't believe me, ask that stupid, fat gossip Hannah Rigsby. She saw me sneaking back in at two."

"Why didn't you just say all that in the first place?" Frankie asked.

Charlie looked at her like she was insane. "Why do you think? Because it proves what I already know! I'm a terrible daughter! I preferred to hang with Iggy than see my own mum for her birthday!"

Then she sniffed dramatically and swept inside while Frankie stood on the LeDoux driveway, staring after her and thinking, *But… if you met Igor here, why was he at your mum's party in the first place?*

~

Merry stared into her freezer, frowning, one hand on her silent mobile, the other on a packet of something frozen. Verity had not answered a single call in over two hours.

The coward.

"Hey, Mum," said Archie, scratching his head as he wandered in. "What ya doing?"

Merry shook the thought away and pulled the mince out. "Trying to work out dinner."

He noticed the mince and said, "Spag bol? Cool! How's the case going?"

"Not great, to be honest, honey. I think it's all over."

"Oh, that's a shame. I was just scoping some Nike Air Max's online last night." He laughed. "Don't worry. I'm proud of you. At least you tried. We can't ask for more than that."

She laughed and pulled him into a tight hug. "Aw thanks, honey.

229

Proud of you too."

He pulled back—the youngest wasn't much of a hugger—and opened the freezer door again, no doubt hunting for a treat. "So, what do you want me to do with the CD?"

"CD?" She was reaching now for the microwave. It was going to take a bit of zapping to thaw this baby out.

"Yeah, the lame-arse tunes that guy recorded." He located a chocolate ice block and pulled it from the freezer. "You know, Mr Wuthering Heights?"

Merry frowned at the treat but was too distracted again to comment. "I forgot all about Heath's music. Any good?"

He scoffed, peeling the paper off. "Nah, lots of poor little rich boy shit—I mean stuff." He smiled, then slurped at the ice cream while she turned back to program the microwave. "There was one weird one though, real dark."

"Oh?"

"Yeah, called 'Shutter Down.' Something about paedos living in glass houses shouldn't watch through windows. Or something."

Merry stopped and swung around, still clutching onto the frozen packet. "Paedos? You mean like paedophiles?"

He shrugged, licked the treat again. "Told you it was dark."

Merry stared at him for a few more moments, gasping, then she dropped the mince, stepped across and pulled him back into a hug, realising now that the case went a lot deeper than anyone suspected. It had roots they hadn't even begun to uncover.

As he squirmed in her arms, she said, "You might be a new Cluedo champion in the making, Archie! I think you've just cracked the case!"

~

Verity was glad it was late summer and the roads were not icy. She had driven like a bat out of hell and was lucky she'd arrived safely. She hadn't even stopped to pack a bag, hadn't really stopped for anything, and now she was hammering on the thick wooden door, like the occupant had just two seconds to answer it.

When at last it opened a good two minutes later, Verity smiled stiffly and said, "Hello, Angus. We need to talk."

Then her smile turned glacial.

CHAPTER 25 ~
GAME, SET…

The sleuths were having what they assumed—hoped—was their final breakfast meeting, but this one was not at Seagrave, and Verity was not in attendance. Just like last time, Merry had phoned and asked to meet in neutral territory, and so they were back at the Games Room Café, but it wasn't at the Cluedo table, and today's choice was not lost on Martin.

"Getting all the pawns lined up, hey, Merry?" he said, staring at the chess board below his cup. "Ready for the checkmate?"

She held two crossed fingers up. "Not quite there yet, but maybe…"

Merry had already revealed what she'd learned from Archie and had then produced a piece of lined paper and read out the song lyrics she'd scribbled down last night, which left them all gasping. Then Frankie had revealed her own information, verifying that Charlie had lied yet again about her alibi.

They now had a pretty good idea who the real culprit was, and they were certain it wasn't Woko. But there were still a few crucial questions to be answered. And, more importantly—especially for Earle—evidence to be gathered. And so they divvied up the final tasks as they polished off plates of cooked eggs and toast.

Then, still chewing, Kila jumped up and threw a twenty-dollar note on the table. "Okay, I'm first cab off the rank. I'd better get going."

"Good luck!" they all chorused as he left them to it.

Merry glanced at her phone again, and her excitement dampened.

"Verity still not responding?" asked Frankie.

Merry shook her head, then confessed her last conversation to the group. "Oh God, I hope I haven't stirred something up!"

"Don't worry about it," said Frankie. "Great theory though.

You could give Martin Chase a run for his money." Then she winked at Martin and reached for the bill that the waitress was now presenting. "Come on, guys, let's get this paid and get on with it. We've got a massive day ahead of us. And Merry, if you can't get hold of Verity, talk to Sir George directly."

"Are we really going to do this?" Merry said, the excitement returning.

"We still have to get the final pieces in place," said Earle, glancing down at the chess board again. "It's not over yet, folks. Not by a long shot."

~

Kila sat on the stiff plastic chair and stared at Woko's sorry face across the table from him. He looked ten years older, like all those drug-fuelled recording sessions had finally caught up with him. They were at the Sydney Police Centre where Woko was being temporarily held, and Kila wasn't sure what Earle had said to Woko's solicitor and what Woko's solicitor had said to the police to grant him access, but he didn't care. Didn't have time to care. The clock was ticking.

For his part, Woko seemed intent on stressing his innocence. "I didn't do it, Kila! You have to believe me!"

"They've got your fingerprints, bro. Your DNA."

"Because I did the shoot! The video shoot, I mean! Shit! I already told you this." He blinked. "Okay, so we had a bit of fun afterwards, Lia and me. I wanted to see how those nice big beds felt. And yes, fine, Heath busted us, but he wasn't mad. Honest to God! He just wanted me to help him put out an EP. That was all it was. An EP for his silence. You have to believe me! I only went there for the video. I never went back to kill anybody!"

"Unfortunately, the DNA doesn't have a time stamp, so…"

"They're pinning it on me. You know yourself, they look for a black man to blame."

Yes, he'd already sung that tune himself, but this time the DNA was very incriminating. The lawyer had already broken the bad news. "There was the betel nut, Woko. It came straight from your gob."

He dismissed this with a sneer. "As if I spit in Lia's house. On her bed! She would kill me!" Then he realised what he'd said and dropped his head into his hands. A muffled voice adding,

"Why? Why they think I do this?"

"Because you were jealous of Lia's relationship with Tawny."

Woko looked up. "This is bullshit! Lia was not into chicks! Ask her friends, ask her sister!"

"I did. Maybe she was bisexual; maybe she never told anyone. You said it yourself—Lia was hiding something to protect the family. That might have been her big secret."

That just made Woko look bleaker. "Okay then, tell me this— even if she was a lesbo, what do I care? Why would I kill her for that?"

Kila's thick lips smudged upwards. The guy made a good point. To men like Woko, Kila even, that only made a woman *more* attractive. It certainly wouldn't make them murderous. Besides, if Woko was killing people who slept with his woman, then he should be leaping across the table, hands at Kila's throat, not staring at him like some kind of saviour.

Kila shook his head. "Look, I don't have time for this, and I don't really think you did it."

A look of relief swept across Woko's face. "Then why you here, busting my balls, bro?"

"The triple zero call, remember? You were going to tell me something."

Woko looked at him confused, then the penny dropped. His eyes lit up, his features softened, and the years suddenly slipped away.

~

As Martin rang Susan's doorbell again, he hoped it would be the last time and that Merry knew what she was doing. He and Frankie had repeated their last conversation with Susan, every lewd innuendo, over breakfast that morning, and one particular snippet had Merry's brain churning. She was thinking in Cluedo terms again and needed Martin to return and inspect the home's layout just like a Cluedo board.

In effect, she told him, he was to look for a secret passage.

So when Susan swung the door open to him, Martin said, "No more games this time, Susan. I need to take a closer look at your cabana." Then, as her eyebrows rose and a small smile flickered at her lips, he quickly added, "And, no, that does not mean I'm flirting."

~

Frankie stepped into the admin office at Saint Augustine's, and the receptionist leapt from behind her desk as though she'd been bitten.

"I'm sorry, Frankie Jo, but Sister Mary has made it quite clear you are not to have any further access to Charlotte Burlington-Brown."

"Oh, I saw her yesterday," said Frankie, tone dismissive. "It's not Charlie I'm here to speak with."

Then she bat her eyelids innocently while the receptionist looked even more alarmed.

~

On the other side of town, on almost identical premises, Earle was parking his car just inside the imposing gated entrance. It was Trinity Ladies College, just down from the Burlington mansion. But, unlike Frankie, he wasn't heading for admin. Instead he got out and walked back to the front of the school and out onto the pavement.

Then he turned around, looked up, and smiled for the first time in days.

~

Merry smiled at her mobile phone as the last RSVP came in positive. Her one job today was to send out an invitation, not unlike the first invitation that had set the ball in motion. But this time she was doing the inviting and Sir George was on the guest list, so too his extended family—or what was left of them.

It was time for... What did Agatha Christie call it? The grand denouement! But unlike Christie, there would be no egg-shaped man at the front, twirling his moustaches with every accusation. This time all five sleuths would hold court, and each of them would play their part to end this sorry saga. She just hoped the jitters would not get the better of her and that Verity would show up because she was a pivotal part of the process.

CHAPTER 26 ~
THE FINAL DENOUEMENT (PART 1)

The collection of luxury vehicles in Seagrave's car park took Merry's breath away, but she wasn't embarrassed now as Otis pulled his old bomb in beside Susan's gold Mercedes. She'd learned enough today—received all the confirmation texts and phone calls—to know that the only person who needed to be ashamed was already sitting inside that house.

She hugged her son tight, then jumped out and waved as he turned the car around and left her to it, the words "You got this, Mum!" streaming out the open window as he departed, far too quickly for her liking.

"He's right, you know," said Frankie, who was leaning on her Audi, waiting for the others outside the mansion. "You are one supersleuth, Merry Kean, and I can't believe I ever doubted you."

Merry smiled and said, "Well, you are just a journalist, Frankie, so I'm sure it's not the first time you got something wrong. I'll forgive you."

Frankie's eyes widened, then she laughed just as the other sleuths pulled their cars in beside them.

Inside the house, the Burlington family were gathered in the Yellow Room, as Merry had requested. Sir George was in his wheelchair, to the right of the main lounge suite, nursing a cup of tea, Charlotte kneeling down beside him, chatting away as if this was just a casual reunion. She had a pretty floral dress on, and her hair in a floppy high pigtail, making her look almost childlike. Susan and Clem sat side by side on one of the lounges, bored expressions on their faces and glasses of something strong on the coffee table in front of them.

And, across from them, on a matching lounge, sat Igor Ivanov, the odd one out. He looked as relaxed as a caged tiger. He was still in his usher uniform, had clearly come straight from the cinema, but even his shaved head and bold tattoos could do nothing to camouflage his nervous energy as his hands played a manic drumbeat against his thighs.

All five of them looked up and glowered at the sleuths as they walked in.

"What is the meaning of this?" demanded Susan, getting to her feet. "And how dare you invite me to my own house! What impertinence! You are nothing but interlopers!"

"Sit down, Susan," growled Sir George, causing her to flinch. "It hasn't been your house in years. Nor mine for that matter. But the people who lived here are now dead, and these five *interlopers* are going to tell me exactly what happened. Or at least I hope they are." He glanced at the sleuths and back. "I've promised to hear them out, and I expect your full attention."

She rolled her eyes and flopped back down beside her husband, who took her hand and made a soothing sound. Sir George turned back to the sleuths who were now clustering together on one side, in front of a well-stocked bar, helping themselves to stools. His eyes shifted from Merry to Frankie and Kila to Martin before resting, finally, on Earle.

"This better be good."

"It is, sir, and we thank you for getting everyone here so quickly."

"Well, it's no thanks to my PA," he shot back. "I can't find the bloody woman! Verity's gone AWOL."

"We don't need her for now," said Earle. "Frankie, would you like to open?"

Frankie nodded and stepped into the centre of the room. She gave the family a wide, confident smile, knew how well that worked for disarming her prey, then said, "Thank you for meeting us at such short notice. And for giving us the chance to set out exactly what we believe happened here, in this house, that horrendous night six months ago."

Her eyes locked onto George. "We also thank you for this opportunity. I'm not sure how you selected the five of us, but as you know, I'm a journalist. I trade in facts. Yet there's been a lot of fiction woven into this case, and it's been difficult—to borrow a phrase from Tawny—to see the wood for the trees. So, tonight we're going to sort fact from fiction and tell you what we think happened here on August 30 last year. But before we can do that, we need to set some facts straight."

She turned to Charlotte. "How are you feeling, Charlie?" Then held a palm up. "I know you hate that question, but there are going to be some difficult questions today, and we need *you*, more than anyone, to be truthful. Do you think you can do that?"

"Of course!" Charlotte said, feigning indignation.

"Good, because the first piece of fiction is your whereabouts on the night your family was murdered. Can you tell everyone, please, where you were between midnight and two a.m.?"

Charlie's cheeks burst with colour, and Igor shifted in his seat.

Sir George just looked confused. "She was at Saint Auggies of course!" he blurted. "Where else would she be?"

So, Verity had not revealed the girl's secret to her boss, thought Frankie. *Interesting.* She crossed her arms and waited, giving Charlotte a chance to answer.

Eventually Charlie said, "Oh, fine! Might as well tell the whole world—I'm a terrible, terrible daughter. I ducked out of school, and I met up with Iggy at Sue and Clem's place." She turned to her stunned grandfather and gulped. "I know it was horribly selfish of me, Gramps, but I wasn't to know they'd all die that night! I wasn't to know I would never get to see them again!"

Charlie dropped her head into her palms.

Sir George stared at her, bewildered. "You snuck out of your boarding school? For this joker?" Before Igor could react, he added, "What kind of school lets a young girl just take off in the dead of night?" Then he turned angry eyes to his daughter and said, "And you welcomed her in?"

Susan rolled her eyes. "Oh, Father, she was going to hook up with him anyway. We just provided a safe space."

"A den of sin!" he shot back, then glared again at Igor. "You lowlife piece of garbage. Taking advantage of a child like that."

Charlie looked up then through tear-smudged eyes and screamed, "I'm not a *child*, Grandpa! And he wasn't taking advantage! We love each other!"

"Rubbish!" Sir George roared back.

"But hang on," said Susan. "Igor was at the party earlier that night. I saw him there." She squinted at the young man. "Why *were* you at the party? It makes no sense."

Igor's jaw tensed. "Tawny invited me. She said she needed to tell me something. Something important."

Susan's eyes squinted back at him, but Frankie hadn't quite finished with Charlie yet.

"You met Iggy at the LeDoux house between midnight and two a.m. Tell us, please, how did you get back to school?"

Charlie stared at Frankie then. Hard. Like she wanted to throttle her. "I told you already. I got an Uber."

"Really? Ubers are getting luxurious these days." Frankie dropped her head to the side. "I know you're trying to protect certain people, Charlie, but your lies are doing you and your family no favours. I spoke with that tattletale, Hannah, like you told me to, and she tells me a different story."

Frankie turned to the others to explain. "Hannah Rigsby is a boarder in Charlie's year; she was also up and about on the night of the murders—don't ask me why, it's not important. I spoke with her just a few hours ago, and she claims she did see Charlie climb back in the boarder's common-room window just after two that morning. But that's not all she saw. She saw Charlie get out of a Mercedes. A gold Mercedes."

And now all eyes were back on Susan, who looked horrified, but before she could protest, Frankie added, "We know you own the gold Merc, Susan, but it wasn't you that Hannah saw through the car window early that morning. She told me it was an older guy with bad tattoos." Then to ward off the glares now directed at Igor, she said, "I also assumed it had to be Igor, but journalists shouldn't make assumptions. Hannah meant someone *much older*. A grown man with access to the Mercedes." She cocked her head at Clem now and said, "Tell us, Mr LeDoux, ever been inked?"

Finally the eyes settled on Clem, who had been watching this exchange with interest but was now scratching the top of his arm instinctively. He gave them all a meek smile and pulled his shirt up to reveal a large French bulldog smudged in black and red ink across his upper bicep.

"*Oui*, it is me. Guilty as charged." His smile turned apologetic. "I helped the young lovers, this is true. I am French; it is what we do." He looked at Sir George then. "I am sorry if I have overstepped, and perhaps Charlotte should not have sneaked out, but knowing that she did, I was making sure the young *amoureaux* returned safely."

Susan just stared at her husband, her face frozen.

Sir George's fury was writ large across his wrinkled brow. "This is completely unacceptable, Clem. You too, Susan. You should not be providing a nest for my granddaughter's indiscretions, and you certainly should have told me all this earlier. Why didn't you mention any of this during the inquest?"

Susan waved a hand dismissively. "I'm sorry, Father, but it was completely irrelevant and just would've confused matters. We told Charlie to keep it to herself. It just made her look bad, and she was going through enough as it was." Then she looked at Frankie and said, "This is all very enlightening, but what has any of this got to do with the murders? If my husband dropped Charlie back at school, how could she possibly be involved? I thought you were going to tell us who did this horrible thing!"

"She's right," growled Sir George now. "You're doing a good job of highlighting my family's lack of morality, but it doesn't explain what happened here that evening."

"Oh, I was just doing some fact-checking," said Frankie breezily. "Correcting a few alibis. My part, for now, is done."

Then she gave Merry a nod and stepped back towards the bar.

Merry took a deep breath and smiled awkwardly as the group all turned to stare at her. She had none of the reporter's natural confidence, so she tried to remember the tips she gave her own kids when they were forced to do public speaking at school.

Speak slowly. Speak clearly. And don't forget to breathe!

She took Frankie's place in the centre of the room, inhaled deeply, then addressed Sir George directly.

"We're not quite there yet, sir, if you'll bear with us a bit longer. In order to explain the murders, we need to make one more detour, to the Snowy Mountains and your ski lodge. That's actually where it all started, you see, last winter. Or at least that's what set it all in motion." She glanced at Martin and added, "You could call this bit the prologue."

He smiled reassuringly while Sir George just looked irritated and Susan grappled for her drink, her expression wary.

Merry said, "We've all suspected for some time that the key to the case rested with an incident that happened during that final ski trip. We thought it was related to an affair Tawny had on the third day of the trip—*after* Heath and Charlotte had returned home. We now know that was a classic red herring."

She flashed a look at Susan, who was now chewing on her scotch glass, a blush creeping into her cheeks.

"In fact, the incident that sparked the murders happened on the *second* day of the trip, when Heath and Charlie were still at the lodge."

Susan looked up, blinking. And so did Charlotte.

"But *nothing happened*," Charlie said. "I keep telling you this! It was just another ordinary day. We skied, we went back to the lodge, sat around playing cards and then we went to bed."

Merry smiled sadly back at her. "Actually, Charlie, something did happen that night. You just didn't know about it. But Heath did, and he told your mum. We believe Heath saw someone looking in through the bathroom window that evening, and that's why Tawny ordered shutters be installed down there. It wasn't to give her extra privacy though. It was to stop someone perving in at her daughter."

"Me?" said Charlotte. "You think someone was perving at me? Like a peeping tom?"

"More like a sick pervert," said Merry, who hated that term. It was too benign, too whimsical. "We also think that's why Heath dragged you home early, Charlie. He was protecting you."

"From *whom*?" demanded Sir George, his patience waning. "Who is this pervert, and why am I just hearing about this now?"

"It had to be someone from the village," said Susan quickly. "Maybe one of the workers? Do you think they followed Charlotte to Sydney and then killed the family?"

"Why would they do that?" demanded Sir George. "That's ridiculous."

"He is right, my darling," said Clem. "You do not kill people for a little peeping! It makes no sense. It is outlandish! And it does not explain why Lia was murdered."

"Oh, I think it does," came a voice from the doorway, and they all turned to see Verity leaning against the doorframe. The missing PA had been leaning there for some time, but no one, it seems, had noticed. She stood up straight and stepped into the room.

"Where the blazes have you been?" demanded Sir George, but for the first time since the team had met her, Verity ignored her boss and turned to the sleuths where she locked eyes with Merry.

"You were right, Merry. Angus did know more than he was

telling, but it had nothing to do with Tawny and any affair she might be having."

"So that's why I couldn't get you!" Merry replied. "You just drove all the way to the Snowy Mountains?"

"And back." Verity fell into a lone armchair as though only just realising how weary she was. "After what you said yesterday, I was determined to prove my innocence. I spoke to Angus, demanded the truth this time. He's a loyal employee you've got there, sir." She frowned at Sir George. "But his loyalty was misguided. If he'd spoken up earlier, none of this might have happened. It took some persuading as Tawny had sworn him to secrecy, but the truth is, the person staring in at the bathroom window that night was..." She paused, sighed, then said the name the sleuths already expected: "Clem."

There was a long silence then, like everyone was trying to catch up, then Susan scoffed loudly and said, "Oh for goodness' sake!" And Charlotte screamed, "No! It's not true!" And Clem leaned back in his seat and shook his head over and over, his eyes staring up at the ceiling.

Verity looked at Clem and sighed again. "It wasn't the first time either, I'm sorry to say. Heath spotted you looking in at Charlie the night before, Clem, but gave you the benefit of the doubt. Assumed it was innocent, that you were just out on that walkway, having a quiet smoke. But when you followed Charlie down on the second night, he knew it was more than a coincidence. You were standing outside, watching her take a shower. Heath told his mum, his mum told Angus and demanded he install the blinds, which is how Timmy spotted Tawny in her negligee and how we all got sidetracked. Merry's right. The blinds weren't put up to hide Tawny's affairs. They were installed to hide her daughter from a pervert."

"Lies! All lies!" Clem roared, now on his feet.

"Sit down!" Sir George roared back, his voice weaker yet somehow more threatening, and Clem sank into his seat while Susan just stared at him, speechless.

Eventually Clem threw his hands in the air and said, "So, I will deny all of this. It is all bullshit. And still it is proof of nothing. It is my word against this Angus. He is not family! He is lying!"

"What about Heath, is *he* lying?" said Merry, turning now to Charlie. "Because here's the really sad bit, honey. Heath left a message from the grave, and no one bothered to stop and listen." She pulled out the disc that Woko had given them and explained what it was to the group. "There's a song Heath recorded on here titled 'Shutter Down.' It has quite a story to tell, but there's one line that really gives me the shudders, and it goes something like this: *'Thinking back to better days when you had no stench. Tell me please, how d'ya say paedophile in French?'*"

There was another stunned silence before Clem was back on his feet. "This is not true! It is bullshit! My nephew, he was deluded! He made a mistake! You tell them, Charlotte, have I ever touched you? Ever?"

Charlie was staring at him, horrified but shaking her head. "No... no... never."

"See! It is all lies. It is poof of nothing. I am not a murderer."

Merry ignored this and said, "That's why your mum suggested a Swiss finishing school, Charlie. She was trying to protect you. It's why she agreed on boarding school because it was so much better than your suggestion—the LeDouxes."

"No!" Clem roared again.

"We also think it's what she was arguing with Heath about in the kitchen the night of the party. Your brother was probably enraged that Clem was there, not you. That Clem was still part of the family and you were the one who'd been banished. We believe Heath gave your parents an ultimatum that evening, and we also believe that someone overheard that ultimatum and knew then that they had to act, and fast."

Clem continued shaking his head throughout this exchange and looked more bewildered than guilty as he turned to his wife. "You tell them, Susan! I would not do such a thing! This is madness! So I accidentally saw a pretty girl while I was having a cigarette. That does not make me a paedophile; it does not make me a murderer. Why would I kill anybody for this?"

"It is rather absurd," said Susan, turning to the sleuths, her voice sounding almost amused. "I mean, ten points for trying and all that, but I really don't think my husband would kill a bunch of people because he got caught peeking through a bathroom window." She glanced at Martin. "Even *you* couldn't make that work in a book."

Martin smiled at her and stepped forward to join Merry in the centre of the room.

"This isn't a book, Susan, this is real life, and it's not the only time your husband peeked at Charlotte now, is it?" He raised his eyebrows towards Clem. "That's why you encouraged Charlotte to meet Igor at your house so you could watch them at your leisure. Did you watch her every time she visited your home or just the night of the murders?"

"What?" roared Sir George.

"Eww!" said Charlie while Igor just looked stunned beside her.

"No, no, no!" yelled Clem. "Like Susan said! We were just giving the lovers a safe space to meet."

"And where was this so-called safe space, Clem? The cabana?"

He blinked back worriedly, then glanced at his wife, but she was staring hard at Martin, a hand to her lips, her cheeks now drained of colour.

Martin explained to the others, "There's a two-way mirror in the LeDoux cabana. Susan showed me earlier today. The cabana is where young Charlotte and Igor hooked up and where Clem sat back and watched."

Young Iggy leapt from his chair then, his hands in fists beside him. "Fucking hell! You dirty bastard!"

But Sir George was staring wide-eyed at his daughter. "Why on earth would you need such a mirror?"

Susan shrank back. "It was just a bit of fun—"

"Fun?" He looked at her like she was vermin, and she gasped.

"Don't you dare judge me, Father! What else am I supposed to do with my time? You pushed me out of your company, handed it all to Roman—"

"I made your life easier, giving you a chance to have children—"

"I don't want *children*!" She spat the word out like it, too, was vermin. "I want some bloody purpose. I'm bored to tears! So if I have a little fun in the cabana with my husband; who cares? It's perfectly innocent!"

"Watching your niece while she's with her boyfriend? This is innocent?"

"No! I never did that. And neither did Clem. It was just at the ski lodge, and he only did it the once. I told Tawny this; it was perfectly innocent."

"Hang on, you *knew*?" said Charlotte, staring at her aunty.

"That he was watching me?"

"No… I mean, it was… innocent…"

"You can keep saying that word," said Martin. "Doesn't make it any truer. And Tawny didn't believe it was innocent either, did she? When you met with her at the lodge the day after." He addressed the others now to explain. "There was another piece of fiction that was fed to us during our investigation, and Frankie and I swallowed it, hook, line and sinker." He met Susan's fiery eyes. "Tawny was sprung with someone in her bedroom at the lodge last winter, and we were led to believe that person was Susan. That Tawny and Susan were having an affair."

Sir George was now speechless.

Martin continued. "This was another red herring. A skewering of the truth. Because you *were* in the room with Tawny that day at the lodge, Susan, but you weren't 'mucking about' as you insisted. Quite the opposite. Tawny was confronting you about your perving husband, demanding you act. Did you tell her you would do so? Did you beg her not to take it to anyone else? To give you a month to sort it out? Is that what led to the climax at Tawny's fortieth?"

Susan's lips were now pinched shut, her eyes glaring upwards at the ceiling.

"We believe it was *you* who overheard Heath's ultimatum to his parents in the kitchen at the party," said Martin. "You knew you had to act, and fast. You had to stop Roman from revealing the truth about your husband to Sir George. And so it was you who arranged to meet with Roman later that night when the party would be over. And it was you who killed them all." He paused for a moment and let those words settle around them like a terrible stench before he added, "Wasn't it, Susan?"

CHAPTER 27 ~
THE FINAL DENOUEMENT (PART 2)

The Burlington family sat back in their seats, each one looking as stunned as each other. Except for Susan. Suddenly, strangely, she just looked bored. A little weary even.

She swept a hand across her skirt as though wiping away crumbs and said, "You people are beyond extraordinary. You must be very desperate for a million dollars. And where, pray tell, is your evidence for all this?"

Like she hadn't just been accused of slaughtering her beloved family.

Martin glanced at the others, incredulous, then Earle stepped forward to join them. He had a grim look on his face.

"You're right, Susan. Evidence would be handy, which is why I'm relieved there's a security-conscious girls' school down the road from here." He looked at Sir George and added, "I'd move Charlie in there, if I were you. At least they have CCTV. I paid Trinity Ladies College a visit earlier today. I was also relieved to find they don't wipe their files regularly. Turns out their camera caught a silver Tesla driving past their school in the direction of Seagrave at exactly 1:37 that fateful morning. About an hour before the murders."

His eyes returned to Susan. "While your husband was watching the young lovers back at your house—a criminal offence, by the way; nothing innocent about it, but that's a conversation for your lawyer." He shook his head. "Anyway, while he was doing that, we believe you took Clem's electric vehicle because it was quieter than your Merc, and you drove back here to Seagrave."

Clem looked at his wife with a start then, like something had just clicked in his head, but she was too busy scoffing to notice.

"Impossible," she said. "Why would I want to do that? Besides, I didn't have the codes."

"You didn't need them. Roman was expecting you. He buzzed you in, and you met him in his study, but you weren't there to make apologies for your husband. You were there to demand Roman back off. Again, I can only assume what happened next, but my guess is he refused and an argument ensued. Things got heated, and that's when you reached for the candelabra and smashed your brother's head in. You then noticed the gun in the open safe and decided you needed to kill the only other people who knew you would be there—Tawny and Heath."

"S-Susan?" stammered Sir George, hand at his throat, eyes wide behind his glasses. "Tell me this isn't true."

"Of course it's not true, Father!" Her tone was one of impatience and indignation. "As if I could kill any of them! As if I could even manage it. Heath would have overpowered me in two seconds! It's absurd! And remember, it was Heath who was splattered in blood, Heath who confessed to everything!"

"Heath probably woke up after hearing that gunshot, the one that killed his mother," said Earle. "Did he run out and find you in the hallway, Susan? Or did you pull him from his bed, half-blind without his glasses? Did you feign innocence? Pretend there was an intruder and drag him from body to body, knowing he'd reach for his parents and contaminate the crime scenes, smatter himself with their blood? In his half-blind, drug-fuelled state, he would have been distressed and confused. Would not have objected if you had led him to the hall, placed the phone in his hand, and then produced the gun, demanding he call emergency services and take the blame."

"Nonsense, all nonsense," said Susan, shaking her head, lips slouched downwards.

"How terrified he must have been when he finally understood what was going on," continued Earle. "With the gun trained on his head, you gave him an ultimatum of your own—confess to everything or I kill you now and then I'll kill your sister. Perhaps he thought he could overpower you, perhaps he didn't believe you'd go through with it. Or perhaps he just agreed to spare his beloved Charlie. In any case, he did exactly as he was asked, and that's when you shot him dead."

A loud clapping broke through Earle's monologue, and Susan was now on her feet.

"Brilliant!" she called out. "Bravo!" She clapped her hands

towards Martin and added, "I hope you've been taking notes, Mr Chase, because this would make one hell of a plot for your next piece of drivel. But that's all it is—drivel. Talk about fiction!" She flashed Frankie a look then. "Pity your evidence is so weak. All you have is a car that looks vaguely like my husband's—not *mine*, I might add. Must be a dozen Teslas in this fancy neighbourhood. Can you actually *see me* in this mysterious, murdering Tesla? Get a number plate? Hmm?"

Earle looked down and she smiled. "Didn't think so. You should know better—it takes more than wishful thinking and a few coincidences to plant a murder on somebody. And what, pray tell, has any of this got to do with Lia? Hm?" She glanced around the group, now looking emboldened. "You're going to need to do better than that, Supersleuths!"

"I can do better than that," came a chirpy voice from the bar, and she swung around to find Kila still perched on a stool, his legs spread out before him, a wolfish grin on his face.

Kila Morea was not actually feeling happy, he was bluffing as he often did, masking his anger. And boy was he angry. This spoilt, smug, sorry excuse for a human had destroyed so many lives, including, most tragically, an innocent woman called Lia.

As he watched Susan's smile falter while her family recoiled around her, not wanting to believe there could be more, Kila crossed his legs over and said, "You should be applauding *yourself*, Susan. Slaughtered half your family six months ago and got off without a second glance. What'd I say to you, Merry? You *dim-dims* really can get away with murder."

He shook his head and got to his feet.

"Your only problem was Lia. The pesky housekeeper, and Tawny's bestie. You could never be sure what she knew. Had Tawny told her about Clem's perving that winter? Would Lia eventually tell somebody? That's where you made your first mistake—feeding Martin that clue, pointing him in the direction of Lia. Couldn't help yourself, you needed to know what the housekeeper knew. You hoped Martin would be bright enough to find out but not bright enough to link you to the killing. Pity he's such a smart bloke. A true intellect."

Now Kila offered Martin a conciliatory grin before turning back to Susan. "Your second big mistake was lying about Lia's sexuality, then backflipping on it. You must have given the police that fake tip-off just to ram home Woko's supposed motive and confuse the issue. Why you then contradicted that lie to Martin and Frankie is beyond us. Maybe you wanted to add to the confusion, maybe you can't keep all your lies straight. But the truth is Lia wasn't bisexual. Woko knew that. So did Eva. So did I."

Then he shoved his hands into his pocket and his tone darkened. "What we don't know, and probably never will, is exactly what Lia knew about the murders, but I've got a hunch she suspected Clem. She was scared of somebody, that I do know. But instead of acting on this, poor lovely Lia acted up instead—partying hard, trying to forget. Trying not to make things even worse for Sir George and young Charlotte. Because how would accusing Uncle Clem of anything make things better? But it was eating her up inside.

"And then I came along, a kindly compatriot she might be able to unburden her secrets to. If only I hadn't put my own needs first, she just might have. Were you watching her that night? Did you see me go in and then leave again the next morning? Was that when you decided to kill her? It was Clem she was scared of, so she probably let you in without a second thought. I'm hoping Lia never knew what hit her."

Susan sniffed and shook her head and said, "Don't know what you're talking about. Again, I'm not hearing any evidence. Last time I looked, it all pointed at your dodgy *compatriot* Woko."

He half smiled. "Oooh that was a stroke of brilliance—planting Woko's betel nut at the crime scene." He looked at Martin. "Definitely include that in your next book. Did you follow Lia to Woko's studio one day, Susan? Or was it me you followed? That morning I left Lia's apartment to meet with Merry, we ended up talking to Woko in the studio laneway. He was down there spitting betel nut all over the place. Were you watching us then? Wouldn't have been hard to wait until we went inside, then scrape some up and plant it on Lia's body, stitch someone else up while you were at it."

Earle cleared his throat then and added, "It's only a matter of time before we find a camera that puts you in the vicinity of Woko's studio, Susan."

Her lips smooched south again, and she reached for her handbag. "Well, until that non-existent day comes, I think I might take my leave." She stood up and glanced around as if only just noticing how distraught her family looked and said, "It's not true, you know, none of it is true! And, again, not one shred of actual evidence, so unless you've got—"

"How about testimony from Heath?" said Kila, causing her to swing back around. "Will that do?"

She looked at him, bewildered. "He's been dead for six months! What did he do? Send another message from the grave?"

"Kind of." He reached into his jacket and produced a small digital recorder.

"Oh God, not another woeful rap tune!" She exhaled dramatically and slouched back into her seat beside Clem who leaned back, like he really wished she wouldn't. "That's hearsay, isn't it, Earle? Can't be used in a court of law, last time I looked."

"No, but the triple zero call can," he replied as Kila stepped across to join them in the middle of the room. "You were lucky. The police never had this properly analysed because they were singularly focused on your nephew. They couldn't work out his last words, didn't think they mattered, so they settled on what we all agreed we heard, which was, 'So sorry, sis.'"

"That's *not* what he said?" asked Charlie now, her voice barely a whisper.

Kila offered her a sympathetic smile and placed the recorder on the table in front of Susan. "I asked Woko to analyse Heath's final words, properly this time. You see, Woko's not just a dodgy compatriot, Susan, he's also an audio engineer. A bloody good one as it turns out. He was able to remove all the superfluous noise, which revealed the background info. We now know what Heath said as the gun went off. Turns out he wasn't saying sorry to Charlie—although I'm sure he was." He flashed Charlie another sad smile. "He was telling the world who killed his parents and who would go on to kill him and then Lia."

He gave her a moment to dispute this, but Susan had gone deathly quiet, her eyes fixed on the recorder, her complexion almost grey. So he leaned down and clicked Play, then stepped back as the now-familiar distress call came through the recorder's loudspeaker.

"Emergency services, what's your emergency?"

"I, um… I'd like to report a… a murder, please. Two murders."

As Heath ran through his so-called confession, his tone so clearly distraught, Sir George made a deep, guttural sound and Charlie started weeping softly.

Just as it reached the final words, Kila leaned down and pressed the Pause button.

"You ready for this?" he asked them both.

They nodded, although their expressions suggested otherwise, and he clicked Play as Heath's final words rang out:

"All you need to know is I killed every last one of them and now..."

"And now? Sir?"

"And now I'm going to kill myself, or so Susan thinks."

Kila paused the tape again, giving them a moment to digest that, then in case there was any more confusion, he repeated the words loud and clear:

"Or so Susan thinks."

Then he clicked Play again, and they all jumped as the remnant sound of gunshot filled the room.

Sir George was the first to react. He was wheeling frantically towards his daughter, his expression one of immeasurable pain.

"Why?" he demanded. "*How* could you do such a thing? To Heath? To your own brother? To poor, beautiful Tawny—"

"Tawny, Tawny, Tawny!" she bellowed back, no longer smug and calm. "That's all you ever cared about! Roman and Tawny and their perfect fucking children!"

He stopped wheeling, looked at her, aghast, as did Charlie.

Susan shook her head. "You stupid old fool! None of this needed to come out, but you couldn't believe one of *them* could be guilty, so you had to push it! Had to make sure I got the blame! But it was all *their* fault! Don't you see? They threatened me!"

"What?"

"Heath and Roman and Tawny! Even Lia! Giving me those sideways looks like I was married to a monster. After everything Tawny got away with! She was the vile one in this family."

"You cannot possibly be comparing Tawny's sexuality with paedophilia!" Sir George said. "What Tawny did was not illegal! She was upfront about it. Roman knew. We all did. She was not hurting anybody! She didn't deserve to die for that!"

"She *threatened* me, Father. So did Roman. Said they'd go to the police, take Clem away from me. It was their own damn fault!

They all asked for it!"

Then she stopped, gasping as she realised what she had just confessed, before bursting on, words now tumbling out along with decades of pent-up resentment.

"Tawny and Roman were such hypocrites! Why couldn't they just leave it alone? I told them I'd take care of it. But Roman said that wasn't good enough. Roman insisted I meet with him after the party that night. He said you'd disinherit us! He opened the safe, showed me your will. Said there was a provision for family scandals. Like Tawny was some *innocent*!

"He demanded I divorce Clem and report him to the police. How *dare* Roman ask such a thing! He had absolutely everything—this house, the business, the children, Tawny! Hell, he even got the better, grander name. Roman. Me? I get boring old *Susan*! But that was fine. I accepted that. All I wanted was Clem; that's all I ever asked for from this family. I just wanted to be happy, and I *was* happy until Heath stuck his nose in! I told Roman to take the inheritance, but please, don't go to Daddy, and don't go to the police! Don't take the one thing I had left! Clem!"

She reached across to grab Clem's hand, but even he looked horrified, like he couldn't comprehend it. Susan read his horror and gasped back at him.

"I did it for you!" she screamed. "For us!"

"I... I did not ask you to kill them... I did not want you to kill them..."

"But I had to, don't you see? It was them or you!"

He shook his head and edged away and could no longer look her in the eyes, and so she turned hers to Charlie.

"You understand! Iggy doesn't belong here either, but you'd do the same for him!"

"No!" Charlie cried. "No, I would not, and nor would he ask me to!" Beside her Igor was shaking his head madly. "But my mum *did* accept him; she loved him in the end."

"Because she hoped he would look out for you, Charlie," said Frankie, a voice of calm breaking through the hysteria as she joined the sleuths in the centre of the room again. "Your mother loved you very much. She wanted you to be with Iggy. It was safer than hanging with your creepy uncle."

"Shit! She was going to tell me!" Igor said now, sitting forward, finally finding his voice. "*That's* why she invited me to the party! I think she was going to tell me about Clem, but we never got a chance to talk. Perhaps if she'd told me, I could have..."

Frankie shook her head. "If she had told you, you might have ended up dead, along with Lia."

"Poor Heath." Charlotte gasped now. "My poor, poor brother. All he did was try to help me. He tried to save me from Clem."

"But Clem didn't *do* anything!" Susan cried. "All Clem did was look at his beautiful niece. Where's the harm in that? He never would have touched you, Charlie! I know that!"

"It was *illegal*," said Earle again, his deep, gravelly voice also like a balm. "And how can you be sure that's all it would ever be? Where is Charlie living right now, Susan? At your place? In the *cabana*?" The woman's eyes shifted frantically. "By killing Charlie's true guardians, you handed your niece over to a paedophile on a platter."

And with those words, pandemonium broke out.

Sir George was now charging his wheelchair at Clem, roaring out the word "monster!" while Susan had buckled over and was gasping like she was taking her final breaths.

Verity managed to intercept Sir George before he made it to a stunned-looking Clem while Charlotte fell into Igor's arms, crying and shaking uncontrollably, as Igor stared at the door like he wanted to escape.

And the five sleuths all stared at each other, looks of relief now etched across their faces. Then Earle reached for his phone and dialled the number for DI Morgan.

When the detective picked up, he said, "Hey Morgs, got a minute? My team and I just straightened your case out, and it's now looking a lot less wonky. I think you better get yourself to Seagrave. And fast."

CHAPTER 28 ~
HOME IS WHERE THE HEART IS

"Oh, they look lovely!" said Beryl, reaching across to take the bouquet of baby pink peonies from her husband. "But don't you go blowing all the money on foolish things like flowers."

Earle offered her a sheepish grin as he pulled his jacket off and followed her into the kitchen. "How d'you know I got the money?"

"I always knew you'd do it, dear, if it could be done. I just didn't mind either way, that's all I was saying. I've always been happy with my lot. You know that."

He nodded. Slumped into a kitchen chair. "I got a bit lost towards the end there, didn't I, love?"

"Nah, you were just blinded by the money, and bored. Big time. Have been since the day you handed in your badge." She laughed as his eyebrows swept upwards. "Like I didn't notice! And I don't blame you, dear. You're a good detective. Your talent is wasted on the golf course. Maybe you could have a chat to Morgan, see if he can farm some more work out to you."

"Ooh, I don't think Morgs is too happy with me right now, Beryl."

He chuckled, thinking about the uneasy conversation he'd had with the detective back at Seagrave. Morgan and his team had arrived soon after the kerfuffle, heard the whole story and shuffled Susan and Clem away, but not before a rather heated conversation with the sleuths that included words like "hindering an investigation" and "perverting the course of justice" and "interfering bastards". But Earle knew they'd done the force a favour and his wife was right; he still had some fuel left in the old tank. Perhaps he'd put part of the windfall into setting himself up as a police advisor. Or maybe he'd look into teaching…

"But what are you doing back here so soon?" Beryl asked, reaching into a lower cupboard to search for a vase. "I thought you'd be celebrating the end of the case with your new buddies. Like you always used to."

"Nah, the only one I fancy celebratin' with is right here in this house."

She found a vase and filled it with water, then said, "Shall I frock up and see if we can get a table at the bowling club? Tess tells me they have a fancy new bistro. Half-decent chicken parmies."

"If it's okay with you, I thought we'd stay in. I could really slaughter another plate of your world-famous sausages and mash."

Beryl looked up from the vase. "Are you patronising me, Earle Thomas Fitzgerald?"

He laughed. "I wouldn't bloody dare!"

She handed him the vase and said, "Right, well, while I get that cooking, how about you make yourself useful. Pop these in the lounge room. Gruff needs feeding too. Then you could mix me a lovely scotch and dry and I'll meet you out on the deck in a bit. There's a fresh packet of chippies you could open while you're at it."

He nodded and said, "I'm onto it. But first I'm gonna call Tess. See if she'd like to join us. Maybe she could bring her lovely partner, Fiona. 'Bout time those two came out of the closet."

Beryl stared at him surprised, then her face lit up like it was Christmas.

~

Across town, Merry was shouting her children a lavish meal out, or at least that's what it felt like. They were at the steak house just two blocks down the road and had been here plenty of times before, usually to celebrate a birthday or some sporting achievement, but this time Merry didn't stop them from ordering the fanciest steaks on the menu, and she shouted herself the best bottle of wine, which she now shared with Otis.

"Let's raise a toast to Mum, hey?" he said, reaching for his glass. "She's a bloody legend!"

The younger two held their soft drinks high, and Merry swelled with pride.

Like Beryl, she knew the money didn't really matter. Merry was the richest woman in the world, had everything she needed right here, at this table, raising their drinks towards her. But she also knew she couldn't hold on to them forever. They needed their own lives, and so did she.

"Can I have two desserts tonight, Mum, now that we're millionaires?" asked Archie, smashing a forkful of chips into his mouth.

"Don't be such a *pig!*" said Lola as Merry laughed and shook her head.

"That money's going to something more important than your belly, mister. But I'll tell you what we can do. We can grab some chocolate on the way home and have a game of Cluedo if you like."

"Really?" said Otis, eyes wide. "I thought you didn't play anymore."

"Well, I've got to practice if I'm going to have a chance of winning next year's championship."

The kids squealed, more excited by this news than the money, and so the glasses were lifted again and there were cheers all round as Merry thought, *It's as good an ambition as any.* But the truth is, she wasn't doing it to fill her time or even give herself some purpose.

Merry needed to find where she had left her smile, and she had a hunch it was somewhere between Las Vegas and the Patio.

~

Frankie read the article through one more time, then pressed Send and pushed herself back from the office desk, smile widening. There was definitely a book in this, maybe even a Netflix doco, but for now a series of probing Frankie Jo exclusives would have to suffice. At least Sir George had approved that in his sad and shattered state.

Verity had turned very efficient soon after the house had exploded, shepherding Charlie, Igor and Sir George into the kitchen where she set about making strong coffee, laced with something even stronger. She then buzzed the police in and handed Susan a number for the family solicitor. Sure, the woman was a monster, but she was Sir George's monster and he would want her well represented.

Then, finally, she'd turned to the sleuths and offered them her congratulations. "I will be in touch very soon with your remittance," she said, and Kila had scoffed at that.

"Better be more than a few croissants and some coffee."

She'd laughed. "A deal's a deal, and you pulled it off."

That's when Frankie had negotiated the articles, not really giving Verity a choice in the matter. "Like you always say, the story will come out eventually. Better to have someone in your corner."

Frankie would work on approval for the book deal later. For now, it was time to get back to her own life. She reached for her tote and scooped out her trusty iPhone, flicking through what looked like a hundred messages still waiting to be answered, most of them from the Boss.

Frankie's mind went to Tawny and Lia then and also to Tawny and Susan and all the confusion over what their relationships really entailed. It was so easy for people to get confused. Half the *Herald* assumed Jan was Frankie's lover, but it wasn't like that, never had been, although it often felt like a marriage, a rather warped, 1950s-style one. Frankie was the harried husband who came home late at night, Jan the good wife on call with food and advice. And stories of their past which were really just thinly veiled threats.

But what was Frankie so afraid of?

She glanced around the bustling office and thought of her Walkley journalism award then. Of the lies she had told to win it and how Jan had backed her up. Because Jan was right. That drunken politician had used the words "off the record" several times, yet she'd ignored him and published his story anyway. She'd won the gong and he'd been ousted from parliament. Two weeks later he took his own life. Frankie had tried to pretend it wasn't her fault. At least that's what Jan had told her. And seven years of therapy. But now she knew differently, and now she was ready to face her own facts.

Frankie thought of her job then, one she adored, and of her beautiful, expensive apartment that she might have to give up. Then she felt her heart flutter.

Was she really prepared to lose everything?

Scrunching up her face, she groaned, then tapped in the familiar number. When Jan picked up, Frankie added a smile to her voice and said, "Hey Boss, have you got a moment?"

~

Martin returned home hours later to find little trace left of Tamara. He dropped into a chair and reached for the TV remote and tried not to think of their last ugly argument.

Tamara had watched from their bed as he dressed to meet the others at the Games Room Café that morning. But she didn't bother asking where he was off to this time; she just shook her head at him sadly.

"I know you're not having an affair, Martin. You wouldn't have the courage."

He looked up from the laces he'd been tying and said, "Courage?"

"Yes, Martin. *Courage*. It's not just for fictional characters like Flynn Bold. You're too scared to break up with me so you have to invent a fake lover to drive me away."

"You think that's what I'm—"

"*Of course* that's what you're doing! You're such a scared little boy! Too scared to show who you really are, with your fake hair and your fake literary ambition and, worst of all, your fake name." She smirked at him and added, "Braxton Wicks."

It was just two words, but Martin felt like he'd been pummelled. He leapt from the bed, one hand to his reconstructed nose, surprised too that she'd left that one out, and said, "How did you…?"

"I'm not stupid, Martin, although you never stopped to find that out. I know who all those loony letters are from, and I know why you keep them. They're from your mother, aren't they? She just wants to reconnect—"

"You've been *snooping* on me?"

"What choice did I have? You share nothing with me, Martin. Treat me like a secondary plot. Pretending there's someone else, when all there is, is a poor desperate woman trying to reach out to her son."

"Shut up, Tamara. You don't know anything about it."

She glowered. "I know more than you think. I know you come from a small, hick town and that your real name is Braxton Wicks. I know you changed it to Martin Chase around the time you got an agent. Chase is slam bang in the middle of Jane Austen and Agatha Christie on bookshelves—that's why you did it!"

Actually, it had more to do with Lee Child, but he didn't get a chance to tell her that. Or the fact that he didn't just come from a hick town, he came from a hick family, the son of a violent high school janitor and a timid teenage mother who took off hours after his delivery, but not before slapping him with a name that pretty much summed up his fake and painful life. How his mother ended up pregnant didn't bear thinking about. It was his family's ugly backstory, whispered to him once by a vindictive cousin. A story his father fought hard to hide—including with both fists on a rusty old tinny boat. And it was a story that Martin fought even harder to keep from the dust jacket of his books.

But Tamara wasn't listening now anyway, the silent treatment long forgotten. "I think that's just pathetic," she rolled on. "Sad too, because I prefer Braxton Wicks. At least it's original and authentic and doesn't sound like everybody else out there in *literary world*. You're a fraud and a phony, and you don't even trust your own story, let alone your fiction. Have to try to snag readers while they're looking for someone else."

Okay, that one hurt.

Martin slumped down on the bed. "What's your point, Tamara? What do you want me to say?"

She stared at him, incredulous. "Don't say anything, Martin! I don't trust a word that comes out of your mouth. And I don't trust this relationship; I wonder if it was ever real. It was for me... once." Her eyes welled with tears. She blinked them away. "So I'm going to make it nice and easy for you."

And with that she swept her lovely long legs from beneath the covers and walked out of his life. And now all that remained was the sweet smell of sandalwood and a hunch he'd just let the best thing that ever happened to him slip away.

Martin stared at his bleak reflection in the flat-screen TV, his father's face staring back at him, then dumped the remote and got to work. He marched into the kitchen and flicked on the kettle, then strode into his office and brought his computer to life, bringing up his twentieth manuscript. It was time to heed Tamara's words and stop being a coward.

It was time to kill off Flynn Bold.

But first he needed to throw a lifeline to a drowning woman. He reached for a pen and some stationery and began to write to his mother...

~

Trevor repeated Kila's order, his eyebrows raised. "A bottle of *my finest*? What does that even mean?"

"Buggered if I know," Kila replied. "Isn't that what you order when you're celebrating?"

"What're you celebrating?"

He hesitated, grinned and said, "Got my PI license back."

Sheila had just called to deliver the good news, adding, "Morea, I've never met such a lucky bastard! I don't know how you keep avoiding charges, but for the love of God, no more stashing prawn heads in cheating husband's convertibles, okay? I know the guy's a pig—it's the reason you got off—but here's how it's supposed to work: Your clients wreak their own revenge and you just take their money, got it?"

He'd laughed and assured her he'd behave, but they both knew he was lying. Damsels in distress were Kila's kryptonite. You could blame his sister for that. Or the murdering bastard she'd hooked up with really, the one who picked her up in a bar and took her life away. But he tried not to think of that. He was in too good a mood, and it had little to do with the windfall. Like he'd told the others, he'd never been motivated by money.

"So, French champagne?" said Trevor, still hovering. "Is that what you're after?"

Kila shook his head. "Nah, can't stand the stuff, just make it a lager. And don't forget my sister's—"

"Lemon squash, yeah, yeah, I'm onto it." His eyes swept upwards. "You think she watches you from up there? Your sis? Think she'd thank you for wasting your life in seedy bars, rescuing young girls from sleazebags, putting them in cabs, getting them home safe?"

He shrugged. "Not a waste, mate. Not if I save just one."

"Fair enough," Trevor said, stepping back before shifting his eyes to the door. "I'll add a gin and tonic to the order, shall I?"

Kila turned to find Frankie walking towards him, tote bag under one arm, sheepish smile on her beautiful face.

"Hey," she said. "Figured I'd find you here. Mind if I join you? I've just put the story to bed and wanted to celebrate."

"Pull up a pew. Trevor's just getting me a bottle of his finest. Make sure it's French, hey Trev?"

Trevor looked at him, laughed, and headed off while Frankie took the empty stool beside him.

"Well, that was a challenging experience," she said. "Talk about mission impossible. Can't believe we solved it! And we did it in less than a fortnight."

She nudged him with one shoulder. "How are you feeling?"

"I'm alright. Thought you'd be celebrating with your buddy. What's her name?"

"Jan, her name is *Jan*." Frankie smiled tensely. "That's all she is, nothing more than that."

He looked at her confused, and she winced and said, "I just called her. Told her we'd be seeing a lot less of each other from now on."

"How'd that go down?"

"Let's just say I've had to switch my phone off."

"Ouch."

She nodded. "I know it's going to hurt, but it's time to cut the apron strings." If that meant destroying her career in the process, then so be it. If the truth came out, the truth came out. It was time to live in the light, and she felt so much lighter for it.

Trevor appeared with the bottle and two glasses, and as she watched Kila peel the top off, Frankie said, "How about we get something to eat after this. I'm famished."

He looked at her sideways. "You asking me on a date, Frankie? Isn't that sexual harassment?"

"In your dreams, Morea. Besides, I've seen how your lovers end up."

"Ouch," he said again, one hand to his heart.

"Sorry, that was a low blow, even for me. Let's just call it the beginning of a beautiful friendship."

"Friendship?" He looked at her, confused again. "Like, when you just meet and talk and can't actually touch each other."

"Yes! That is generally what friendship means."

He raised his eyebrows and handed her a flute and said, "Talk about mission impossible. But hey, I'm up for the challenge."

Then they clinked their glasses and he thought, She'll be in love with me before the end of the bottle.

~~ *the end* ~~

ACKNOWLEDGEMENTS

I'd like to thank the usual suspects, including my family and publishing team—Annie Sarac at The Editing Pen, Elaine Rivers, my whip-smart reader, and my talented new cover designer Nimo Pyle. Thanks for always having my back.

I'd also like to say a very special thank you to my beloved newsletter subscribers who answered the call to provide fresh character names for this book. There were so many weird and wonderful suggestions, I barely knew how to choose. But choose I did. And so we can thank the following people for adding that extra splash of colour. They each receive a free copy of the book and get to see their chosen name in print!

Take a bow…

- Charlene Zall Capodice, New Jersey, USA for BURLINGTON and FRANCESCA
- Merry Chapman, Florida, USA for MEREDITH
- Brenda K. Sage, Arkansas, USA for BRAXTON
- Beth Helm Remington, Virginia USA for TAWNY BROWN
- Linda Hastings, New Mexico, USA for IGOR
- Susan Morris for ROMAN
- Ellie Herman for POOKIE
- Josile Reigle for LeDOUX

If you'd like to take part in future competitions like this one, or receive news, views and the odd free eBook, just sign up to my author newsletter: **calarmer.com**

Printed in Great Britain
by Amazon

86549356R00154